A
LITTLE
NIGHT
MURDER

Other Books in the
Blackbird Sisters Mystery Series

How to Murder a Millionaire

Dead Girls Don't Wear Diamonds

Some Like It Lethal

Cross Your Heart and Hope to Die

Have Your Cake and Kill Him Too

A Crazy Little Thing Called Death

Murder Melts in Your Mouth

No Way to Kill a Lady

Little Black Book of Murder

Novellas in the Blackbird Sisters Mystery Series

Slay Belles

Mick Abruzzo's Story

A
LITTLE
NIGHT
MURDER

A BLACKBIRD SISTERS MYSTERY

NANCY MARTIN

AN OBSIDIAN MYSTERY

OBSIDIAN
Published by the Penguin Group
Penguin Group (USA) LLC, 375 Hudson Street,
New York, New York 10014, USA

USA | Canada | UK | Ireland | Australia | New Zealand | India | South Africa | China
penguin.com
A Penguin Random House Company

First published by Obsidian, an imprint of New American Library,
a division of Penguin Group (USA) LLC

First Printing, August 2014

LIBRARY OF CONGRESS CATALOGING-IN-PUBLICATION DATA:

Martin, Nancy, 1953–
   A little night murder: a Blackbird sisters mystery/Nancy Martin.
      p. cm—(Blackbird sisters mystery; 10)
   ISBN 978-0-451-41527-1 (hardback)
   1. Blackbird Sisters (Fictitious characters)—Fiction. 2. Women detectives—Fiction. 3. Murder—Investigation—Fiction. I. Title.
   PS3563.A7267L585 2014
   813'.54—dc23   2014003885

Printed in the United States of America
10 9 8 7 6 5 4 3 2 1

Set in Bembo

For Cassie and Sarah—
new moms who have taught me just about
everything about mothering

A
LITTLE
NIGHT
MURDER

CHAPTER ONE

As I waited in the frigid backseat of a limousine, watching the front gate of a women's prison on an otherwise beautiful July afternoon, I wondered if I could tap politely on the door and ask the warden to please incarcerate my sister. Just for a few days of peace and quiet.

She was sitting beside me, skimming the newspaper and driving me crazy. Which I could do nothing about, because I had asked her to do me a favor, and as usual she'd agreed faster than she could touch up her lipstick.

"Why on earth," Libby demanded, "are some men so infatuated with their man parts that they take pictures?" She rattled the offending newspaper. "Really, Nora, here's another story in your paper about a fellow who photographed himself and sent the picture to fourteen women in his workplace. His colleagues called him Thunder Dick. I think that probably just encouraged him, don't you?"

Distracted, I said, "Uh-huh."

"If Mr. Dick truly wanted to arouse the interest of a woman, he should have photographed himself washing dishes. Now, *that's* sexy! These days, a picture of a man lathered up with Palmolive suds would make me faint with desire."

"Uhm," I said.

"But maybe he could be pictured without his shirt." She began to stare off into the distance, her eyes going dreamy, her lips turning slack. "Bare chested. With a splash of lotion on his skin to catch the candlelight. Because—"

I finally began paying attention. "Are you having a stroke?"

"—let's face it," she said as if I had not spoken, "the right lighting can conceal a lull in a person's gym routine or a temporary overindulgence in burritos. What is it about men and burritos? I find it puzzling, don't you? I mean, why have a burrito when you could have chocolate? Does That Man of Yours use lotion?"

I blinked, pretty sure I'd missed something important. "What?"

Libby finally folded up the paper and sighed. "Nora, your hormones have addled your brain. By the time your baby is born, you won't be able to keep two thoughts in your head at the same time."

During the past several months, she had repeatedly volunteered to help guide me through my pregnancy. So far, her most practical advice was for me to scrub my nipples to toughen them up for nursing.

"I'm a little distracted at the moment, Libby."

She pointed out the front-page article that had started her rant. "Why is your newspaper on such a penis kick this summer? I liked it better when journalists got obsessed with fun things like movie stars and shoes. Why don't you write a nice article about summer sandals?"

I love my sister—both of them, that is—but sometimes I wish we were back in the days when I could lure Libby into a closet with a Butterfinger bar and lock her up for ten minutes of solitude. My solitude, that is.

In the front seat, the chauffeur had been studiously ignoring my sister's rambling discussion of male anatomy. But suddenly he said, "There she is, Miss Blackbird."

The door of the stark prison building opened from the inside, and my best friend stepped out into the sunlight. If her first instinct was to wince at the searing sunlight, she suppressed it. But then, Lexie Paine, as close to royalty as anyone in Philadelphia got, was all about self-control. She put on a pair of very dark glasses and squared her shoulders. Then, wearing the same black Armani suit she'd worn in court the day she'd confessed to manslaughter, she walked briskly toward the fence that separated the free world from the prison where she'd been incarcerated for nine and a half months. She carried a ragged manila envelope, which I presumed contained all that remained of her considerable fortune.

"She doesn't look fat at all." Libby leaned over me to peer out the window. "I hear they serve white bread at every meal in prison. I might as well glue white bread directly to my thighs. One jay-walking citation and I'd be a poster girl for Jenny Craig."

I opened the car door and bailed out onto the hot, cracked asphalt of the parking lot. "Stay here," I said to Libby. "And remember what I told you. No reporter can find out where Lexie is going, okay? Don't tell a soul."

"What do you take me for? I am perfectly capable of keeping a secret when it's—"

I closed the door on my sister's next volley of claptrap.

For the past several days, since hearing of my friend's upcoming release, surprising Lexie had seemed like a good idea. Now, though, I had every expectation she might slap my face and hitchhike out of there. For my role in her incarceration, I might have deserved that.

She walked straight through the gate, and from behind her sunglasses she said coolly, "Nora, I knew you were pregnant, but isn't this overdoing things just a bit?"

3

"Maybe a little." Noting that she did not hug me, I said, "Lex, we need to get in a car right away."

Lexie did not obey my request. She stood still, back stiff, head high. I could not see her eyes behind the glasses. Back when she was young, after a blue-blooded cousin broke her bones and assaulted her, Lexie had reinvented herself into the girl who'd never be a victim again. She became the smartest student in her Ivy League class. Then a powerful woman who crushed the competition on Wall Street. Now that she'd been to prison, I wondered how she planned to reinvent herself one more time.

She said, "Why should I get into your car?"

"Because you're going to be the hottest news story of the summer," I said, "and you'd hate that. We're trying to protect you from the reporters. Lex, please get into the car."

A long, awful moment stretched, and I wondered whether the most important friendship of my life had ended.

"No," she said. She turned her face up to the sun. "No. Just for a minute, let me breathe."

With her face tilted to the sunlight, she reached out and took my hand. Clutched it, really, and her chilly facade crumbled. "Thank you, sweetie. I was afraid my mother might show up today, and there are times when you just can't face your mother. You're such a welcome relief, I can't tell you."

I felt the bubble of tension break in my throat. She had stuck by me during the worst time of my life, and I intended to do the same for her.

For now, I said, "I brought Oreos."

She laughed unsteadily and let me go. "You're a lifesaver. But you shouldn't be doing this. It's not going to be easy being my friend now."

"You think I'm a stranger to scandal?" I asked with a smile.

"Good point." She removed her sunglasses and brushed something that might have been a tear from the corner of her eye. "Your tribulations have made you stronger, haven't they? All right, let's go—but why three limos?" She gave the three idling black cars and two hired taxis a composed inspection.

"Television trucks are waiting out on the street, and so are about a dozen print journalists. There's even one man with a camera on a motorcycle. We're going to do our best to lose all of them before they can figure out where we're going. And Libby's going to stage a scene to attract their attention."

Libby chose that moment to rap her knuckles on the car window and wave brightly at Lexie.

Lexie waved back, trying to conceal her trepidation. "What kind of scene?"

"I thought it best to leave the details to her. But I'm sure whatever she dreams up will do the trick. This way."

Lexie followed me to the second limousine. "Has your beau plotted all this?"

"It was a team effort. Ready now?" I opened the rear passenger door for her.

Our escape was touch and go. I thought the reporters spotted us. But in the rearview mirror we saw Libby bail out at a traffic light and feign a shrieking meltdown—scattering the contents of her handbag, which might have included several rubber snakes. Later she told us that reporters called an ambulance because they thought the chauffeur was having a heart attack. I also learned that my sister scored a date with a traffic cop who stopped to help.

A few days after that, Lexie was still successfully concealed from the press, although lounging around the pool at her mother's summerhouse felt more like a vacation at a luxury spa.

"Who knew you had such a cunning side?" Lexie said, seated in her bathing suit at a glass-topped patio table under a striped umbrella.

I was drifting in the cool bliss of the swimming pool, on a large pink noodle. "It's a recessive gene I inherited from my parents."

"Ah, yes," Lexie said. "Are they still in Argentina, avoiding tax extradition?"

"They're on a cruise at the moment. I imagine them stowed away in a first-class cabin and dining with the captain every night."

"They certainly know how to live the good life," Lexie said. "So does my mother. Not that high living made her a bad parent. She did help me avoid the creepy math tutor who kept wine coolers in his briefcase. And her advice about majoring in business instead of fashion merchandising was very sound, too. But to her dying day, she'll shout that going to jail was my own fault. And she'd be right. I think I need help, sweetie. You have to help me relearn all the lessons of civilized society. You always do the right thing."

Maybe because I was floating so comfortably, my first thought popped out unbidden. "I try to do the right thing because I screwed up once. And Todd died."

She set her tea down on a table, and she got serious fast. "Your husband got himself killed with drugs and stupidity, Nora. That wasn't your fault."

It felt like my fault, though. I hadn't done enough, hadn't dragged him to the right doctors, hadn't locked him up or tied him to a bedpost—anything to keep him away from cocaine. In my worst moments, I feared I had enabled him.

I didn't want to make the same mistake with Lexie—do nothing, that is. When I'd heard a judge intended to release her for reasons too complicated for anyone to understand yet, I had telephoned her formidable mother and asked to be the one to pick her up. I suggested Lexie be allowed to go into hiding at her mother's palatial summerhouse on the Delaware, just a half hour's drive from downtown Philadelphia and a few miles from my home. Here, I intended to keep watch on my friend.

Except for the occasional cutting remark that seemed to pop out of a hard, angry place inside, she seemed to be a little better every day. My biggest concern was that Lexie was being denied her best recovery strategy—her work. She'd heal faster if she could be allowed back into her office.

But that was impossible.

Lexie went on. "For a woman so concerned about appearances, my mother certainly has no qualms about her own reputation. She's on her fourth husband—have I told you? The polo player went back to South America, so she married a yachtsman from Newport. She's an enthusiastic wife, but mothering never suited her. Does that worry you, sweetie? The possibility of evolving into a terrible mother now that you're hatching one of your own?"

"Most of the time I'm too hungry to worry," I said. "Tell the truth. Do I look like a manatee?"

She tilted down her sunglasses to make a better examination of me wallowing in the water in all my pregnant splendor. Diplomatically, she said, "That swimsuit is very flattering, Nora."

She looked elegant in a black bathing suit with a black lace cover-up designed by an artist who knew how to make a woman's nearly naked body look chic, not tarty. I, on the other hand, was simply glad there were no harpoons handy, since it would be easy to mistake me for a great white whale.

I said, "I have eight weeks to go. We Blackbird women get big early."

"Well, you look happy," she said. "Having a family has always been important for you, hasn't it? Just don't let it overwhelm you, please. Women who have nothing to discuss but diapers bore me to tears."

She wasn't herself, I said inwardly. It wasn't her nature to be hurtful. She had spent the last months holding back her thoughts and emotions. Letting other people make all the decisions for her must have been excruciating for a woman who had commanded a fast-paced investment firm. But her usual control had cracks now, and I was the recipient of her lapses in kindness. This phase would fade, however. After Todd died, I had been alternately a crazy bitch on wheels or a lump under the coverlet. Lexie moved in with me—against my wishes—and fed me, talked with me, stuck by me until I could function again.

She slipped off her cover-up and waded down the steps of the shallow end. With the seemingly unshakable composure of her *Mayflower* forebears, she put her palms flat on the surface of the water and canted her face up to the sun again. Her black ponytail hung down between shoulders just starting to tan. She inhaled a deep, cleansing breath of fresh air and let it out on a sigh.

She said, "The press continues to be baffled about my where-abouts?"

"So far, so good." I didn't want to bother her with the details, but there was a full-scale hunt going on—complete with baying hounds and irate letters to editors from former clients whose fortunes had been ruined by the millionaire investment whiz who got out of jail thanks to a team of mobbed-up lawyers.

"I'm grateful for your help, Nora," she said. "Although I miss my own digs."

"This is the right place for the moment," I said.

"I'll probably have to sell my house, you know. To help with the Cause."

"I hope not, Lex."

She shrugged. She had taken to making light of her effort to repay all the clients who'd been swindled by her former partner at the Paine Investment Group. I knew she was obsessed with getting the hundreds of stolen millions back into the hands of investors who had trusted her firm with their life savings. After all, she said, it was her name on the brass plate that still hung on the building in the center of Philadelphia, not her larcenous partner's. But it was going to take time. And sacrifice.

Meanwhile, she admitted to feeling guilty about her luxurious hiding place. Her mother's mansion—one of many pieds-à-terre around the world—stood on a Bucks County bluff overlooking the river. This little-used summerhouse was only a convenient few miles down the road from Blackbird Farm, my family's formerly grand but now crumbling estate. The differences between the two properties included air-conditioning—my house had become a sweltering oven in July—and the sumptuous swimming pool, which had been built before the Great Depression by one of Lexie's robber baron relatives. It resembled a Roman bath. The mosaic on the bottom of the pool depicted a Bacchanalian banquet scene. The surrounding garden was guarded by two marble Praetorian Guards, spears in hand, glaring stalwartly off into the woods behind the mansion.

Indoors, the great house's many gracious amenities included a billiards room with cigar burns courtesy of J.P. Morgan, a salon where polo teams could be plied with cocktails and a servant's wing with forty numbered bells in the hallway. That wing was currently empty, since Lexie couldn't afford more than the services of her longtime houseman, Samir, who had taken a deep pay cut to continue to loyally shop, cook and keep house. Lexie confided to me that he had accepted the job offer because he was writing a book in his spare time—subject unknown so far—and he was glad to have his own sprawling suite in the essentially empty house for staring glumly at his computer screen. To our tremendous gratitude, Samir made our lunch every day and regularly appeared with frosty pitchers of herbal tea.

It was not Samir, however, who came through the diaphanous curtains of the French doors and stepped onto the bluestone terrace of the pool, carrying our refreshed iced tea pitcher in one hand and pinning a portfolio under his other arm. Rather, it was a tall, hulking man with an infamous reputation.

He said to Lexie, "I think I just scared the bejesus out of your butler."

"Don't worry, darling," Lexie called to him, "he recovers quickly. Michael, is Nora expecting twins, do you think?"

The father of my baby put the fresh pitcher on the table. "Doctor says just one. Last month, she showed us the pictures to prove it, 'cause I had my doubts." He ambled to the edge of the pool and smiled down at me. "How was yoga class?"

I paddled over to the stairs. "Great. Baby Girl loved it, too. She was very peaceful." I put my wet hand up to him.

Michael Abruzzo, who had sworn he was getting out of organized crime, was still frequently mistaken for a wanted criminal. He had big shoulders and a broken face, and in public he often kept up a kind of benign menace that could scatter a crowd. But he helped me out of the pool as if I were precious glass. From a nearby lounge chair, he pulled a towel and clasped it around as much of me as it could cover.

I stretched up on tiptoe and gave him a kiss. "Did anyone follow you?"

He raised one eyebrow. "You're kidding, right?"

"After that masterful display of evasive driving during last week's escape," I said, referring to Michael's command of the lead car in our prison escape plan, "I don't mean to cast any doubt on your criminal expertise, but—"

"I didn't have any reporters on my tail today. Lexie's undisclosed location is still a secret." He kissed me again. "Did you tell her?"

I smiled up into his blue eyes. "I was waiting for you to get here."

Lexie perked up. "Tell me what? Are you two keeping secrets?"

I clasped his hand, and he squeezed mine back. I took a deep breath and faced my friend. "We're getting married. A week from Friday. We picked up the marriage license yesterday."

"Darlings!"

Lexie leaped from the pool and hugged us both, leaving a wet splotch on Michael's shirt and me feeling tearily happy.

With her eyes shining, too, she cried, "After all this time, all your ups and downs—how romantic. Friday? Where? What can I do? Lord, I can't afford an extravagant gift, so it will have to be a service of some kind—anything."

"The main service? Don't tell my sisters. Either one of them. We're trying to do this quietly, and you know Libby. Given enough time, she'll rent a circus tent and hire the Harlem Globetrotters to officiate, so I'll wait until the eleventh hour to invite her."

"Of course. Not a word from me. But—could we invite friends here for a shindig after? It might have to be hot dogs and potato chips, but I bet there's some of Mama's champagne in the cellar. Let me throw you a reception."

"I don't think that's smart. The press will certainly view our wedding as something out of *The Godfather*, and there would be photographers in helicopters who would spot you. So, no, we're going to see a judge in her chambers. Judge Scotto—do you know her? And maybe you'd sneak out of here long enough to be a witness? We need two. It will be very quiet."

Suddenly Lexie had real tears in her eyes—a flash of her former intuitive, empathetic self. More than anyone, she understood the complexities of my relationship with Michael—all the reasons why I had been afraid to marry him, share a life and family with him, as well as the sometimes irrational rationales that compelled me into his arms. Although Michael and I came from different worlds— different kinds of dysfunctional families—we shared the desire to create a stable family for ourselves. Lexie recognized that.

She gave me another, gentler hug. "You're getting married before the baby comes. Very wise. I wish you both all the happiness you deserve. Of course I'll be a witness. And I'll keep your secret, I promise. Libby would certainly make a big production, indeed. I won't breathe a syllable."

"Not to anyone." Michael hooked his thumb back at the house. "Not even to the person I brought along today."

"Who did you bring?" I asked, surprised.

"Somebody to meet you. She's in the house, powdering her nose."

I had already noted that he'd come wearing an old white dress shirt, sleeves folded back over his forearms, the tail untucked over his usual jeans. The look was a significant sartorial upgrade from his customary black T-shirt, which alerted me that he had brought someone important. "Maybe I should go put on something more suitable?"

"You look great. She'll be here in a minute. Meanwhile," he confessed, "I need to talk to Lexie."

Although intrigued about who had come with him, I said, "What are you two working on? Is Lexie teaching you all there is to know about business?"

Lexie gathered up a towel for herself. "Your groom doesn't need me to play teacher, sweetie. I've mentored MBAs with less insight into the financial world. In fact, it's the other way around this time. And he's keeping me sane. If I didn't have something complicated to think about, I'd be going crazy."

I decided not to take offense, patted myself dry and reached for my T-shirt. But her words gave me pause. Was this the reinvention I had been expecting? With some humor, I said, "Should I be worried?"

Michael didn't respond as he settled into a lounge chair. He fished his reading glasses out of the pocket of his shirt and opened the portfolio of papers. Also in the portfolio was a small laptop, which he flipped open.

Lexie said, "Since I can't get a job to save my life—not with my licenses revoked and all my former associates pretending I have the plague—your groom and I thought we'd put our heads together on a project."

"A project," I said lightly. "Is it legal?"

"In some countries." Michael matched my tone. "Do you want to know more?"

"The less, the better. I don't want to be served with a subpoena in the maternity ward."

Lexie bit her lip, but Michael smiled at me. "That's my girl."

I sat in the chair next to his. For all our jesting, I trusted he wasn't going to break any laws. His own precarious legal status—on parole for racketeering with the rest of the notorious Abruzzo family, and at risk of returning to prison if he so much as sneezed in the wrong direction—was worth minding. But I wasn't sure where Lexie was headed.

I pulled on the T-shirt. Due to my dire financial straits, I had been forced to dig into my sister Libby's collection of hand-me-down maternity clothes, which meant I was bending my fashion rules considerably. Libby's taste ran to gaudy items with funny sayings printed on them.

Today's bright yellow T-shirt read LET ME OUT, IT'S DARK IN HERE. I had counted on nobody seeing me except my close friend, but here I was, stuck looking ridiculous.

Michael sent me a sideways glance and smothered a smile.

"It was free," I reminded him.

"It's not bad," he said. But any minute he was going to burst out laughing.

Saving me from further embarrassment, my cell phone rang in the depths of my beach bag, and I struggled up to reach for it.

Lexie saved me the trouble. She found my phone, saying, "You're working hard these days, Nora, despite our lazy afternoons. Is the social season heating up?"

"It never cooled down," I said, accepting the phone. "But my editor has been on vacation. Now that he's back on American soil, he's shouting for my head."

"Why?"

"I misbehaved while he was away. It's time to pay the piper."

But the phone stopped ringing in my hand.

Of all the people who phoned me, only my editor was so impatient that he'd hang up after only two rings. I checked the caller ID. Yes, Gus Hardwicke was obviously back from Australia.

"Why is he shouting?"

"In his absence, I may have exceeded my station."

"I like what you've been doing lately," Lexie said. "The article about the ten best charities and the ten worst? That took real reporting. If that sort of thing is your new direction, I think it's great."

"Mr. Hardwicke may not think so. There have been irate letters to the editor about the ten worst charities. People complained that I discouraged donors."

She was impatient. "Why give money to a charity that sends less than five percent of the funds they raise to their actual mission? They're giving all their income to professional fund-raisers! That's outrageous."

"Even five percent is better than nothing, some might say."

My phone chirped—a signal I had received a text. I checked. From Gus.

Where is Lexie Paine???

I should have guessed he'd already be hot on the trail of Lexie's story. I put the phone away before she could see the screen.

I knew I should call him back, but instead I decided to put off the inevitable for just a few more minutes. I dried my legs while Michael asked Lexie a convoluted question about currency exchange and offshore bank accounts. I sipped tea and tried not to think about large-scale international money laundering.

But their financial confab was interrupted by music from the house next door. From the distance of two football fields away, the trilling of opening chords on a piano rose over the treetops. I couldn't see from our poolside vantage point, but I heard a pair of voices join in, singing warm-up scales.

Lexie rolled her eyes. "Cue the howling dogs. The music is starting early today."

Michael glanced up from his computer screen to listen. "What's going on?"

"It's my neighbors." With one hand, Lexie indicated the half-hidden mansion that stood behind a screen of tall trees. "Back in the day, my great-grandfather and his brother built these twin houses up here. The brother sold his to Toodles Tuttle."

"Toodles?" Michael grinned.

"You know all about credit default swaps, but not Broadway theater?" Lexie demanded.

To Michael, I said, "Toodles Tuttle was a very famous composer. He wrote musicals."

"Tap dancing and chorus girls, right?"

"Exactly," said Lexie. "He made a fortune at it, too, which was how he could afford the house. But Toodles died a few years ago. Now his wife lives next door, the old harridan, with a slew of minions who obey her every command. The gardener told me she recently discovered one of her husband's unproduced musicals, and they're trying to get it ready for the stage. She's looking for investors, if you're interested."

Just then one of the singers hit a flat note, and Michael winced. "Sounds like a losing proposition to me."

But Lexie looked thoughtful. "A totally new Toodles musical? It might be very lucrative."

"From what I've heard these last few days," I said, "the songs are pretty good. We can't see the dance rehearsals, of course, but—"

"Uh-oh." Michael's expression changed. "Dance rehearsals? I think I just figured out something."

"Yoo-hoo!" a voice called musically from the house. "Is everybody decent? Or are you skinny-dipping?"

Michael got to his feet and said to me, "Brace yourself."

The woman who came up the stairs was a tall, sixtysomething redhead with impossibly long legs, displayed in a leopard-print skirt much tighter and shorter than anyone her age should be seen wearing. She also wore bright blue eye shadow and livid red lipstick and had piled her fiery hair high. Maybe my mind was already on Broadway, but my first thought was that she looked like a woman ready to take center stage.

Lexie scrambled up and extended her hand to her newest guest. "Hello, I'm Lexie." She skipped her last name.

"Hiya, doll. I'm Bridget O'Halloran. Great to meet you at last!" She pumped Lexie's hand with enthusiasm. "Mickey has told me all about you. Except he didn't mention you were such a looker."

"Mickey, hmm?" Lexie sent Michael an impish look.

Which he missed, because he was pulling me to a standing position. "Uh, Bridget, Lexie's just a friend. This is her house. But here's Nora."

Off-balance and unwieldy, I wobbled in the tall shadow of Bridget O'Halloran, shielding my eyes against the glare of the sunlight to look up into her face. She was exactly the kind of woman who appeared on *The Real Housewives* of some-such place—lots of extra hair that couldn't possibly be natural and clothes that managed to look both expensive and very cheap indeed. She was wearing false eyelashes, but the vivid blue of her eyes gave her away. I knew instantly who she was.

She inspected me, too. From the curl on her lip, I could see she wasn't pleased with the picture I made. To keep the chlorine out of my hair, I had configured a less than chic topknot with a cheap banana clip. I had liberally coated my nose with white sunscreen, too. And my silly shirt wasn't going to win any runway accolades.

I smiled bravely, however, and put out my hand. "How do you do?"

"How *dooo* you *dooo*?" she parroted back at me, then laughed. A laugh with an edge of hostility. "You sound like you've got a silver spoon shoved up your—"

"Nora," Michael intervened, "this is Bridget O'Halloran. My mother."

Lexie made an involuntary squeak in her throat and shot me a wide-eyed stare that managed to say, *His mother?*

Michael had been born the son of Big Frankie Abruzzo—the boss of most of the organized crime that still operated in southern New Jersey—and Big Frankie's paramour, an exotic dancer who had willingly handed over her child to be raised with the rest of the Abruzzo boys by Big Frankie's wife. Michael referred to his biological mother by her first name, and he told me he'd been in touch with her off and on his whole life. Whether Bridget still saw Big Frankie, I wasn't sure, but judging by the diamond bracelet on her wrist and the large designer handbag on her toned arm, I guessed she was accepting generous presents from somebody with very deep pockets.

She looked around the pool. "Nice joint you've got here," she said to Lexie. "I once had a boyfriend who had a pool like this. He was a champion Olympic swimmer. He wanted to marry me, but I didn't like the idea of living with a man who wore a Speedo all the time. You don't have any guys in Speedos, huh? Because they're kinda fun for the short haul."

"Not today," Lexie said with a smile.

"So," Bridget said to me, "how come you won't marry my son?"

Her blunt question shocked me into a stutter. "Uh, I—I—"

To Lexie, Michael said, "Bridget speaks her mind."

Bridget's glare turned even frostier on me. "He says he asks, and you say no. Now you're as big as a cow with his kid, and you still won't get married? How come? You too good for him?"

"Why—of course not."

"He says you're cursed or something, and that's why you're putting off a wedding. What's that all about?"

"The Blackbird curse," I said.

"What kind of curse? Is it for real?"

"My family—that is, all the women in my family—tend to be widowed young. And although I really don't believe in that kind of thing, I admit I worry that something terrible might happen when—"

"Nothing's going to happen to me," Michael said. "Back off, Bridget."

"Hey, I'm not making judgments," Bridget said, raising both hands as if the local sheriff had commanded her to reach for the sky. "I just don't like the idea of some rich society girl thinking her shit doesn't stink."

"Bridget!"

"How about some iced tea?" Lexie interjected before Michael could further object to his mother's choice of words. "Or—is it too early for gin and tonics?"

"Gin and tonic would hit the spot," Bridget said. "Plenty of lime. Light on the tonic."

"Coming right up!" With an apologetic look thrown over her shoulder, Lexie fled toward the house.

Michael's cell phone rang in his pocket. He took it out and glanced at the screen before apologizing to me. "Sorry. Business. I gotta take this." He walked to the far end of the terrace before answering his call. If I'd had a towel in my hands, I'd have twisted it up and used it to strangle him.

As both of them abandoned me to fend for myself, I was left standing in front of Bridget O'Halloran while she dug into her handbag and rooted out a stick of gum. She peeled it open, giving me another chilly once-over that made me feel like the fat lady at a carnival sideshow. Dropping any pretense of politeness, she said, "How far gone are you?"

"Seven months," I replied, mustering good cheer.

"Still puking every morning?"

"No, I'm past all that. I feel wonderful, actually."

"It's a girl, Mick says."

"Yes, we're delighted."

"Girls can be trouble. I sure gave my parents the runaround. Got a name picked out yet?"

"Not yet. Michael is cautious about giving a name to someone we haven't met yet," I said, although I wondered if his mother might change her mind about me if I offered to name our firstborn after her.

"I once had a boyfriend who was the superstitious type. He was a swami, wore beads, real in touch with his feelings. But he ran off with a hippie chick, and last I heard he was telling fortunes outside a circus. I said good riddance." She folded the gum into her mouth, continuing to squint at my silly shirt. "You and my Mick aren't exactly a match made in Vegas, know what I mean? Like, the odds aren't good."

"We couldn't be happier," I assured her.

"Wanna know what I think?" She glanced around to make sure we weren't being overheard. Then she glared straight into my face. "I think you're a gold digger holding out for something better to come down the pike. You're broke, right? And he's just starting to hit it big. Well, he's more than the dough he carries in his pocket, lemme tell you. Mick's the best of the best. You should grab him before he goes back to one of the real women he used to date."

The gold-digger crack infuriated me. But her last remark side-tracked my sputtering temper. "The real women he——?"

Bridget turned her back on me and walked to the edge of the terrace, toward the piano music. "So, what's the story next door?"

"Just a minute," I said.

But she bulldozed over me. "I hear they're auditioning for a musical. A Broadway musical. What do you know about it?"

"They rehearse a lot, but other than that——"

"You know anybody over there?"

"At the Tuttle house? Why do you ask?"

Bridget turned on me, tall and aggressive. "Do you know any-body who could get me in?"

"Ah," I said.

Her eyes narrowed dangerously. "What's that supposed to mean?"

"You came here to get an introduction to the Tuttles," I said, unable to keep the note of accusation from my voice. "You want an audition."

She lifted her chin. "And why not? I'm still damn good on my feet, babycakes. And I can belt a tune as good as anybody. They'd be lucky to get me in their little show."

I had my doubts that any Toodles Tuttle musical could be called "little," not even if it had been discovered long after his demise. But with another look up and down Bridget O'Halloran's spectacular body, I had to agree with her. She might look very good indeed on a Broadway stage. She had presence and sex appeal and a certain well-traveled womanliness that said *star quality*.

She said, "Mick tells me you're connected. That you know ev-erybody who's anybody. So how about getting me an introduction to your friends?"

"They're not my friends," I said. "I'm barely acquainted with the Tuttles."

"But you do know them, right?"

"Not enough to ask a favor."

She glared at me a little, then finally smirked. "Well, sometimes a girl has to make her own opportunities." She lifted the latch on the pool gate and let herself out. "I once had a boyfriend, a big-shot psychiatrist in Hollywood who had kind of a mommy problem, if you ask me, so we worked on that, him and me. Good times. Anyways, he always talked about seizing the day. So I'm gonna do a little seizing."

"Wait! You can't just walk over there and expect an audition."

"Can't I?"

"Surely it's unprofessional—"

Bridget stepped through the gate and headed across the lawn. Over her shoulder, she said, "Tell Mick I'll be back in half an hour, babycakes."

CHAPTER TWO

I ran to find my sandals, determined to chase Bridget across the lawn. But I had to sit down to put them on, and with my ungainly belly it was almost an impossible task. By the time I managed to wrestle one on, Bridget was out of sight.

Michael came across the pool's flagstones, pocketing his phone and looking annoyed.

"Everything okay?" I asked, panting with the struggle to reach my feet.

"It's complicated," he replied, still distracted by his call.

I decided I didn't have to be sympathetic. I gave up on my sandal and threw it at him. "You had to leave me alone with your mother?"

He caught the sandal one-handed and looked genuinely apologetic. "Sorry. I have a couple of pots on the back burners, and one of them just boiled over. Where'd she go?"

Lexie appeared, carrying a tray with bottles and glassware. "I don't have any limes! I hope lemon will do. Oh, dear— What happened to—? Where did she—? Was it something I said?"

"Nothing anybody says ever bugs Bridget." Michael went down on one knee to help me with my sandal. "She's indestructible."

Lexie set the tray on the table. "She's not exactly what I expected."

I stuck out my foot to make Michael's job easier. "I'm not sure what I expected, either, but she certainly isn't it. Will she tell anyone about Lexie?"

"She doesn't read the news, so she probably doesn't know who Lexie is." He slipped my sandal onto my foot and looked around. "Where did she go?"

I said, "I think she went to audition."

"For the play?" Lexie cried.

"I knew it!" Michael got up and was suddenly pacing around me. "I should have figured out she had another motive for coming here today. Is this going to upset the neighbors?"

"They're a bunch of crackpots themselves," Lexie said. "They probably won't notice the arrival of one more. It's like a screwball comedy over there—music and dancing and cocktails at all hours. If Fred Astaire were alive, he'd be swanning down the staircase in a tuxedo."

"Well, there's no stopping Bridget when she gets an idea in her head," Michael said grimly. "I better go after her before she accidentally tells the whole world where Lexie is. You should have seen her the time we waited at a stage door to get the *Phantom* guy to autograph her blouse. She practically mugged him."

"You saw *Phantom of the Opera*?" I said, thinking there were still things I didn't know about the man I was about to marry.

"Half of it. When I was a kid, she dragged me to shows all the time. Mostly, I fell asleep, except when the girls in little outfits came out. *Phantom* was the show when she finally let me start waiting in the lobby. I learned to play poker from the guy who sold tickets."

"How old were you?" I struggled to stand up.

He helped me to my feet. "Seven or eight. He cleaned me out of my allowance. Bridget got it back for me, but I don't want to know how she did that."

With a wicked grin for me, Lexie said, "You can find out when you have holiday dinners together, Nora."

The thought of sharing holidays with Bridget O'Halloran set off a siren in my head. That's when we heard a bloodcurdling scream from across the lawn.

"Oh, shit," Michael groaned. "She sucker punched somebody."

We could hear shrieks coming from over the rooftops of the adjacent mansion. The shrieks changed, though, and didn't sound like the cries of neighbors who'd let the wrong person through their front door. This was fear and panic.

"Someone's hurt," I said. "Or in trouble."

"Stay here, both of you," Michael ordered, already heading across the flagstones. "Call 911."

He boosted himself over the wall and ran across the sloping lawn. Just as fast, Lexie and I had our cell phones in hand, but she was quicker at hitting the numbers. I heard her speaking to the emergency call center, so I went across the terrace to the gate. The screams diminished to loud wails, no less disturbing. I found myself steadying Baby Girl with a trembling hand.

"What do you think has happened?" I asked Lexie when she arrived at my side. She was still holding her phone to her ear. Together, we watched Michael disappear around the Tuttle hedge.

Lexie put her palm over the phone. "Old Mrs. Tuttle and her daughter have been moldering in that house since Toodles died. Maybe the old lady finally kicked the bucket. I've asked for an ambulance. I'm on hold, but— Nora, wait!"

I couldn't stop myself. I lifted the latch on the wrought-iron gate and went through. Lexie followed, phone still to her ear. We hurried across the lawn together, passing the overgrown flower borders full of blowsy peonies and tall foxgloves in a riot of pinks and lavenders. I couldn't move very fast, and by the time we arrived at the other house, the wails had diminished to loud weeping. We found ourselves on a wide stone patio very much like the pool deck of Lexie's house—except no pool. Someone had secured colorful duct tape to the tiles, as if marking off a performance area. Fourth of July streamers still fluttered overhead, looking faded. The second-floor windows of the house were cranked open, and we could hear voices raised upstairs.

"Hello?" I shouted up at the open windows.

A distressed female face appeared above us, and the woman called down, "It's Miss Jenny! We think she's dead!"

"Jenny?" Lexie was shocked. "That's Gloria's daughter!"

The woman disappeared, and Michael stuck his head out the window.

He said, "Did you call 911?"

Lexie pointed at her cell phone. "Yes, I'm still on the phone with them. The ambulance should be here soon."

He looked grim. "Too late for that."

"Can we help?" I asked.

He hesitated, then nodded. "Come up. Maybe you can talk these people down off the ceiling."

We hurried around to the front of the house, where an extravagant blue Bentley was parked in the curve of the driveway. We rushed past it and through an open door. Inside, the mansion had exactly the same layout as Lexie's. The only difference was in the decor and condition of the home. Where Lexie's digs looked as if a Roman emperor had just moved out, this one looked as if it had been decorated by Busby Berkeley. Art deco furniture and sconce lighting, marble floors in a checkerboard pattern. But the walls hadn't seen a fresh coat of paint in decades. The once-elegant furniture was shabby, and the floors needed a thorough cleaning.

In the front hallway, Lexie and I almost fell over a piano bench. Gathered around the baby grand stood a group of weeping young people, all of them dressed in rehearsal clothes and dance shoes. They were crying in one another's arms, with all the drama you might expect of a theatrical troupe.

I didn't see Bridget among them.

Lexie and I rushed up the staircase—she was much faster, but I doggedly tried to keep up—past a row of dusty-framed theater posters that advertised old Tuttle musical productions. We headed toward the sound of raised voices.

On the second floor, Michael shouldered his way past another weeping couple, who embraced in the corridor. Looking unnerved, he indicated a bedroom with a jerk of his head. "I'm not good with hysterical women. And there's a bunch of them in there. I'll go wait for the ambulance."

Lexie and I went into the bedroom.

On the floor lay a dead woman.

It's hard to upstage a dead body, but old Mrs. Tuttle, widow of the famed Broadway composer Toodles Tuttle and the star of quite a few of his shows, had what it took. Seventysomething years old, but looking every day of ninety, she stood over the deceased while clutching her throat as if to hold back sobs of grief.

The main thing about the old woman?

She was blue.

Her skin was an inhuman shade of indigo.

Perhaps the strange color of her skin was enhanced by her green satin turban, decorated with a crusty emerald brooch pinned drunkenly over one eye, and her swirling green paisley caftan, belted with what appeared to be a coiled drapery tieback. She looked like an ancient blue Scarlett O'Hara wearing curtains from a Sunset Boulevard mansion. Except her skinny blue legs were encased in a pair of knee-high compression stockings that sagged around her bird-like blue ankles. Her blue feet were crammed into gold mules with moth-eaten marabou on the toes. Jungle red lipstick had escaped the outline of her mouth, and her mascara looked as if it had been accumulating for months. Her rheumy eyes bulged with melo-drama.

She croaked, "My life is over!"

To the rest of us, it looked as if her daughter's life was the one that was over.

The elderly woman gave another incoherent cry of sorrow. With one blue hand clamped around her blue throat in a gesture that originated before movies had sound, she reached her other desiccated claw for my help as she swayed precariously between conscious thought and a bad actress's imitation of fainting. "My precious little girl is dead!"

Her daughter was neither little nor a girl, but she was definitely dead. And the mother was definitely alive, but in danger of collaps-ing right down on top of the corpse. I took a firm grip on her skinny blue arm and said, "Mrs. Tuttle, let me help you sit. I'm Nora Blackbird. Remember me? You used to sing duets with my father at parties."

"Oh, yes." She let me assist her down on a frayed ottoman beside a lumpy reading chair. She peered up at me. "Your father isn't much of a singer, but he makes up for it with charm. He's a mensch. And what a dancer! He can really cut a rug. But your mother—she's a shiksa with more chutzpah than most, isn't she?"

"Yes, Mrs. Tuttle."

"And your grandmother never liked us—Toodles or me. Oh, she acted real polite, but she couldn't hide it. She hit me in the schnoz with a champagne cork once. Call me Boom Boom. That was my stage name, you know. I'm reviving it for the new show. *Bluebird of Happiness*. It's going to be a blockbuster."

I was not the only person in the room who noted how easily

Boom Boom Tuttle was distracted from her daughter's demise. A large woman in Hollywood's idea of a nurse's uniform stood frowning at Boom Boom, and the couple who had been weeping together in the hallway came in and also stared doubtfully at the lady of the house. Even Lexie seemed unable to mask her surprise at Boom Boom's eagerness to forget her daughter's death in favor of a new Tuttle musical.

To be certain, I knelt down and reached to touch Jenny Tuttle's neck. Although I had met Jenny a few times, I wouldn't have called her a friend. But I remembered her.

Specifically, I remembered Jenny, middle-aged and self-conscious, playing the piano as invisibly as a church organist while her father charmed an audience with his songs.

My thoughts went back nearly twenty years to a time when I was home from boarding school for the holidays. Christmas greenery and lavish ribbons disguised the peeling paint and crooked banister of Blackbird Farm. My parents preferred to entertain rather than spend their time doing mundane things like fixing leaky toilets and replacing burned-out bulbs, so the glow of candles usually hid the worst of their deferred maintenance. Back then, the house was alive with music and champagne and much laughter. Parties were a weekly occurrence. But one night we had a special guest.

Handsome even in his later years, Toodles Tuttle had breezed through the front door of our sagging homestead, bringing a cloud of sparkling snowflakes in his wake. Out of that cloud had appeared shy Jenny, wrapped in a cape that looked like a horse blanket beside her father's dapper tuxedo.

Toodles went straight into the living room to spontaneous applause, but my father—elegant even in his tatty dinner jacket—gallantly helped Jenny off with her cape. Tossing it over his arm, he bent down to kiss her cheek. "Happy New Year, Jenny."

Daddy didn't usually pay attention to the plain women. He spe-

cialized in pretty, vivacious females who reflected back his efferves-
cent ways. He must have experienced an unusual moment of kindness
that evening. Jenny Tuttle, plump and otherwise colorless, had
turned pink at his kiss. She couldn't find her voice.

Daddy led her off into the living room, bending over her as if
she were as fascinating as a beautiful princess. "You'll favor us with
some music tonight, won't you, dear? Nobody can tickle the ivories
the way you can."

Daddy flattered Jenny onto the piano bench in a shadowy corner, where she sat for the rest of the night playing one Toodles
Tuttle tune after another. Her father sang his own jaunty lyrics, and
the guests alternately sang along or danced in the living room,
where the moth-eaten carpet had been rolled up. That night, nobody noticed Jenny. When Daddy asked me to, I prepared a plate
from the buffet laid out on silver platters in the dining room and
delivered a midnight meal to her with a glass of champagne. Remaining at the piano, she ate and drank in snatches between musical numbers.

The only time I remember noticing her after that was when my
parents danced together—just the two of them performing for the
crowd, Daddy spinning and dipping Mama, who laughed and
didn't miss a beat. Jenny fumbled a few notes, though, as she
watched my glamorous parents in each other's arms.

At the time of the party, we had no servants in the house anymore. Although Grandmama was quietly selling off her silver and
jewelry, we no longer had the money to pay household help. So as
midnight neared, it was my grandmother who struggled to open a
bottle of champagne for thirsty guests. She squeezed her eyes shut
and put her thumbs awkwardly against the cork. With an explosive
pop it had sailed into the crowd, and champagne foamed onto the
floor. Laughter erupted, and then applause. I hadn't recalled where
the cork had landed, but Boom Boom had obviously not forgotten.

I remembered Jenny that long-ago night being . . . pathetic. Collapsed on the rug now, she looked even more pitiable.

I intended to feel for a pulse, but as soon as my fingers touched her flesh I knew she was gone. Jenny had been dead for some hours.

Her body lay on a small area rug beside the bed, feet bare, nightgown twisted around her crumpled legs. With one hand, she had seized a handful of the fabric over her heart, and although the muscles of her fingers had loosened in death, the message was unmistakable: A pain in her chest had come on suddenly.

On the floor beside her pocket lay a small, faded photograph. I looked closer. It was a typical school portrait of a child—maybe six or seven years old, a homely boy with a fringe of dark hair he was clearly trying to hide behind. He had a knobby chin, and his front teeth were missing. Clearly, though, the photo had meant something to Jenny. She had kept it close, and it was in her hand when she died.

I knew better than to touch the photo—or anything else—but I couldn't stop myself from closing Jenny's half-open eyes.

"Her heart," the nurse said, standing over me. "She had a weak heart."

Boom Boom wrestled a crumpled hankie from a pocket and sniffled into it. "I never thought Jenny would go before me. I only hope God took her gently."

Gently? Glancing around, I thought Jenny's death had been anything but gentle. Her bedclothes were twisted. The jumble of bottles and cans on her bedside table had been knocked awry in the throes of her agony. Her cell phone lay yards away on the carpet. I wondered if she had brushed if off the table and had been trying to reach it to call 911 when she was fatally stricken.

The only corner of the room that seemed undisturbed held a small shrine to Toodles Tuttle. On an upright piano sat a large framed photo of the famous Broadway composer. He wore a tuxedo and smiled beguilingly at me from across the room. Every day, Jenny Tuttle must have awakened to her father's smile.

"Poor Jenny," sobbed the man behind me. "Poor, poor Jenny!"

The woman with him had a corona of blond hair with the texture of cotton candy. Her voice was squeaky. "Don't get hysterical, Fred. You'll trigger one of your asthma attacks."

I looked up at the couple and wracked my brain. They looked familiar to me. He was sixtyish but working to look younger. He wore loose-fitting trousers on extraordinarily long legs with saddle shoes and had tied a scarf jauntily around his neck. His thinning hair was as jet-black as an advertisement for hair dye.

She was younger—a spritely character from Dr. Seuss with a pink-cheeked face beneath the halo of bright blond hair tied up with a ribbon. Her petite body was encased in a purple leotard with a matching tutu around her hips, tap shoes on her tiny feet. A mad grin seemed stamped permanently on her face.

The man finally snuffled up his tears and gave me a trembling smile. He put his hand down to me to shake. "How do you do? I'm Fred Fusby. I'm the music director of the show."

The baby-voiced woman with him said, "You probably recognize us. We used to be Fusby and Fontanna, the famous dance duo? Fred and I starred in seven Tuttle musicals. I'm Poppy Fontanna."

"Hello."

Poppy Fontanna almost curtsied as she shook my hand. Out of her mouth spilled what sounded like a string of well-memorized words from an old review. "People say I embody everything Toodles wanted musical theater to be—lively and sophisticated with a touch of sexy panache."

"You were on Broadway?" I asked, striving to be polite as we spoke over the dead body of their idol's daughter.

"Yes, *Sunlight before Rain*? *Happy Heels*? Now Fred and I do road shows—you know, the traveling companies, bus and truck revivals of the old musicals. He has arthritis in his feet, though, so he stopped performing with me and conducts the orchestra instead. Anyway, when Boom Boom called and said she'd found a brand new Toodles Tuttle musical—of course Fred and I were on the first plane here. We're thrilled to help bring to life *Bluebird of Happiness*."

Fred wiped his eyes. "We were so excited. But now—oh, this is a terrible tragedy. Jenny won't be here to enjoy the—the—"

"To enjoy her father's final work," Poppy finished for him. As he dissolved into sobs again, she gathered Fred into a comforting hug and patted his back as if he were a child.

"Oh, I dunno," Boom Boom said from the ottoman. "Maybe we'll find some other music Toodles left behind. This old house is chock-full of his stuff."

"Miz Tuttle," the nurse interrupted briskly, "I think it's time you had a lie-down, don't you? I'll make you some tea, and you can pull yourself together."

"Okay, okay, Higgie." To me, Boom Boom said, "This is my nurse, Miss Higginbotham."

Just then the paramedics appeared at the doorway with their gear and a wheeled stretcher. The first paramedic took one look at Boom Boom's blue skin and said, "Wow, I've never seen anybody so cyanotic before. And still be conscious, that is."

The second paramedic elbowed his partner aside and saw me on the floor. He grinned happily. "Great! I haven't delivered a baby in months!"

"There's no baby. Not yet, anyway." I moved aside so he could see the body of Jenny Tuttle sprawled out on the floor. He lost his smile and went down on one knee to feel for a pulse, just as I had.

Michael helped me up off the rug. The scene in the bedroom broke up quickly, but not before I decided that I had witnessed exactly that—a theatrical scene. Fred and Poppy slipped out of the room with the precision of a dance team that did everything smoothly. Lexie gave me a wide-eyed look that indicated we had more to discuss, but she stepped forward to help the nurse assist Boom Boom off the ottoman and out the door. I could hear Boom Boom's nattering voice as they led her down the hallway.

The paramedics took over, and Michael bent to help move their equipment. I faded to the back of the bedroom. The drama of the last several minutes suddenly hit me in a wave of nausea. I felt a little woozy. To my left, I saw a half-open door and slipped through it. I found myself in a lady's dressing room with an adjacent bathroom.

Unsteadily, I sat down on the slipper chair at the dressing table. In the makeup mirror, my reflection looked pale. I tried to shake the nausea off, but my head continued to spin.

To compose myself, I focused on the dressing table. It was crowded—not with makeup, but with cans of soda pop and prescription bottles. A lot of prescription bottles. I couldn't help looking at the labels, and I discovered that the bottles contained an assortment of diet pills—many of them the same prescriptions I had encouraged my sister Libby to dispose of a year ago when she went on a crash diet. No wonder Jenny had appeared smaller than when I saw her last. She'd been trying to lose weight. The rest of the bottles seemed to be vitamins and supplements—some of the labels in Chinese. Others from pharmacies with Canadian addresses. The wastebasket at my feet was filled with more empty soda cans. I recognized the name of an energy drink I had been warned to stay away from during my pregnancy.

Michael stuck his head around the door, his face full of concern. "You okay?"

"So-so."

He came to my side. "The paramedics are calling the coroner.

33

We can't get out through the bedroom right now. The door is blocked by their gear. So we're stuck. You might as well stay here and calm down."

"I'm calm. Except—my goodness, have you ever seen anything as bizarre as Boom Boom Tuttle?"

"You mean Mama Smurf? Was she wearing blue makeup?"

"She seemed to be blue all over. Do you think her color has anything to do with the show they're working on? It's called *Bluebird of Happiness*."

"She's sure got the blue part down."

"Have you found Bridget?"

"Not yet. But the cops are on their way, and she has a sixth sense about cops. Maybe she beat it already." His gaze grew concerned. "You're not going to faint, are you?"

"I'm not going to faint," I said. "But I—I knew Jenny Tuttle a little. She used to come to the parties my parents threw. She was very sweet. It was a shock seeing her like that."

Michael looked contrite. "I'm sorry I called you up here."

"No, I was glad to help. But perhaps we should give the family some privacy now." I glanced through the adjacent Jack-and-Jill bathroom to a second door on the other side. "Maybe there's another way out of here."

In Lexie's house, most of the bedrooms shared a connecting bath. I got up and went to the other door. I tried the knob, and it turned. Michael came behind me as I opened the door.

We walked through a small bathroom and into another bedroom.

And found Michael's mother on the bed with a man.

CHAPTER THREE

Bridget sat on the bed, slipping on her shoes. From a standing position, the man was stepping into his loafers.

Michael stopped dead. "Oh, hell, Bridget. What have you been doing?"

I thought it was pretty obvious, but his mother smiled up at him from the bed. "Don't get the wrong idea, Mickey."

"Wrong idea?" Michael's voice went up ten notches. "Is there any other idea?"

I touched his arm. "Michael—"

"It isn't what it looks like." With the flourish of a magician's assistant, Bridget indicated the shoeless man. "Meet Mr. Oxenfeld. He's the producer."

Oxenfeld had taken one look at Michael, and all the color had drained from his face. He snatched up his shoes and backed himself against the closet door, hugging his loafers as if for protection.

Bridget said, "He promised me an audition."

"In bed?" Michael demanded.

"A singing audition," Bridget insisted. "Dancing, too. We came up here to discuss it in private. There was a lot of shouting going on downstairs. We couldn't hear ourselves think."

Michael said, "You weren't the least bit curious about the shouting?"

"Don't be rude." Bridget mustered a motherly tone. "I was in labor with you for two days."

"Only because you didn't want to leave the roulette table. A lady was found dead in the next room."

"Dead!" Oxenfeld squeaked. "Who? Boom Boom?"

"I'm sorry, Mr. Oxenfeld," I said as kindly as I could, "but it's Jenny Tuttle who's gone. It looks as if she had a heart attack."

"Jenny! Oh my God!"

If Oxenfeld had looked shaken at being discovered in a compromising position, he suddenly appeared to be on the brink of a heart attack of his own. He ran past us into the connecting bath, then had second thoughts and made an abrupt about-face to dash back into the bedroom. Clutching his shoes under one arm, he yanked open the door and fled into the hallway.

Bridget called, "Hang on, babycakes!"

But when Oxenfeld didn't come back, she turned to me and said, "Thanks for nothing. I had a perfectly good audition going, and now you've ruined it."

Michael grabbed his mother by the elbow and hauled her to her feet. "Forget the audition. We're getting you out of here now."

"But—"

"The cops are due any minute. Do you really want to get mixed up in a police investigation?"

After a second's consideration, Bridget said, "You've got a point. I—uh—have a few speeding tickets they might want to discuss."

"I thought so."

"Have I ever told you about the boyfriend I had with three hundred speeding tickets?"

Michael said, "You know I don't like hearing about your boyfriends."

The three of us skulked into the hallway. There, Lexie was just letting herself out of another bedroom. From inside, we could hear Boom Boom's raised voice. Her nurse argued back.

Lexie shook her head. "Boom Boom's in there fussing about which wig to wear on opening night. Who's going to notice her hair if the rest of her is blue?"

Michael said to her, "Let's get you off the stage before the curtain goes up."

We hurried down the stairs and past the same crowd of weeping dancers still gathered around the piano. We got out the front door in time to see the Bentley make a hasty escape down the driveway—probably Ox Oxenfeld exiting stage left as if pursued by the proverbial theatrical bear. Passing the Bentley on their way up toward the house, though, came two police cars, lights flashing.

Michael cursed. "It's going to look worse if we leave now. Let me talk to them, okay? Maybe I can explain we're just good Samaritans."

The first officer out of his cruiser was a state trooper named Ricci, whom Michael and I had gotten to know over the winter during Michael's house arrest. Today Ricci and Michael shook hands—if not exactly as friends, then as longtime acquaintances.

I hated handing Michael the job of explaining our presence on the scene. But Lexie was officially an ex-con—an inexperienced ex-con, to boot—so letting him do the talking might save us unnecessary complications.

To make matters worse, from behind the police cars roared a familiar red minivan. My sister Libby tooted her horn before jumping the sidewalk and pulling to a stop. She bailed out into the sunshine wearing a sky blue skirt with a low-cut T-shirt on top, belted at the waist to enhance her voluptuous figure. In sequins, the T-shirt read BUDGET BUNNY.

"Nora!" She waved her hand as if to flag down a speeding train. "I haven't seen you all week! And you've grown another size already! Oh, I used to love wearing that shirt. It's one of my favorites. So cute!"

"Lib, this is an awkward time for—"

With a squeal, Libby shot past me and gave Lexie an exuberant hug. "Lexie, my dear, you look marvelous! Being indoors for so long obviously does wonders for the complexion. Did you learn to meditate? Or make friends with terrifying people? We must have lunch someday, so you can tell me everything. I hear all that time alone can be spiritually uplifting. Orange is the new Zen! And who's this?"

Libby sized up Bridget O'Halloran and obviously recognized a soul sister. Before I could introduce them, Libby blurted out, "Whoever you are, I love your fashion flair. Leopard is universally stylish. You could wear it with a nun's habit and be welcomed anywhere. It adds a soupçon of pizzazz to every outfit. Like cinnamon."

Bridget took in my sister from the top tufts of her auburn hair, caught up in a fetching bouffant ponytail, to the besparkled peep-toed shoes on her feet, and she instantly warmed to Libby. "I don't know about soup, but I think leopard says 'I'm available.' At least, that's what all my men friends tell me."

"Do you have many men friends?" Libby asked brightly. "A few to spare, maybe?"

"Libby," I intervened before the two of them could get down to the business of exchanging dating strategies, "this is Michael's mother, Bridget O'Halloran."

Intrigued and delighted, Libby shook Bridget's hand. "I have ne'er-do-well sons, too! Sometimes I think they'll be the death of me, but at other times I realize they add a certain je ne sais quoi to life."

"Like cinnamon," Bridget said.

"Or vodka," Libby replied. She finally noticed the hubbub unfolding around us. Her testosterone detector perked up as she realized several handsome policemen were moving purposefully into the Tuttle house. "What in the world is going on here? I have a delivery to make."

"A delivery?"

I had already seen the new decal stuck on the driver's side door of Libby's minivan. In bright letters, the decal read BUDGET BUNNY. The accompanying picture showed a smiling rabbit delivering a basket to the front door of a delighted housewife. The same smiling rabbit appeared on Libby's T-shirt.

"Have you started another new business?"

Libby proudly thrust out her bosom to display her T-shirt. "This week, I'm helping a friend who's a franchise owner for a wonderful company with plenty of upward mobility. I'm giving it a whirl before I decide to invest. Assuming any banker would back a single mother whose only credit reference is Costco. The job is not the spiritual experience I usually seek in my enterprising endeavors, but I've already met the most charming people. The Tuttles have been especially friendly, even though Boom Boom says Grandmama Blackbird was her sworn enemy. Something about hitting her with a champagne cork. Don't you think they're delightful? The Tuttles, I mean?"

"If you like the color blue," Lexie said. "Have you laid eyes on Boom Boom?"

Libby didn't blink. "You mean her skin cream? Lately I've been trying out a night cream that's green. It may help with wrinkles, but it smells like anchovies. Every night, I dream about pizza. Maybe I should ask Boom Boom about hers."

"I don't think it's a cream. I think it's her skin that's blue."

"Libby, what kind of services are you providing?" I asked, cutting through her diversionary baloney. Libby had once tried peddling sex toys without a permit, which had landed her on the Bucks County most wanted list for weeks. I feared she might have found another dubious pursuit.

"Oh, get that frightened look off your face!" She mustered some irritation. "We run errands, that's all. So far, I've made a few deliveries, done some personal shopping. My friend will even take your car for an oil change, specializing in Lexus models, because—did you know?—the Lexus service department gives massages while you wait. There are lots of hidden perks in this job—"

Lexie cut the sales pitch short. "What are you doing for the Tuttles?"

Libby popped open the tailgate of the minivan and stood back to reveal her cargo. Inside, we could see several cases of the same energy drink I had seen in Jenny Tuttle's bedroom.

Lexie observed, "Somebody's very thirsty."

"Jenny Tuttle," Libby reported. "I swear, she's addicted to the stuff. This is my second trip for her this week. She tips well, though."

"About that tip," I said. "Don't get your hopes up today, Libby."

"Why not?"

"Jenny died this morning."

"Died!" Libby clapped one hand over her bosom. "What happened?"

"She had a heart attack."

"Just my luck!" Libby wailed. "One minute I have a reliably steady customer, and the next minute I'm stuck with a huge hole in my schedule."

Bridget said, "I know what you mean. Just when I think I've caught a break in my career, somebody rudely interrupts my audition." She glared in my direction.

"Who were you auditioning for?" Libby asked.

"Ox Oxenfeld, the Broadway producer."

"Oxy is a producer?" Libby's face lit up. "He never mentioned that to me!"

Bridget blinked. "You know Ox?"

"He's one of my customers. Actually, he was my very first. I delivered a chilled bottle of champagne to his house for his lunch. Three days later, he invited me to stay for crab salad—I just love crab salad, don't you?—and I got to telling him about my quest for spiritual vibrancy. He became very interested and said he was on a similar path. We did some breathing exercises together. Some men just need to be taken by the hand, don't they? They're so helpless."

Bridget had begun eyeing Libby with a distinctly cooler expression growing on her face. "Yeah, helpless all right."

Libby missed the warning and continued to burble. "Oxy sent me home with crab salad leftovers, and I gave him some other exercises to try. At first, he thought I meant push-ups. Well, that just goes to show he has a lot to learn about *me*!" She laughed liltingly. "My philosophy? Exercise is such a dirty word, I have to wash my mouth out with chocolate!"

While Libby laughed, Bridget folded her arms. "Good philosophy. Do you know how much money Ox Oxenfeld has?"

"Money? Well," said Libby, dimpling, "he did give me a tour of his house. I saw everything from the fancy cars in the garage to the heated towel racks outside the sauna. There's nothing like a sauna to bring a glow, is there?"

I decided we'd better change the direction of this conversation before Bridget strangled my sister with the leopard print bra peeping out from beneath her tight sweater.

"Libby, I'm feeling a little exhausted. Why don't you drive us all over to Lexie's house?"

"Now?" Libby gave the busy police officers a glance of longing. "Well, we don't want to endanger your child, I suppose. This way, everyone."

Bridget called shotgun, and we all piled into the minivan.

In Lexie's driveway sat a car I didn't recognize—a little white convertible with red upholstery. With a curt word of thanks to Libby, Bridget threw her expensive handbag into the convertible's passenger seat and climbed behind the wheel. She slammed the door and revved the engine before tearing out of the driveway. Zooming past us, she raised one dismissive hand as a good-bye.

"Good grief," said Libby as we watched her abrupt departure, "for a mob boss's mistress, you'd think she'd have more people skills. We're lucky she didn't run over our toes, aren't we?"

Lexie wound her arm through mine. "Nora, let's get you in out of this heat. You look pale. Libby, can you join us? Or do you have more deliveries to make?"

Libby shrugged. "If Jenny Tuttle is dead, I'm done for the day. But I'm not ready to face my children yet. Nora, are you going to work? I'll drive you into the city. I could go for some recreational shopping to raise my endorphins."

I had to be at the offices of the *Philadelphia Intelligencer* in an hour and a half, and there was no telling if Michael could get away from the police in time to drive me, so I thanked Libby for her offer. While Lexie made drinks, I hauled myself upstairs to change.

With relief, I stripped off Libby's maternity T-shirt and took a fast shower to rinse off the pool chlorine. Refreshed, I put on a linen maternity dress—one of the few that didn't reflect Libby's preference for low décolletage. Nor did it make me look as if I only needed a Wonder Woman lunchbox to carry to kindergarten. Why did designers of maternity clothes believe pregnant women wanted to regress to their own toddler wardrobes? It was hard to find something that made me look remotely professional. This sleeveless, trapeze-style dress was a cheery shade of pink, though, and I'd had it hemmed to show off my legs—one feature that hadn't ballooned up. Yet. I had found an antique seashell button that worked as a closure at my neckline and matched the subtle embroidery around my throat. I checked the mirror. With a pair of kitten-heeled slingbacks, I looked pretty good. Almost normal from the back. The side view was an eyepopper, though. Could I spend the next two months backing into rooms?

Trying not to think about my silhouette, I combed out my hair and redid it into another cool updo. My face had a touch of sunshine—a few freckles had bloomed on my nose—so I added lip gloss and mascara and hoped I didn't look too pale. After seeing Boom Boom's bizarre complexion, I felt as if I looked pretty normal.

Downstairs, Lexie and Libby were finishing glasses of iced tea in the breakfast room.

"Michael didn't come back yet?"

"He must still be talking with the police." Lexie gave me a hug. "Try to put this afternoon out of your mind, Nora. It's awful, but really, people die every day. It's natural, the circle of life and all."

"I know." But it felt unnatural to me. I remembered Jenny as she had been years ago, her eyes shining with gratitude for my father's kindness. She had been a real person to me, not a stranger. And her death was not something I could shake off in an hour or two.

Briskly, Lexie said, "Thanks for coming today, sweetie. You're good medicine for me. And for keeping me out of the public eye—you're wonderful. For the rest of the day, think about your baby and—the future." She smiled, careful not to mention next week's wedding in front of Libby. "See you again tomorrow? The weather's supposed to be perfect for dipping our toes in the pool."

"You know I love to dip with you." I gave her a good-bye hug.

Libby picked up my swimming bag and led the way to her minivan. "Lexie says there were plenty of spiritual opportunities in prison, but they all required sitting on folding chairs, which sounds awful. I mean, why risk hemorrhoids, even for metaphysical nirvana? Give me a therapist's office with a comfy couch any day. If nothing else, you get a nice nap. That door handle is broken," she said when I reached to let myself into the vehicle. "I'll have to open it for you from inside."

When we were both in the van, I said, "What's wrong with this door handle?"

"I left the van parked on a side street in New Hope, and somebody tried to break it off with a crow bar. Imagine! In broad daylight! That town just isn't safe anymore."

"Really?" Our little village had always seemed perfectly secure to me. The only crime I had ever witnessed was when one of my mother's friends broke the fashion rule of wearing white to a wedding.

"Rawlins says there's suddenly more crime in the neighborhood. It's a good thing That Man of Yours is staying at your house. You must feel safe there now that we're having a crime wave."

"I do." Especially after Michael had gone overboard and spent some money on a security system. We had also argued about getting some large dogs to protect the property. So far, I was winning that battle. We had enough animals to look after already. But hearing Libby's report of increased crime in our area, I appreciated Michael's concern.

Libby said, "I hope Lexie's safe where she is, all by herself."

"She has Samir. And she's not afraid to call 911 in an emergency." A thought struck me. "Libby, you haven't forgotten we need to keep Lexie's location a secret."

"I haven't breathed a word!"

"Thank you. If the press finds her, they'll eat her alive."

"She would be a big story," Libby agreed. "I love attention as much as the next person, but not the kind where the press makes you sound horrible. Although, technically, Nora, aren't you the press?"

"Well . . . yes."

"Is it some kind of career no-no that you're keeping her whereabouts a secret?"

Although I had been taking an online journalism course lately, I was still enough of an amateur not to know for sure. "Let's hope not."

Within minutes Libby and I were speeding down I-95 toward Philadelphia. Libby's phone erupted into the song "Call Me Maybe," and she answered.

"Oh, thanks," she said to her caller. "But I won't be needing any more energy drinks, after all. Bye!" When she hung up, she said, "Poor Jenny. All that work to lose weight, and where did it get her? She's still fat, but now she's dead, too. It's a cautionary tale, isn't it? I guess I'm lucky I'm just voluptuous, not in a coffin."

I sighed. "Do you remember Jenny, Lib? She came to Blackbird Farm with her father for a New Year's Eve party."

"Well, I remember her father. What a charmer! He came to several parties. But Jenny? She's hazy in my memory."

"She played the piano," I said. Which explained why Libby hadn't noticed her. At the parties our parents threw, Libby usually thrust her way into the center of the action—sitting on the piano with her chin propped fetchingly in her hands while someone sang to her. Or dancing in front of the crowd. Anything to put herself on display. On the other hand, Jenny rarely did anything to draw attention to herself.

Libby said, "It's too bad she died. She had a heart attack?"

"Looks that way. She was taking diet pills."

Libby said, "And drinking all that energy stuff? What a bad combination."

"Especially if she had a weak heart."

"Some people will do anything to get thin," Libby said. "This just goes to show that diets can be deadly."

While Libby chattered, I thought of Ox Oxenfeld's reaction when he heard the news that someone had died. Which reminded me of seeing him with Bridget, and then I made the mental leap to my sister spending time in the company of the shoeless Broadway producer.

I turned to Libby. "Tell me more about Ox Oxenfeld. All that crab salad and champagne—are you dating him?"

"Dating?" Libby asked vaguely. "What's a date? I have five children, Nora. I can't date. I'm lucky I can break away just for an hour to get an emergency pedicure. Where would I be without Rawlins to babysit Lucy and Max while I try out the errand-running business? I just wish he wasn't also making a list of the expensive things he wants me to buy for him before he goes off to college in a few weeks. And the twins got themselves summer internships at the medical examiner's office, which I thought would be fine—you know, doing some office filing, maybe—but of course they talked their way into a lab, which means I have to pay for the disposable suits they wear to wheel bodies around. Those suits cost such a pretty penny, too. Honestly, why can't they talk their way into a nice job bagging groceries or making coffee? Today they're learning how to scrape DNA from under the fingernails of a cadaver. I suppose I'll have to pay for that somehow, too."

I recognized the signs. She was steering me away from the subject of a potential new boyfriend by throwing conversational bombs in my path. I couldn't help being distracted. "Lib, the twins are only fourteen. Do you think it's wise for them to be scraping cadavers?"

"How can I stop them? The twins got away from me a long time ago." Libby rolled down her window long enough to tousle her hair and freshen up the air in the minivan. Or maybe to give herself time to concoct a story I might swallow. At last she said, "I'm feeling a little overwhelmed these days. Seeing you so happy with That Man of Yours, and your baby coming, too—well, I can't help feeling a little down."

"I'm sorry that you're feeling low," I said with all sincerity.

"I'm not trying to make you feel guilty," she replied at once. "I'm being honest, that's all. Here you are, happy with a new man in your life and children coming, not to mention a glamorous job where you see beautiful, sophisticated people every night, while the only break in the monotony of my life seems to be an exterminator who can't get rid of my carpenter ants. He brought burritos again last night after the children refused to eat the low-calorie asparagus soup I spent hours making. They acted like he was Zorro, coming to rescue them from the food police—me!"

Suspicions aroused, I asked, "Did the exterminator stay after dinner?"

"I did not invite him to stay," she reported. "He's perfectly happy watching television with the children, but where I'm concerned, Perry Delbert lacks a certain . . . spark."

"The last guy with spark was that fireman who set fire to your bedroom curtains with a scented candle, remember? It was a lucky thing he didn't burn the house down." Catching myself, I said more kindly, "I've seen the way Perry looks at you, Lib. He has plenty of spark."

"Well, I wish he'd be a little more demonstrative! Honestly, I have to drag more than two syllables out of him."

"Surely he says something?"

"He says he likes my size! He says he likes a woman he can hold on to! Now, what kind of compliment is that? So when Oxy pays me genuine compliments and offers to rub my feet—"

"He rubs your feet?" I asked. "I thought you were just delivering champagne!"

"Don't judge," Libby snapped. "I work hard for my family. I deserve something nice once in a while. At the end of an excruciating day running silly errands for people who have more money than anybody should, an occasional foot rub is a small reward. I bet That Man of Yours rubs more than your feet."

"Libby—"

"I'm jealous! There, I said it. I'm in a rut at the moment—a very expensive rut—and you're deliriously happy, aren't you?"

"Well, yes. We're overjoyed about our daughter coming. And we're delighted to be adopting the baby that Rawlins and Zephyr Starr are giving to us—"

"Oh, let's not talk about that!" Libby interrupted, even more irritably. "That's the worst!"

"The worst?"

"For me, it's awful! I'll start crying if we discuss my becoming a g-g-grandmother." With heat, she burst out, "I just can't face it, Nora! You might be happy about that baby, but she is part of my current state of mind."

Maybe a big part. I realized I'd been so wrapped up in keeping Lexie out of the limelight that I had missed all the signs. Libby's eldest son, Rawlins, a good kid with a sensible head on his shoulders most of the time, had made a mistake in judgment last winter during his senior year in high school. He ended up fathering a child with a woman who—there is no other way to say it—deliberately seduced him to get herself pregnant, and then went to prison for murder. Rather than try to raise the baby himself, Rawlins had asked Michael and me to adopt the child, and we had accepted with enthusiasm. The baby was going to be born within a week of my own due date, which was a little daunting, but also exciting.

But for Libby, the coming baby meant she was going to bear the disheartening label of *grandmother*.

"I'm too young to be a gr-r-r—I can't even say it! I'm not even forty yet! It's not fair!"

"All right," I soothed. "We don't have to talk about the other baby."

"We have to *talk* about her," Libby cried, exasperation boiling over. "We can't ignore her for the rest of her life! I just don't want to hear the G-word anymore, okay?"

"Okay," I said before Libby could burst into a storm of tears. "From now on, she'll be your niece—how about that? Nobody needs to be reminded that she's your—well, that she's a child that Rawlins brought into the world. She'll be my daughter. Your niece."

"Niece." Libby gradually brightened. "That's very much nicer. Thank you, Nora."

"And we're delighted to adopt her, Libby. Your life will come together soon, too, I'm sure. With Rawlins going to college, and Max starting nursery school, Lucy growing up, and the twins going to high school—"

"It's probably best if we ignore the twins. There's no telling what trouble they can get into in high school." She snuffled up her tears. "High school means girls and access to dangerous substances in the chemistry lab. I can't bring myself to think about what they could blow up."

"Then think about yourself for an afternoon," I said. "A little shopping might be just what you need. There's a new lingerie shop on Walnut Street. I think you'd really love it."

She sighed. "You're so insightful sometimes, Nora. Yes, it's time for me to stop wallowing and take charge—get my life back on the right spiritual trajectory. I've got a new career and maybe a new man on my horizon. I know! I should study up on Broadway musicals! I think I have a tape of *Camelot* somewhere. And *West Side*

Story. Remember those cute summer dresses they wore in the movie? If I had enough cash, I'd update my whole summer wardrobe."

The thought of my sister rechanneling her annoyance with the exterminator and devoting all of her suppressed sexual energy to Mr. Oxenfeld gave me a stab of pity for the poor fellow. And if Bridget O'Halloran had decided to target him, too, he might be in mortal danger.

"Maybe you shouldn't go overboard with the new man, Libby. Why don't you let nature take its course gradually?"

"To hell with that," she said. "At his age, he might die, and I'd have to start all over again with someone else. That's just poor time management. No, I think I'd better get cracking where Ox Oxenfeld is concerned. Strike while the iron is hot! Off to the lingerie store! Would you like to come along? It would get your mind off Jenny Tuttle."

"No, thanks. I have work to do. Have fun without me."

"I wonder what Ox's favorite color is?" Newly energized, Libby sent the minivan swooping off an exit ramp, and we arrived in Philadelphia.

CHAPTER FOUR

The good news was that if my batty sister was focusing her considerable energies on Ox Oxenfeld, at least she wouldn't be planning my wedding.

Libby dropped me in front of the Pendergast Building, and I was soon through security and zooming up the elevator to the offices of the *Philadelphia Intelligencer*, the rag that still paid my salary.

As soon as I stepped off the elevator, I knew Gus Hardwicke was back with a vengeance.

Although most of my colleagues usually headed home around four in the afternoon, the whole newsroom was still buzzing with busy reporters. Either we had big breaking news—perhaps a celebrity had been arrested for indecent exposure—or our editor had thrown a tantrum and every writer on the staff was trying to prove his or her value by staying late. All heads were bent, faces turned to computer screens, fingers busy on keyboards—hot in the pursuit of a lurid story for tomorrow's edition. I heard the clatter of keystrokes and the low hum of reporters intent on saving their jobs.

I bumped my desk with my belly but caught an avalanche of envelopes before they cascaded to the floor. I didn't stop in the office every day to check my mail, so invitations to social events sometimes piled up. It was often more efficient for me to arrive at events directly from home, and I wrote my stories in the back of a car that whisked me from place to place. I communicated often with the features editor by phone and e-mail—a system that worked well for us.

Sometime during the last couple of days, someone had sent me a vase of flowers along with an invitation to a summer gala. The yellow roses were drooping just a little. I scooped up the vase and cradled it in my arm, intending to walk it directly to the ladies' room for a drink.

But a loud voice boomed across the newsroom like the crack of a bullwhip. "I'm so glad you could finally join us, Miss Blackbird!"

I spun around, arms full of invitations and flowers. The whole newsroom looked up from their tasks, too, as if everyone had been anticipating this moment when our temperamental boss finally laid eyes on me, the late arriver.

Gus Hardwicke stood at the open door of his office, his freckled arms crossed on his chest, wiry dark brows thunderous as he glared with barely controlled rage. He was tall and athletic, wearing an open-necked dress shirt and linen trousers, bristling with Australian brio and the temper of a managing editor ready to prove he hadn't missed a step during his vacation. His narrowed gaze involuntarily left my face, though, and slid lower to land on my distended body.

I saw Gus's green eyes widen. His shock morphed into revulsion before he pulled himself together. "Come into my office, please. We have things to discuss."

I left the invitations at my desk. Walking across the floor felt like a trek across the Sahara as all my fellow employees either sent sympathetic looks my way or made little effort to hide smirks. I guessed they had already a formed a pool to bet on whether I was going to be fired.

Determined not to be intimidated, I breezed into the editor's office and presented him with the vase of flowers. "Welcome home, Mr. Hardwicke," I said in a clear voice that I hoped carried out to the newsroom. "I trust your vacation was restful despite all the globe-trotting. You look a little sunburned. Did you get in any spearfishing? And how was the biking in Paraguay?"

He slammed the door, and we were alone in his office. "The only living creature I felt like spearing was my father. Fortunately, he has bodyguards." He dropped the vase of flowers directly into the trash can beside his desk, then swung around to give me another appalled stare. "Good God, Nora, what the bloody hell happened to you?"

I lifted my arms to better show off my enormous figure. "Do I need to explain the facts of life?"

"I'm well acquainted, thank you. Maybe you need to learn how to avoid this unfortunate outcome. I reckon you're big as a boomer."

I knew Gus Hardwicke was more bark than Aussie bite. So I said with good humor, "We've been over this, Gus. I'm deliriously happy about this baby, and I'm allowed six weeks of maternity leave."

"I thought that wasn't happening until the end of summer."

"We Blackbird women get big early."

"Spare me the gory details. Crikey, I've seen kangaroos carrying two half-grown joeys, and they're not nearly your size."

"Some people actually say pregnancy agrees with me."

"Don't expect me to lie. You look appalling."

"Is this how you treat the ladies Down Under? If so, I can understand why you were thrown out of the country."

"I left voluntarily. More or less."

"I was beginning to wonder if you had decided to fight your way back into your father's good graces and stay in Australia. Or won't he have you?"

"Actually, he's trying to buy some media outlets here in the states. Or hadn't you heard?"

I had heard indeed, but I didn't feel I could press Gus about his media mogul father, who owned at least four television networks and half the newspapers around the globe. Making a move into the U.S., he was bidding to buy a cable company, a handful of tabloids and a radio station or two—all of them owned by a triumvirate of old dragons here in Philadelphia.

But he had encountered a setback with the fire-breathing sellers, so the rumor mill said, and he was regrouping before staging another assault. Like everyone else, I wondered what the senior Hardwicke's next move might be—a full-scale attack or a more wily strategy. I knew the dragons slightly—they had been protégés of my grandfather Blackbird—very patriotic, ring-wing fossils. I guessed they resented someone from another country making a bid for their assets, which they seemed to think were as American as the Liberty Bell and should remain so. But, of course, money talks, even to dragons. And Gus's father had a lot of money.

Gus didn't wait for me to answer his question.

He said, "My current goal is keeping this sinking ship afloat a little longer. While I was away, the bludgers around here started slacking off again. This newspaper is actually on the brink of disaster. I have to fight to earn back every quid I made here all over again, or we're out of business. I need news. Got anything good?"

"You mean more sordid stories about male body parts?"

He laughed. "In the States, dongers do seem to sell newspapers. It's a great country, isn't it?"

Gus leaned against his desk, the only stick of furniture in the office. It was my observation that he preferred to work on his feet, pacing and shouting, rather than sitting in a comfortable desk chair like a normal human being. Which meant there was never anywhere for me to sit. The walls were decorated only by large sheets of blank newsprint, where he scrawled his ideas for the next day's edition. Each night he ripped down the previous day's work and hammered up fresh paper to begin anew.

He folded his arms over his considerable chest again and said, "We will now have a natter about your dubious contribution to journalistic excellence while I was away."

"You were reading my work while on vacation?"

"*On holiday* doesn't mean *brain-dead*. I read your piece about the ten worst charities."

"It was the ten best, actually. I added the ten worst because—"

"The worst are what kicked up reader interest. Which I like. As for the rest of your work, all I can say is there was certainly a lot of it."

"Everybody checks news on their electronic devices so often nowadays that I thought we should frequently post something to keep readers interested."

"News about the blithering social scene? Or what frock somebody's empty-headed secretary wears to a ladies' luncheon?" Scorn dripped from his words. "You call that news?"

"I call it content. Content that readers want to see. Yes, updates from Washington are more important, but what a stylish office worker wears to a fund-raising lunch is what keeps people coming back. Our online advertising is up eighteen percent," I said, pleased to have pried the number from the ogre who ran the advertising department. "I don't think that's only because the public wants to read about exhibitionists. My frequent social posts keep readers coming back, but they make advertisers take notice, too."

He did not argue with me. "I hear you were the one who insisted Tremaine post my video clips in the online edition."

"I did not insist. I suggested. The results were phenomenal. Readers loved everything. Who knew Paraguay was so scenic?"

"I sent those videos to Tremaine because he's a bike enthusiast himself. I intended them to be seen only by him. I did not give permission—"

"Our page views were better than ever," I said. "Maybe it was those shots of you in tight shorts, but I truly believe our readers are interested in what the rest of the world looks like. Your video clips were a perfect example of how we could expand our view of the world. I wish you'd sent more."

"Are you free for dinner? I can show you all my sightseeing photos." His temper was definitely cooling, because a gleam of naughtiness began to shine in his green eyes.

Gus had made a serious bid for my affections when he first came to Philadelphia. I thought I had successfully diverted his efforts, and now here he was playing his game again.

I maintained my composure. "Despite the graciousness of that invitation, I must decline. I have several events to attend this evening. In fact, if you're finished with me now, I should get moving."

He gave me a wry look. "Are you off to lift a coldie with your Pommy friends?"

"Cocktails at an apartment around the corner. It's a party to raise money for leukemia research. Some of the Phillies will be volunteer waiters."

Gus grabbed a white linen jacket off a peg by the door and swung into it. He opened the door and held it for me. "I've been cooped up here all day listening to your lazy colleagues whinge about their work. Let's go. I could use a drink, and I don't care what local cricket player gives it to me."

A Little Night Murder

Reporters surreptitiously watched us walk to the elevator. Gus punched the button, and we took the plunge together.

He said, "How's your jailbird friend? Lexie Paine, the murderer? You know where she's hiding out, I suppose? First on my list of things I want now that I'm back on the job is an article about her."

"You won't get it from me."

"Have you seen her?"

"Not lately," I said, thinking *not in the last hour.*

"Do you know where she is?"

"Why do you need to know?"

"Because like half the city I want the confessed murderess to explain why she's out of jail several years early."

"She confessed to manslaughter, not murder."

"In this pistol-packing country, doesn't that simply mean she cut some kind of shady deal? That's what she does, right? Shady deals? And what is she up to now? More unscrupulous plans to get even richer?"

"She was a respected investment adviser before things went . . . a little crazy. She never cut deals. And she's not unscrupulous."

"You're such a lamb, Nora. You always assume the people around you are just as innocent. Your friend is corrupt," Gus said flatly. "How did she acquire her home, for example? It's in some kind of historic location, correct? And the rest of the buildings have been owned by boating clubs for—what?—centuries? So she pulled strings to get it. And what about bilking her clients of their life savings? She's a notorious public personality now. And you—the blue blood who knows everybody important—are the perfect reporter to get all the nasty details of the story."

"She did not bilk her clients. Her partner did."

"And she killed him for it."

"It was manslaughter, not—" I caught myself and said more calmly, "I am not going to write about my friend."

"I assumed as much. So I assigned Hostetler to start mucking about."

Hostetler was a particularly unpleasant weasel who shoveled up the worst sort of mud that Gus liked to print. Plus he stole other people's food from the staff refrigerator, which ranked Hostetler very low in my book—especially now that I seemed to be hungry all the time.

I said, "Has Hostetler run out of penises?"

Delighted, Gus gave a rollicking laugh. "Anywhere in the world there's a woman with a hatchet, Hostetler can get her on the phone for a quote. It makes me uneasy about his childhood, but I gave him a raise anyway." As we stepped off the elevator, he said, "I hear your thug is back to his life of crime."

Exasperated, I burst out, "How long have you been back in Philadelphia? Twelve hours? And already you want to make up tales about Michael?"

Gus put one finger to his lips to indicate we should not let ourselves be overheard by the lobby security guards. As we crossed the lobby, he lowered his voice. "It doesn't take long to hear the buzz about the Abruzzo family. I've even seen the photos. He's hanging around with petty drug dealers now? Care to make a statement to the press? An insider's view of current mob activity?"

I kept my voice down, too. "Michael doesn't deal drugs. Never has, never will."

"And the rest of the family?"

I remembered Michael saying some of his pots had boiled over, but I said, "His father and his brothers are serving sentences for some misdeeds, and that's all I know."

"Nora—or shall I call you Pollyanna for all your pretending to know nothing?—let me explain. Abruzzo père, Big Frankie, is in jail, so your thug has been promoted. Except instead of making a fortune in illegal gambling, he's breaking up the old gang. Putting longtime employees out into the street, poor dears, ending the rackets, the numbers, the whole enchilada, as you Yanks say."

"Is that so?"

"That's what I hear," Gus said blithely. "Except it's not going smoothly."

No, it wasn't. I knew quite well that Michael was trying to dismantle his father's crime domain. It seemed a wise course of action now that we had a family on the way. But his cousins were angry. They didn't want the flow of easy money from sports betting and the car-theft ring to end. So Michael had been maneuvering a lot of pieces around the chessboard, working things he didn't want me to know about.

But what photos showed Michael with petty drug dealers? That was news to me.

Gus said, "Think your thug will be around to see your baby born? Or will the rest of his family take action, and parts of him will float up in a secluded billabong someday soon?"

Without a word, I put on my sunglasses and stalked out through the revolving door of the building and out onto the sunny sidewalk. I walked away from Gus.

He caught up and fell into step beside me. "Sorry," he said.

"That was uncalled for."

"I apologize. I'm a bullying sod, I admit it. And you're probably in no condition to be toyed with."

If he'd punched me in the nose, I couldn't have felt more stunned. His words were very cruel. But I was determined to show no weakness. "You must be very angry with me to say a thing like that."

"I am," he admitted, sounding far from unhappy. He put his hands into the pockets of his trousers, and we walked together with the throngs of people heading home for the day. "You made a spectacle of me in the newspaper during my absence. Otherwise, you did your job exceedingly well while I was away. I was also pleased to hear you stepped up while Stan took ill. Lending a hand around the office—that's unusual for you."

"Unusual? Of course I'd help Stan."

"What I mean," he said as we walked, "is that you don't normally take editorial initiative."

"I'm hardly qualified to take any initiatives. I'm a social reporter, not Pulitzer material."

"How will you ever get ahead, Nora, if you have so little ambition? Do you want to report on weddings the rest of your career? Haven't you heard?" Gus asked. "Women need to lean in, not step back when opportunities arise."

"I can't tell. Are you happy with my work or not?"

"You're doing your work commendably. But you disobeyed my order."

"Which order?"

"The one about not putting yourself in any newspaper photographs."

I stopped short on the sidewalk and took off my glasses to stare at him. "That's what had you sending me furious text messages from the other hemisphere? One silly photo?"

"It wasn't silly. It was you—a reporter—on the same page with the people you were covering. You compromised the story by making yourself part of it."

"The story? Gus, it was a party! A party for expectant mothers, raising money for the March of Dimes! Not exactly breaking crime news or political intrigue. I thought it was a nice cross-section of mothers from Philadelphia. Not just a highbrow crowd. What on earth do you imagine I was compromising?"

"I don't want your photo in the paper," he said, flushing.

The photograph in question had been a lark. At a garden party full of friends, I had indeed impulsively posed along with half a dozen equally pregnant young women—all of us laughing over the size of our bellies. It had made a darling picture, nothing worth getting red in the face about.

"You're not making sense," I said. "Your photos brought us readers. Is my picture totally repulsive? What do you have against pregnant women?"

"I have nothing against pregnant women." He reached out and distractedly touched the shell button at my throat. Then he shook himself and took me by the elbow instead. He turned and walked me down the sidewalk again. "I have something against you being pregnant, that's all. And I don't want it in my newspaper."

I laughed. "You're squeamish! Didn't you know where babies come from?"

"I don't like the idea of his baby coming from you," Gus clarified. "Under different circumstances—well, things would be different. Between us. And you know it."

"Things aren't different," I said evenly, keeping up with his brisk pace. "I'm with Michael—for life. You and I agreed not to do this anymore, Gus. We work together, and that's the extent of our relationship. If you had a change of heart while you were away—"

"I can't deny I thought about us," he said. "But good God, a satellite can see you're as big as a buffalo with his child, so you've made your choice."

"I have."

"So I won't be chasing you around the desk," he said. "It's undignified. I don't like looking ridiculous."

"You're not ridiculous," I said, feeling kinder. "It's actually very flattering. At my size, I don't feel very desirable right now, so you— it's nice to know somebody still finds me appealing."

"He doesn't?" Gus demanded.

"Could we slow down, please? I can't catch my breath."

I was hot and sweaty, too, not to mention feeling as if things were getting slightly out of my control.

Gus immediately checked his pace, but he didn't apologize. In a different, more dangerous tone, he said, "I can't see you and not imagine what you did with him to get into that condition."

"Gus," I said.

"And I hate the way the two of you look at each other," he said, voice still quiet, but intense. "It sickens me. I resent him. No, I despise him. I'd knock his teeth through the back of his head, if I got the chance. But I'm not pining for you, so relax. We'll work together, and I'm going to make you work very hard indeed. Your column is one of the few successful bits of this newspaper, and you do know everybody who's important in this damn city, so we're going to make the most of you. Is this your party?"

We had arrived at a crowded spot on the sidewalk outside a handsomely refurbished townhouse that probably dated from the days of the Continental Congress. The freshly painted door was open, held by a smiling young man in a tuxedo shirt and bow tie, dress slacks and a baseball cap. Well-dressed partygoers wished him luck for the rest of the baseball season as they streamed past him into the house.

"Gus," I said again, holding him back by his arm.

He shook free of my touch. "That's all I have to say on the matter."

He put his hand on the small of my back to help me up the staircase until we reached the lavish condominium on the second floor. The walls were white, the ceilings very high, the floor plan an open concept with one gracious room opening into the next. Tall windows looked out into the leafy trees of the park. Blazing afternoon sunlight splashed on the sparkling surfaces of mirrored furniture, the silver chandelier, the polished granite countertop big enough to hold all the food and beverages to serve a hundred people. Rich, pale carpets lay on the mahogany floor. The upholstery was done in soft tones that had been selected by an expert in relaxed luxury.

Gus said, "Take some sexy pictures. Not pretty dresses, but tits and famous people with drinks in their fists, got it?"

With that advice, Gus let his hand fall away from my back as we entered the party.

Our host was the fortysomething father of a teenager who had famously made his family rich by designing popular cell phone apps. The son was nowhere to be seen—perhaps they kept him chained in his bedroom with his computer. The father greeted us at the door. Either he was a geek himself or he had embraced his son's success by dressing in a slovenly T-shirt and cargo shorts with hiking sandals. His hair was long, and his black eyeglasses completed the picture of the wealthy techie. He shook Gus's hand and was surprised when Gus asked an astute question about the new app. They went off for a confab in a corner beside some tall bookcases.

Our hostess was no lockjaw Old Philadelphian or even a New Money babe pumped full of Restylane. Instead, she was an average-looking mom slightly overdressed in a flowered Dolce and Gabbana frock, with maybe too many diamonds for daytime. Her haircut was smart, and she had brand-new blond highlights, but otherwise she appeared to be unspoiled by her newfound wealth. I had heard she was a former kindergarten teacher. A cocoon of longtime friends gathered festively around her and admired the large cocktail ring she showed them—a sure sign she was settling just fine into the lifestyle of the newly rich.

I introduced myself and told the hostess how lovely her home was. She laughingly admitted to having turned the project over to a designer, who had made the place picture-perfect. "I don't have any talent for decorating. And I got sticker shock shopping for bath-tubs."

I liked her for that and asked how they became involved in the leukemia organization. Without a blink she told me about a brother-in-law who had died of the illness.

"We just want to do something useful now that we have the resources," she said.

Her friends jumped in to tell me about how she had been just as sweet before she got rich.

I took notes, then snapped some photos. With my thumbs on the keyboard of my phone, I sent photos of baseball players to the *Intelligencer*'s online editor, who would post the pictures on the newspaper's Web site within the hour.

The room was very hot, and I dabbed my forehead with a cocktail napkin. The party wasn't a big fund-raiser, but rather a feeder event, a gathering of people who might, if properly encouraged, bring more moneyed guests to a bigger gala with an expensive ticket price. There were no high rollers out at this hour. The hedge-fund guys were still at their desks, and the top socialites didn't stoop to midweek disease-related events anymore. Instead, I counted a handful of ornamental Junior Leaguers who were probably just breaking into the social scene or looking to meet men. Also, a scattering of good-hearted people from the medical community, plus some of the professionals who made it possible for the social set to put themselves on display: two important dermatologists, a well-known hair dresser, a pair of hungry Realtors, a spa owner and a formal-wear buyer from a big department store.

I avoided one busy, hard-faced young woman who was launching her career as a social publicist. People who wanted to be famous hired her, I'd heard, to get their names and faces in the media. By Twitter, she had already tried to push one of her clients on me—a suburban restaurant owner's pretty wife who had no claim to fame, as far as I could see, except her good looks and ambition. Knowing who's who in the philanthropic world was useful for me, but I hadn't quite decided how I felt about social climbers hiring personal publicists. If there was a good philanthropic purpose to that, I hadn't discovered it.

From studying the crowd, I deduced that the app family hadn't been rich long enough to attract many wealthy friends, but it wouldn't take long for the social back-scratching to begin. Within a year, I guessed, they would be seen at top fund-raisers several nights a month. They'd be generous with their money, but they'd probably also get their nips and tucks and German cars like everyone else in their social circle. I wondered if they would publicly compete against their new friends to see who could spend the most money at luxury raffles. I hoped the mother gained more self-assurance by then, or she'd be knocking back chardonnay by lunchtime every day. Maybe the father would upgrade his wardrobe and learn to play golf. Would they be happier, though?

After a few minutes, I met an old friend in an alcove. Chandler Ann Rudiak was flipping distractedly through a book of bird prints that had been displayed on a glass-topped table.

She glanced up and saw with obvious relief that I was someone she knew in the sea of guests. "Nora! You look . . ."

"Big," I supplied. "Please don't ask if I'm having twins. I'm not."

She laughed. "Okay, I won't. Sit down. Rest a minute while we get caught up."

Gratefully, I sank into one of two clear Lucite chairs at the table. "You look wonderful, as always. That skirt—is it Chanel?"

"Yes, last year's collection. The blouse is from Talbot's—on sale."

I laughed. "You have a knack for mixing."

"You don't look half-bad yourself. Still pulling clothes from your granny's closet?"

When I had first started attending parties for a living and needed elegant clothes every night of the week, I climbed the attic stairs to look through my late grandmama Blackbird's collection of vintage couture—items as varied as Gucci miniskirts that Twiggy would have envied to beaded Dior ball gowns worn to Palm Beach galas with movie stars. I made good use of her carefully preserved clothes. Two of her friends soon gave me more fine garments, so I had a lot of valuable and classic pieces to choose from.

"Not at the moment," I said. "I'm borrowing a lot of my sister's maternity clothes. My taste isn't quite the same as Libby's, but I'm making do."

"You always make it work." She looked more carefully into my face. "Are you okay?"

Chandler Ann was a couple of years older than me, but I had dated her famously handsome brother Dylan for a while. I had bonded with the whole Rudiak family, and even after Dylan went on to date New York socialites far out of my league, I enjoyed the family's traditional day-after-Thanksgiving brunch, to which they invited a hundred people every year. A while back Chandler Ann and I had practically camped out together to buy tickets for the touring show of dresses worn by the late Princess of Wales.

So I felt comfortable telling her the truth. "It's been a complicated day."

"What's up? Everything hunky-dory with your baby?"

"The baby's fine. Perfect, in fact." I had been friends with Chandler Ann for a long time. "But something awful happened today. Jenny Tuttle passed away."

Beneath her fringe of stylish blond bangs, Chandler Ann's fine-boned face went through some almost comic gymnastics as she absorbed the news and tried not to show her first reaction. "That's so sad! I know—knew—Jenny pretty well, in fact. She was a client of ours. I saw her every week for almost a year when she was coming to the clinic."

Past generations of the Rudiak family had been respected Philadelphia physicians. But Chandler Ann's father had an entrepreneurial streak as well as a medical degree, and he'd opened a weight-loss clinic so popular that he franchised it nationally. All his children now worked for the lucrative company. Chandler Ann was the black sheep who hadn't gone to medical school, so she was the chief financial officer and kept the books for the multimillion-dollar business. I reflected that diets must be doing better than ever if she could afford Chanel.

Chandler Ann said, "I'm so sorry to hear Jenny died. I— Can I ask how it happened?"

"We think she had a heart attack."

My friend turned pale at that news. "Thank heavens she stopped seeing Dad a while back. I wonder if she— Do you think she was still dieting?"

I didn't want to gossip or admit that I had snooped among the bottles on Jenny Tuttle's dressing table. And I was unwilling to spread rumors that could turn ugly, so I said, just as ambiguously as before, "She looked slimmer."

Shaking her head, Chandler Ann said, "She was desperate to lose weight. But my dad's natural methods weren't fast enough for her. He rarely prescribed medication, for example, which is what she kept asking for. She really wanted to be thin for this summer, so she left our clinic. I presume she went somewhere else to get the medications she wanted."

I said, "I saw a lot of energy drink cans around the house, too."

"No!" Aghast, Chandler Ann clapped one set of fingertips to her mouth. "Those are so dangerous! Especially for someone in Jenny's state of health."

"Her mother mentioned she had a heart condition."

"She should have avoided all caffeinated beverages." Chandler Ann reached out to touch my arm. "You look really upset about this, Nora."

"It was a shock seeing Jenny," I admitted. "I find myself thinking how sad it was that she never really had a life of her own."

Chandler Ann nodded. "Yes, after Toodles died, her mother was really Jenny's focus. She didn't have a job or a boyfriend, let alone children. That's why I was pleasantly surprised to see her at the clinic. She was finally doing something for herself. Getting healthy. She hinted that she had something big coming up soon, too."

"Something big?"

"I don't know what. She only blushed and laughed me off when I asked. But I got the impression she wanted to look nice for whatever was on her horizon. She even asked me if I used a stylist to help me shop for clothes."

"Maybe she meant the opening night of the new Toodles Tuttle musical."

"There's a new musical? My parents love those Toodles shows!"

"I understand they found an unproduced musical Toodles wrote before he died."

"No wonder Jenny wanted to look good. Too bad her self-improvement efforts contributed to her death."

Hearing my friend say it, I was shocked. "Do you think that's true?"

She lifted her shoulders. "I can't say for sure, of course. But caffeine drinks and diet pills? Plus some of the crazy supplements people buy on the Internet? That's a lethal combination. How did her mother handle her death?"

"Her behavior seemed . . . inappropriate this afternoon."

"She's nuts," Chandler Ann diagnosed. "At least, that's the impression I got from Jenny."

I thought about my relationship with my own mother. It was surprisingly distant, perhaps, by the standards of people from outside our socioeconomic group. She had always been a hands-off parent who sent us to boarding schools at a young age and left our day-to-day care to our grandparents' housekeeper. I remembered her more as an exasperating sort of in-family party planner, but not a source of any real support. If I felt the need for actual guidance, I had always turned to my grandmother. By no means would I describe my mother as "nuts." Eccentric, maybe, but not crazy.

Before we could further explore the topic of mothers and daughters, a baseball player arrived at our table to offer fresh drinks. Chandler slanted a flirtatious glance up at him and asked what position he played best. He took the question seriously before figuring out she wasn't asking about baseball.

"Nice try," I said when he eased himself away.

She sighed. "He's probably ten years younger than I am. I'll be thirty-five soon, and I'm still single. You are probably right to start a family before you walk down an aisle with that—I mean— Sorry, Nora." Unable to stop herself, she let her gaze slip to the diamond on my left hand—a ring too big to ignore. "Are you married to your scary guy or not?"

"He's not scary," I said. "He's protective."

She took my hand and tipped the ring toward the sunlight to see the facets sparkle. "He sure has lavish taste in jewelry. It might be nice to have somebody looking after me—especially if he likes diamonds. These days, most of the guys who invite me for drinks end up staring at their cell phones the whole time. I hate thinking I'm less interesting than Angry Birds or text messages from their bosses."

"Michael spends a lot of time on his cell phone, too."

"Oh." She looked disappointed. "He ignores you, huh?"

"No," I said truthfully. "He doesn't ignore much of anything."

"So—are you planning to tie the knot with him? Have a big wedding in Vegas, maybe? Or not?" Chandler Ann looked over my shoulder into the crowded party behind me. "Because that hunk you came in with is kinda yummy."

"That's my boss," I said. "My editor."

She perked up. "The Australian guy? I've heard about him. I saw those pictures of him bicycling in Paraguay. I bet he likes women more than his cell phone." She continued to admire Gus from afar. "Is he single?"

"Very."

She heard my tone and laughed. "I get it. He's a tomcat?"

"What a nice, old-fashioned expression," I said with a smile. "Go get him, tiger."

We promised to touch base soon, and Chandler Ann told me to take care of myself. I sent my best wishes to the rest of her family. I went to say my good-byes to our host and hostess and met them in the kitchen just as their computer-whiz son made his appearance. He was a tall, lanky boy with frizzy hair and a wrinkled T-shirt. Disinterested in the activity around him, he elbowed his way past one of the baseball players, yawning as if he'd just rolled out of bed. I caught a whiff of him. He hadn't bathed in a while.

He snapped, "Mom, I need a smoothie."

"Right this minute, Jakey?"

He sighed impatiently. "Well, yeah. I'm starving!"

His mother lost her smile and rushed to the refrigerator to gather ingredients while his father said jovially, "Where's your new girl-friend, Jake?"

"If you must know, she's putting her clothes back on."

The father did a double take that I probably wasn't supposed to see. A moment later, a very tall young lady arrived in a minidress so short it almost showed whether or not she was wearing panties. Barefoot, she dangled a pair of high-heeled sandals from one finger. I recognized her as an up-and-coming local model. She draped her skinny arm around the boy's shoulders and nibbled his neck while he waited for his mother to make his smoothie. His expression didn't change as the girl's lips traced a path to his earlobe.

Sixteen, as rich as a prince, and already going to bed with models.

To make Gus happy, I should have snapped their photo, but I couldn't. I didn't have the tabloid killer instinct. Time to go. Halfway out the door, though, I encountered Brenda Monroe, a local television newsreader.

"Nora, great to see you! You look great! We should have lunch." Brenda spoke rapid-fire and was constantly in motion. She reached into her shoulder bag with one hand while gripping my wrist with the other. "Listen, if you happen to see Lexie Paine, how about giving her my card? I'd love, love, love to talk to her. We're all wondering what her next move will be. I'm sure she has a plan to make scads of money. Maybe we could all have lunch together? Just us girls. Here. Tell Lexie to keep me in mind."

Two seconds later, she was gone like a gust of wind. Somewhat dazed by the encounter, I put Brenda's card into my handbag. Every reporter in town was hungry for an interview with Lexie, and I shouldn't get caught looking like a deer in the headlights when they asked me about her.

In the fading sunshine, Gus was waiting for me, leaning on a parked car and yelling into his phone. He terminated the call when he caught sight of me. "You're holding out on me again."

"Now what?"

"I hear a famous person died this afternoon. And you were on the scene."

"She wasn't famous," I said, automatically going into protection mode. "Her father was famous."

"Toodles Tuttle's daughter, right? The composer fellow who wrote that sappy stage tripe."

"His shows are not sappy. They're charming."

Gus said a rude word. Then, "How did she die?"

"Don't get your hopes up. There's no seedy celebrity story to print in the paper."

"The police must disagree. They assigned her case to the Homicide squad."

For a split second, I didn't respond. Of course, Jenny's death had been caused by a heart attack. But I had seen the faces of her mother and the nurse. I had heard the strange pitch in the voices of the dancers who'd been on the scene when I arrived. And from the way Ox Oxenfeld had run out of the house—well, it all added up to something I wasn't quite ready to accept. But Gus's information brought all the impressions together in my head. I knew there was something fishy about Jenny Tuttle's slip from the surly bonds of earth.

Gus's gaze sharpened. He gripped my arm so suddenly that I bit back a startled cry. He said, "It *was* a murder, wasn't it? And you were right there when it happened."

"I wasn't there when it happened. I arrived much later. I don't know anything."

He gave me a frustrated shake. "Dammit, Nora, didn't you understand what I said this afternoon? The *Intelligencer* is going under unless I can bring things back from the brink of disaster. That was supposed to be a call to arms. I want a story from you, young lady— not a do-gooder piece about cheating charities. It's time you earned your keep. Either you write about your friend Lexie Paine or you write about this Tuttle woman."

"I won't write about Lexie."

"Then you're choosing the Tuttle murder? Excellent. A dead body is even better than Paine hiding from the clients she screwed." His editor's brain was already humming. "To get the public interested, we can start with a piece about her father. We'll build the big picture from there. I'll put together a standard obit for her. See what you can dig up about him to add. Not the usual happy crap. Something juicy. Call me later."

CHAPTER FIVE

B efore I had time to protest, we parted ways at the corner. Gus strode back toward the office, presumably hot to write something contemptible about Jenny Tuttle's untimely death. The thought made me feel genuinely ill.

I walked half a block before I realized my cell phone was ringing. Out of breath, I stopped and sat on a shady park bench to answer the call.

"Hey," Michael said in my ear. "It's me. How are you?"

"It's been a weird day."

"Ain't that the truth," he said. "Sorry I couldn't drive you to work. I talked to the state cops for more than an hour. They're suspicious about the way the Tuttle lady died."

"They aren't the only ones. Gus Hardwicke is back. He needs a hot story for the dog days of summer, and if it's not Jenny Tuttle's death, he wants a juicy article about Lexie."

"Oh, hell. You're not going to do that, are you?"

"Of course not. He put an especially unpleasant dog on the hunt for Lexie, though."

"Well, maybe Hardwicke will be diverted by the Tuttle story. It just heated up. The cops say a sixtysomething woman dying of a heart attack wasn't all that unusual. But she was famous, and she had money, plus a lot of different prescriptions were sitting around in plain sight—some of them written to her mother—so they ordered an autopsy. With a tox screen. The good news for us is that they interviewed all those dancers hanging around the house, who said we arrived after she was dead, so we're in the clear. But Homicide is starting to dig. And guess who they want to talk to first?"

"Who?"

"Bridget."

My heart lurched. "Your mother? Why?"

"It seems today wasn't the first time she tried to get an audition for this Tuttle show. She's been communicating with the Tuttle family for weeks. Not exactly cordially."

"Oh, Michael."

"Yeah. And now she's done one of her disappearing acts. All I need right now is my mother getting press coverage in a murder case. Pretty soon the papers will dig up some of the old pictures of her."

"What kind of pictures?"

"You don't want to know."

Before I could stop myself, I said, "Gus says he's seen new photos of you. With petty drug dealers."

I must have caught him off guard, because he said, "Who took the pictures?"

"Does that matter?"

"Yeah, it does." Then he said, "Hardwicke's hoping I'll go to jail so he can carry you off on his surfboard."

"Don't change the subject, please," I said. "Can you tell me what's going on?"

Michael hesitated. "Don't worry about it. I'll explain tonight. I'll pick you up at nine, as planned."

"Okay. Good luck finding your mother."

"Thanks. See if you can figure out who might have wanted the dead lady gone, okay? It might keep Bridget out of jail."

I knew he was joking, but I said, "I'll see what I can do."

He told me he loved me, and we ended the call.

I sat for a moment, gathering my thoughts. In my mind's eye, the image of Jenny Tuttle collapsed on her bedroom floor floated up again. Maybe it was my impending motherhood, but I found myself thinking of Jenny and her mother. Had their relationship been as fraught with conflict as I had guessed? My curiosity was piqued.

Then I remembered the photograph. I don't know why it had slipped my mind until that moment. Maybe I had been too surprised by Boom Boom's blue skin. A small photo of a boy had fallen from the pocket of Jenny's bathrobe. Who was the child? And why had Jenny kept his picture so close?

Suddenly my baby gave me a kick, and I smiled. Already, my daughter was reminding me that there were more important things to think about. I gave her a rub and felt her wriggle under my touch. I smiled. Soon I'd be holding her, feeding her, dressing her in the soft pink onesies that seemed to come every day in the mail from generous friends. I could hardly wait for my maternity leave and the long, happy weeks of getting to know our child.

I walked through shady Rittenhouse Square, where a threesome of small children was trying out new roller skates under the watchful eyes of indulgent parents who chatted while holding cups of iced coffee. Along with the early evening crowd of city dwellers strolling out to dinner in the local restaurants, I went a few more streets into the city's cultural district. The theaters were already lit up for the evening performances. Neon lights flashed to entice audiences, and large posters shouted the names of coming productions. I wondered how many times Toodles Tuttle had seen his name in such lights.

A grandfatherly passerby with a briefcase spotted me trundling toward one of the theater doors, and he lunged forward to open it for me. "You look beautiful," he said jauntily.

He gave my tummy a rub as if summoning a genie from a bottle.

One of the strangest parts about being pregnant was how public my body had become. Complete strangers felt they could make personal remarks and touch me, which was very disconcerting.

If being touched by strangers was weird, it was not as dreadful as the labor and delivery horror stories so many women felt the need to share with me. If I heard about one more long, agonizing tale full of pushing and screaming and doctors suddenly deciding to perform cesarean sections in the nick of time, I might decide not to go through with it all.

But a second later, I was in the cool, air-conditioned lobby of the city's great performance space. A creatively dressed crowd milled around a bar that had been set up to serve a few elite donors who were being honored for their support of the current show running in the theater.

"Nora!"

I headed for the committee chair, who had invited me, and she gave me a hug while gushing over my size. She was a wealthy, middle-aged theater lover who gave various charities profits from her family's patio furniture fortune.

Eventually I sidetracked her baby discussion and got the lowdown on the party while snapping a few photos for my weekly print column. Wealthy contributors might be altruistic in spirit, but it never hurt to give them good publicity in the newspaper. Attention in the media not only drew public interest in good deeds but also increased charitable giving in general. For me, this tenet was the mission of my column, and I was careful to single out the people who gave the most hours or money. First-time donors also responded well to a little stroking. I could do my part to see future donations rise. Even if Gus was taking the *Intelligencer* down a deplorable path, I was determined to keep my own standards high for as long as possible.

But the online readers didn't care about rich old people—my father called them the Nearly Deads—who gave money to good causes, so I skipped sending photos to my online editor. I'd save the pictures for the print edition.

Work accomplished, I went around the edges of the crowd, looking for a certain someone who might have been invited to this party—someone I thought might be able to tell me more about the Tuttles.

At last I sniffed him out. Nico Legarde and Herman Jones had carried their drinks to the balcony, where they could spy on the party from above and probably gossip. They were both dressed in very stylish skinny summer suits—oozing sophisticated nonchalance and handsome enough for a magazine shoot for men's cologne.

"If it isn't Nora Blackbird." Nico smiled with his usual wry gentility. Which, I suppose, is another way of saying he was one of those people who mistook sarcasm for wit. He looked like urbane European royalty once removed—which he was. He made the most of his genetic haughtiness by raising his eloquent brows. "What made you think we'd love the silver salad tongs you sent for our wedding?"

"They're elegant, which I adore," Herman answered for me in his Georgia drawl. He towered over Nico, and he propped his elbow on the other man's shoulder in a gesture of jaunty possessiveness. "And you love anything expensive—even better if it has a pedigree."

"In your own ways, I knew the two of you would appreciate the tongs," I said. "They came from my grandmother's collection. She bought them from the Duchess of Windsor's estate."

Nico's little bud mouth popped open in surprise. "Get out of town! Well, now, Herm, you were right to find a proper place to display them."

"It drives Nico nuts that I'm still such an Atlanta boy," Herman confided in his deep, sonorous voice. "I'd like every square inch of our apartment to be decorated to the hilt."

"Do you also display your collection of Super Bowl rings?" I teased.

"Two does not make a collection," he corrected, with a twinkle in his dark eyes. "Will you pay a call? Come for lunch?"

"Perfect. I'm starving all the time. In fact—"

Herman caught my longing glance and his southern manners kicked in instantly. "Sit down, and I'll go get you some canapés. Another drink? What are you having? Tonic and lime?"

"Thank you, Herman."

To Nico, Herman said sternly, "Don't ask her any uncomfortable questions. She's a lady."

As the former wide receiver eased off to find me food and drink, catty Nico wasted no time asking me a very uncomfortable question. "So, Nora, what do you know about Lexie Paine? Did she survive prison? And what's she up to now? Has she moved to Borneo to bilk unsuspecting natives for another fortune?"

I bit back a snappy retort and said, "As far as I know, she isn't allowed to leave the country."

Nico gave me a sideways frown. "You're disappointingly discreet."

"Yep."

"Well then, how are things going between the beauty and the beast?"

I sat down in the nearest chair. "I don't know who you're talking about."

"You and your Mafia Prince, of course." Nico remained standing and pulled out his slender cigarette case. "I suppose you have nothing to say about him, either. Never mind. I approve, you know. My father used to say the Blackbird girls always chose the wrong men, but a woman as otherwise polite as you needs forbidden love in her life. If you didn't have a scoundrel in your bed, you'd have to do something else extraordinary. It gives you a necessary dash of piquancy." He squeezed my arm, probably intending to take the sting from his words.

For someone who made his living in the cutthroat business of running posh nightclubs in New York and London as well as Philadelphia, he only occasionally let his softer side show, and I should be thankful for the squeeze. But I never really liked hearing editorial comments about my private life.

I said, "Nico, I need some gossip."

He laughed, chose a cigarette and closed the case. "Not so discreet after all, are you? Well, you've come to the right man. But only if it's off the record."

I could use his information as deep background and not mention his name in print. "It is. I must ask you to keep it to yourself, too. It's about Jenny Tuttle. I think your parents knew her father."

Nico's powerful father had owned a big theater in the city, and Nico had loved the stage since he was a small boy—which was why he donated to theatrical causes now that he could afford to be philanthropic. I was betting he might have some info about the Tuttle family.

Nico sat down with me on the bench. "They did know Toodles. So did I. In fact, he helped me get started in the club world. He even played in my first establishment. If not for him, I might be running a string of seedy strip clubs instead of attracting celebrities with live music and thousand-dollar bottles of vodka."

"I doubt it would be strip clubs."

He allowed a small smile as he put the cigarette between his lips. He didn't light it. "As for Jenny—I met her a few times. We weren't exactly close, but I knew her."

"You heard she died today?"

Nico removed the cigarette and held it in his fingers, his usual dispassionate demeanor fading. "It was on the five o'clock news before we came here. I heard the word *homicide*. What happened?"

I told Nico what I knew about Jenny's death, and he shook his head.

"What a shame. It's hard to imagine anyone would want to kill her. Jenny was remarkably unremarkable, don't you think?"

"That's unkind."

"But honest. If you met her at a party, you'd send her to the piano as soon as possible, right? She was comfortable playing background music. It was the metaphor of her life, wasn't it? She had some talent, but not like her father. Toodles was the life of every party he ever attended."

"You knew Toodles well?"

Nico surprised me with a wink. "In every sense of the word. He was one of my first."

"Nico! Are you suggesting Toodles was . . . ?"

"Bisexual? Yes. And quite energetic. He chased skirts and trousers with equal zest. He practically used chorus girls like his own private harem. I told you, he was the life of the party. Don't tell Herman."

I was pretty sure Herman knew all about Nico's previous dalliances. I said, "Did you know the Tuttles are working on a new musical? An old one Toodles left behind?"

Nico gave a gentlemanly snort. "If Boom Boom or Jenny found any decent music or lyrics in that mausoleum, I'll eat my sombrero. What's the show called?"

"*Bluebird of Happiness.*"

He laughed. "That proves it. Toodles would never have stooped that low."

"Wait," I said. "You don't believe Toodles left an unproduced show?"

"Nora, not only was Toodles a marvelous composer and a delightful raconteur, plus an adventurous spirit in his personal relationships, but he was an astute businessman, too. He advised me extensively in business, so I should know. A genuine Tuttle musical? I'm sure he'd have left it safely in the hands of experienced theater people—not his nut of a wife."

"Are you sure about that?"

"His final show—*The Flatfoot and the Floozy*? Not his best material. If he had old work lying around, he'd have produced it then, instead of that stinker."

"If he didn't write this new show, where did it come from?"

Nico's brows gathered. "Is it any good?"

"I've only heard rehearsals. Despite all those years of symphony subscriptions and Todd dragging me to jazz performances, I'm still not very discerning when it comes to popular music."

"Todd's idea of jazz was—well, never mind." Nico had the good grace not to speak ill of the dead. "Who's directing? Sometimes it's a ghostwriter."

"The music director is Fred Fusby."

"Freddie?" Nico scoffed. "The tall, skinny daddy longlegs of a hoofer? He's no director!"

"I got the impression he was trying."

Nico wagged his head. "So they're producing it on the cheap. The whole thing sounds like a disaster. What do you bet Boom

Boom is squeezing some discarded songs into a lame book she's written herself?"

I doubted that theory. Boom Boom didn't seem capable of creating much of anything. Maybe whatever had turned her blue had also affected her mind.

Herman returned with a waiter carrying a tray of food and more drinks. They had gathered a selection of the best of the canapés, which the waiter set down on the low table before me. It took all of my self-control not to seize a stuffed mushroom right away. Herman tipped the waiter and dragged another chair closer for himself. When he was seated, the three of us dug into the feast. I avoided the oysters, saying I was supposed to skip raw seafood, so the men enthusiastically gulped all of them in short order. They told me stories about the people we could see at the party below and their donations to the current show. None of their anecdotes had information I could write up for the paper—too many off-color insider jokes for the public to appreciate. Nico and Herman were very entertaining, however. I enjoyed their company and was sorry to have to tear myself away.

"Let me call you a cab," Herman said with concern when I told them I needed to start walking to my next event. "You shouldn't be out on the streets in your condition."

"Don't be silly." I stretched up to give him a kiss on the cheek. "The walk will be just what the doctor ordered."

Besides, a walk might help me organize my thoughts about Jenny's murder.

My mind was sidetracked, though, when I left the building and noticed a man loitering on the corner. Although he ducked his head and pretended to throw a cigarette into a trash can, I recognized Hostetler, the reporter Gus had assigned to locate Lexie Paine. With a pang of dismay, I realized Hostetler had decided to follow me in the hope I might lead him to my friend.

Well, there was no way I could take off running down the nearest alley and lose him, considering the shape I was in. I'd just have to think of a way to send him on a wild-goose chase. For the moment, I pretended not to notice him and walked in the opposite direction.

My next stop was a dinner for a politician who should have retired long before he dodderingly started spouting century-old political views about women. The dinner promised to be as dull as beans.

But I arrived to discover that the hotel had been almost entirely taken over by an extended Indian family celebrating a wedding. The lobby was full of lively ladies in magnificent silk saris and dignified men decked out in traditional sherwani, although many had swapped out the usual leggings for Western trousers. Feeling underdressed, I cut around a group of young women and teenage girls who were elaborately hennaed and wore gold bangles on their arms. When one of them stepped into my path, I recognized a woman I had met before. In her native finery, though, I couldn't recall her name. She reintroduced herself as Priyanka Sengupta, and I realized she was a doctor I'd encountered at some hospital fund-raisers.

"May I take your photograph?" I asked her after we exchanged greetings. "Your sari is lovely."

Priyanka agreed and asked her friends to join her, so I was able to snap several photos of their exquisite makeup and clothing. One photograph of the young doctor's arm—covered in a serpentine henna design that looked like a beautiful, though temporary, tattoo—was going to look great at the top of my weekly wedding roundup.

She said, "Nowadays, it's usually just the bride who has the mehndi design. The darker the henna, the happier her marriage will be. But we all got into the ceremony yesterday, so we were all painted. Very pretty, don't you think?"

"Beautiful."

"The bride has her husband's initials painted in henna some-where secret on her body." She dimpled as she smiled. "It's his job to find his own initials on the wedding night."

It was a serendipitous and charming encounter. I had been want-ing to jazz up my wedding coverage with something other than white-bread events, and this would be a good addition. I thanked them all and wished them a happy evening.

In the ladies' room, I pulled a light jacket out of my bag to for-malize my linen dress. I swapped my sturdier shoes for a pair of dressy heels and touched up my lipstick. The final effect wouldn't get me noticed at the Indian wedding, but it was a definite im-provement.

I headed down a long hallway to one of the more distant ball-rooms to find the retirement party. As the cocktail hour was end-ing, I snapped a picture of the tanned and beaming honoree. He had one arm clamped around his mortified wife, who managed to keep a smile frozen on her face. His clueless sons were already drunk. With his antiquated views, the man of the hour had of-fended women everywhere, so very few were in attendance. Only a handful of former political allies had showed up to wave the guest of honor into the sunset. They had all benefited from his favors over several decades, but now many were too afraid of being tarred with the same sexist brush to show up to thank him.

I wasn't crazy about attending, either. But I dutifully found the table in the back of the room where I had been seated with some other journalists covering the retirement.

As I sat down, one of the television reporters said, "Hey, Nora. Tell us what you know about Lexie Paine. Is she really living in a Red Roof Inn on I-95?"

"I have no idea," I said as plausibly as I could manage.

Another newspaper reporter grinned. "I hear she's hoarding

stray cats in a dump in Roxborough. She's fallen a long way from the caviar buffet at Vendre's. If you see her, tell her I'll bring her a sausage pizza in exchange for an interview."

Someone made a sausage joke, and the other men roared with laughter. I wanted to defend Lexie, but that would only make them push harder for information they could print. Better to let the insults fly over my head.

"Since when has your paper started paying for interviews?" I asked.

A particularly dyspeptic older reporter had smuggled a pint of booze under his rumpled jacket, and he poured liberally into any glass that was pushed his way. "We gotta compete with the *Intelligencer* now. The Awesome Aussie is buying photos, I hear. This is what happens when the tabloids take over. In no time, the front page will be nothing but dick pics and perverts."

"I'm sure it won't go any further than it has already," I said.

From their smirks, I could see nobody at the table believed me. They spent most of the dinner checking their cell phones and madly texting whomever. During the laudatory speeches, they muttered wisecracks to each other. There was no love lost for the retiree.

I used my time to sketch out a quick article about Toodles Tuttle, as Gus had requested. I found all the facts online and wrote briefly but glowingly about the Broadway star. When finished, I hit "send" and it went to Gus.

A tepid burst of applause erupted, so I used the moment to slip out to the ladies' room to check my voice mail. No messages, but a lot of missed calls.

Including one from my sister Emma. I almost hit "redial" immediately. But I needed to have some privacy before I called her back. I hadn't seen her in weeks, and there was no guessing what kind of shenanigans she might be up to.

A Little Night Murder

On my way back to the ballroom, my cell phone rang, and I saw Gus Hardwicke's name on the screen.

Reluctantly, I answered. "Yes?"

He said, "You were supposed to call me."

"I'm at a dinner. You're making me miss the fond farewell speech."

"You can thank me later. I got the Toodles piece you sent. Can't you dig up some dirt?"

I had learned that Toodles was bisexual, and Nico had suggested he had been an avid philanderer, especially with chorus girls. But that was not the kind of information I was going to share with Gus just yet. I said, "I'm told his last show, *The Flatfoot and the Floozy*, was not his finest work."

"That's the best you can do?" Gus moaned. "Well, I've been trying to roust up interesting tidbits for his daughter's obit. Utter failure. Has there ever been a more boring woman? Even I can't make her sound interesting. What about you? Know anything scandalous?"

"I have nothing to offer. And I'm going home for the night."

"Not yet, you're not. Where are you?"

I told him the name of the hotel but added, "I'm leaving in twenty minutes."

"I'll be there in five."

He must have been having a drink in a nearby bar, because he showed up in the hotel's lobby just four minutes later with his coat slung over one shoulder and his sleeves rolled up. He was listening to someone on his cell phone. Whatever he heard, he didn't like. Abruptly, he hung up and headed my way.

"Bugger me," he said when he approached me sitting in a lobby wing chair. "I think you're even bigger than you were this afternoon."

"I'm too tired for any more jokes about my size."

"You do look a bit wilted," he observed, standing over me with a momentary air of indecision. "Do you—? Can I get you something?"

"No," I said tartly. "But thanks for asking. It suggests you're actually human."

"Don't tell anyone." He kicked a chair closer, sat down and crossed one long leg over the other. "Instead, spill everything you saw when you walked in on the dead woman."

I rearranged my face. "She was on the floor in her bedroom in her nightclothes. Flannel, not black lace. No smoking gun, no bloodied knife. She had a heart attack."

Gus leaned back in his chair to get a better look at a pair of slender young ladies in saris who were walking by. He said, "My police contact says they're running tests for toxic substances."

I knew that already from Michael. "Oh?"

"I think that's promising. Maybe she had an addiction to something interesting. My contact also says there was a photograph on the body. Did you see it?"

The photo of the little boy. Conscious that Gus had begun to eye me with suspicion, I decided to play dumb. "What kind of photograph?"

"A kid. Cops think it must have fallen out of her hand when she died. They're faxing me the picture so I can put it in the *Intelligencer.*"

"What?" Startled, I said, "Why would you do that?"

"Because I need something to print, of course. I'm going to put the photo in the paper and ask people to help identify the kid. Who's the mystery boy in the photo found at the crime scene?"

"Gus, you can't do that." I struggled to sit up straight.

"Why not? It's interesting, isn't it?"

"Look, I didn't know Jenny very well, but she was a very private person. She'd be horrified to be part of a manufactured news story. You can't do it."

person. She'd be horrified to be part of a manufactured news story. You can't do it."

"Bloody right I can," he shot back. "We need to get the public's motor running. So we'll start with the kid."

I choked down my distaste and said as calmly as I could, "Please don't do this. Using children—it's disgusting."

He grinned with delight. "Nothing sells newspapers like disgusting."

"Some newspapers sell because they print the news. Jenny Tuttle doesn't deserve to be abused. She was a quiet person. A very nice person."

"She was a useless sort of person, and nobody's going to miss her. Not unless we juice up her life a bit." With a cold smile, he said, "You could always write about Lexie Paine instead."

I wanted to snap at Gus. To tell him to leave Lexie alone. But a wave of pregnant-lady exhaustion swept over me. I checked my watch. Five minutes before nine.

Gus noted my glance. "Am I keeping you from a hot date?"

Unable to rock myself out of the deep chair on the first try, I blushed and attempted to boost myself up by bracing my hands on the upholstered arms. No luck. Smirking, Gus took pity on me and pulled me to my feet.

I stretched my back to ease the stiffness that had set in during the dinner. "My ride is due any minute."

"You can't go yet. We haven't strategized."

"I oppose all your strategies. Anyway, I need sleep. I'm punching your time clock." I headed for the hotel's exit and tried not to waddle.

Gus followed me out. "You've lost your stamina, Nora. How am I going to burnish your star if you can't stay out past sunset? Do you plan to go into your coffin as dull as Jenny Tuttle?"

I reached the curb. "There's an old saying here in Philadelphia.

You don't want your name in the newspaper except when you're born, married and dead."

"What kind of life is that?"

"Old-fashioned, I admit. But at this moment, it's exactly what I want."

From half a block away, a set of headlights popped on, and a massive vehicle slowly approached the hotel. The driver pulled to the curb and left the noisy engine running. The vehicle was a gigantic SUV that looked capable of roaring through tangled jungles or across searing sand dunes. It had some kind of large metal protrusion on the front, in case a herd of elephants might need to be pushed out of its marauding path.

Gus squinted and recognized the driver. "Your chauffeur is off house arrest?"

"No, but the terms are more flexible now."

"And where did he steal this vehicle? From the Secret Service? That's his line of work, right—stealing cars?"

"He stole one motorcycle when he was sixteen. What were you doing at sixteen?"

"Packing my suitcase for Oxford." Gus saw Michael come around the hood of the beast and took an involuntary step back from me. "Good evening, Abruzzo. How's the life of crime?"

Michael kept both hands in the back pockets of his jeans. His face was still, his eyes lazily lidded. Bad to the bone. Without trying, he managed to exude an attitude of casual menace. "Hello, Hardwicke."

I stood between them—Michael on the street, looking like a criminal who'd just slipped his handcuffs, and Gus on the sidewalk, looking like an Oxford-educated man of the world. To get the surly scowl off Michael's face, I leaned out and gave him a kiss on the mouth. He met my gaze and smiled. With it, his eyes lit up.

It was an intimate smile, one that communicated a dozen

messages—how happy he was to see me, how pleased he was about the coming baby that would seal us together forever, how eager he was for our wedding in a week . . . and the night ahead of us. It made me warm inside, but I realized it was the look Gus hated. He'd told me so, and now here it was.

"Ready?" I said to Michael.

"Let's go."

"Good night," I said to Gus.

Michael opened the passenger door and helped me up into the seat with a boost on my butt. Gus didn't say a word.

I was still struggling with the unfamiliar seat belt when Michael got behind the wheel and closed his door. He helped me with the buckle. I looked out the windshield and saw Gus watching us, his face blank. Abruptly, he turned on his heel and went back into the hotel.

When the buckle clicked, Michael said, "How's Baby Girl?"

"Michael," I said, "there's blood on your shirt. What's wrong?"

"Nothing's wrong with your powers of observation, that's for sure. How do you like this truck? I'm test-driving it."

He put the huge SUV in gear and slid into traffic with the ease of a tank barging into a raging river.

"Can we afford to buy anything, let alone this monster?"

"It's not a monster. And it's a business expense. For Gas N Grub. The finances are loosening up now, so, yeah, we can afford it."

Michael had been fighting his way back to solvency after one of his employees embezzled considerable money while he was in jail. To avoid going completely bust, he'd been forced to borrow capital from his infamous brother, Little Frankie—the brother best known for faking being dead to avoid prosecution for various crimes. The money had saved us from certain bankruptcy, but I was still nervous about how Little Frankie wanted to be repaid.

Sitting in the passenger seat, I felt as if we were riding in the lead fire truck of a parade. "What is this thing, exactly? Gus said it looks like a Secret Service vehicle."

"Close. It's an Escalade. The governor ordered it—with bullet-proof glass and body armor that's supposed to resist rockets." Michael couldn't disguise his delight. "Except the state decided it was too expensive, even for the governor, so I'm giving it a try. We can get it at a discount."

What kind of discount he meant, I didn't want to know. "Do we need bulletproof glass?"

"No, but it's cool, right?" Michael maneuvered the Escalade around a corner. "And check out how many kid safety seats we can put in the back."

I looked into the yawning rear cavern of the SUV. He had already strapped one baby car seat in place. I said, "We're having a family, not transporting a platoon."

"It's really safe," he insisted. "It'll survive a crash test with a train."

"Are you thinking of crashing into a train?"

He shot me a grin as he pulled through an alley shortcut to reach our route out of the city. "No, but you never know if some old lady in a Prius is going to back into you at the grocery store."

I really had no opinion about cars. But I could tally up a list of strikes against this Escalade. Its size seemed ridiculous. The gas mileage was probably budget busting. And I'd never learn to drive something this big. Of course, I was still trying to overcome a tendency to faint at inappropriate moments, so I was barred from even applying for a Pennsylvania driver's license, but I had hopes of getting behind the wheel before our children needed transportation to school.

Michael had been researching various vehicles for weeks, making notes about crash tests and repair records. I knew he was looking for a car that would be perfect for our coming family.

He was glancing up at the rearview mirror and finally said, "Is somebody tailing you?"

"What?"

"Nobody'd tail me unless they had a death wish, so it must be you. There's an old guy in a blue Honda behind us, and he's made every turn I have. Use the side mirror. Who is he?"

All I could see in the side mirror was the blur of cars in traffic, but I could guess who was behind us. "Gus told another reporter to find out where Lexie is. I think he was following me earlier. He's a very unpleasant person. What should we do?"

"You want me to lose him? Or break his face?"

"Michael—"

"I'm kidding. We'll lose him."

"I don't want to be in a car chase!"

"Me neither. Here. Lucky break."

On the next block, two city police officers on bicycles were stopped in the street, talking to another officer who sat in a cruiser that idled at the curb. Without concern for the cars behind us, Michael pulled up beside the police. He used a button to roll down the passenger window, and he leaned across the console to speak past me to the officers.

"Sir," he said to a cop who looked to be about twenty years old. "See that old guy in the Honda behind us?"

Only one officer looked at the Honda. The other two kept their eyes trained on Michael.

Sounding impossibly harmless, Michael went on, "I don't know who he is, but he's been bothering my wife tonight."

One of the bike officers came over to the Escalade and used a flashlight to look us over. When the light landed on my large belly, he turned it off and stepped back as if startled by my size.

Michael said, "Do you think he's a weird sex offender or something?"

The bike officer nodded and said, "We'll check it out."

Playing along, I smiled brightly at him. "Thank you."

Michael rolled up the window and pulled back into traffic. Behind us, the police waved the blue Honda over to the curb. The cruiser's flashing lights came on, and I knew Mr. Hostetler was in for an evening of unpleasant questions.

Cheerful again, Michael said, "See? Much easier than a car chase."

I didn't have the energy to discuss his extensive understanding of tailing and losing bad guys, so I said, "Okay, whose blood is on your shirt? You hid it from the police just now, but I can see it plain as day."

He gave up trying to stall. "Promise you won't go crazy."

"Have I ever gone crazy?"

"It's my blood. I didn't have time to go home to change." When I didn't respond, he glanced across at me. "Are you counting to ten?"

"Twenty." I took a deep breath to steady myself. "What happened?"

"No sugarcoating—I get it. Okay, I got shot."

CHAPTER SIX

"Shot!" I cried.

"Winged," he hastily corrected. "On the arm."

He pulled up his shirtsleeve to show a bandage wrapped tightly around his forearm, just below his elbow. "It's not serious. And it's got nothing to do with your Blackbird curse, so don't start—"

"What happened? Where were you? Is this why we need a bulletproof car?"

"I'm okay, everything's okay. I was talking to a guy at the diner in New Hope. Just when we finished, some kid came at us with a Glock. Where the hell does a kid get a Glock, I'd like to know? What's this world coming to?"

"That's what concerns you?" I cried. "Where the gun came from? Just last week you told me to stay away from that diner. Why am I supposed to stay away, but you can waltz in there anytime you please?"

"I never waltz," Michael said. "Me waltzing would be like a

dancing grizzly bear. I'm fine. See? It's hardly a scratch. I went to the hospital, got a couple of stitches."

"What about the other guy? The man who was with you?"

"He's fine, too. The windows of the diner are a mess, that's all. The shooter needs to spend some time at the range before he goes taking potshots at—"

"Michael! Do you hear yourself?"

"Sorry. I know you're upset. But it was a chance thing."

"If you went to a hospital, the doctor had to report a gunshot wound. What does that do to your parole?"

"Nothing. The guy I was with is a friend of my parole officer."

I counted to twenty again. "Michael, what's going on? Gus said you're mixed up with petty drug dealers."

"One thing about Hardwicke is his consistency," Michael said. "All right, I said I'd explain it all tonight, so here it is: I agreed you and I could live at Blackbird Farm because I figured it was as safe as neighborhoods get. I thought things would get even quieter if I terminated all the Abruzzo operations in the area. So I put a bunch of guys out of business—which means nobody's going to give me a free beer at the family reunion—"

"No sugarcoating," I warned.

"Anyway," he continued, "as soon as my cousins cleared out of town, we've suddenly got stupid kids robbing stores and selling dope, and you know how I hate dope. It can mess up a perfectly good neighborhood in a couple of weeks. So not only do we have a crime wave getting started, but it features a bunch of dimwits who think guns are cooler than skateboards. They are a hell of a lot more dangerous to the general public than my cousins taking a few bets on football games."

I thought about Libby's door handle. "Are these the people Gus saw you with in photographs?"

"Probably. I'd still like to know who took those pictures. Police or press?"

"What does it matter?"

"Because if it's the cops, they're flashing pictures around to reporters for reasons I'd like to know about. And if it's the press, the cops probably don't know they're doing it, which is equally dangerous. I don't like not knowing which problem it is because it means I have to work plans for both. How did Hardwicke get to see them?"

"I don't know, and you're changing the subject again. Why did you get shot? You were talking to one of these criminals?"

"I was winged, not shot. And the guy I was talking to is a cop. Believe me, I'm not happy about this." He held up his arm as Exhibit A. "It's going to put me out of the basketball league for a week or two."

In the last several months, Michael's weekly pickup basketball game at the local Y had grown into some kind of league of middle-aged men whose skills weren't as sharp as their competitive spirits. Michael was considered the ringer in a team comprised of local doctors, a history professor and a fiftysomething chiropractor. Without Michael, the team could sink so low in the rankings they might never recover. Meanwhile, he pretended to be amused by the competition, but I could see he was every bit as bent on winning as his older teammates were.

I was happy knowing he associated with a chiropractor. Bad kids who carried Glocks—another story.

"Why were you talking to a police officer?"

"Well," he said, and stopped.

"Michael?"

He kept his gaze on the road ahead. "You have to keep quiet about this, Nora. Not tell Hardwicke, I mean. They—the local cops—asked for my opinion."

"Your opinion?"

"My advice," he corrected.

"The police need advice from you?" I couldn't keep the astonishment from my voice.

"Why is that so surprising? I run legitimate businesses in town. The fly-fishing store, the garage, the tattoo shop—"

"Don't try to sell me on the idea that you're the newest member of the Rotary Club. Less than a year ago you pleaded guilty to racketeering. Now you're best friends with the local police?"

"Not best friends. They still hate me, and it's mutual. But there are things I know how to do that small-community law enforcement doesn't."

That didn't sound good to me. "Like what?"

"Like how to discourage—uh, extraneous crime. And this undercover cop wanted to, y'know, get some tips. Except after today he isn't so undercover anymore. It's kinda funny, isn't it? The cops coming to me for help?"

"What kind of help?"

"Just talk," he assured me. "I told them I'd think about ways to intimidate the kids out of business. I don't want a drug trade going on in our backyard any more than they do. There's probably a way to work it."

I fell silent. *To work it.* I knew the phrase and what it meant. He loved to plot. Working the angles, playing one side against the other, toying with dangerous people to make them do what he wanted— that was Michael's special gift. He was the grand master of figuring out a crime.

"I'll be careful." He glanced across at me and measured the level of my distress. He reached for my hand. "Nobody knows better than me how close I came to screwing up my life, Nora. Now I've got everything I ever wanted and a lot of stuff I never knew could be so great. I'm not going to risk any of it."

"But—"

"I saw the kid coming at us, and I hit the deck almost before the gun went off. The shooter was more scared than anybody else. The cop drew his weapon, and the kid literally wet his pants. And me, I was already on the floor, hiding under a table. The whole thing was like a comedy routine, honest."

I realized I was gripping his hand tightly enough to hurt him. I tried to relax.

"You make all of these horrible things sound so ordinary."

"It wasn't ordinary," he admitted. "But it wasn't as bad as it sounds. My arm is fine. I'll be holding our daughters in a few weeks."

I let him squeeze me into calm.

Finally, I noticed we weren't on our way home. The headlights were lighting a highway I didn't recognize. I looked around to get my bearings.

"Where are we going?"

Michael let me go and hit the gas again. "We've got an errand to run. Emma called me. You better try phoning her now. Maybe she can explain better than I can."

I remembered the missed call I'd had from Emma. My younger sister, the most wayward of the Blackbird sisters, had spent the last few weeks on the edges of the show-jumping circuit, trying to restart her career as a rider of fine horses owned by very finicky owners. When I'd last heard from her, she was in Florida, working a short-term stint at a respected barn.

To Michael, I said, "Is she still in Florida? Is she in trouble? Or drinking again?"

"I don't think so."

I hit her number and listened to her phone ring.

All three of the Blackbird sisters had endured tragedy in our lives. Not long after our parents ran off with our trust funds and started their grand tour of South American dance competitions, the three of us had lost our husbands. Mine was executed by his drug dealer, ending a long, horrifying nightmare of drug addiction and emotional abuse. Libby's was shot trying to escape a murder charge. And Emma's husband, Jake, an NFL quarterback who shared her love of fast living and hard parties, had died in a car accident, the cause of which still hadn't been determined.

After our losses, Libby and I had gradually found ways to kick-start our lives again, but Emma had struggled. While pretending she was strong, she still went on alcoholic binges and dated all the wrong kinds of men. Her reckless behavior had culminated in a love child last year, and we still weren't sure she had done the right thing for herself by surrendering the baby to his father. Worse yet, she had committed arson, and I thought her run to Florida was partly to avoid being questioned about the fire.

She didn't answer her phone. I dialed again and listened to it ring. Where was she?

Finally Michael said, "Here we are."

He pulled the big Escalade through a pair of stone gates and up the curving driveway of a Main Line mansion with a fountain spurting out front. Dramatic lighting illuminated the Palladian windows and an impressive front door. The expansive lawn and elaborate shrubbery were surely maintained by a landscaping service. The grass was as carefully trimmed as a golf course.

"Oh, dear," I said when I realized where we were.

We might have had time to plan what to do next, except the front door swung open and light from the foyer chandelier spilled outside.

Hart Jones, a high-stakes stockbroker and the lover who had impregnated my wild little sister in an elevator, came out and stood on the front porch as Michael and I climbed out of the SUV.

Hart's well-tended face was tense. "Hello, Nora. I'm sorry to drag you out so late."

"Hi, Hart," I said, coming around the front of the Escalade. "Is everything okay?"

His eyes widened when he saw me in the glare of the headlights. "Wow. You're—I thought your due date was a few months away."

"Seven weeks," I said, managing a smile. "As you can guess, I can hardly wait."

"You look wonderful. It suits you." He gave me a kiss on the cheek. "Hello, Abruzzo."

Michael shook Hart's hand. He kept his voice neutral. "Hello, Jones."

Hart seemed too embarrassed to meet Michael's eye, so he turned back to me. "Thank you for coming. I'm sorry about this. I'm at my wit's end tonight."

From the moment we'd arrived we could hear the baby screaming inside the house. The sound sent my blood pressure soaring, and it made Michael go tense with suppressed anger.

Before he could act on that, I said to Hart, "Can we help somehow?"

He glanced over his shoulder into the house but spoke to me. "It's Penny. Her ankle acted up again, and she's having trouble with the pain medication. It's so hard to quit. The pills give her a lot of relief, but—we don't function as a family very well when she's taking so much. I think I've got her talked into going back to rehab. She needs help."

Listening to him, I heard all the same words I'd used when I had uselessly tried to justify the drug behavior of my husband Todd. Making excuses. Placating. Shouldering part of the blame. Dodging, softening, hoping everything would turn out all right without anyone being forced to make hard choices.

Hart said, "She might go in the morning, she says. Or the next day. But Noah—he won't sleep. He cries and cries, and it drives Penny crazy. He's making everything worse for her. I admit I'm not very good with him, either. . . ."

I knew Hart's preferred strategy when parenting problems arose. He went to his office to work. Or to hide.

Another sharp wail rose from inside the house, and we could hear Penny's infuriated voice snap in response.

Michael moved to cut past Hart, but I held him back. If we played it wrong, we could escalate a difficult situation.

Gently, I said, "What can we do to help, Hart?"

"Can you take him—Noah? For the weekend, just long enough for me to drive Penny to the facility." Thinking on his feet, he changed his mind. "Or maybe for the week? While she gets settled? That way I could— There's an important deal on my desk. If I could get it squared away—"

Michael started to say something, and I knew what words were in his mouth. Hart and Penny couldn't go on treating Noah like a football, passing him off to us when he became inconvenient. Several times during the past few months, we had taken Noah off their hands, against our better judgment. Each time his visits seemed to stretch longer and longer, and when it came time to give him back, the pain was more difficult to bear.

Maybe we were enabling, I thought. Maybe we should have pushed Hart and Penny to solve their own problems. But we couldn't do it, not when Noah was the one who suffered. It was Noah who mattered most to us.

So I said quickly, "Of course we'll take him. We're happy to do it."

Hart said, "You've got other things on your mind, I'm sure." He indicated my pregnant belly. "But if you have a few days to spare, it would mean a lot."

"Of course," I said again.

From the grand foyer, the sound of Noah's crying came closer, and Penny appeared. She was very thin, and her hair was scrunched into an unflattering ponytail. Her face, bare of makeup, looked tight and angry. Gone was her patrician beauty. Her skin looked blotchy. Dark circles smudged the flesh beneath her hard eyes. Her jaw tightened when she saw us standing on her doorstep.

In her arms, Noah writhed and shrieked. He tried to throw himself away from his adoptive mother, but she gripped him even harder. Her hands were white with tension. The baby's shirt was sopping wet with tears and drool.

"Hey," Michael said.

He wasn't speaking to Penny.

Noah's little head twisted around at the sound of Michael's voice. He let out another scream, but the emotion behind it was different. With hot tears streaming down his chubby cheeks, he flung his arms imploringly in Michael's direction.

Something ugly twisted in Penny's face. Rapidly, she paced forward and almost threw the baby at Michael.

Who easily scooped him up. The little boy instantly molded himself against Michael's chest, and his crying changed to an exhausted moan.

"Take him," Penny snapped. "Get him out of my sight. He's not my son. He hates me. I never want to see him again!"

She spun around and ran back into the house. We saw her flee up the curved staircase and disappear. On the second floor, a door slammed.

Hart said, "She doesn't mean it. That's the drugs talking. She'll calm down. She'll be okay."

"I'm sure she will." I accepted the diaper bag Hart proffered and ignored the enraged glance Michael sent to me. "We'll look after him, Hart. Don't worry. You concentrate on taking care of Penny."

Already, he was backing into the house. "Great. Thanks, Nora. You're a lifesaver. I'll be in touch tomorrow, I promise. I'll call."

He closed the door, leaving us on the doorstep.

"The hell he'll call," Michael said, steel voiced. "It'll be next week before we hear from him again."

"Shh. He might be listening."

"He knows what I think."

Michael turned and went down the steps with Noah in his arms. I followed, noting that the baby's crying had finally stopped. Michael opened the passenger door and, one-handed, boosted me into the seat. Then he gently eased the baby into my arms. Noah gave a croak of dismay, but he was too exhausted to protest.

Michael took his time going around the SUV. When he got behind the wheel, he had his anger under control.

I said, "We need to put Noah in the car seat."

"Give him a few more minutes to calm down. We'll just sit."

"Look, he's getting a tooth. Two teeth, see?"

"Hey, yeah. How about that?"

We both looked at the two bottom teeth that had pushed through since the last time we'd seen him. No wonder he'd been crying.

Noah put his hands out to Michael again.

I bundled the baby over to him. Noah heaved a wavering sigh and snuggled close. He put his fist into his mouth and blinked up at Michael.

We sat for a time, just listening to the baby breathe.

I should have been happy. I loved Noah. I loved taking care of him. With us, he was a happy child with a glint of humor in his expressive eyes. And when I held him in my arms, it felt as if I was also taking care of Emma, something she'd never permit.

A Little Night Murder

As we sat together in the darkness, however, a cold dread oozed up from deep inside me.

I knew what was going to happen.

One of these days when it came time for us to hand over Noah to Hart and Penny, Michael wasn't going to give him up.

CHAPTER SEVEN

In the morning, Libby telephoned.

"I just dropped the twins off to watch an autopsy of a man who died a month ago. They were more excited than when we went to Disney World. Do you think they need counseling?"

"Couldn't hurt," I said, washing breakfast dishes. "Libby, have you spoken with Ox Oxenfeld since Jenny Tuttle was murdered?"

A pregnant pause. "I haven't seen him, if that's what you mean. But we did have a . . . conversation."

My suspicions were aroused. "What kind of conversation?"

"Let me ask you something instead. What exactly constitutes phone sex?"

"Libby!"

"We *talked*," she said. "We kept our clothes on. At least, I did. Whether or not he—"

"Never mind." I pulled a clean dish towel from its drawer and began to dry the Beatrix Potter dish that had been handed down in my family for generations. Noah liked the bunny pictured on it, so I'd pulled it out of the butler's pantry for his cereal. "I was just wondering if Ox might have said something about Jenny."

"Like what? Do you think they were having an affair?" Her voice was sharp.

I very much doubted their relationship was anything sexual. I said, "I'm curious, that's all."

"Hm. Would you like me to pose some discreet questions? I should probably call him today, anyway. I could ask him for business advice. I'm still considering the Budget Bunny franchise. Let me go change my shoes first. I'll call you if I learn anything interesting."

Why she needed to change her shoes—well, I didn't want to hazard a guess. Libby hung up before I had a chance to ask if she'd heard from Emma lately.

With a few minutes alone, I fired off some photos to the online editor for posting later. I was just starting to research blue people when Michael came down holding Noah.

He said, "Changing diapers is a lot like changing tires in the pit at an Indy race. Getting the job done fast is a matter of having all the supplies in the right place."

I laughed and shut off the computer. On his way to work at Gas N Grub, Michael drove Noah and me over to Lexie's house to soak in the pool.

"Noah slept for twelve hours," I told Lexie after we had splashed in the water and had our lunch. "And he ate like a champion this morning. He's happy with us. We're happy with him."

"That's sweet, Nora. But . . . ?"

We had tucked Noah into a beautiful white wicker bassinette Lexie had said was a gift for Baby Girl from her mother. Today it was the perfect place for Noah to snooze in the shade by the pool. Yards of eyelet lace fluttered in the breeze while he drowsily played with one of the many stuffed toys we kept for him at Blackbird Farm. The pink bunny with the googly eyes was his favorite.

I leaned back in my lounge chair in the shade. "Michael is trying to teach him to walk already. He thinks Penny keeps Noah cooped up in a cage all the time."

"He's kidding, right?'

"For the most part, yes. I shouldn't tell you this," I said to my friend, "but last winter, just after Noah was born, we had a feeling that Penny tried—that she was giving him something to make him sleep so she didn't have to cope with him."

"You mean a drug?" Lexie sat up straight in the sunshine and whipped off her sunglasses. "Nora!"

"We can't prove it. And judging by the scene at their house last night, she's certainly not doping him anymore. But Michael is suspicious of everything she does. He is almost pathological about safety now that our own baby is coming, but it spills over into feeling protective about Noah, too. I told you about the deluxe security system he had installed on the farm?"

She put her dark glasses back on again. "I don't blame him. A women's prison is bad enough. But he has seen things and known people who must make him fear the worst for— Never mind." She suppressed a shudder, and I knew she was shaking off her own prison experience. "The two of you should have adopted this little boy in the first place, sweetie."

"We're not legally married yet, and Michael is a convicted felon. Adoption laws in Pennsylvania have loosened considerably, but it's still complicated. The only reason we have permission to adopt Rawlins's baby is that Rawlins and the mother of his child have relinquished their parental rights and made it clear the child is related to me and I should be his mother. But what judge would have approved our adoption of Hart's son, if Hart objected? The bottom line is that Hart is Noah's father."

"Not if he cares more about his office than his offspring," Lexie said. "How does Emma feel about this?"

"She has abdicated any responsibility."

"That's Emma," Lexie agreed. "Ignore the problem, or drink it away."

"Yes," I said. "I'm almost afraid she'd never come back if Michael and I had her child. She doesn't want to see him. But now I'm also worried Michael won't give Noah back to Hart. And although I don't disagree with him, we can't just decide Noah is ours. There are laws."

"Your groom is accustomed to breaking laws."

"I know," I said on a sigh.

Lexie gave me a consoling pat. "Let's not get ahead of ourselves. Nothing's happened yet."

Lexie's houseman came outside and set a tray on the small table between our chairs. A dish of strawberries, a bowl of whipped cream, a plate of scones—all decorated with folded yellow napkins and some daisies in a slender vase. He refilled our glasses of iced tea without being asked.

"Thank you, sweetie," Lexie said to him. "How's your book coming this morning?"

"I baked instead," Samir said curtly. Because I had worn another one of Libby's crazy shirts—this one read I GROW PEOPLE. WHAT'S YOUR SUPERPOWER?—Samir carefully avoided looking at me. He gathered up our wet towels and took them into the house. When he was out of earshot, Lexie cast a despairing glance at the scones and whispered, "Carbs. I'm so sick of carbohydrates after prison. Biscuits, white bread, pancakes—it all makes me flash back to being stuck behind bars. I don't have the heart to tell Samir that I feed all his baked treats to the birds."

"Michael feels the same way about scrambled eggs."

"So he said." She popped a strawberry into her mouth. "Your

groom has been a good listener for me, Nora. Thank you for sharing him."

Part of me felt a little jealous that Lexie could talk about her emotional prison experience with Michael but not with me. Perhaps his input on her jail time was more insightful than mine, but it still bothered me just a little. I wanted to help.

I also wanted some reassurance that they weren't concocting something illegal during their clandestine meetings. I took the bull by the horns and asked, "How is your project going? The one you and Michael are working on together?"

"It's going," she said, smiling.

Another stop sign. I tried to ask again, but across the lawn at the Tuttle house, someone began plunking on a piano. Nobody sang, but the piano banged.

"Hardly Mozart's *Requiem*," Lexie said dryly.

On the table between us lay the day's edition of the *Philadelphia Intelligencer* with the blaring headline BROADWAY HEIRESS DEAD. Below that was a fuzzy version of the photo I had seen sliding out of Jenny's pocket as she lay on her bedroom floor. The face of the nameless boy smiled shyly up from the newspaper alongside a smaller headline: HELP IDENTIFY MURDERED WOMAN'S OBSESSION.

Lexie and I had already lamented the objectionable word *obsession*. Nobody knew who the boy was, let alone his connection to Jenny Tuttle. I guessed every con artist worth his salt would be telephoning the *Intelligencer* now. And I could only imagine Jenny's reaction, if she were still alive.

Again, my protective nature was stirred. I wanted to save Jenny's reputation before it was slung through the media mud. But I needed to learn more about the circumstances of her death before I knew how to head off the worst of the publicity.

"I have an idea," I said to Lexie. "Why don't I take the scones over to Boom Boom Tuttle?"

Lexie was not fooled. She eyed me from behind her sunglasses. "What's your ulterior motive?"

"It's simply a kind gesture," I protested. "I should pay a condolence call."

"And?" she pressed.

"My editor," I admitted, "seems to think it would be a good career move for me to investigate Jenny's life."

Lexie was easily diverted by career talk. "I like hearing that he's interested in your future, sweetie. Last I heard, he was trying to pinch your bottom by the water cooler."

"We have reached détente where that kind of behavior is concerned. Instead, he's trying to make me more ambitious."

"That could be a good thing, Nora. Don't be offended. He's trying to help you along. You could use a mentor. Or maybe a work spouse."

"A what?"

"A work spouse is different from your real spouse. You might have a husband or wife at home, but at the office you need a trusted ally, too. Somebody who has your back, who can act as your confidant. A person you can count on as completely as your husband. A work spouse, see? Just don't get the two confused. That's when trouble starts."

"I can imagine." But I shook my head. "I'm gradually learning to do my job, but I'm not sure I can handle being the kind of reporter Gus wants me to be."

"He's a bit of a loose cannon," Lexie conceded, "and the *Intelligencer* isn't exactly the *New York Times*. In fact, I'm a little surprised he's merely editing a tabloid here in Philadelphia when there's a whole Hardwicke empire to run."

"I have a feeling he's doing more here than working on the *Intelligencer*. His family is trying to buy a bunch of media companies in the Philadelphia area."

Lexie sat up with the keen interest of a woman being denied the delicious daily excitement of her office. "I wondered. Television, cable, newspapers—it's all going to be one consolidated media in the end, and the Hardwickes have the money to buy a lot of it. Is he the local negotiator for his father? The embedded family representative?"

"I don't know for sure. He may be the black sheep of the family, but it makes sense that he's here for more than running a tabloid."

"You could learn a lot from him, you know."

I groaned. "I don't have the stomach for defamation. I want to protect Jenny Tuttle, for example, not drag her name through the mud."

"That's one of your best qualities, sweetie. But you also have a healthy sense of curiosity, and that's a good thing in a journalist. In this case, I must admit I'm curious about the circumstances of Jenny's death, too." Lexie gave the neighboring house a contemplative stare. "For one thing, Boom Boom didn't seem terribly distressed that her own daughter is gone."

"Maybe by now reality has set in, and Boom Boom is grieving for Jenny. Maybe I should go over now—to be a good neighbor."

My friend grinned. "And if we have time to ask some innocent questions, what's the harm?"

"We? Lex, there might be reporters at the Tuttle house."

Lexie swung her slim legs over the side of her chair. "You're not leaving me out of the action. I'll ask Samir to bring his manuscript out here so he can watch over Noah while we go next door for a few minutes. Honestly, I can't take being trapped in paradise much longer. Can you make that plate look like a gift?"

I was already pulling a satin ribbon from the heap of wrapping that had encased the bassinette. I tied the ribbon around the plate and stuck a couple of daisies through the bow.

Meanwhile Lexie pulled a black sundress over her head. Then she gave me a doubtful smile. "Maybe you should slip that shirt inside out?"

Anything was better than being seen in public in my super-power T-shirt. "Good idea."

Within a couple of minutes, Lexie and I rang the bell at the front door of the Tuttle house.

From out back, we could hear the thunder of tap-dancing feet and someone's strident voice shouting out numbers.

We rang again and knocked louder. In another minute Fred Fusby opened the door and stood there, towering over us. By the look of his face, he'd been crying for hours. His eyes were swollen and red. Or maybe somebody had slugged him.

"Mr. Fusby, I'm Nora Blackbird, and this is Lexie Paine. We were here yesterday afternoon . . . during the crisis. Is there—are you okay?"

"I'm fine." He looked embarrassed. "We thought you might be more people from that awful newspaper story. Or the police again. We haven't had a half hour of uninterrupted rehearsal all day."

"I'm sorry things are so difficult."

"A tabloid ran a photograph this morning and implied the person had something to do with Jenny." He mustered some outrage. "Half a dozen crazy people have come knocking at the door, hoping they've inherited millions."

"How terrible," I managed to say.

Lexie stepped inside without being invited, and I followed. Through the French doors at the back of the foyer, we could see ten or twelve dancers wearing top hats and sweating as they pounded their feet and twirled in unison on the patio. They were the same people who had wept around the piano, but now they danced their hearts out. An excitable, limber man shouted at them as if they were a herd of animals. He was dressed in a tight shirt, loose trousers and saddle shoes. His top hat lay squished on the patio as if he'd stomped on it in a rage.

"The choreographer finally showed up," Fred said, sounding doleful.

I had the distinct feeling that we'd fallen through a rabbit hole and ended up on the set of a sophisticated but madcap showbiz movie. Any minute, Gene Kelly was going to slide down the banister and land at the feet of a winsome young lady with stardust in her eyes. They'd fall instantly in love and tap-dance across the marble floor and out into the sunshine.

"Nora and I don't want to interrupt," Lexie said, "but we brought some food. Perhaps not enough for everyone, but—"

At the sight of Lexie's proffered plate, Fred teared up all over again. "Jenny used to love scones."

"Then take them," Lexie said. "Enjoy them."

I was glad to see someone genuinely sorry Jenny was gone. I said, "We'd also like to pay our respects to Mrs. Tuttle. If she's not indisposed, may we see her?"

Fred had been in the act of accepting the plate with weepy pleasure, but at the mention of Boom Boom, his demeanor cooled. "She's upstairs. Follow me."

"You all seem so hard at work at rehearsing," I said as Fred led us up the stairs. "No time off to mourn?"

"Some of us are more affected by Jenny's death than others," he said with another sad sniff. "But if the show is going to open on schedule, we have to keep working. The choreographer and I are doing what we can to move forward, but we're in limbo at the moment."

"In limbo because of Jenny's death?" I asked.

"No." As he neared the bedroom doors, he dropped his voice. "According to some, Jenny's death is just a pothole on the road to a

Tony Award. Problem is, we're still waiting for the rest of the money to come in. We can't hire more people without the big cash."

"The big cash?"

"From the backers. A show like this is astronomically expensive to produce. Not all the money is lined up yet."

"I thought Ox Oxenfeld was the producer."

"He's the managing producer." Fred led us along the upstairs hallway. "That means he does a lot of work but doesn't fork over much cash. Boom Boom says we have big money coming from a very important financial backer, but he hasn't sent the check."

"Who is the big backer?" Lexie asked.

Fred put his hand on one of the bedroom doorknobs but didn't turn it yet. He looked at Lexie and said with great dignity, "I'm told that's none of my business."

Before we had time to sympathize or ask more questions, he opened the door and waved us into the inner sanctum. The large, dim room was dominated by a gigantic canopied bed upon which Boom Boom Tuttle was laid out like an Egyptian mummy, complete with bandages over her eyes and perfumed smoke wafting in the air. The smoke did not obscure the color of Boom Boom's skin—still very clearly blue.

Without moving from her prone position or out from under the strips of material on her face, Boom Boom snarled in a raspy voice, "Who the hell is there? What are you doing? I'm having my treatment!"

Fred said, "It's some of the neighbors."

"Freddie? What's wrong with your voice? You softie, are you still all *verklempt*? Why don't you go bake something and take your mind off everything?"

Fred's tears overflowed all over again, and he let himself out of the bedroom with a bang.

I pulled a tissue from a conveniently placed box and held it over my nose and mouth to avoid breathing the smoke. I approached the bed cautiously and moved the tissue long enough to speak to Boom Boom. "It's me, Nora Blackbird, Mrs. Tuttle. And my friend from next door. We've come to pay our condolences."

"Your what? Oh, right. You mean because of Jenny. Sorry, I can't get up right now. This is my two-hour pheromone treatment. It's part of my invigoration program. I'm getting in shape for the show. Building energy. I'm playing the starring role, you know."

Lexie crossed the room and opened a window.

Boom Boom had elastic wraps around her chin, and both skinny arms were encased in towels that appeared to be soaked in some herbal liquid. Her bare blue legs were smeared with an ointment that gave her skin a ghastly sheen. Greasy socks did not disguise the bunions on her bony blue feet. In addition to the smoking pots, a humidifying steamer sat on the bedside table, directing a moist flow of damp air directly at her nostrils.

In a chair beside the bed, her bored nurse sat leafing through a magazine. Higginbotham wore a pair of eyeglasses on a chain and a medical mask to avoid breathing all the fumes. She met my eye and shook her head, as if despairing of Boom Boom's irreparably lost youth.

The rest of the bedroom had been set up like a theatrical dressing room, dominated by a lighted mirror over a makeup table. Every other horizontal surface was cluttered with framed photographs of Boom Boom in her younger, pre-blue days. Sometimes she posed with famous people. A few of the pictures showed her with Toodles. But most of the photos were of Boom Boom herself.

She had been very pretty in her heyday—a perky face with a keenly flirtatious gleam in her eye. There was a series of shots of Boom Boom in her single television role as the wisecracking wife in a comedy about a talking dachshund. For that role, she had been seen most often wearing an apron and rhinestone-rimmed eye-glasses. In one picture, she appeared to be clowning around—pretending to strangle the dog while laughing wildly. In all the pictures, her skin was perfectly normal.

Lying on the bed, she was disconcertingly corpselike.

"We're very sorry about Jenny," I said, trying again. "She was a lovely person. Everyone's going to miss her."

"She was never going to be a star, but she was a nice kid. Too bad about her heart."

"How long did she have a heart condition?"

"Always," Boom Boom said promptly. "From the time she was little. Good thing all she ever wanted to do was play her piano. She played it day and night, all the time. Between her and Toodles, it drove me crazy. Never a quiet moment."

It felt a little strange to be talking to a motionless body stretched out on a bed, steaming with stinking chemicals. But I said, "Was Jenny playing the piano for your recent rehearsals?"

"Sometimes, but that's what Fred's for. She was a pain in re-hearsals. A real balabosta. Always making everybody stop and do things over. That's no way to get a show up and running."

Lexie had taken her time looking at all the framed photos, but finally she spoke up. "Fred mentioned you're waiting for a backer to come through."

"Fred should keep his mouth shut." Boom Boom moved rest-lessly. "Him and Jenny—they've been bugging me for weeks about one thing and another. We need money for a director, to hire more dancers, to pay a costumer. Hell, I got a money guy, but he's a little late, that's all. He's—right now, he's in England. Probably going to those fancy horse races where the shiksas wear big hats. But he'll be here soon."

"Meanwhile, Mr. Oxenfeld is financing the rehearsals," Lexie prompted.

"Yeah, Ox threw in the gelt to get us started, but he's the stingy type. He takes care of the business side of things. He was a big help to Toodles."

"And a good friend to you?" I asked.

"Naw, he wasn't my type. I like 'em brawny."

A brawny man might snap frail Boom Boom like a dry matchstick, but I didn't say that aloud. I couldn't imagine her stepping on a Broadway stage in her condition.

Instead, I said, "I understand you've been bothered by people who have read this morning's story in the *Intelligencer*. About the photograph that was in Jenny's pocket at the time of her death."

Another dismissive wave from the bed. "The people downstairs are answering the door and the phone. It's not my problem."

"Do you know anything about the photograph?"

"I never saw it," Boom Boom replied. "It's a kid, right?"

"Yes, a small boy. Do you know who he was?"

"Who knows? Every once in a while Jenny sent money to lost causes. You know, a few bucks here or there to help a poor kid in some backwater place or other. It was probably one of her charity things."

Lexie said, "The newspaper hinted there might be money coming to the boy in the photo."

"He'd have a hell of a job proving it. Say, maybe I should check about Jenny's life insurance. Maybe *I* got some money coming!"

Without glancing up from her magazine, the nurse made a disparaging noise with her lips.

Boom Boom said sharply, "Higgie, shouldn't you be organizing my pills or something? I don't pay you to sit around on your *tuches*."

Higgie sighed and heaved herself out of her chair. She lumbered over to a dresser topped with a tray packed with pill bottles. She took the eyeglasses from the chain around her neck and perched them on her nose so she could read the labels on the bottles. Methodically, she began selecting various pills and lining them up on a plate.

A doorbell gonged from the floor below.

On the bed, Boom Boom stirred like an old dog that had caught a whiff of its dinner. "Hey, if that's some reporters, I should invite them up here to talk about my comeback."

"Nora's a reporter," Lexie said.

At that news, Boom Boom sat up and removed her mask. Behind it, her eyes were pink holes in her otherwise blue face. She stared at me with stunned interest. "You're a reporter? Maybe you could get us some press for the show?"

"Well—"

"Absolutely," Lexie said, nudging my foot with hers. "Nora's column would be a perfect place to give you some buzz."

"Okay," I said. "Maybe I could interview the cast?"

"And me!" Boom Boom said. "I could tell you all about my career."

"Of course. And everyone else who's been staying here to work on the show. "

"Nobody else is very interesting. Hey!" Boom Boom snapped her fingers. "You want to come to the preview on Monday? We're performing parts of the show for some money guys Ox has rounded up. You could take some pictures, maybe get us on TV?"

"I'm with the *Intelligencer*," I reminded her. "Maybe I could put you on our online edition, but I'm not—"

Lexie said, "Nora will do her best to get you all the publicity she can manage."

"Right," I said.

"Great! The preview's on Monday. Don't forget. Between now and then I'll dig up some of my old scrapbooks for you."

Lexie and I went out into the hallway together and breathed deeply of the fresh air. We could have gone down the stairs then, but I paused on the carpet.

Lexie cut her eyes toward the bedroom where we had found Jenny the day before. "What are you thinking?"

"I wouldn't mind taking another look at Jenny's room. Boom Boom has given us permission to investigate, hasn't she?"

"Interview, yes. Investigate, no. But it's a fine line, isn't it?"

Together, we crept into Jenny's bedroom and eased the door closed. Immediately, I noticed that someone had removed the area rug on which she had died. It gave me a pang.

But time was limited. Not sure what I was looking for, I began opening the dresser drawers. I found clothes—mostly beige. Same with the closet. A few hanging blouses and pants, a couple of sensible dresses—all arranged in descending sizes. She had obviously been losing weight for many months. I caught the faint whiff of mothballs. An assortment of old garden hats and beige handbags were untidily arranged on the shelf above the hanging bar. No photo albums.

On the floor were two large boxes. I opened the top one and discovered it was full of music—large sheets of it covered with notes and scribbles.

Lexie peered over my shoulder. "That's a conductor's score, with the composer's notes, see?" She pointed at the scrawled words on the margin.

"One of her father's scores?"

"I don't know. Do you recognize the title?"

"Lover, Sing Me a Tune." The title didn't mean anything to me. I dug down past it into the box and found more music. "Wedding Belles"; "I Love You for Always, My Dear." The box was stuffed with pages of it.

"Lex, maybe these are more undiscovered Toodles Tuttle songs!"

"If so, the Tuttles have a gold mine on their hands. But look. His signature's not on any of the pages."

I flipped through many of the large sheets. "No signature at all," I reported.

Lexie turned away to look through the things left on the bedside table. Over her shoulder, she said, "I remember more stuff being here."

"The police must have taken evidence." I peeked into the adjacent dressing room, where I had rested after discovering Jenny dead. All of her prescription bottles had been removed. Someone had emptied the trash. All the energy drink cans were gone.

Lexie opened the drawers of the bedside table, then flipped through the books that were stacked there. Something fell out of one of the books and fluttered to the floor. She bent to retrieve it. "Here's an envelope."

I went to her side, and we looked at it together. Jenny's name and address on one side, no return address, a forever stamp that had been processed by the post office. Figuring my fingerprints were all over the room already and that I had nothing more to lose, I took the letter from Lexie. "How many federal laws will I break by looking at this?"

"Nobody would send a woman as pregnant as you to federal prison. You'd take up too much space."

"That's comforting." The envelope had been slit as if by a knife or letter opener. It was easy to slip out the letter and unfold it.

Dear Miss Tuttle,

How come I have'nt heard a word from you? I thought you said I could audition for your show, but you have'nt called? I think you and me both know I could make things tough for you, so how about coming through for me? Or else.

The scrawled signature was none other than Bridget O'Halloran's. "Oh, great," I muttered.

Lexie read the note over my shoulder. "Bridget knew Jenny? Before she died?"

I stuffed the note back into the envelope. "Michael's going to be peeved about this."

"Not as peeved as the police. Nora, this note sounds threatening." Lexie's eyes were wide. "Do you think . . . that Bridget could have murdered Jenny?"

"How?" I asked. "Bridget arrived in the house just minutes before the body was found. And Jenny had been dead for some time."

"They could have met the night before Jenny was found, though, right? And maybe Bridget—did what? Slipped Jenny a poison? Or some drugs?" Lexie took the envelope from me and used it as a fan to cool herself. "This note implies a lot."

Reluctantly, I handed the book to Lexie, and she tucked the envelope back inside.

My only hope to clear Bridget from the list of suspects was to keep looking. I headed for the upright piano. Since Jenny's death, someone had taken the framed photo of Toodles and put it face-down on top of the piano. As if nobody wanted to see his smiling face anymore? I opened the piano bench. Empty. I closed the bench and sat on it, thinking. At that moment, I noticed the layer of dust on the piano keys. I touched one, and a sour note sounded from inside the piano.

"Somebody will hear you," Lexie warned, low voiced.

"This piano is out of tune. And judging by the dust, nobody has played it for a long time."

She noticed my frown. "So?"

"Everybody has told us that Jenny played the piano. But she obviously didn't play this one."

"Maybe she played the baby grand downstairs?"

"Maybe," I said. "There must be a bunch of pianos in this house."

"Why do you want to know what piano she used?"

My thoughts were jumbled, and I tried to make sense of all my impressions. "Things don't add up, Lex. Fred seems to be the only one who's sorry Jenny is gone, yet it looks as though somebody might have hit him. Why? And this Tuttle musical is going to be big and important, but the backer of the show isn't anywhere to be seen. Why again? I was told Toodles would never have left unproduced music behind, but there's scads of it here. Plus, Boom Boom is blue, for heaven's sake, but nobody around here seems to notice! And we've heard how much Jenny played the piano, but if she wasn't playing for rehearsals and she didn't play in this room, where did she go?" I turned to my friend. "This house is exactly like yours. Where could we find another piano? The basement?"

Frowning, she shook her head. "A basement is too damp for an instrument. And the attic is probably too dry. And the rooms in the service wing are all too small. Why are you so concerned about what piano she was using?"

"I don't know. I just— Everything seems muddled."

She said suddenly. "The folly!"

"There's a folly?"

"The little building out behind the house. My great-grandfather and his brother loved classical architecture. Out behind my pool house, there's a kind of miniature Roman temple. It's where my mother keeps all the pool furniture in the winter."

I went to the window and tweaked the shade aside. I could see down into the back terrace, where the chorus line appeared to be taking a break. The dancers lounged on the serpentine stone wall,

all fanning themselves with their top hats. Beyond the rehearsal terrace, I could see the rotunda roof of the folly as it poked up from behind a thicket of trees. It looked like the kind of place where vestal virgins awaited their fate.

At my shoulder, Lexie said, "We'll never get there without somebody noticing."

From downstairs, we suddenly heard angry voices rise.

Lexie said, "If that's reporters, I better make myself scarce."

I went straight to the door and listened before opening it. I recognized one of the voices. Bridget O'Halloran's.

Lexie and I left the bedroom as we had found it and hurried toward the landing. Cautiously, we peered over the staircase to the foyer below. Bridget was pushing her way into the house.

CHAPTER EIGHT

"You can't come barging in here!" a girlish voice cried indignantly.

"You can't stop me, babycakes." Bridget's deeper voice carried easily from the front hall. "Where's Mr. Oxenfeld? He said he wanted to see me dance today."

Tiny Poppy Fontanna stood squarely in Bridget's path, creating a small but determined blockade. The diminutive dancer's face was pink with anger, and her small frame vibrated with outrage. "Mr. Oxenfeld isn't here. Besides, we are in the middle of rehearsal. You can't interrupt."

"What's the matter, short stuff? You afraid of a little competition?" Bridget cut around Poppy and stalked into the house, her heels clicking sharply on the marble floor. She looked like an Amazon, dressed in a tight white skirt with a zebra-print blouse tied at her trim waist.

"It would hardly be a fair competition," Poppy said. "You're a complete amateur. I have twenty years of experience on the stage."

Bridget swung around, eyes narrowing with raptor intensity. "I thought you were some kind of chorus girl. Now you want the lead role?"

"Boom Boom is playing the lead," Poppy snapped with pride. "I'll be her understudy."

"Understudy? You mean the one who sits backstage and never gets to shine?"

From above, I saw the gleam of ambition in Poppy's face and knew she had two key things figured out: first, that Boom Boom Tuttle might make a grab for the lead role in her husband's musical, and second, that Boom Boom was too old to actually go on stage. Poppy planned on opening the Broadway show herself.

Primly, Poppy said, "I'll do what's best for the show."

Bridget made a rude noise and poked her long forefinger into Poppy's chest. "What's best for this show is me. Jenny Tuttle told me so herself."

Poppy was full of scorn. "When did you ever meet Jenny Tuttle? At a rest stop on the Jersey Turnpike?"

"She got out more than you think," Bridget said. "On Friday nights, she was the first one at the bar at Del Marco's Crab Paradise—where I was the headliner all last winter. She heard me do my set. Said I'd be great in *Bluebird of Happiness*."

"If that crazy story is true, how come you haven't been rehearsing with us?"

"Because Jenny said she had to keep her old lady happy for a while—until she raised enough dough to get the show off the ground."

"We don't have the money yet. So you can shove off, lady."

Bridget gave Poppy a little push. "I'm here to claim my role, short stuff. So back off."

A red flush crept up the dancer's neck, and Poppy batted Bridget's hand away. "Jenny doesn't have anything to say about this show anymore. Go back to your crabs."

"You'd like that, wouldn't you?" Bridget intended to give Poppy's poofy hair a derisive flick of her fingernail, but she must have flicked harder than planned. The hair suddenly bounced off and hit the floor, exposing Poppy's bare head. Without her wig, only thin white strands of hair barely covered her pale skull.

Poppy shrieked with rage, steam almost bursting from her ears.

Lexie and I were halfway down the staircase, hoping to break up a girl fight before it started. On the bottom step, Lexie shoved me out of the fray and made a leap to grab Poppy just as she launched herself at Bridget with her claws bared.

Bridget took advantage of Lexie's inadvertent help by taking a roundhouse slap at Poppy's face.

At that moment, who should come through the open door but Michael. He grasped the situation instantly and lunged to stop his mother.

As if in slow motion, I saw Bridget swing her hand at Poppy just as Michael seized her other arm. Bridget couldn't stop her forward motion, however, and the blow came around and connected hard with Michael's face. His head snapped back, but he also had the self-control to pull his mother close and subdue her before she could inflict any more violence.

In the following heartbeat of silence, I picked up Poppy's wig from the floor and handed it to her.

Poppy snatched her trademark blond hair from me, her face a mask of fury. "I'm calling the police!"

She jammed the wig sideways on her head, stalked around us and disappeared up the stairs.

"Jeez, Bridget," Michael said as he released his mother, "you can't go around hitting people. You're going to get yourself arrested."

"I didn't hit *her*. I accidentally hit you." Huffy, she straightened her zebra blouse. "And you're not going to press charges."

"Give me a minute to think about that," Michael said.

I said, "Let's get out of here before the police show up again."

When we got back to Lexie's house, Michael and Bridget retreated to the far end of Lexie's patio for a private discussion. As I relieved Samir of babysitting, my cell phone rang. I sat down on one of the lounge chairs and answered. I plugged one ear to block out Bridget's strident voice.

"Where are you?" Gus demanded. "We needed you here four hours ago!"

"It's Friday. I don't go into the office on Fridays because I have so many evening events."

"Don't you know that putting in time at your desk will get you ahead in your career?"

"You ran the photograph," I said, already guessing the cause of his temper, "and now all hell has broken loose."

"I never took you for an I-told-you-so kind of person. But yes, our phones have been ringing off the hook. I've declared all hands on deck until the calls slow down."

"All your callers are claiming to be Tuttle heirs and demand their rightful inheritance?"

"The stories have small variations, but they all want money, yes. Don't gloat. I'll admit I was unprepared for the number of phone calls from avaricious opportunists. One money-grubber in particular says he won't speak with anybody but you."

"Who is he? What does he want?"

"He wants to talk to you!" Gus roared. "So call him!"

"Do you have a number where I can reach him?"

Gus reeled off the phone number, and I scrambled to jot it down on my pad. I said, "Have you reversed it? Tried to find out who this number is registered to?"

"I'm a journalist," Gus snapped. "Of course I tracked down the bloke. His name is David James Kaminsky. He's a twenty-eight-year-old schoolteacher in rural Delaware. He owes fifty thousand dollars in student loans and four thousand dollars on a used Volvo. No speeding tickets, no arrests. No guns registered to him. As a side business, he makes zithers."

I thought I'd heard wrong. "Zithers?"

"Which he sells at something called a Ren Faire." Gus spelled that part for me. "In other words, he's an average American nutjob, so he's probably safe. Call him."

Gus slammed down his phone.

I punched in the phone number for David Kaminsky and got a voice-mail system. I said, "This is Nora Blackbird, returning your call to the *Intelligencer*." I gave him my phone number and disconnected.

From his bassinette, Noah gave a sigh and then a squawk, so I picked him up. "Don't become a reporter, okay? Think about becoming a minister. Or a librarian. Something quiet."

He jammed both fists in his grinning mouth and gurgled. But raised voices caught his attention, and he turned around in my arms to watch Michael and his mother renew their disagreement. Before it escalated any further, I gathered Noah closer and took him inside to change his diaper and warm him some milk.

In the breakfast room, Lexie and Samir stood at the window, watching from a safe distance while Michael and his mother hashed out their differences.

"She hit him again," Lexie reported.

Samir added, "She ought to be doing that lady wrestling show on TV. You know, the one where they tear each other's clothes off and try to beat each other's heads against the floor?"

Lexie and I exchanged concerned glances. Maybe her self-imposed house arrest was having a deleterious effect on Samir, too.

At that moment, Bridget stormed off toward the Tuttle house, where she'd left her car. Michael paced around the pool for a few minutes before he came inside. His left eye was puffing up already. Lexie handed him an ice pack. Noah stopped swinging his bare foot to give Michael a long, puzzled stare.

To all of us, Michael said, "Sorry. She gets a little out of control sometimes."

"It must have been interesting," Lexie said, "growing up with her."

"I didn't grow up with her." He applied the ice pack to his eye.

When I knew my voice would sound normal, I said, "I have to go in to work early. It seems the switchboard at the paper is swamped with phone calls, so I'm needed. Can you drive me to the train?"

"I'll drive you into the city," Michael said.

"No, Noah shouldn't spend all his waking hours in a car seat." I handed the baby into Michael's arm and the sippy cup, too. "Take him home. Play with him. I'm perfectly happy riding the train." I turned to go upstairs but hesitated. "Michael, did Bridget tell you she knew Jenny Tuttle? They met at a crab shack where Bridget sings on Friday nights."

"No, she didn't tell me." He gave up on the ice pack and held the sippy cup for Noah. His expression was uneasy. "How long have they known each other?"

"Maybe you could ask Bridget?"

"Before the police do," he agreed.

I went upstairs to change out of Libby's superpower T-shirt and into one of my grandmother's flirty A-line go-go dresses from back in the day when she partied with Ali MacGraw. Grandmama had bought a few choice couture pieces for the years after having her own children when she hadn't quite regained her figure. This one was a pink and tangerine Pucci print, off one shoulder. I had barely enough room for my baby bump in the front, which gave me a butt-hugging figure in the back. I hoped the perky geometric print and my bare shoulder might distract attention from the faults of the dress. I borrowed a squirt of Lexie's lotion to bring out a shine on my shoulder, touched up my lipstick and gave my hair a jolt of hairspray to create some spikes out of the bun at the crown of my head—another distraction from my size.

Back downstairs, I thanked Lexie for her hospitality, and Michael and I took the baby outside, where Michael had parked another gigantic vehicle—this one a monster painted with desert camouflage and with HUMMER printed on its hood.

"Michael, this one is literally a tank! I can't reach to put Noah in his car seat!"

"I'll help," Michael said, but even he had trouble getting Noah buckled in. He finally managed to settle the baby, then hoisted me up into the passenger seat, saying, "It's not a tank. It's a soft skin—no armor. It might be a little inconvenient to get in and out of, but this one is really safe."

"Safe can't be our only criterion," I said when he had climbed behind the wheel and fired up the noisy engine. "What's wrong with a nice minivan? With cup holders and good gas mileage and a backup camera so we don't bump into anybody at a Little League game?"

"I can't be seen driving a minivan!"

"Why not?"

"Because I run the Abruzzo family!"

"I thought you were shutting down the Abruzzo family. Now suddenly you're Tony Soprano again?"

"That's not what I— For the benefit of the local punks, I'm now the top of my family tree. They're supposed to be afraid of me, not laughing about what I drive."

"Why do they have to be afraid of you?"

"Because that's the way intimidation works."

"Intimidation?" I cried. "Michael, what are you doing? Have you hurt somebody?"

"Do you really have to ask me that? Look, I can't go around driving something silly. I'm a mob boss, not working at a Verizon store at the mall!"

We had both raised our voices. Before I could answer, Noah gave a whimper from the backseat. I turned around to look at him, and his lower lip was quivering. Huge tears trembled in his eyes. His parents argued in front of him, and now we were doing the same thing. Pretty soon shouting was going to be a normal part of his life.

I collected myself. With a reassuring smile, I stretched around and gave the baby his pink bunny to play with.

"There must be a happy medium when it comes to cars," I said, endeavoring to erase any trace of the annoyance from my tone when I turned around again. "We should have something that doesn't straddle two time zones."

"Okay, I'll keep looking." Michael sent a chastened glance in the mirror at Noah.

"And we're going to have to figure out a different way of disagreeing."

"Yeah, I know. Sorry, but yelling is still my default option. I'll work on it."

"It's not just you," I said. "I'll work on it, too."

We had reached the bottom of the lane that connected Lexie's driveway with the route up to the Tuttle house. I craned around to see if Ox Oxenfeld's Bentley had reappeared in front of the house. It hadn't. And Bridget O'Halloran's white convertible was gone.

As Michael turned the Hummer toward the train station, I said, "How determined is your mother to get a role in the Tuttle show?"

"Not any role. The lead role. She's obsessed."

"Obsessed enough to threaten Jenny?"

"As far as I can tell, it's Boom Boom she's fixated on. If Boom Boom was dead, I'd be figuring a way to get Bridget to a country with favorable extradition laws."

I decided against immediately telling Michael about the letter I'd found in Jenny's nightstand. "Boom Boom does seem a much more likely target. A lot of people want her out of the picture."

Intrigued, Michael said, "Like who?"

"Poppy Fontanna, for one. She wants to play the lead in the show, too. At the moment she's settling for the understudy, but I think she's only biding her time. Poppy has a temper and isn't afraid to throw a punch. And remember how Ox Oxenfeld reacted when he heard that Jenny was dead? He turned white and ran out of the room."

"Not just because he wanted to get away from my mother?"

"That's possible, too," I said amicably. "But I thought he was genuinely worried about what Jenny's death meant to the future of the musical."

"I got the same vibe," Michael said. "What about the piano man? Fred."

"He's the only one who seems genuinely upset about Jenny's death. That's sad, isn't it? She didn't leave much of an impression behind."

"Did she leave money?"

"She must have inherited quite a bit from her father. Why?"

Michael shrugged. "Usually when somebody gets killed, there's money at stake. A hothead gets greedy and grabs an ax or a knife or a gun. But when somebody dies of drugs or something slow, the killer isn't usually a mook passing by, hoping to score some petty cash. It's somebody close—somebody in the house who wants something more than loose change. Cops always look at heirs or a husband or boyfriend or whatever. Did she have a boyfriend?"

I tried not to think about how Michael came to believe such truths about murder. "I don't think she had a boyfriend."

"Too bad. Nothing makes a person homicidal like love gone wrong."

"Personal experience?" I asked, thinking of Bridget's remark about Michael's romantic past.

He smiled. "No indictments. What about the kid in the photo? Where did he come from? He didn't just pop out of thin air. If he's Jenny's son, who's his dad? Jenny had at least a one-night stand with somebody."

Last evening, I had told Michael about Gus's plan to run the photograph in the *Intelligencer*. "We don't know if he's Jenny's son. But I'll find out about the boy in the picture soon. One of the many people who called the newspaper with some kind of information or question about the photograph is a man who wants to talk to me. He wouldn't talk to Gus. So this should be interesting."

This new development wiped the smile off Michael's face. "Why you? Do you know him?"

"I don't recognize his name."

"Well, don't meet him late at night on any street corners. Take Hardwicke with you. Maybe he'll get himself mugged."

"I'll be careful." I stewed for another moment. The scenery passed in a blur as I mentally sped through everything I had seen and heard. I had been collecting a lot of information and even more impressions, but one question seemed impossible to answer. "Why would anyone kill someone as sweet as Jenny?"

"That's your department," Michael said. "You're the one who knows these people."

Behind us, Noah crooned to himself. He was happy again.

I said, "Noah seems perfectly content when we talk about homicide."

"What do you expect? He's a Blackbird."

"That's not very— Wait—stop!" I twisted my head around to look out the window. "Is that Emma?"

We were passing one of the many beautiful horse farms in Bucks County. A cluster of barns stood beside two large outdoor rings studded with daunting hurdles built out of colorful barrels and white rails. The rolling pasture glowed green with lush grass, and a handful of beautiful horses cantered across it, their riders dressed in exercise gear, complete with helmets. At the back of the group, a gray horse rollicked along with a familiar figure in the saddle.

Michael pulled over, and I clambered out of the Hummer, almost turning my ankle as I landed in the soft gravel on the roadside. I shouted Emma's name and waved both hands over my head to get her attention.

The gray horse wheeled around, and Emma pointed him in my direction. Another moment later, they arrived at the split-rail fence—the horse snorting and sweating, Emma controlling him seemingly without effort.

"Hey, Sis!" She pulled off her helmet and grinned at me. "Looks like you're having a baby!"

I hadn't seen my mischievous little sister in almost two months, but she looked the same as always—stunningly beautiful despite her dusty clothes and riding boots. If anything, her body looked more fit than ever. She had put on a few pounds—all of it muscle. Her skintight T-shirt was wet with sweat under her breasts and arms.

Her horse stuck his nose over the top rail of the fence to me, breathing in gusts. He was a lanky gray with dark stockings and dapples on his haunches. His dark eyes were full of intelligence as he snuffled my hand, but he shifted his weight and swished his tail to show he wasn't entirely a gentleman.

I pushed his curious muzzle away and looked up at my sister. "You look good, too. And it seems you have a job."

She kicked one boot out of its stirrup and hitched her leg up over the pommel of her saddle. She sat as comfortably as if in a rocking chair, not on a hundred thousand dollars' worth of restless, world-class equine athlete. The breeze ruffled her short auburn hair. "The weather's too hot and sticky for me in Florida. I got back a few days ago."

"And you didn't feel like phoning me until last night?"

"I've been busy." Her smile was easy as she rubbed her horse's neck. "What do you think of him? Handsome, right?"

It was hard to stay annoyed with Emma when she was feeling positive. "Very pretty. What's his name?"

"In the barn, we call him Cookie. I forget his registered name, but it's something in German. He's one of Paddy's new purchases, just out of quarantine from Europe. I'm stretching his legs this afternoon. His assigned rider got a better offer, so Paddy asked if I'd like to try. Get him fit, train with him. In a couple of days we'll see if he can jump the way his advance publicity claims."

"You mean you might ride him in competition? Em, that's great!" I was delighted to hear someone might trust her enough to let her ride in important shows again.

"Yeah, we'll see." She gave his neck a rub, and the horse mouthed his bit and shook his head.

"Won't Mr. Twinkles be jealous?" I asked, thinking of her chestnut gelding. The horse stayed at Blackbird Farm with me, where he ate his head off and supposedly strengthened his sore tendons.

"Twinkles still needs to heal a little. So I'll ride Cookie until I can get my own horse back in top shape. And to earn a few extra bucks, I thought I'd run a quick two-week pony class for kids next month before school starts. Does that work for you? Can I use the farm?"

"Sure. The pony classes are fun."

"I'll start working with Twinkles then, too."

A Little Night Murder

The Grand Prix circuit was where Emma wanted to be, and she had purchased Mr. Twinkles herself to compete. But his health problems had delayed her plans. From time to time, Emma's career ambitions got sidetracked by her drinking, too, so I was glad—if a little surprised—to see her literally back in the saddle. Maybe this new horse would take her to the kind of competitions she dreamed of.

But considering her track record, I was also concerned about her personal life. "Where are you staying?"

Her face closed. "Don't worry about me, Sis. I've got lots of offers."

"With anybody I know?"

She laughed harshly. "Nobody you want to hear about."

Between boyfriends, Emma had sometimes lived with me at Blackbird Farm. But now that Michael was making his permanent home there, Emma didn't come around much anymore. I knew they'd had a disagreement last winter, which resulted in him throwing her out. Since then, I'd worried about my sister.

Today, though, sitting on a beautiful horse, she looked surprisingly healthy. And happy.

So I hated to break the mood when I said, "Michael got your message last evening. We have Noah in the car right now."

"Good. Hart called me, asking for help. When I couldn't reach you, I got in touch with Mick."

"Want to see Noah?"

Her gaze traveled past me to the waiting Hummer. It was hard to see through the darkened windows, so she didn't try to get a glimpse of her son. She shook her head. "Nah. He's in good hands. You two may not be a match made in the society pages, but together you're a fortress where that kid is concerned." With a barely different tone in her voice, she asked, "How did Hart look?"

"Upset," I said. "Penny's going back to rehab."

"Yeah, he told me. What else is going on? How's Lib?"

Clearly, Emma didn't want to hear anything more about her son. She was determined to forget she'd ever given birth. So I said, "The usual. The twins are terrifying. Rawlins is going off to college soon. Lucy says her imaginary friend ate one of Libby's emerald earrings. Mostly, though, Libby is worked up about becoming a grandmother. Consequently, I think she's looking for a new man in her life."

"What happened to the exterminator? The dude with flannel shirts and the giant mosquito on top of his truck?"

"He's history. Too many burritos, not enough flowers and champagne. She may be starting something with Ox Oxenfeld."

Emma's eyes popped. "The Broadway guy? You're kidding! He's loaded. What does the bug man say about that?"

"Not enough. She's looking for someone with more verbal skills. Perry's not exactly a great conversationalist."

Emma wagged her head in lament. "He moons for her, though."

"With Mr. Oxenfeld, there's foot rubbing involved."

"Well, foot massage is fleeting. She's got five kids," Emma said with a laugh. "And one of them's heading off to college next month. She's probably thinking of tuition payments. I don't blame her."

"Em! Since when do you think with your wallet, not your heart?"

"C'mon, Nora. Romance might make your blood run hot, but sometimes it's a good idea to think about the bottom line."

"I'm astonished to hear you say that."

"I can support myself," she said. "And I'm not feeding any kids. How's Mick?"

"Fine. We're finally getting our heads above water."

She jutted her chin in the direction of Michael's Hummer. "One look at the monster truck tells me that. What's he doing? Planning on driving that thing into combat?"

"He's concerned about safety. Which is understandable."

"Yeah, I hear things are hot again in the mob world. But he can handle the heat, right?" She rubbed her shoulder as if to loosen a tight muscle. "He was certainly cool when it came time to drive me to the hospital."

"He wasn't the only cool one," I said. Emma had delivered her baby without any fuss. I patted her horse's neck. "Come by the farm when you get a chance. We'd like to see you. Bring your new boyfriend."

With another cold laugh, she put her boot back in the stirrup and gathered the reins. "I don't think you're going to want him around."

"Why not?"

Instead of answering, Emma waved and nudged the gray horse into a canter. Her nonreply made me nervous. Emma wasn't known for her good taste in men. If she already knew this one was trouble, things could be worse than usual.

But I had other problems to contend with. Time to go to work.

CHAPTER NINE

I took the train into Philadelphia, and by the time I arrived mid-afternoon, my lunch at Lexie's was long forgotten. Hungry again, I grabbed an iced orange juice and a salad and carried them into the Pendergast Building. In the newsroom, every telephone was ringing, and my colleagues looked frantic.

Skip Malone and Mary Jude Yashurick had been pulled off the Sports desk and out of the Lifestyle department, respectively, and they shared their tales of woe with me.

"I've talked to eight crazy people today." Skip showed me his notes. "Four of them think they're Jenny Tuttle's illegitimate kid, but only if it means they have money coming. Two say they're her long-lost husband. One claims he's speaking with her from beyond the grave through the voice of his cat."

I said, "I'm just glad there are no penis stories on your list."

"Give me time," he retorted with an eye roll.

Mary Jude was equally aggrieved. "I can top your list of wackos.

I've got one guy who says he's the reincarnated Toodles Tuttle himself."

Skip pointed his pen at Mary Jude. "There's a pool going. Whoever gets the craziest call wins all the money. The pot's up to a hundred and eighty bucks. I'm going to get a doozy to win it all."

His phone rang and he scooted his swivel chair back to his desk, leaving Mary Jude and me alone together in our corner.

Mary Jude and I had bonded when I'd first arrived at the *Intelligencer.* She wrote a food and recipe column, and she had helped me learn the newspaper's computer system. She was still my native guide in a lot of ways. When I'd had a miscarriage last year, she'd been very supportive. In return, I tried to be a good listener when she talked about her travails with her son Trevor.

For a moment, she watched me wolf my salad while my computer warmed up. "You look good these days, Nora. And that's a cute dress."

"Thanks. My clothing situation is getting dire, though. At home, I'm wearing my sister's T-shirts—but only when nobody can see me."

"I think I wore the same stupid shirt for the last two months." She scooted her chair closer. "If you don't mind me asking, what are you going to do about child care once your baby is born?"

I crunched a cucumber and managed to open some computer files at the same time. "I'm not sure yet. We've been looking after Noah again, and Michael and I have taken turns. We're lucky to have flexible schedules. It must be so much harder for you."

Mary Jude opened a package of bagel chips—no doubt one of the many products that food manufacturers sent to her for review. She offered me a chip. "It's getting worse. When Trevor was little, I could almost manage everything. But now that he's older and needs more physical therapy sessions, I'm seriously thinking about going part-time here at work. Or maybe job sharing with some-body. Except I'm barely making ends meet already. I dread cutting back even more."

I bit into the bagel chip. Trevor had a lot of special needs, and although Mary Jude had been quietly courageous about taking care of her son after his father took off, I knew she was stretched thin.

I waved off her offer of another chip. "I'd share a job with you in a heartbeat. But my idea of cooking is still microwaving a Lean Cuisine."

"And my idea of socializing is taking Trevor's caregiver to Mc-Donald's." Mary Jude sent me a sideways glance. "What is Mr. Hardwicke's policy about job sharing?"

"Does he have one?"

"We figured you'd know."

"Me?"

"You've obviously got his ear. Can you ask him?"

I knew my relationship with Gus had caught the attention of my coworkers. I understood him better than most people in Philadel-phia. He wasn't a blue-blood Colonial descendent, but he came from a kind of family I recognized. But I was uneasy, knowing my coworkers wondered if we were forging something else.

On the other hand, maybe I could do some good for somebody. I knew I sometimes took advantage of my relationship with the boss. Was it wrong? Or useful?

"I'll give it a shot," I told Mary Jude.

She gave me a thumbs-up and reached for her phone, which had begun to chirp. I quickly rearranged my files, sending the articles I had written the night before to the Lifestyle editor. A second later, my cell phone went off, too.

When I answered, my sister Libby said musically in my ear, "Are you in the city now? I just happened to bump into someone and we're having a late lunch after a little shoe shopping."

I looked at my watch. It was almost teatime. "You're with Ox?" I asked.

"Why, yes. He'd like to meet you. Under better circumstances than yesterday."

Libby was on the case, all right. She must have called Ox the minute she and I hung up earlier. I got the details from her while closing the lid of my salad. We disconnected, and I headed for the elevator.

Unfortunately, Gus Hardwicke was just stepping off as I started to get on.

"Whoa." He caught my elbow. "Where are you going?"

"To pursue a hot lead."

He pointed at the busy newsroom, where all the phones were ringing again. "We need your help here."

"We? Have you been answering calls?"

He released my elbow and straightened his tie. "I had to represent my father at a meeting this afternoon."

"Merger talks going well?"

"It's not a merger; it's a takeover. And if those old farts haven't figured that out by the time it's all over, I'm going to bend them over a barrel and take a good look at their shriveled freckles before I—"

"I get the picture." I stepped onto the elevator before he could turn coarser. "I'm going to talk to somebody about Jenny Tuttle."

Gus got back onto the elevator to ride down with me. "Who's the somebody?"

"Ox Oxenfeld, the producer of the Tuttle musical."

"Did he poison the dead lady?"

"Poison?"

"The preliminary tox screen says Tuttle died from massive amounts of speed and caffeine. Enough to kill a tribe. Did Oxenfeld shove pills down her throat?"

"I doubt it. But he has been working with Jenny on the show, so

143

he may know her better than most." I punched the "lobby" button, and the doors closed. "Gus, what is the *Intelligencer*'s policy on child care?"

He couldn't stop a glance of distaste. "My personal policy is to not think about it at all."

I ignored his tone. "Why don't we have an on-site day-care center?"

"Are you joking? For one, it would be ridiculously expensive at a time when I'm considering canceling our order for paper clips. And two? Why would we want a bunch of squalling nippers around the office?"

"Workers are more productive if they're secure in knowing their children are being well taken care of. Google has day care and healthy food options and—"

"And allows workers to bring their dogs to the office. The big difference is Google makes money. Our employees would be much more productive if they used a dinger when they go to bed with each other."

"A dinger?" I asked before I could stop myself. "Isn't that a wild dog?'

"That's a dingo. A dinger is a rubber, a love glove, a condom."

The words came out of his mouth just as the doors parted on the eighth floor. A distinguished gentleman with a cane stood outside the elevator with an air of consternation. He was a slender, elegant gent in an expensive suit that hung slightly on his frame, as if life had just begun to drain his flesh away. But his silver eyebrows rose nimbly high on his patrician forehead until he caught sight of me.

"Nora Blackbird! My dear young lady, how is your lovely mother? She is the original party girl. Always smiling." He stepped onto the elevator with pleasure.

"Last I heard, she was taking a cruise to Antarctica to see penguins. Hello, Mr. Dietrich." I shook the old man's firm hand. "What happened to you? You've added a walking stick since I last saw you." From the jaunty way he used the cane, I felt the question wouldn't trouble him.

"I'm ashamed to say I took a tumble off the dock at our summerhouse. I'm finally too old to water-ski. Who's this . . . person?"

Adam Dietrich, one of my father's fellow boarding school alumni, ran a small but exclusive investment firm that catered to people whose money was older than that of most. He also collected extinct birds' eggs, and the Smithsonian had already inquired about a donation someday. There wasn't a way to summarize his whole pedigree during an elevator ride, however, so I said, "Mr. Dietrich, this is Gus Hardwicke, the editor of the *Intelligencer*. Gus, Mr. Dietrich is an old friend of the family."

Gus punched the elevator button again and attempted to regain some courtesy as he shook the old man's hand. "How do you do, sir? It's a pleasure to meet any friend of the Blackbirds."

"Hm," said Mr. Dietrich, who was not easily bamboozled.

I said lightly, "We were just discussing the possibility of opening a day-care center here in the Pendergast Building. If we want talented women in business, we need to remove the barriers that keep them from working, don't you think?"

"I absolutely agree," Mr. Dietrich said without hesitation. "One of our oldest partners just retired, and his former office suite is available. It's on the floor below the newspaper. It might serve your purpose very well."

I concealed my amazement at being taken seriously when—if I was being honest with myself—half my purpose in bringing up the subject was simply to annoy Gus. "Would you be interested in exploring the possibilities? Perhaps sharing a facility with us?"

"Exploring can't hurt. Let's set up a meeting." He reached for his breast pocket but frowned thoughtfully. "Nora, I have an empty seat on the board of the Dietrich Charitable Foundation."

"Would you like me to mention the vacancy in my column?"

"Heavens, no." He smiled fondly at me. "I wonder if you might consider taking it?"

A seat on the board of a major charitable institution? One nearly as old as the city? I barely contained my surprise. After a heartbeat, I managed to say, "I'm very flattered."

"Let's talk about it. My assistant saw your newspaper piece about disreputable charities, and it got us thinking about you for the foundation. Our focus is family matters—education, child services, that kind of thing. We need a young career woman's perspective." He pulled a silver case from his pocket and handed over his business card. "Call Lemetria and make arrangements for a lunch with me? We could discuss your day-care plan at the same time."

"I'll call soon," I promised as we reached the lobby.

"Excellent." On impulse and smiling, Mr. Dietrich reached out and patted my baby bump. "Lovely to see you, Nora. Good day, Hardwicke."

"G'day, sir," Gus said to the gentleman's departing back. To me he said in an undertone, "What was that about?"

I was still staring at the vellum business card in my hand. "I must be coming up in the world."

"You barely have time for your job, let alone some do-gooder project."

He was right. And with children on the way, I was going to be even more pressed for time. But I was dazed by the honor Mr. Dietrich had suggested.

I stepped off the elevator. "Exploring, that's all we're going to do."

Gus stayed where he was, stubbornly propping open the elevator doors. "I haven't agreed to your cockamamie day-care plan. We haven't got a spare drachma to spend on anything, and besides, I don't want a mob of children around."

"Don't say no yet."

"Nora, there are several things we need to discuss in more detail."

"I don't have time now."

Two men in suits had crossed the lobby and boarded the elevator without looking up from their cell phones. One reached past Gus to hit a button. "C'mon, buddy, kiss your wife and make up so we can all get back to work."

Gus looked mortified and released the door. I laughed and waddled out to meet my sister.

Around the corner at one of the city's most elegant hotels, I ran a gauntlet of bellmen rushing luggage for arriving guests. I used the bronze hand railing to hoist myself up the staircase and went through the open doors to the cool cavern of the lobby. The hotel had once been a bank, and the bones of a grand marble monument to commerce remained.

"Whoo-hoo!" Libby's voice echoed from a table in the bar. She waved using her fingers only. Two large shopping bags sat at her feet, and she was wearing a pair of striking purple sandals with laces around her trim ankles.

I stepped around a champagne bucket and leaned down to give my sister a kiss on her fevered cheek before sitting down at the banquette Libby shared with a pink-faced Ox Oxenfeld.

"Hello." I shook his hand. "I'm Libby's sister Nora."

"Yes, I remember." Ox continued to blush. "We didn't have much time to talk when—at the Tuttle house."

"It was a very upsetting day, wasn't it?"

"Yes, very. I hope you'll excuse my less than cordial behavior. I wasn't myself." He poured champagne into a spare glass and passed it my way. He gave me a nervous sidelong glance, and I realized he was probably trying to decide if I planned to embarrass him by bringing up his assignation with Bridget O'Halloran in front of Libby. I sent him a steady, blank-faced gaze in return and kept my mouth shut. Visibly, he relaxed.

Libby had picked up her fork again and made a show of cutting a smidgen of cheesecake from the long, narrow plate of elaborate desserts before her. She looked very festive in a low-cut blouse with a long silver necklace that rode the crest of the wave of her bosom. Her hair was a coquettish tangle, her lipstick lush.

"Would you like some cheesecake?" Ox asked me. "My parents owned a Brooklyn deli, so I'm a bit of a connoisseur where cheese-cake is concerned. The stuff they serve here is first-rate."

Libby forked up a bite. "Here, try this one, Oxy."

She fed him from her own fork.

I watched my sister pat his mouth with her napkin. Clearly, things had moved faster than expected between the two of them. Like maybe Mach 3.

To Ox, I said, "Why don't you tell me about the new Tuttle show? Isn't it a miracle that Boom Boom found one of Toodles's old scores?"

"Yes, a miracle." He couldn't quite meet my eye as he reached for his champagne to wash down the cheesecake. "But the music's great, and they're working hard to make the production a hit."

Ox was a short man—barely my height, I guessed—but he sat with the body language of a powerful person accustomed to com-manding money and prestige: upright posture, shoulders square, head high, one hand resting on the table at all times. As befitting a Broadway impresario, he wore flashy rings on his pudgy fingers. Otherwise, he had a round face and a bald head with a neatly trimmed white fringe around his prominent ears. Put him in a red sleigh and a false beard, and he'd make a pretty good Santa Claus.

I said, "I suppose finding Boom Boom's daughter dead was very upsetting for everyone connected with the show."

Libby sighed again. "Such a gruesome subject!"

Ox patted her hand. "The show is my livelihood, Elizabeth."

She smiled fetchingly. "The show must go on, Oxy?"

"I hope so," he replied, gazing deeply into her eyes.

I cleared my throat before they started canoodling right in front of me. "There's something I have to ask you, Mr. Oxenfeld. Have you noticed anything strange about Boom Boom?"

"You mean her color?"

"Exactly. I've seen earlier pictures, and she wasn't always blue. What happened?"

Ox said, "She was taking some dietary supplements that caused the coloration. She's hoping it will fade, but . . ."

Libby said, "I ate too many carrots on a carrot diet once, and my palms turned orange." She held up her perfectly normal palms. "That was just one of many reasons for me to condemn dieting forever."

To Ox, I said, "When did it happen?"

"Let me see. About two years ago, I guess. It started gradually. Then suddenly she was blue, and—well, now she has a nurse to help keep her medications straight."

I swallowed a comment about closing the barn door after the horse was gone and instead said, "I've been invited to Monday's preview. Boom Boom said I should bring cameras. What's the purpose of the preview? Can you tell me about it?"

He swung around to me again, unable to conceal his surprise. "I wasn't expecting any media coverage. I'm not sure it's the best— Well, if Boom Boom feels strongly about it, I can hardly protest, can I? The purpose? I've invited some influential people to attend. We're still hoping to find backers. And—well, everybody connected with the show seemed to think a preview might be a nice send-off for Jenny. Boom Boom vetoed a funeral, you see. The cast is rehearsing tonight in the theater's rehearsal space. The main thing is making sure they can do the show without Jenny. Her loss will be a great hurdle to overcome."

"Why?" Libby asked. "What did she have to do with anything?"

I said, "Jenny was a vital part of rehearsals, wasn't she, Ox?"

"Yes. She had— She rewrote some of the lyrics that didn't work, made a few adjustments to the music." Ox seemed torn between keeping information from me and impressing my sister. "That happens a lot during the creation of any show when the composer is present, you understand, but without Toodles around—well, Jenny was extraordinary at interpreting the spirit of her father's intent."

I said, "Might she have contributed to the songwriting back when Toodles wrote the show?"

Ox struggled with an answer and finally said, "As far as I know, she did not. *Bluebird of Happiness* is one hundred percent from Toodles. Jenny was a big help, though. Without her, we'll unfortunately have to rely on Fred Fusby now."

"Doesn't Fred have the talent to pull the show together?"

"I fervently hope so. But he's only the music director—the one who conducts the musicians and coaches the singers. We still need a stage director, too—and a whole team of theater pros: lighting designers, a costume staff, that kind of thing. Unfortunately, we can't afford anyone else just yet."

I said, "You're waiting for the big investor to bring more money to the production."

"Uh, yes. Boom Boom has promised he's on his way, but—well, we need the money soon or the production will fold. Which is why we're hoping to encourage other investors at the preview."

Libby frowned. "I thought you were the producer, Oxy. You

said you wear a tuxedo and go to lovely restaurants with famous actors and—"

"I am the managing producer." He regained his expansive demeanor. "But I'd be a fool to sink all my capital into one basket. I must save my eggs for expenses that are more important to me personally."

He smiled into her eyes, and she leaned close and glowed.

I interrupted the tunnel-of-love moment by asking, "Ox, do you know who Boom Boom's big investor is?"

"No, but I trust her," Ox said, perhaps a shade too quickly. "We've known each other a long time. She may be losing a few steps at her age, but she still has relationships with the important people we need. I'm sure she has lined up someone reliable."

I asked, "Is she really going to play the lead role?"

Ox again grabbed his champagne glass and raised it to his mouth, only to belatedly realize it was empty. As efficient as a geisha, Libby reached for the bottle to replenish his glass. While she poured, he said, "Boom Boom had a lot of talent in her day. But, uh, it's a very demanding role. It requires a singer–dancer with skill and stamina. And someone who isn't . . . blue. Out of respect for her past accomplishments, however, we continue to . . . indulge her."

"I suppose the big investor wants Boom Boom to play the lead?"

"He's the financial linchpin, but the addition of new backers may change the casting. Everybody comes in with new opinions. It may be a better box office strategy to offer the role to someone with the star power to sell tickets—someone from television or the movies, perhaps."

Libby swallowed a mouthful of cheesecake and leaned closer, resting one breast on Ox's arm. "I'd love to meet Neil Patrick Harris. Isn't he adorable?"

To Ox, I said, "You're stuck with Boom Boom for the time being."

Libby sighed irritably. "Boom Boom is a bitch on wheels, from what I heard when I made my deliveries. Everybody hates her. But they're also terrified of her."

"That may be overstating things," Ox said without much conviction.

Libby licked her fork, then speared a raspberry with it. "You told me it's a wonder she wasn't the one who died. You said you were actually afraid somebody might kill her."

Ox's resolve crumbled. He gave up trying to snow me. "Honestly? She's more exasperating than any actress I've ever known. It's a miracle somebody didn't strangle her a long time ago."

"What about Jenny?" I asked. "Did anyone want to strangle her?"

"Jenny was her mother's polar opposite. She was very much liked."

"By everyone?" I pressed.

"Almost," he said, and couldn't go on.

I said, "Fred liked her. But Poppy didn't. And neither did Boom Boom."

"True," Ox said unwillingly. "But that doesn't mean they killed her."

"Ox, do you know the boy in the photograph? The photo Jenny carried in her pocket?"

"I have no idea who he is."

"Can you guess?"

Libby said, "Betcha he's her son. A love child. The result of a wonderful but doomed romantic relationship with—well, I don't know who. Did Jenny sleep around?"

"Of course not." Ox began to look unnerved by the way my sister and I were peppering him with questions. "Jenny was a very quiet woman—a woman with a spotless reputation. She was a paragon."

Libby said, "A paragon? That's usually a word that means she wasn't much fun."

I thought of Jenny hanging around crab shacks listening to the likes of chanteuses like Bridget O'Halloran. Maybe she wasn't as much of a paragon as people believed.

"If she did have a romantic relationship," I said, "who might it have been with?"

Ox shook his head firmly. "I can't imagine Jenny being interested in romance. She seemed single-minded about the music. Where's the waiter? We should order more cheesecake."

As he snapped his fingers to call a waiter, it hit me that maybe Ox was trying to gloss over his relationship with Jenny for my sister's benefit. I wondered if he and Jenny had ever—? Had he used the proverbial casting couch?

Instead of pursuing that idea aloud, I asked, "Did Jenny support your idea that Boom Boom should star in the show? Or did she prefer Poppy Fontanna?"

Still looking around for the waiter, Ox said, "We all agreed Poppy isn't right for the role, either. Not powerful enough. Not a showstopper."

I asked, "So who will get the part? Not—Bridget O'Halloran?"

At the mention of Bridget, Ox turned colors all over again. "As much as the delightful Miss O'Halloran would like to be the lead, I'm only the producer, not the director."

"So Fred will decide?"

Ox considered the question and looked rather surprised by the answer that occurred to him. "Until yesterday, I'd have said that Jenny would have decided. She wasn't the official director, but she was making the creative choices. And she was the only one who would have eventually stood up to Boom Boom."

"So," I said, "if Boom Boom feared her daughter might prevent her from getting the role, what might Boom Boom have done?"

He couldn't summon the words. By his expression, though, I guessed he believed Boom Boom might have gone to any length to play the lead in *Bluebird of Happiness*.

Libby slid her hand over Ox's. She leaned close to his ear and whispered, "Let's not talk about murder anymore. We have much more exciting things to consider."

When Libby set her sights on a man, he was usually a goner. As she stroked his hand, Ox seemed to lose his ability to concentrate before my eyes. Any minute, he was going to start thinking about all those hotel rooms within close proximity. And I wondered if Libby was thinking about her unmet need for intimacy. Or—as Emma had suggested—her need for financial help paying college tuition for Rawlins.

I couldn't stand to watch anymore. Abruptly, I thanked them for the champagne I hadn't even sipped and stood up to excuse myself.

Libby cried, "You're going already?"

Ox rose to shake my hand. The light of the chandelier gleamed on his bald head, highlighting the age spots. He had twinkly Santa eyes, which were discernible through his saggy eyelids. For an old guy, he was courtly.

To me, he said, "Those are very attractive shoes you're wearing."

"Oh. Thank you."

Libby jumped up from the banquette. "I'll walk you to a cab, Nora. Ox, order us more desserts, and I'll be right back."

She wobbled on her new strappy sandals as we crossed the lobby. Outside, Libby gasped and leaned against the hand railing. "Nora, please slow down. I think I'm going to explode."

"What's wrong? The new shoes?"

"Not just the shoes." She clutched her stomach as if she'd been stabbed. "I bought some new Spanx. The Spanish Inquisition could have used this thing! It's killing me. And how are Spanx any different from that girdle Grandmama took to wearing, I'd like to know? I was seduced by the naughty name. Now all my internal organs are getting squished!"

She did look a bit as if she'd been poured into her outfit like sausage into its casing. I said, "That couldn't have anything to do with the cheesecake."

"What's wrong with you?" Libby blinked, looking as wounded as a fawn.

"Seeing you practically sitting in Ox's lap is—is—honestly? I can't stand it." I spun on her. "One day you're delivering his lunch, and now he's suddenly buying you sexy shoes!"

"You asked me to talk to him!"

"Talking is different from . . . from throwing yourself at the man. What are you thinking? Do you even *like* him? You're acting like he's some kind of meal ticket!"

"I'll have you know he told me more than he told you. You didn't ask him who got Jenny hooked on energy drinks. Well, it was him! He was totally addicted himself, and he encouraged Jenny to try them, too. But he started getting heart palpitations, so his doctor ordered him to stop. Meanwhile, he got Jenny hooked on caffeine!"

"Then what in the world are you doing with him? He might have killed her!"

"Not on purpose!"

"How do you know that?"

"I just do, that's all. He's too nice a man to hurt anyone, let alone a lady."

"You're blinded by love, is that it?"

Her spine stiffened at my sarcastic tone. "He's an attractive man who could use an attentive woman in his life. Why not me?"

"Why not? For one thing, he must be twenty-five years older than you are!"

Two bright spots of color appeared on her cheekbones. "That just means he's worldly and smart and—"

"You've got him wondering how fast he can get his hands on a Viagra prescription." I could hear myself getting angrier by the second, but I couldn't stop myself. "And what about that spiritual fulfillment you're always babbling about? That goes out the window when you see dollar signs?"

Libby snapped to attention and quivered with affronted pride. "Out of the goodness of my heart, I came out here to warn you not to exhaust yourself with worrying about Jenny Tuttle's death. But I can see your hormones are completely out of control—"

"The only thing that's out of control around here is you. You've sunk to seducing a man to get to his money!"

Libby sucked in a breath and raised her head high. "I think you've said enough, Nora. If you'll excuse me, I have to find a ladies' room and take off these Spanx before I rupture an ovary. Which I might need if I decide to marry Ox Oxenfeld! Good-bye."

She stormed back into the hotel, leaving me standing there in openmouthed astonishment.

Had I heard correctly? She was actually thinking of marrying Ox Oxenfeld?

CHAPTER TEN

I left Libby to do whatever the hell she wanted with her life, and I tried to calm myself by walking several blocks toward the Chinatown section of the city. Although still furious with my sister, I told myself I needed time to process what I had learned from Ox Oxenfeld. But my thoughts were so muddled by anger at my sister, I ended up thinking that the only person without a motive to kill Jenny Tuttle was me.

I passed the best Peking duck restaurant in Philadelphia and a few more tiny shops before stepping through a doorway beside a former Chinese laundry that was now the take-out window of the Fu Manchu restaurant.

I took the long flight of narrow steps to the second floor. Halfway up, I encountered an old woman gripping the banister and carefully making her way down the stairs. With a start, I remembered her. Dorothea Mitt Scanlon. In her day, she had been a very famous Philadelphia socialite and a friend of my grandmother's. Now at least ninety, she attended only a handful of high-society social events a year—those with ticket prices of five thousand dollars and up, and which required the haute-est of haute couture. She was still stick thin and as tanned as cordovan leather, but her cosmetic procedures could no longer fight gravity. Her face was tight at the edges, and filler had puffed her mouth into duck lips, but everything between had gone slack. It was a shame, because she'd probably have aged very gracefully if not for surgical intervention. We said hellos but kept going our separate directions. The light was so dim and her eyesight was so poor, I was sure she didn't recognize me—certainly not in my current round shape.

At the top of the stairs, I knocked, and Krissie Wong opened the door to her modest apartment.

"Hi, Nora. Thanks for coming. Wow! Is that a real Pucci?"

"Inherited from my grandmother." When I had closed the door behind myself, I said in a stage whisper, "I just met Mrs. Scanlon on the stairs. Can you tell me what she's wearing to the hospital ball?"

Krissie put one finger to her lips. "She'd be humiliated if it got out, but she's recycling old dresses."

"Hey, that's the story of my life," I said with a smile.

"But not hers. Poor thing, she lost all her money. Lexie Paine stole it."

"Lexie didn't steal anything," I immediately objected. "It was her partner who did all that."

"But her partner's dead, and Lexie's still alive, so that's who people blame. I feel sorry for Mrs. Scanlon. She doesn't have any children, and her husband is long gone. Her friends are paying for her ticket to the gala to cheer her up. She must sell her house and downsize."

I felt sorry for Mrs. Scanlon, too. At her age, she was probably afraid of ending up destitute. But it was unfair of people to blame Lexie for her partner's terrible crime. I kept my objections to myself, though. It was hard to defend someone who was living in the lap of luxury—even if that luxury was borrowed.

Krissie's tiny apartment was jammed with clothing that hung on hangers and racks and lay folded over the furniture. Some of the items I recognized right away—elaborate silken costumes from the opera company's coming production of *Carmen*, obviously sent to Krissie for alterations. The other pieces ranged from prom dresses to business suits and beautiful beaded gowns I'd no doubt see in the coming months at formal functions around the city. Despite her modest atelier, Krissie did quality work for quality clients.

Her furniture consisted of folding chairs, several old sewing machines and a well-used ironing board, all crowded together so that there was little room to move except for a small cleared space in front of a three-way mirror. The room smelled faintly of machine oil as well as the cooking fragrances that floated up from Fu Manchu.

From the half-open kitchen door waved Krissie's tiny, smiling grandmother. The former proprietor of the long-gone laundry business downstairs, she was now a diminutive, wrinkled lady who always seemed to sit in Krissie's cluttered kitchen reading a Chinese newspaper. Her gnarled fingers ran lightly across the printed symbols.

Judging by the bare-bones nature of her apartment, I suspected Krissie sent money to support many relatives abroad.

Krissie didn't notice the mess around her and cheerfully asked, "How about some tea?"

The idea of drinking hot tea in the hot apartment didn't appeal, so I thanked her and declined. "How are my dresses coming?"

"I wanted you to try on the St. Laurent one more time. I'm still not sure we have it right."

I slipped into the bathroom that served as the dressing room and pulled over my head a voluminous chiffon dress. When I came out, Krissie fastened the gown at the back and led me to the mirror. Together, we studied the mint green Yves St. Laurent design with critical eyes. I had inherited it from an actress who had battled her weight, so the dress had been intended for a larger woman. Its long, sweeping lines and wealth of fabric were intended to camouflage figure flaws. The elegant neckline was a simple silver ring that exposed my pale shoulders. The chiffon flowed over my belly in a graceful cascade of mint green and touched the floor at my feet. Krissie had lightly basted her alterations so that the dress fit my figure.

But Krissie frowned at my reflection and finally shook her head. "It fits, and the color's great on you, Nora, but it still overwhelms you, doesn't it?"

I sighed. "I look as if I'm swimming in key lime pie."

"I hate to suggest this, but what if we cut it short? If it were cocktail length, it wouldn't be a St. Laurent anymore, exactly, but it would suit you better. And it would be more multipurpose."

It felt like a sin against fashion to change the spirit of the original St. Laurent design. On the other hand, I really needed something nice to wear during the next two months.

Seeing my indecision, she said, "Let me pin it up, and we'll look at it again."

While she worked, I stood still and let my gaze rove over some of the costumes hanging around the room. There were many saucy peasant dresses and bright military uniforms with plenty of braid. "Looks as if you have *Carmen* under control."

She laughed around the pins in her mouth. "I think so. I didn't make the costumes, you know—I'm just altering pieces from the opera company's costume shop. They send me work when their staff gets overwhelmed."

"Do you work on other kinds of shows? Musicals, for instance?"

"Just alterations, never original designs. I have a rush job on my hands at the moment."

"*Carmen*? Or for a preview of *Bluebird of Happiness*, by any chance?"

She blinked up at me. "*Bluebird*. How did you know that?"

"I've been invited to see the preview on Monday night."

"I thought that preview was supposed to be top secret. Here, look again. What do you think?"

The hem was bulky with extra fabric, but I could see what Krissie had in mind. With high heels, the dress might be flattering, and a little bit sexy, too.

I said, "May God and Coco Chanel forgive me. Let's hem it."

Krissie laughed, and I went back to the bathroom.

Next up was an off-white Galanos gown that I'd been saving for years. It had been my grandmother's when she was expecting my mother. Not for that reason alone did I hold the dress in special esteem. The designer had been born in Philadelphia, and my grandmother had known him well. Although she never said so, I had heard an aunt whisper that she had been one of the great designer's muses.

I slipped on the dress and caught my breath at my reflection. It was simple, elegant, very chic, with a slim silhouette that might have suited Claudette Colbert in an old movie. A pregnant Claudette, that is. The fabric was a creamy silk with satin ribbon that was embellished with tiny crystals. The shape of my belly was clearly visible, but was not an ungainly bulge. The designer had taken pains to minimize my grandmother's pregnancy, and his extraordinary skills were clear. The neckline was demure, the bias cut feminine. The best part was that the very low-cut back of the dress featured an exquisite oval of rose-shaped satin cutouts that made a feature of my otherwise naked back. As if they had been cut out of the fabric, appliqued roses fluttered down the back of the dress into the slight train. The total effect was . . . romantic.

I hadn't planned on wearing white to the judge's chamber, but the cream-colored Galanos masterpiece was the kind of dress in which a woman could start a new life, a new family. I looked at myself in the mirror and felt myself tear up. My dear grandmother might well have been standing at my shoulder, smiling at me. She had been the woman who most shaped my life, and I felt as if I honored her memory by wearing her beautiful dress to my wedding.

Filled with happiness, I soon felt guilty for having yelled at Libby. Who was I to judge her situation? Maybe she saw something in Ox I hadn't observed yet. I needed to apologize to my sister.

"You need help in there?" Krissie asked from the other side of the closed door.

"I'm fine. Just a sec." I found my handkerchief and dabbed my eyes. Maybe my hormones were more out of control than I thought.

"This is more like it!" Krissie said when I emerged from the bathroom. "Let me adjust the hem. And maybe I'll tweak the fit of the bodice. This dress demands perfection."

Down on her knees, she began pinning the silk. "Since you're going to the preview on Monday night, I wondered if there's any chance you knew Jenny Tuttle?"

Her question surprised me. "I knew her slightly. I was in her house just after her body was found."

Krissie sat back on her heels. "Maybe you can help me with a problem. In addition to the costumes I was altering for the show they're working on, I have a couple of dresses that belong to Jenny."

"You do?" I was startled all over again.

"Not like this." She gave the Galanos a respectful tug. "Dresses she ordered online. She brought them here for alterations. Now that she's gone, I don't know who to send them to." Krissie gestured at something hanging in a plastic bag from a doorframe. "A little blond lady brought the costumes, and I was thinking I could send Jenny's dresses back with her, but—"

"A blond lady with a baby voice?"

"Yeah, that's her. The one who looks like Shirley Temple and talks like she just took a hit of helium." Nettled, Krissie said, "But she acts like a drill sergeant—giving orders and never saying thank you."

Poppy Fontanna. "I wouldn't send Jenny's dresses back with the drill sergeant. They could go to Jenny's mother, I suppose. Krissie, did Jenny tell you what the dresses were for?"

"Yeah, she said they were for the opening night of her musical. She couldn't decide which dress would be best, so she left both of them here."

Her musical, I noted. "Could I see the dresses?"

"I guess discretion doesn't matter anymore." Krissie had finished crawling around me and clambered to her feet. "Right this way."

She opened the garment bag and showed me two long gowns on hangers—not couture pieces, but mother-of-the-bride dresses someone might pick up in a department store. They looked a little matronly to me, but elegant. One was black, one silver. Both with beading. They were showier than the clothing I had seen in Jenny's closet. She had planned on making a splash.

Krissie said, "Jenny thought the black was more slimming, but she was hoping to diet her way into the silver one."

"When was she going to pick them up?"

"She said she wouldn't need them for a few more weeks. Come to think of it, that was almost a month ago. When is her opening night going to happen?"

"It's not a firm date yet. Krissie, did Jenny actually call it 'her' show? Or her father's show?"

Krissie screwed up her face to think. "I'm pretty sure she said it was hers."

After dressing again, I thanked Krissie profusely for her hard work on my gowns and asked if I could pick them up on Wednesday. She agreed. I waved good-bye to her smiling grandmother and went back down the narrow stairs to the street.

Outside, I almost didn't hear my phone over the roar of a passing bus. I ducked into the lobby of a tourist hotel to answer.

"Nora Blackbird, hello?"

"Uh, Miss Blackbird? From the newspaper?"

I plugged my other ear so I could hear the soft male voice on the other end of the line. "Yes, that's me."

"It's David Kaminsky. Sorry about playing phone tag. I was at band camp and had to wait until the kids were dismissed for the day."

Band camp? I made my way to a sofa in the lobby and sank down into its squishy softness. Too late, I realized I might have to flag down a passerby to get my bulky self out of the deep cushions.

My momentary silence prompted my caller to add, "I'm the assistant high school band director this year." He named a school district in nearby Delaware. "It's only a few extra bucks, but I love it. Did you play an instrument in high school?"

"The cello," I said.

"Oh, cool. Actually, my first love is strings. I play them all, give private lessons. Band camp is just something to do in the summer. I'm a music teacher, in case you didn't guess."

"Mr. Kaminsky, my editor tells me that you called the newspaper this morning."

"Yeah, I did. Hey, I'm coming up the expressway, almost to the city. Can I meet you somewhere? For a drink or something? Just to talk, that is. Hey, that sounds like a Match-dot-com hookup, huh? But I'm not trying to pick you up, honest."

A Little Night Murder

I hadn't planned on taking any chances, but the voluble David Kaminsky sounded like the kind of callow youth I could be perfectly safe with.

I was about to suggest he meet me in the hotel lobby, but I felt my stomach gurgle and instead asked if we could meet at the Reading Terminal—a kind of indoor food court popular with tourists. I walked a couple of blocks to get there and stood in line for a dish of Bassetts cinnamon ice cream. On such a hot day, the line was full of locals as well as out-of-towners. At a nearby stall, the Amish girls were packing up their leftovers. One of the coffee vendors was already closed for the day and had put a GONE FISHING sign on the counter. I passed it and went to the back of the terminal to find a semiquiet table to enjoy my treat, feeling only slightly guilty.

When I finished the last creamy slurp, it felt good to do nothing for a while. Sitting quietly, I wondered if maybe I was pushing myself too hard. I had felt energized during my middle trimester, but now perhaps my body was telling me to slow down a little.

My caller showed up in a rush. I recognized him instantly. Except for his front teeth, he didn't look much different than he had in his childhood photograph—all elbows and the big chin and floppy brown hair. He wore nondescript khaki shorts with sneakers and a short-sleeved polo shirt with the name of the high school band embroidered on it. He took off a blue baseball cap and put his hand down for me to shake.

"Wow." He recoiled from me when I struggled to my feet. "I guess you're having a baby soon."

"Yes." I caught my balance on the back of my chair. Judging by his tone of voice, he thought my condition might be contagious. "Do you want to go somewhere for a drink? Or is this okay?"

He looked around the busy space. "This is great. Can I get you something?"

"How about a bottle of cold water?"

"Coming up!"

When he returned with two bottles of water, I said, "When you phoned the newspaper, Mr. Kaminsky, you asked to talk to me, personally. May I ask why?"

He put his baseball cap on the table between us. "Call me David. My mother told me to phone you."

"Do I know your mother?"

"Nah, she just reads your stuff in the paper. Even if the *Intelligencer* is getting a little wacko lately, she said I could probably trust you. She lives in Exton, right outside Philly. She says the picture in the paper is my first-grade photo. It just about gave her a heart attack, though, opening the *Intelligencer* and seeing my old picture there."

"I'm sorry about that. What makes her think it's your photo?"

He laughed. "Well, you know. Moms know everything. She recognized it. She has a copy at home, right there in the dining room. In one of those frames with all the circles and a picture for every year of school? Anyway, she said I should call you. So here we are. What's this all about?"

The ball was in my court. I had stewed about how to approach a potentially delicate subject. Cautiously, I asked, "Do you know who Jenny Tuttle is?"

His smile was broad. "Sure. She's my mother, right?"

I must have looked flabbergasted, because he said quickly, "My birth mom, that is. I'm adopted. So I'm guessing she's my real mother."

"Can you prove it?"

"That I'm adopted? Well, I don't carry the papers with me, but—"

"No, I mean can you prove that Jenny was your mother?"

David cracked open his water bottle and took a thirsty slug before answering. "Mom was required to send my picture to the adoption lawyer now and then—we guess to keep my file updated, but maybe it was to send to the birth parents. That's the only reason I can think why she had a copy. Mom always said she would help me look up my birth parents anytime I wanted, but I never did, you know? Because, hey, they were never really my parents. My adopted parents, they're my real parents. Actually, I have two moms. Mom and Mimi. They're lesbian," David said the word without batting an eye. "Both of them are music teachers, too, like me. I didn't want to hurt their feelings by digging around for anybody else. Does this make any sense?"

"Yes, it does."

"So I could find out, I guess. But why would that lady have my picture unless she was my mom?"

"I don't know." I peered at David for a moment, trying to see any resemblance to Jenny Tuttle. But my last glimpse of Jenny now clouded my impressions of her physical appearance when she was alive. If David's eyes were the same color as hers or if their noses matched, I couldn't be sure. He was certainly shaped differently than she. He was lean and knobby, while her figure had been well padded.

But his interest in music. Could that be hereditary?

I said, "Do you know who the Tuttles are?"

"Well, yeah. Toodles Tuttle?" David couldn't hide the sparkle in his eyes. "Who doesn't know who he is? The composer. 'Begin with My Lips'? And 'Usher in the New Year'? Great songs. I saw *Kick Step Change* when I was ten. Mom and Mimi took me up to New York for my birthday. I think I played the CD, like, a thousand times. Is it crazy to hope I could really be related to him?"

I couldn't hide a smile. This high school music teacher wasn't dreaming of a big monetary inheritance. He was thrilled about the musical connection. "I don't think it's crazy."

"So what's next?" he asked. "I know Toodles is dead, and Mom says that this lady is gone, too."

"Well, if you think it's time, you should find out who your birth parents really are. From your end, that is."

"Mom says the lawyer who handled the adoption is still alive. He probably still has all the papers."

"That's the first step, definitely."

David looked into the distance for a moment, letting his imagination fly. He was smiling. "How cool is this?"

"Pretty cool," I agreed.

My cell phone rang. I checked the ID. Gus was on the line.

I said good-bye to David Kaminsky and asked him to call me when he learned more about his adoption. Running late, I took my phone outside and flagged a cab before returning Gus's call.

He said, "Where the hell are you?"

"I'm on my way to my first event."

"Come back to the office. I need to talk to you."

"I can't. I'll be late."

He growled. "I should meet you somewhere else, anyway. This is a personal matter."

My antenna went up. "What personal matter?"

"Between you and me, of course," he said with exasperation. "That's what personal means. Plus I want to hear what you learned about Oxenfeld. What time will you be finished with whatever tea party you're attending?"

"An hour," I said without responding to his tea-party crack. "What's this about?"

"I find it necessary to discuss it face-to-face."

"All right." Curiosity on high, I said, "I'll call you in an hour."

"Do that," he snapped, then hung up.

The tea party was exactly that—a children's tea party in the sleek, modern entrance space of the new Barnes Foundation museum. I crossed over the moatlike reflecting pool and entered the blissfully cool lobby. Once I was inside the normally serene building, the party noise and mayhem practically hit me in the face.

Dozens of foster kids had been seated at darling little tables decorated with pastel paper cups and plates. The guests were supposed to be genteelly passing cucumber sandwiches while listening to a local author read from her newly released children's book. But the audience was far more interested in pulling apart their sandwiches and pouring their juice from cup to cup than in hearing about two shy frogs on a picnic. The parents watched nervously from the sidelines and tried to signal commands to their charges.

The only parent who seemed above the fray was the regally tranquil woman I had met a few times at past events for foster kids—a cause in which I was becoming increasingly interested. My new acquaintance went by the name of Miss Patty, and I had learned she was the foster parent to fourteen children.

Miss Patty waved to me, and I slipped into a seat beside her.

"Nora," she whispered, "you always look so pretty. Where do you get such fine clothes?"

"I'm a big believer in hand-me-downs."

She chuckled. "You and me both. Do you have enough baby things for your little one?"

Touched by her concern, I quickly reassured her. "My sister has bags and bags. She promises I won't have to buy so much as a sock."

"Well, when you're finished with those things, you know where to send 'em."

She caught me by surprise. "Miss Patty, do you mean you're fostering babies again? I thought you were only taking older children now."

She wagged her head. "I know I am too old to take in babies, but they won't stop sending me the ones that are hard to place."

"You're never too old for babies, right?"

"No." She turned serious. "I have to think about my longevity now. I take vitamins and go for walks in the park. There are a lot of children who need homes."

The beleaguered author looked up from her book and frowned in our direction, so I gave Miss Patty's hand a commiserating squeeze.

The short conversation about leaving children behind got me thinking about Jenny Tuttle and David Kaminsky. If he really was her son, how had she gone about giving him up? Had she found a home for him herself? Or simply surrendered him to a lawyer? And if so, who was the boy's father? Had he factored into her decision at all? Had the decision to give up the child been mutual? Or Jenny's alone?

A shriek from one of the children's tables drew my attention. The tea party was fast degenerating into a brawl, so I got up and found the event committee chair, an acquaintance whose husband owned many lucrative fast-food franchises. She was a pretty blonde who had started out flipping burgers in one of his drive-in joints because she needed to support her orphaned younger siblings. She'd married the boss and now devoted her time and considerable money to children's charities. I conducted a whispered interview before requesting permission to take photos. I snapped pictures of the decorations and several of Miss Patty's kids before calling it quits.

I noted the time and hit the street. In a hurry, I threaded my way through the hot, Friday rush-hour pedestrian crush toward my next event. On the way, I phoned Gus, but he didn't pick up. I left a message to tell him where I'd be for the next half hour or so.

At a popular Pine Street restaurant best known as an LGBT hotspot, I arrived with the first rush of guests, which gave me only a few minutes to talk with the chairperson as she helped string a banner in front of the hostess station at the last minute.

"Hi, Nora! You look great! When are you due?"

"In a few weeks," I reported, with a smile. I mopped sweat from my forehead with a cocktail napkin. "How's the party shaping up, Elle?"

Elle Maslowski and her mother had cofounded the unfortunately named Center for Women's Pelvic Health after both of them struggled with cervical cancer. Elle's mother had since passed away, but Elle—back at her job at an advertising firm—was still fighting for a cure. To prove her worth to the local organization, she was hosting several small events leading up to a big annual fund-raiser. Judging by my previous experiences with Elle's party throwing, the restaurant would soon be filled with dozens of young career women with checkbooks in hand and ready to pose for their close-ups. With her masterful networking skills, Elle had the makings of a major philanthropist for the future.

I got the party lowdown from Elle and took photos of her with the first few women who arrived. I sent the pictures to my online editor for immediate posting, and within a few minutes everyone at the event seemed to be sharing photos on their cell phones. Over the heads of guests, Elle happily shouted that even more people were showing up just because of my coverage. I suspected she was encouraging me, not really telling the truth, but it was a nice compliment.

Someone turned up the music and the big doors to the sidewalk were rolled up to let the afternoon sunshine pour in. With it came the heat. Elle's banner fluttered in the hot breeze—a cartoon drawing of a uterus dancing alongside the words CENTER FOR WOMEN'S PELVIC HEALTH.

Everyone was beautifully dressed in a rainbow of pastel colors—showing off plenty of well-maintained skin and admiring each other's high, sexy shoes. Women might dress nicely for the men in their lives, but they really pulled the best from their closets when seeing other women.

Elle circled back from greeting more newcomers. "For real, how's pregnancy?"

"For real, it's pretty great, thanks. How are you doing these days?"

She knew what I meant and tried to keep her smile in place. Her eyes turned glassy, though. "I'm okay. Losing Mom was hard. A friend told me that when your mom dies, you have to start being a grown-up all by yourself. These days I am thinking a lot about the kind of woman I really want to be."

I gave her a hug. "Your mom would be proud of what you're doing today."

We were interrupted by the arrival of more guests. Soon I felt rather than heard my cell phone go off, so I excused myself to answer the call. I expected to hear Gus's shout when I picked up, but instead it was Michael's voice on the phone.

"Everything okay?" I asked him when I found a spot on the hot sidewalk where the music wasn't blaring.

"We're great," he said cheerfully. "We stopped at the garage for a while. I think Noah's going to be a Corvette man."

Smiling, I could imagine Michael, Noah in his arm, at his garage with the usual dubious roughneck employees who hung out there. "Will you be teaching our daughters about car maintenance, too?"

"You bet. How's the murder investigation going?"

"I'm thinking of murdering my sister Libby. Does that count?"

"What's she done now?"

"She thinks she's falling in love with Ox Oxenfeld."

"That won't last," Michael predicted. "The bug man's head over heels for her."

"But he's broke, and she has tuition bills—not to mention cheesecake—on her mind." Fearing the purpose of Michael's call, I asked, "Have you heard from Hart Jones?"

"Nope," Michael said. "Jones doesn't have the guts to call me. You?"

"No."

"Then I guess we'll be keeping Noah for a while. Listen, I just wanted you to notice what time it is."

I checked my watch. "Almost six."

"Yeah. One week from now, we're going to be walking into the judge's office together. You and me, getting married."

My heart swelled, and I laughed, delighted that he'd thought to call me at this very moment. He sounded very happy.

"I'll be there," I promised. "That's a wedding I won't miss."

He said he loved me and hung up. Still smiling, I turned around and almost bumped into Gus Hardwicke.

He'd heard what I'd said on the phone. Sharply, he asked, "Whose wedding?"

CHAPTER ELEVEN

could have made up a lie. But with the heat, the noise of the party and the swirl of young women around us, not to mention the dancing uterus and Baby Girl suddenly giving my bladder a kick, the whole sensory kaleidoscope made my brain short-circuit and I said simply, "Mine."

A storm crossed Gus's face, and then he blinked. A heartbeat later he grabbed my arm and pulled me into the bar. There, along the wall, he found two empty seats in the far corner. He pointed at one of the stools and said, "Sit."

The swivel stool looked high and precarious. "I don't think I can climb up there."

He helped me up and waited while I steadied myself before sitting next to me. He said, "You're marrying your thug? When?"

"I'm not telling you."

"You can't do it."

"Gus, I've had a lot of time to consider this step. Believe me, I know all the pros and cons. But Michael and I want a family together more than anything. Now that it's actually happening, we're getting married."

"It doesn't matter to you that your rug rat will be born into the mob? That someday it might be in danger from—"

"If anyone can protect us, it's Michael."

"You're not a fool," Gus began, "but there are circumstances to consider. Nora, I—"

"Is this the personal matter you wanted to discuss? My wedding? Because I'd rather talk about Jenny Tuttle's son."

Gus's expression changed, and he sat up, all attention. The bartender noticed and came over. Gus ordered himself a scotch, and I asked for a tonic and cranberry juice. When the bartender went away, Gus said, "Tell me everything."

I reported that David Kaminsky and his mom believed David might be Jenny Tuttle's son. The adoption bulletin delighted Gus. "Just as I hoped! But the Kaminsky kid doesn't know for sure?"

"Not yet. He's not a kid, either. He's a teacher, remember? He's going to check with his adoption lawyer and get back to me."

"Who's his father?"

"David hopes to find out when he talks to the lawyer."

"This changes the story very nicely, doesn't it?" Pleased, Gus rubbed his palms together. "We have the beginning of a summer saga, see? Readers will love it!"

"We don't have any solid information yet," I cautioned. "It will be Monday until David can see his lawyer, and surely it will take a few more days before we'll be able to confirm—"

"The hell with that. Did you take his photo? An updated picture, that is, not the kiddie version. One we can run in the morning?"

I was starting to feel railroaded again. "Aren't you listening? There's no new information."

"Of course there is. We've got a cliffhanger for the murder story, and we'll have readers running to buy the paper every day to hear if he's really the Tuttle heir or not."

"He's not interested in the Tuttle money. Well," I corrected myself, "at least that wasn't his first thought. He's delighted to think he might be related to Toodles. It's the music that thrilled him."

Gus snorted. "Then either he's a total wanker, or you don't recognize when you're being conned."

The bartender returned with our drinks. I stopped myself from making an imprudent remark and instead sipped the cranberry tonic and looked around for some peanuts. The bartender noticed my glance and skimmed a fresh dish in front of me.

"Gus," I said when I was crunching nuts, "we can't use David Kaminsky this way. He's a music teacher, for heaven's sake. He's not tabloid fodder."

"He'll learn to love it."

"It feels dirty to me. Like exploiting Jenny Tuttle when she can't protect herself. We're smearing her reputation, and now his is—"

"She didn't have a reputation," Gus shot back. "She was too boring."

I was starting to think Jenny wasn't boring at all. She had led a quiet life, perhaps, but now I could see she had hidden a lot from the people who knew her best. She had hung out in a bar, listening to Bridget O'Halloran. It seemed she'd had a child—presumably out of wedlock. And Ox Oxenfeld had practically admitted Jenny was directing the new musical. My friend Nico had planted the idea that Jenny might have also written *Bluebird of Happiness*, and Krissie had almost confirmed it.

Before I could argue with Gus, Baby Girl chose that moment to make one of her violent, flying trapeze moves, and I instinctively put one hand down on my belly. I used the other to grab the edge of the bar to keep myself from being rocked off the stool. "Ooh!"

Terror flashed on Gus's face. "What's wrong?"

I gasped. "It's the baby."

He let out a curse and whipped around as if to flag down a passing ambulance.

I quelled his panic by grasping his hand, laughing a little as I caught my breath. "No, I'm fine. Every time I drink something with sugar in it, she does a somersault. I shouldn't have ordered the tonic." *Or the ice cream,* I thought guiltily.

He continued to look at my belly in shock. "Does it hurt?"

"Of course not. It's just startling. Here." Impulsively, I guided his hand to my baby bump just in time for Baby Girl to give him a solid Abruzzo kick.

He pulled away immediately, holding his hand in midair as if to allow germs to drip from it. "Good God, Nora, that's disgusting."

"It's not disgusting; it's natural," I said. "Don't you have any urge to have a family of your own?"

"To procreate? Seed the world with more Hardwickes? As if there aren't enough?" He slugged back some of his scotch. "Of course not."

"Can you tell me what's really going on with you?" I asked, curiosity getting the better of me. "In addition to running the *Intelligencer,* are you really tending to Hardwicke family business? Is that where your future is?"

He swallowed more scotch and shook his head, refusing to answer.

"Nobody at the *Intelligencer* believes you'd actually leave us to ourselves for a whole month just to go bicycling. You went home to strategize with your father."

Gus still didn't meet my eye but let his gaze roam around the bar, taking in the scene for the first time since he'd arrived and perhaps deciding how much he could trust me. "My father called a war council for me and my siblings. He wants us all at battle stations for a big media buy."

"The one here in Philadelphia?"

"That, and others."

"Such a story would blow Jenny Tuttle off the front pages."

Gus gathered his composure and said, "For reasons I'll get to in a moment, I'll trust you not to repeat any of what I'm about to say. Yes, he's expanding the empire. Naturally, my siblings and I are vying for top honors—a division of our own, perhaps. And an opportunity to become the *capo dei capi* when our father is gone. That's what's really at stake. And none of us are patient about waiting around for a chance to steer the big ship. I have two capable brothers and two very daunting sisters, all of whom would be better chief executives than me, according to my father. I'd like to prove him wrong by making this Philadelphia deal happen."

He talked about his father's vast holdings as if they were pieces of a particularly delicious pie. But I wondered how much influence all those radio stations, television networks and newspapers added up to. Whoever owned them would be empowered with a lot of information and could choose how it should be presented to the whole world.

Was Gus the right person to control worldwide communication?

Gus had begun to frown with puzzlement at our surroundings. "I'm doing my damnedest to make this bloody buyout happen. You, by the way, probably know half of the Philadelphians in the playbook. They're all as old as Thomas Jefferson, and just as prickly. What kind of party is this, exactly?"

I understood more than what he was saying. The ne'er-do-well son had decided to hang up his surfboard to become a leader within the powerful family corporation. To me, it was a familiar story. Except in Michael's case, getting into the family business wasn't something he particularly wanted.

"This party?" I said. "It's a fund-raiser. I can see how badly you want to be a part of the family business. I hope you succeed."

"Do you really care?" He turned back to me.

"I'm just curious," I replied calmly. "You seem to be concerned about your father's opinion of you."

He studied my baby bump with less distaste than before. "I'll admit my behavior would give a Freudian analyst a field day. I'm aware of my subliminal motives. Which brings me to the personal matter I mentioned."

"Yes?"

He hesitated.

"Gus?"

"It's about my negotiations with the Thomas Jeffersons."

"Oh?"

Still he hesitated. "May I touch that again?" He put out his hand uncertainly.

I felt as if we were on the brink of friendship. So I allowed him to touch me, even guiding his long fingers to the spot where Baby Girl was still rhythmically nudging me from the inside, perhaps encouraging me to quit while I was ahead where Gus was concerned.

He and I sat in silence for a minute, sharing a funny sort of pause that I optimistically decided to interpret as a new phase.

He pulled his hand away and took another drink. "It's still disgusting."

I laughed. And asked, "Do you need help with your Thomas Jeffersons?"

"Yes."

I appreciated his honesty. "What can I do?"

"In a sense, you already have. But it's time I came clean."

Just then Elle bebopped over to us, holding a cocktail and enjoying the music. "Nora, this must be your baby daddy. Hi, I'm Elle. What do you like most about becoming a father?"

Gus flushed and shook her hand while I explained, "This isn't my husband, Elle. This is Gus Hardwicke, my editor."

Her face lit up. "Oh, right! I saw you on TV a few weeks back. You look much handsomer in person. Say something in Austrian."

"I'm from Australia."

Elle didn't hear him. "Has Nora told you about the Pelvic Fund?"

"The——?" Gus squinted as if he hadn't heard correctly.

"We're raising awareness—and money, of course—for the Center for Women's Pelvic Health. Maybe your newspaper could do an article? I bet Nora could write it. She's a big supporter."

I thoroughly enjoyed Gus's revolted reaction to what he heard from perky Elle. I said, "There's nothing I won't do for good pelvic health."

For once, Gus was speechless. Abruptly, he got up from the bar, threw some bills at the bartender and departed without another word, striding past the dancing uterus with a determined air. By the time he reached the sidewalk, he had regained his Aussie swagger and kept going without a backward glance.

Elle was startled but soon laughed with me, and I left her party with the promise of giving her plenty of space in my online column. I'd do my best with the print edition, but I had a feeling Gus would veto any coverage of pelvic health.

Feeling high-spirited, I walked a few short blocks to one of the city's most prestigious private clubs for the final event of my night. I climbed the marble steps and thanked the uniformed attendant, who took a formal look at my invitation and made a production about unlocking the bronze doors for me to enter. He swung them wide, and I passed into the hallowed halls.

I made a beeline across the checkerboard floor for the ladies' room. The club was so old that it had only recently added its first ladies' room. Fortunately, it had spent a lot of money to make up for its antiquated membership policy. The bathroom featured marble and beveled mirrors, and heavy lamps swagged on bronze chains. A towel warmer contained a dozen small linen squares for drying ladylike hands.

Alone, I dug into my bag and came up with everything I needed to transform myself from a casually dressed reporter to a woman who'd been permitted to enter one of the most revered dining rooms in the city. I put on dressier shoes to upgrade my Pucci dress. I redid my hair and makeup, adding a little more lipstick and mascara for evening.

As I was tucking my makeup back into my bag, the door opened and a long-legged woman in a short black dress and a punk haircut barged in. Emma.

My sister stopped dead in her tracks at the sight of me, then grinned. "I should have known you'd be here."

"What a pleasant surprise. We can troll for appetizers together. Or do you have other duties?"

"My duties are to look good for an hour." She went into the first stall and talked to me over the door. "I'm here at the orders of Paddy Horgan. He wants to look like a wheeler-dealer to everybody else. I was hoping to duck out before the stupid dinner starts. I can only stand so much good behavior. Think you could stage some labor pains and give me a good excuse to leave?"

She flushed and came out of the stall.

"Sorry, I haven't felt one twinge," I said with complete honesty. "Em, you really look fantastic."

As she washed her hands, she eyed herself critically in the mirror. "Yeah, I've been working out. Two hours in the gym, plus a lot of riding. And a whole bunch of nutritional stuff. Why does healthy food taste so boring?"

"The taste will grow on you." The best thing about her physical transformation might be the clearness of her eyes, I thought, but I said, "I like your dress, too. Where do you shop?"

"Target. I cut off the cap sleeves. I look like a linebacker in cap sleeves."

The sleeves had been hacked out of her dress with a pair of shears probably used to cut unruly horsetails. I noticed she had in-flicted the same damage to the hem. The shorter length was perfect—midway up her lean, muscled thighs—and the dress looked surprisingly chic. She was wearing a pair of earrings that might also have come from Target. Or from Tiffany, for all I knew. She looked like a dangerous woman who'd mugged an unsuspecting fashion designer.

While she dried her hands on one of the linen squares, I handed over my lipstick. "Nobody looks good in cap sleeves."

She finished drying her hands, then applied lipstick in broad strokes. "You got that right." She eyed her reflection and tossed me the lipstick. "C'mon, if we're stuck here for the night, let's get some drinks."

I went out into the lobby with my sister, and we followed a meandering crowd down the corridor to a ballroom with a high, wedding-cake ceiling and three matching chandeliers that would have looked right at home in a Vienna palace. A large portrait of William Penn frowned down from one paneled wall. A more convivial painting of Queen Charlotte, beloved wife of George III, gazed from the opposite wall. If I recalled correctly, she and her husband had fifteen children, so I felt a certain kinship with her this evening.

The dining room's large round tables had been set with white linen and the club's monogrammed china and silver. The center-pieces were old trophies that had been filled with sprays of fragrant white flowers with lots of ferns for greenery. The all-white decor would have been uninteresting, except in this case, it was meant to showcase horses. At the front of the room, a large screen spun with a slideshow of equine photographs—all staged like the iconic animal portraits by painter George Stubbs. Each horse stood on the end of a long line held, presumably, by an attentive groom who had been cropped out of the picture.

Most of the crowd had grabbed drinks at the bar. The men wore a range of summer-hued ties and stood admiring the horse photos and talking among themselves. The women were more toned down, fashion-wise, wearing once-fashionable dresses—classics. They buzzed about horses, too. Even Emma's gaze strayed to the pictures, and when an admiring murmur arose from the crowd, she joined in.

"That's Whistleblower." She pointed at the screen, her eyes glowing with appreciation for the beautiful animal. "He was a spectacular jumper, now a great stud."

Emma had been first boosted into a saddle before most little girls popped Barbie dolls out of their packaging. While I was reading Nancy Drew and the Baby-sitters Club books, my little sister was fearlessly jumping ponies over fences taller than she was.

Watching her now, I realized I sometimes forgot how much she loved the equestrian world. For all her drinking, risk taking, and wildcatting with one unsuitable man after another, she was still the girl who loved nothing more than a good horse.

She caught me looking and winked. "I'm an expert on studs, y'know. What can I get you to drink?"

"Something with no sugar or caffeine."

"Living large, huh, Sis?" She strolled away to score some cocktails.

In search of photos and quotes—not to mention food—I wandered among the other guests. They were all members of an elite but informal fraternity of wealthy horsemen who bred, traded or trained thoroughbred racehorses or the fine animals that competed on the Grand Prix circuit. Not the usual scrappy small farmers who raised horses in the tristate area, this unofficial group numbered fewer than a dozen members, but it looked as if each had brought along an entourage.

Eventually I bumped into Paddy Horgan, the gruff stable owner who hired my sister from time to time. I introduced myself to him—he had forgotten we'd ever met—and his friendly expression turned cautious.

"I saw Emma on one of your new horses today," I told him. "He was a gray—and very beautiful."

"Right," said Horgan. "A valuable animal. He has real potential. I'm giving Emma a shot with him." Glaring at me from under bushy eyebrows, he added, "I don't want her screwing up."

"Does she ever screw up?" I asked.

"Frequently," Horgan said just as sharply. "She's damn good with horses when she puts her mind to it. But she drinks too much to be reliable. And she should keep her dates off my property. That guy she's seeing now? I ordered him off my place twice. Next time I'm going to call the cops."

"I don't know who you mean, but I'm sure—"

"He's a crook, I'll bet you that," Horgan said. "Shifty eyes and asking all the wrong questions. I don't want him near my animals—or my employees. You can tell your sister I'll fire her ass if I catch him around again."

Before I had time to protest, Paddy Horgan lumbered off to harangue somebody else. I stood for a moment, fuming.

Emma returned with her fingers pinching together three drinks—two for herself and a glass of soda water with an impressive array of fruit on skewers for me.

I bit into an orange slice first, barely holding on to my temper. "Paddy Horgan is his usual charming self."

"What's lit his fuse tonight?"

"Your current boyfriend," I said. "Paddy doesn't like him, who-ever he is."

Emma shrugged that off. "Paddy is still mad that I didn't roll him in the hay a couple of years ago."

"He seems to think your new horse has a bright future. After riding him, what do you think?"

Emma warmed to the subject more easily than usual. "Cookie's pretty great. A few bad habits we'll work on. He's strong, though—really strong, so I need to keep going to the gym. I'm thinking about getting a trainer. Funny, huh? Both the horse and the rider need professional training now. And the gym is a hoot."

"What kind of gym?"

"A suburban meat market. The women come in cute outfits with their hair and makeup done, hoping Prince Charming will notice them on the StairMaster. The guys watch themselves in the mirror when they lift. It's hilarious. But annoying that you have to run this gauntlet of hair-gel dweebs to get out of the place. Now I go at five in the morning, when everybody's serious about exercising. The only drawback was an old coot who doesn't realize he's flashing his balls when he pedals the stationary bike. Now I'm in a kickboxing class." Her grin widened. "Anything to get away from Mr. Sad Sack on the bicycles. Kickboxing is more my style anyway."

"And it might come in handy when you run the gauntlet of dweebs," I said, making her laugh. Emma looked very strong her-self at the moment.

A young man in a sharp suit who had been strolling around the edges of the party suddenly noticed Emma and headed our way. I noticed that his hair was elaborately gelled. But he caught a gander at me and stopped short. Hastily, he turned around and walked off.

Emma laughed. "Hey, Sis, maybe I need you to fend off the hair-gel dweebs."

I patted Baby Girl. "I'm the poster girl for what happens when you have sex. And I'm hungry again. I don't suppose you saw any real food? I might kill for some appetizers."

"The kitchen's backed up at the moment." She sat down with me at the table. "When I was pregnant, I should have invested in Kellogg's stock. The amount of cereal I ate could have filled a dump truck."

"Every time I reach for a cereal box, Michael makes me a plate of steamed vegetables from the garden." I glanced around, feeling increasingly desperate. "They're not even serving cheese and crackers?"

"Booze. That's it until dinner."

"I may not make it that long." I searched my handbag for an emergency granola bar.

Emma watched me dig. "What's this I hear about you discovering Jenny Tuttle's body?"

"I was there, yes."

"Did you faint?"

"It was a close call," I admitted.

Emma watched me start another search in all the interior pockets of my handbag. "How did she die?"

"Somebody helped Jenny overdose on caffeine. Or diet pills. Or both."

"Who would do that? And why?"

"Who? I don't know yet. Why? Well, the Tuttles were working on a new musical. *Bluebird of Happiness*. And it wasn't going very smoothly. Dear heaven, I'm starving!"

"Eat the rest of the fruit in your drink."

"I'm frustrated, too," I admitted once I had gnawed all the orange slices to their rinds and gobbled the cherries, too. "My editor says the newspaper will fall apart if I don't contribute some kind of story—either about Lexie Paine or about Jenny Tuttle."

Emma raised her eyebrows. "What about Lexie?"

"She's staying out of the public eye. Regrouping. Working on a plan to help her former clients. And something else. Something with Michael."

"What kind of something?" Emma asked. "You sound worried."

"Not worried, but—well, you know his tendencies. And Lexie needs a business challenge at the moment, so they—they're thick as thieves. Thing is, my editor is pressuring me to write something that will sell papers. He either wants a story about Lexie or about Jenny Tuttle. But short of breaking onto the Tuttle property to look for clues about Jenny's death, I've run out of material. I'm feeling frustrated."

Emma sent me a stern sisterly glare. "You're not breaking into anything, Miss Marple. Not in your condition."

I hadn't been serious. But I remembered Ox saying the show-business people would be rehearsing at the local theater tonight, singing and dancing their way through Jenny Tuttle's wake. Ox had told me about it. With luck, nobody would be at the Tuttle house this evening. The more I thought about it, the more I realized I had an opportunity.

Emma's expression went from disapproval to amazement. "I know what that face means. Forget it. You're not doing anything crazy."

I grabbed her glass as she lifted it to her mouth. "How many drinks have you had? Is this your first of the night? Can you drive?"

"You can't be serious."

But I was. And twenty minutes later, we were pulling out of a Philadelphia parking garage and heading north in my sister's rattle-trap pickup truck. Me with a giant pretzel I had purchased from a cart, and Emma slurping mineral water from a plastic bottle.

"This is a really bad idea," Emma was saying. "And when I'm the voice of reason, you should know exactly how bad."

"I only want to take a look into the folly behind the Tuttle house. I have a feeling that's where Jenny worked. There's bound to be something interesting there."

"At least let me do the dirty work. I'll play detective."

"Are you kidding? After what you did last spring, setting fire to a neighbor's farm? I should trust you?"

"It was for a good cause."

"It was nuts, and you're lucky the police haven't come looking for you."

"They have already," Emma replied, reaching for her cigarettes. She had second thoughts, though, and tossed down the pack. "They asked me some questions because I was on the Starr property the day before the barn burned. The insurance company is miffed about parting with their money. I'm pretty sure the only reason I'm not in jail already is because the policy owners are either dead or in the slammer. But eventually the cops are going to get serious."

Emma's rash behavior when our nephew's future was at stake hadn't been her finest hour. But now maybe she was on a path of recovery, and nothing should jeopardize that, to my way of thinking. I said, "All the more reason for me to do the snooping tonight."

"Yeah, if you get caught, you can plead temporary insanity."

CHAPTER TWELVE

t felt strangely exciting to be the irrational Blackbird sister for once. I kicked off my shoes and rolled down the window to let the warm air blow around me. I told Emma about Boom Boom Tuttle's blue skin. Emma kept a stash of apples in her truck, and I crunched through two of them during our drive and felt less famished with every mile we covered. Rush-hour traffic had thinned, and the evening sunlight was turning gold. I was feeling rejuvenated.

So I said, "What are you doing next Friday night?"

"Why?"

"I was hoping you'd have the evening free. I need a witness."

"A witness for what?"

"We need two, actually. Lexie said she'd come, and I was thinking you might be willing to stand up with us for—"

"Holy shit," Emma said, already leaps ahead of me. She turned and stared. "You're finally getting married! For real?"

"If you tell Libby, I will positively kill you."

Emma laughed delightedly. "Hey, this is good news! Does Mick know?"

"Of course he knows. We planned it. We have the license and everything. We're going to see a judge in her chambers."

"Hey, this is great. Maybe he'll be able to stop going to confession every time the two of you make sinful whoopee. Do you have rings?"

"I have one for him. With the price of gold so high, I had to be creative, so when I found Granddad's gold band in a drawer, I grabbed it. I had it sized. And it's a beautiful ring. It came from his grandfather, you know, so it has a lot of good marriage mileage on it. I hope Michael is okay with that. Do you think it's kosher to use it?"

"Recycling a ring makes economic sense, so it's right up Mick's alley. And Granddad—he might have actually liked Mick. They have the same kind of entrepreneurial brain, even if Mick's is a little warped. In a good way."

"We'd be very happy if you'd join us."

Emma cackled with pleasure, then got serious. "What about Libby? You're not inviting her? Sis, she'll be crushed."

I still felt guilty about snapping at Libby about her love life. But not guilty enough to tell her what Michael and I had planned. Not yet anyway. "I'm not inviting her until the last instant. You know what will happen if she has even five minutes' notice."

"Yeah, you'll find yourself getting married in the middle of Broad Street with a hundred Mummers playing banjos. If she doesn't have time to plan anything, you're safe."

"That's my hope. So, will you come?"

Emma stole a glance at me. "Is it okay with Mick?"

"Yes," I said. "You're my sister. I want you there. So does he. Just don't bring a banjo."

"I won't," she promised, still grinning. "But—are you sure? I mean, are you sure this is the smart thing to do?"

"Are you referring to the curse?"

"You know it as well as I do, Sis. The Blackbird curse puts Mick's life in danger."

"It's an old wives' tale," I said firmly. "It's not real."

"I hope you're right," Emma said, but her tone said she had doubts.

By the time we turned into the shared driveway between Lexie's temporary home and the Tuttle house, I had revealed our whole wedding plan. Dusk had gathered, and the long shadows thrown across the lush grass by the trees on the two properties were fast melting into darkness.

"How do you want to play this?" Emma asked, foot on the brake at the bottom of the driveway, where the single lane split into two. To the left, we could see the glow of lights at Lexie's place. To the right, the twin mansion looked dark. Out of instinct, Emma killed her headlights.

I pointed. "How about if we leave the truck behind that hedge? You stay here, and I'll walk up to the house myself."

Emma pulled her pickup alongside the ragged hedge and shut off the noisy engine. "No way I'm letting you do anything alone."

I popped open the passenger door and climbed out of the truck. "I'll be okay. Stay here."

Emma got out, too, and met me at the hedge. She planted her hand on my chest. "If things were the other way around, would you let me go alone?"

"No," I admitted.

"Okay, then. Here. I've even got a flashlight. It'll be pitch-dark soon. Let's go."

We started up the driveway and soon reached a gate I hadn't

noticed before. Tonight it was closed and locked, barring our path. Emma clambered over it easily, leaving me on the wrong side. She faced me between the rails, smiling through the gloom. "This looks like the end of the road for you, Sis. Tell me what you want me to do, and I'll be back in a jiffy."

"I won't know until I see what the options are. I have to go, too."

Determined, I stepped up on the bottom rung of the gate and teetered there, trying to figure out how to get my leg over the top bar without rolling my rotund self into the dust below. I reached for help. "Give me a hand, Em."

She deliberately misunderstood my meaning and began to clap. "Here's a round of applause for you, Humpty Dumpty."

"Come on! You won't know what to look for. Help me over."

"Nora, this is the universe's way of saying you're not supposed to go breaking into anybody's house tonight."

"If you won't help me now, I'll do it myself! I've been going to yoga class, and the instructor says I'm very supple." I stepped up on the next couple of rungs and with an involuntary grunt tried to boost myself over. When that didn't work, I attempted to heave my leg sideways, but my belly got in the way. I tried the other leg. No luck. It soon became apparent that I wasn't going to manage getting my large self over the top rail. Feeling a bit like Winnie the Pooh stuck in the honey tree, I realized I couldn't seem to get down, either. Panting, I hugged the top rail. My belly was just too big to budge. I was hanging on for dear life.

Emma smothered her laughter. "Supple doesn't help if you're the shape of an eggplant. Wait, let me get my phone out. I want to take a picture. This is prime blackmail stuff."

"I have plenty of blackmail material on you, too, remember. And I could tell Libby you want the full bridesmaid package. In a heartbeat, she'll have you looking like a porn version of Little Bo Peep. Help me, dammit!"

"Okay, okay, just don't fall. Here, put your other leg over this way."

I felt her grab my ankle and push. "Wait! I can't—"

"No, no, *this* way. Forget about being so damn prissy for once, will you? I've seen your underwear before." As I finally managed to push my right leg over the top rail, she added, "I've just never seen a pair that big until now. When did you start going in for granny panties?"

I tried giving her a kick but slipped and barely caught my balance. The next thing I knew, Emma had a grip on my shoulders, and she hauled me over the gate. With a yelp, I fell—arms and legs pinwheeling—but fortunately Emma was there to break my fall. I landed softly on top of my sister. Emma somehow landed face-first in the dirt and cursed.

"Shh!" I scrambled to my feet and brushed myself off. "Do you want to wake the whole neighborhood?"

"Me?" She got up and spat dust. "It was you who— Oh, never mind. You okay?"

I gathered my dignity. "Fine."

"Well, we're surely over the worst. Let's go."

We walked up the long driveway together—both of us in heels and dresses, Emma's face smeared with dust and me feeling meekly guilty that I had come this far. Not speaking, we listened for any clue that our less-than-clandestine arrival had been heard. I strained to hear a sound that might indicate the house was occupied. I hoped Ox Oxenfeld had been right—that the whole cast of characters had gone to the theater to rehearse for Monday night's performance.

For once, no cars were parked in the circular drive in front of the Tuttle house, and no music came from any of the windows.

Someone had turned on the hanging lantern in the portico over the front door—as if to light their way home after the rehearsal.

Reassured, I led Emma quietly across the terrace to the patio out back, where a stone retaining wall separated the improvised rehearsal space from the garden beyond.

"Where are we going?" Emma whispered.

I pointed. "See that roof behind the tall bushes? It's a folly. Let's try this way."

I found an overgrown garden path and pushed past some spindly foxgloves. We stepped over the remains of a peony hedge now slumped with rotting blooms. Emma shoved me aside and went first. Even with the flashlight, it was hard to see where to go. Underfoot, the weeds on the gravel path were worn down as if by recent foot traffic, however.

"This better not be poison ivy," Emma said over her shoulder. "All I need right now is a rash on my ass. This dress is too damn short."

"Whose fault is that?"

Together, we pressed through the jungle of the untended garden and finally emerged on the other side. We found ourselves standing on a grassy spot in front of a shabby building.

The folly had been constructed to look like a small Roman temple. It was round with a rotunda-style roof held up by a series of Doric columns that hadn't been painted in a long time. Between the columns were plinths where statues of nymphs might once have frolicked. Tonight all the plinths were empty but one. On it stood a single marble statue of a robed woman who looked straight at us with blank white eyes. The beam of Emma's flashlight played from her bare feet up her nearly naked body. She had a lyre in one hand, holding it to her shoulder. At one time the other hand might have been raised to pluck the strings, but the whole right arm was now missing.

"Creepy," Emma said.

"I think it's pretty. I'm sure Jenny appreciated it."

"So this is it? Her secret garden?"

"Let's look inside."

With her flashlight, Emma pointed out the path that circled the building. I went first and followed the way to the back. My heart leaped when I saw a door. It was a recent addition to the temple—a modern screen door with an aluminum door on the inside. Miraculously, it was unlocked.

Behind me, Emma said. "Not exactly top security."

An eerie blue glow greeted us.

In the middle of the round room stood a baby grand piano with a lava lamp sitting on top. Inside the lamp, a blue blob of goop bubbled up, creating a weird glowing circle of light. By that creepy illumination, I could see we were surrounded by file cabinets covered with silly magnets, a messy desk, and a frumpy, rump-sprung upholstered chair with an ottoman, where someone had obviously spent many hours. A collection of old bottles was lined up on the windowsill. A handwritten musical score stood on the piano's music stand. Near it, a wide-mouthed jar—a lumpy, hand-thrown bit of pottery—bristled with pencils that waited for the composer's hand to grab one and begin scribbling on the pages again.

Jenny's hand, I was willing to bet. This was her creative lair. She had come to this place to be alone and to create her own music.

Emma played her flashlight on the far wall. She cursed softly.

Across from the piano, someone had hung a collage of photographs. The collage was studded with darts that had been thrown at the person featured in all the pictures.

"Who's the broad?" Emma asked, staring at the dozens of defaced photographs.

"Boom Boom." My voice hardly made its way out of my throat as I stared at the photos. "Jenny's mother."

Emma let out a slow whistle. "Looks like Jenny wasn't too happy with mom."

Several of the photos had been balled up or torn in pieces, but someone had reassembled them and stuck them back on the wall so the collage could go on serving as a dart board. Some photos had been scrawled with curse words. On others, Boom Boom had been slashed with mustaches or devil horns. One particularly large picture of Boom Boom in her pre-blue prime—posing in tap shoes and a short dress with a top hat—had been scribbled over with two words:

DIE BITCH.

On the central photo, Boom Boom's head shot, a large, gleaming carving knife had been plunged directly into Boom Boom's face.

The rage on the wall was so powerful that it blew me down. I caught my balance on the piano and plunked onto the bench. Jenny hadn't just disliked her mother. Her hate was scrawled and spewed and stabbed onto the collage.

I found myself staring at the wall through a forest of aluminum cans—cans of energy drink that stood around the lava lamp. More empty cans lay in a small trash basket beside the piano's bench.

Emma sat down on the bench beside me. "You okay?"

I nodded, unable to speak. I may have been exasperated with our mother from time to time, but I had never felt the kind of profound rage that pulsed off the wall before us.

Emma arranged her fingers carefully on the piano keys. She struck a quiet chord. The notes rose around us—a beautiful sound in that small, enclosed space with the open rotunda over our heads.

She said. "Judging by the shooting gallery, Jenny and her mother didn't get along, huh?"

"Boom Boom bullied her, belittled her. She probably wanted to keep Jenny firmly in a subservient role so Boom Boom could go on being the star. If Jenny wanted to break out, become a person on her own, she had to come here," I guessed. "This is where she could be herself. Compose her own music."

"Okay," Emma said. "What thirteen-year-old doesn't get mad at her mom once in a while? But hanging all those pictures and throwing darts at 'em—this is bad juju."

"Yes," I said. "She wanted Boom Boom dead, didn't she?"

"Pretty obvious," Emma agreed. "Did somebody know that? And bump off Jenny first, before she finally worked up the courage to whack her own mother?"

"I don't know." I picked up one of the sheets of her music. The paper shivered as my hands began to quake. Maybe the shy, quiet piano player I thought I'd been trying to help had actually been some kind of psychopath.

To learn more, I got up from the piano bench and wobbled over to the desk. I opened the top drawers and found pencils, a pitch pipe and a shallow clutter of blank note cards. But in the last drawer there was a copy of the photo of the boy—the same as the one that had fallen from Jenny's pocket.

I pulled out the photo and held it up to the light of the lava lamp. No, it wasn't quite the same photo. I peered closer. It was a different child. Or a different year. Under that picture lay a few more. I pulled them out. Two, three, four, five, six school photographs of little boys. And two girls.

I stared at the pictures and tried to make sense of what was in my hands. All those children. What did it mean?

I wasn't paying attention as Emma got up from the piano bench and went snooping around the small, cluttered room. "There's a big blue bottle of something over here. Looks medicinal. And, hey— there's a little fridge." Emma picked her way around the ottoman.

"Whoa. Somebody dropped a plate of cake. There's icing all over the—Oh, my *God*!"

Emma backpedaled toward me, cursing a garbled streak.

I dropped the photographs in my hand. "What's wrong?"

"Holy shit, holy shit! There's a *dead* lady over there!" Emma did a dithery dance of horror beside me.

I pushed past Emma to look on the other side of the desk. On the floor in front of the small refrigerator lay a woman—Boom Boom's nurse. I recognized her uniform and her braided hairdo. She lay sprawled on the floor much as Jenny had—one hand clutching her heart. She must have fallen as she was stricken. A plate, a fork and chunks of what was surely a piece of chocolate cake lay scattered around her.

In the next second, Emma and I were standing outside the folly, holding each other and jabbering with panic.

"We've got to call the police," I said when my wits began to return.

"Screw that! I say we close the door and get the hell out of here. I don't want to get caught at a crime scene."

"Crime scene?"

"You don't think she died of natural causes, do you?"

No, I didn't think that. And the police weren't going to, either.

With hands shaking so hard I could barely manage, I found my handbag and dug out the card from the state trooper who'd helped me last winter. Ricci picked up immediately, and when I identified myself, he listened to my story without interrupting. When I finished, he said curtly that he was close by and would arrive within a few minutes.

I ended the call with trembling fingers. Suddenly I felt horrible. Light-headed and nauseated. My knees turned to water. First Jenny, and now Boom Boom's nurse. From far, far away, Emma called my name. But the gloom of the garden closed around me, and the scent of rotting flowers became overwhelming. I felt the dark vegetation rush up around my face, and I could hardly breathe.

When I came around again, I was sprawled in a patio lounge chair and a blur of people moved around me.

Emma told me to breathe. She had a bottle of water, and she pushed it into my hands. "Drink this," she ordered. "It's from my truck, so it's safe. It might be Poison Central around here."

I sipped the water. Choked on it. Tried again but couldn't swallow. My brain finally stopped spinning and I sat up unsteadily. The police had arrived, and the whirling lights from all three cars flashed around the patio, turning it into a bizarre carousel.

Over my head, Ricci spoke with Emma. Beneath his Mountie hat, I saw his hard expression, but I couldn't hear his voice. Those dancing red lights were deafening. Which didn't make sense.

Michael arrived like the cavalry charging into battle.

He shouldered Ricci aside and went down on one knee in front of me. He grabbed both of my hands. His tight grip pinched me back into full consciousness. His worried face swam into focus. The swelling around his eye where his mother had hit him looked worse than ever. He said, "You okay?"

"I think so. I fainted, that's all." I touched my belly and felt Baby Girl give a reassuring wriggle.

"What the hell is going on? Em?" He glared up at my sister. "Are you an idiot? You let Nora romp around in the dark like this?"

"We weren't romping." Emma's harsh tone matched his. "Anyway, it was all her idea. I couldn't stop her. Now I think she's in shock."

I realized I was wearing a blanket that must have come from the trunk of Ricci's cruiser. I pushed my way out of it. "I know we shouldn't have come," I said, sounding maddeningly feeble. "I couldn't get over the fence, and Emma saw my underwear but then—then we found the nurse. She's dead. Just like Jenny. Except there's cake on the floor. Is it my fault?"

Michael looked stymied. "Why would any of it be your fault?"

"I should have done something, I think. But I—I can't seem to— Wait." The first sensible thought shot up through my woolly brain. "Where's Noah?"

"He's at home," Michael said gently. "Rawlins dropped by. So when Emma called, I asked him to babysit."

I hadn't been aware of Emma calling anyone. A lot had happened, and somehow I had checked out. I put my hand on Baby Girl again, and she gave me a reality-restoring kick. She was safe.

Reassured but still dizzy, I said, "We haven't discussed appropriate babysitters. Rawlins is okay, but Michael, there's a lot we haven't talked about. Little things, maybe, but important to discuss sensibly, no yelling. Binkies, for instance. Should we let our child suck on a binky? And what about nursery schools? Even though that's a few years away, we should definitely be thinking about nursery schools."

Michael and Ricci exchanged a look and reached some kind of silent agreement.

"Noah's fine," Michael assured me, helping me to stand. "You, I'm not so sure about."

With the blessing of the police, Michael took me out onto the driveway and helped me into another monster truck—this one cherry red with NICKY'S TOWING SERVICE printed on the side.

Inside, a hundred different lights glowed like the cockpit of a jetliner. I said, "Why do we need a tow truck?"

"It's not a tow truck." Michael started the engine with a high-octane roar. "It was previously owned by a towing company, that's all. It can be fixed up any way we want it. It's really . . . safe."

I sank down into the passenger seat and realized I could not see over the dashboard. My feet barely touched the floor. I felt helpless and stupid and pregnant and sick. And ridiculous.

I burst into tears.

Michael reached across the great divide between us and put his arm across my shoulders. "This wasn't your fault, Nora. You know that, right? The lady died, and you found her, that's all. Let's go to the hospital and get you checked out."

"I don't want to go to the hospital. I'm fine."

"Let's be sure."

I cried for a while and my head got all jumbled again. Michael did his best to soothe me, but finally he gave up and let me cry it out.

Eventually I snuffled up my tears. "I don't need to go to the hospital. I'd just like an ice cream cone."

"Ice cream? Now?"

"Y-yes, please."

With respect for my hormones, Michael drove, and I used a handkerchief to wipe off my runaway mascara. I knew I was muddled up, but focusing on ice cream seemed to settle my churning emotions. Finally, we pulled into a local shop, Greta's Ice Cream Store. I had composed myself at last, and we went inside to the counter. I asked for a single scoop of butter pecan and studied the tin ceiling while a lady in a stained apron spooned my treat. She gave Michael's black eye an uneasy look as she handed over my cone.

My father had often brought us to this ice cream shop. He bought us cones, and we always asked for a pint of Mama's favorite flavor—pistachio—to take home to her. Why hadn't she ever come along with us? I couldn't remember. But thinking of her made my head flash with the pictures Jenny Tuttle had slashed and stabbed on her wall. Her feelings had been terrifyingly clear.

Maybe my mother had been an exasperating narcissist, and my sisters and I still had mixed emotions about her even now. Maybe all children did. But not all children allowed their emotions to fester and boil.

Michael pocketed his change and turned to me. "How about the hospital now?"

I took a restorative lick of ice cream and pulled myself together. "No, I'm fine. Much better, really. Let's go home."

We went outside into the warm evening, Michael twirling the truck keys on one finger and me with an ice cream cone in my hand.

In the glare of green-yellow neon light, I saw that three teenage boys had appeared since we'd pulled in. They sat on the hood of a dilapidated car with a faded peace-sign sticker half-peeled off its bumper. The boys were dressed in jeans and hooded sweatshirts, which even I could comprehend were the wrong clothes for the hot night. The stink of marijuana hung in the air. Their smirks were confident.

My heart skipped.

"Yo." The ringleader jutted his chin at Michael. "You be Mick Abruzzo, right?"

Easing me past them with a firm, propelling hand on my back, Michael gave the kid a long look and didn't answer.

"Hey," the kid called again when we had nearly reached the truck. He slid off the hood of his car and swaggered after us. "Hey, man! Whassup? You scared of talkin' to me?"

I was pretty sure the boy had been educated in the local school system, so his attempt at gang-speak was almost laughable. But his pimply buddies moseyed after him, the three of them making a wall of threatening young muscle. If alone, I'd have run back into the ice cream shop for help. Over my shoulder, I saw the counter lady rush out from behind her display to lock the front door. She turned off the lights.

Michael wasted no time boosting me up into the seat of the truck and closing the door behind me. Then he swung on the boys and moved toward them so fast that the threesome scattered like a flock of startled birds. The ringleader reeled back for a second, then tried to stop Michael by kicking at his knee, karate-style. He missed but held his ground despite Michael's looming size. Then the kid put his right hand on the belly of his sweatshirt.

The gesture was unmistakable. He had a gun.

I dropped my ice cream cone and seized my handbag. I groped inside it for my cell phone. I hit 911.

But not before Michael swung a slow, left-handed slap at the kid's head. It connected—not hard enough to hurt the boy or even throw him off-balance. It only surprised him for a second, then made him angry. For an instant I thought Michael was in terrible trouble. The boy laughed rudely, puffing up his chest like a rooster. His hand dove under his shirt, going for the gun.

But Michael's slap had been a diversion. As soon as the boy made the grab for his weapon, Michael's right fist came out of nowhere and struck the kid under his jaw. The force of the blow blew the boy up and off his feet. Then he went down, out cold before he hit the ground. The gun skittered out of his limp hand onto the cracked asphalt. With his foot, Michael nudged the weapon under the rusty car, where it disappeared. Then he spun with athletic ease to face the other two boys.

They stood frozen for a heartbeat, expressions childishly astonished, before they turned in tandem and bolted into the darkness.

It was over in a nanosecond.

Michael turned around to me, face set so dangerously that if I hadn't dropped my ice cream already, I'd have done it in that moment. I knew other people saw a frightening man when they looked at him, but I rarely did. Until now. Through the closed window, he snapped, "Call the cops."

The dispatcher picked up my call just as he spoke the words. I talked to the dispatcher and gave her our location while opening the door to go to Michael. He resisted my instinct to get out of the truck by gently pushing the door closed again. The violence had erupted out of him like an explosion—flashing one second and gone the next. His face was still, his eyes chilly. He wasn't even out of breath.

But I was shaking harder than ever.

With a spray of gravel, the local constable arrived in a cruiser. He stepped out of his vehicle, took one look at the kid on the pavement and called for an ambulance. Then he pulled a set of handcuffs from his belt and headed for Michael.

CHAPTER THIRTEEN

Michael laced his fingers behind his head in an obviously well-practiced routine. He stood still as the cop approached him. For a horrible few minutes I was sure he was going to be arrested. That was all we needed now—an arrest for assault, even if he'd been the one who was threatened first.

But after a short conversation, the constable put the cuffs away. I watched from the truck, unable to hear their exchange. They stood and talked for a while longer over the sprawled-out teenager, who didn't move a muscle. Michael tipped his head toward the old car, and the constable went over to retrieve the gun from underneath it.

A plainclothes cop arrived in an unmarked car next. The ambulance was right behind him. The EMTs were all business as they attended to the unconscious boy. I breathed easier when I saw him stir and groan as they loaded him onto a backboard and into the ambulance. Michael and the constable and the plainclothes officer watched, talking among themselves. The second cop went over to the boys' car, wrote down the license plate and scribbled in a note-book. Then he made some phone calls.

It was twenty minutes before Michael got back into the truck. By then, my ice cream was a puddle on the floor.

I indicated the mess at my feet. "I need more napkins."

Michael sent a glower at the locked door of the ice cream shop. "I think the chickenshit proprietor has closed shop for the night."

"She was scared," I said. "But it's a big mess. Maybe we should stop at a gas station to get some paper towels to—"

He was impatient, though. He started the engine. "It's not our problem. The truck's not ours."

"Michael, those boys. The one that you— The one in the am-bulance. Was he the one who shot at you before?"

"I doubt it. That one's probably still in custody. This bunch must be part of the same gang, though."

"So a whole group of kids wants to hurt you now? It's a gang?"

He pulled the truck out of the parking lot and headed north. "More of a Cub Scout troop. You saw how the other two ran off like rabbits." In the next moment, Michael sounded tired. "What I just did was really stupid, though."

"Did you have a choice?"

"I didn't think it through. I wanted rid of the gun, so I moved too fast. I should have talked him down or—or something. Now he's just going to be pissed off, and that's not good."

"What else could you have done?"

"I was working on a gag for two of my lunkhead cousins to pull in a few days—ski masks and baseball bats and a laundry basket. It's a classic, but I didn't pull the trigger fast enough, so—"

"What's the laundry basket for?" I asked before I could stop myself.

"It's not for anything. Just show. It's— Never mind. I should have sent them last night, but I didn't, and now this."

A Little Night Murder

I had accepted the idea that Michael had been asked by the local police to help clean up the adolescent crime wave, but I hadn't expected him to become a target. I found myself going cold all over. Not just from seeing a gun or how quickly Michael had disarmed the kid. But from how the violence that unnerved me didn't seem to faze Michael in the slightest. If anything, he was calmer now than he'd been before it started.

He had done what had to be done as soon as he knew about the gun, but even now I was trembling like a sapling in a storm. What was wrong with me? How could I be a good mother if I reacted like a ninny in a crisis? What if I fainted when my baby needed me?

I was hardly aware of Michael driving toward the farm. My thoughts steamed and bubbled, and I grew more and more unnerved with every mile. A rush of nausea was suddenly in my throat.

"Stop the car," I said, fearing I was going to be sick.

"What's the matter?"

"Just stop the car!"

"Okay, okay."

He pulled over, and I popped open the passenger door and landed on the sandy berm of the road. I took deep breaths and willed down my nausea. Holding the guardrail, I walked away, past the front of the vehicle. I stumbled out onto the road into the beam of the headlights.

"Nora!"

I barely heard his door slam or his footsteps behind me. Michael grabbed my arm and pulled me around into the glare of the headlights and the orange flash of his emergency lights. A steamy fog rose from under the truck like the breath of a dragon.

"What's wrong?"

"Me," I blurted out. "I can't do this."

"Can't do what?"

"Have this baby. You—you can handle it. Deep down, you can do anything. And what you don't already know, you're ready to learn. But me—I'm too afraid to do the things that have to be done."

"What things?" He looked completely baffled. "What are you talking about?"

"Protecting us. Even if it's wrong, you have the courage to do it anyway. But me—I'm thinking about consequences or—or—"

"Nora, you've had a bad day." He tried to pull me close. "Let's go get you checked out by a doctor. After that, you need to relax and have something to eat and—"

I pressed my face into his shoulder. "I don't want to be a bad mother. Emma knew her deficiencies. She knew better than any of us. Some people just can't do it. My own mother, for instance. And Boom Boom was a horrible mother. Penny, too. And Jenny Tuttle—she might have given a child away, maybe more than one, because she was afraid she'd be a bad mother, too."

"You're going a little gonzo," Michael said with impossible calm. "We're not giving our baby away."

"No," I agreed shakily. "No, but I'm scared."

We were on a stretch of road that swooped in and out of the dark trees. Branches loomed over our heads, and I was aware of scudding clouds but no moon. We could hear the distant rush of the Delaware River, but I thought the sound of my panicked heart was even louder.

Michael's hands were gentle on me, but he looked up at the sky as if hoping to find some answers there. He said, "Do you think anyone would notice if we moved to Iceland?"

"Iceland?"

He pulled me against his chest, and this time I let him do it. He said, "It looks pretty in all the pictures. We could soak in those hot springs. Maybe do some fishing. There's fishing in Iceland, right?"

My unsteady laugh turned into a hiccough.

He said, "This has been a really weird night."

I felt guilty for making a scene. I knew Michael was doing his very best for me. I hugged him then, filled with gratitude for his patience when I was clearly out of my mind.

"We'll get some brochures about Iceland." I lifted my head to look up at him. "I'm sorry. I've overdosed on estrogen, haven't I?"

"You always seemed so sane compared to Bridget." He started to smile. "But lately . . ."

"I'm sorry," I said again. I managed a smile, too. "Let's go home."

When we were back in the giant SUV, I said, "About getting a new truck?"

"Yeah?"

"I want the bulletproof one."

"You got it."

Within a few minutes we were driving through the new security gate at the farm. When the electronic arm went down behind us, Michael headed up the lane that ran around the side of the house. He parked in the gravel lot between the back porch and the barn. Lately, we'd been working on fixing the barn up after last spring's fire. The cleanup was over, but repairs were going slowly. In the shadow of the barn sat the little vintage sports car Rawlins was driving these days. And beside that was Bridget O'Halloran's convertible.

I looked at it and said, "You said something about a weird night?"

Michael was gazing at her car as if it might explode any minute. "She came around asking me to hide her from the cops."

"Is hiding her a good idea?"

"It's a really stupid idea."

"But you couldn't say no?"

"She keeps reminding me how long it took for me to be born. Every time she tells the story, it gets a few hours longer."

I got out of the truck. For a moment, I stood listening to the wind in the two-hundred-year-old oak trees. From out in the pasture, I heard the muffled whickers of Emma's ponies as they settled down for the night. The evening breeze rustled in my garden, stirring up the scent of compost. My home was peaceful. But any minute I felt it was going to go ka-blooey. We were teetering on the brink of destruction as long as Bridget O'Halloran was on the property.

Michael came around the truck and took my hand. In the dark, we couldn't see the loose fieldstones or the sagging roof of the house. The peeling paint was hidden from view, and so were the missing roof tiles. The warm glow of a kitchen light shining through the wavy window glass looked deceptively welcoming— not as if my soon-to-be mother-in-law lay in wait for us.

But it was my seventeen-year-old nephew, Rawlins, who stepped out onto the porch. From the triangle of light that spilled from the kitchen, he called, "Can I be off duty now?"

Michael and I headed in his direction. Michael said, "Do you have a date or something?"

"Or something," Rawlins said, controlling a grin. He already had his car keys in hand.

Michael pulled a couple of bills from his jeans and tucked them into the front pocket of the loose flannel shirt Rawlins wore over a thin T-shirt. "Just don't take her to the ice cream shop. It's closed tonight."

I stretched up and gave my nephew a kiss on the cheek. I noticed he had shaved recently. He'd grown at least another inch since graduation, too, and his general teenage cleanliness had gone up a notch. "Are you dating Shawna again? Is she home from Harvard this summer?"

He shrugged. "We're just hanging out. She says she's committed to some dude from Atlanta. Except he's spending the summer working at his dad's Mercedes dealership." Rawlins rolled his eyes at the idea of competing against a boy with access to as many Mercedes cars as he wanted.

Michael said, "She's here at the moment. That's in your favor."

"Yeah, it is." Rawlins sent Michael a comradely smile. "Uh, about an hour ago your mom grabbed a bottle of wine and went upstairs. She said she was tired from being on the run. Does that make any sense?"

"Too much."

"Aunt Nora, I showed her the room Aunt Emma usually uses—the one at the end of the hall with the bathroom. Is that okay?"

"Perfect," I said. "Thanks for taking care of Noah, too, Rawlins. We really appreciate your help."

"He's cute. And what's a couple more hours of babysitting? My mom's got me in indentured servitude."

I patted his arm. Rawlins had grown up a lot in the last two years. Okay, he wasn't perfect—but if not for his slip in safe-sex judgment, we wouldn't be getting our second daughter in a few weeks.

I gave my nephew another kiss. "Thank you. Tell Shawna hi from me."

"Sure thing."

He jumped down off the porch and jogged lightly to his car. I waved good-bye, feeling sentimental. Michael held the kitchen door for me. Inside, we hesitated in the kitchen, listening for Bridget. If she intended to ambush us, we were ready.

But she didn't make a grand entrance, so we breathed in relief.

I gave Michael a kiss and said I loved him.

He tucked a strand of hair behind my ear. "I'm going to go back outside to clean the ice cream out of the truck. And maybe move her convertible into the barn. Why make things easy for the cops? Plus I've got some calls to make."

Calls he didn't want me to overhear.

Upstairs, the open windows were already clearing the heat out of the house. A breeze that blew through the cooling leaves of the oak trees was welcome indeed. I peeked into the room across the hall from ours to check on Noah. In a diaper and clean T-shirt, he was sleeping soundly in one of the cribs we had readied for the coming babies. He looked angelic with his thumb in his mouth. I leaned down to kiss him. He smelled of baby shampoo and talcum powder. Rawlins had taken good care of him. I covered Noah's bare feet with a blanket, eased his thumb out of his mouth, and slipped from the room.

In the hall, I listened for Bridget again. There was no sound, though, and no light shining under her door. I concluded she was either an early-to-bed person or she was plotting something. I said a quick prayer for the first option.

I ran a bath, and while the tub filled I carefully hung up my dress on its padded hanger. After I'd climbed over a gate and landed in the dirt, my Pucci needed a trip to the dry cleaners. I dropped my so-called granny panties into the laundry hamper—with a grumble. As I pinned up my hair, I looked down into the backyard. Michael came out of the barn and began pacing around the garden in the dark, cell phone to his ear. I couldn't hear his voice. I wondered if he was talking with the police. Or with his retaliation-minded cousins.

I soaked in a tub full of tepid water, breathing the refreshing scent of lemon and restorative herbs from a jar of bath salts Libby had given me. Trying to relax, I leafed through the pages of a novel, but the story couldn't sidetrack my thoughts. When I heard Michael come inside downstairs, I tossed the book onto the floor and started thinking about Jenny Tuttle and the dead nurse until my brain began to whirl all over again. Cake on the floor. Energy drinks stacked up. The blue bottles of something left behind. The hatred on the wall of photos Jenny had created.

My thoughts must have spun for a long time, because I finally realized the bathwater had grown cold. I put a wet washcloth to my face and tried to force down the tears that had risen in my throat. Could I have prevented the nurse's death somehow? Had she been killed by the same someone who killed Jenny?

And even more puzzling: all those photos of children in Jenny's drawer. What the heck was that all about?

I heard Michael on the stairs and hastily composed myself. He didn't need to see me breaking down again. I pulled the plug and let the water run out of the tub while reaching for a bath sheet. I was shy about showing my enormous naked body these days, so I was out of the tub and wrapped in the towel by the time Michael poked his head into the bathroom.

"I brought you some dinner," he said. "You want it in bed?"

"Thank you. That sounds wonderful."

I brushed out my hair and slipped into one of Libby's maternity nightgowns. It was yellow and low cut, short and frilly, with lace around the thighs and satin ribbons at the shoulders—her style, not mine, but I couldn't afford to be choosy. At least it didn't have some ridiculous words plastered on the front. Wearing it reminded me that I owed her an apology. I vowed I'd call her first thing in the morning.

I slid into the bed, feeling almost myself. Michael had a tray on my lap in no time. A quick stir-fry of shrimp with sugar snap peas, plus a slice of whole wheat toast with butter. A glass of milk, too.

While I dug in, he went into the bathroom and I heard him brushing his teeth. When he came back, his shirt was unbuttoned and my meal was nearly demolished. He went around the room and turned off all the lights except the lamp on the bedside table.

Earlier in the day, I had sorted through some of the toys Libby had sent over, and the bed was still covered with little stuffed animals. Michael gathered them all up and dumped them back into their cardboard box. He missed one little duck, and when he picked it up, it gave a surprised quack. With the toy in hand, he climbed onto the bed with me.

"Did you make some dinner for yourself?" I asked when I belatedly realized he didn't have a plate.

Michael kept his voice down so as not to disturb our houseguests. "Rawlins and I had hoagies before Bridget showed up." He made a hammer of his fist and tapped his chest. "I've got heartburn."

"Maybe not from just the food." I asked, "Is your mother moving in with us?"

"No way. Look, I figured it was easier to let her stay here for a night than convince her to give herself up and talk to the cops. I'll try talking to her again in the morning."

"Are they still looking for her?"

"Yep. From what I hear, she's number one on their hit parade."

We should have been talking about the incident at the ice cream shop, but neither one of us wanted to do that now—not in our bed, where we had some time ago established a no-stress zone. In the half-light, Michael appeared worn out. The swelling around his eye looked sore. He had been taking good care of me lately, and I wasn't keeping up my end.

He said, "Bridget says the cops are putting a real kink in her show-business plans."

I said gently, "Michael, I don't think she's going to get into a Broadway show."

"Why not? She doesn't have what it takes?"

"I don't know about her singing and dancing, but Ox Oxenfeld says they need somebody with star power—the kind that sells tickets, that is."

He cocked an eyebrow at me. "Are you going to be the one to tell her that?"

"I see your point." I set aside the crust of my toast. I had learned so much during the day, and all the facts were starting to get jumbled. I sighed. "I should call Gus before I fall asleep. He'll be furious if he learns I was at another crime scene and didn't tell him all about it."

Michael dug into his pocket and handed over one of his disposable cell phones. Then he relaxed back into the pillows, tossing the duck into the air and catching it.

"I'm sorry," I said.

"Hey, it's your job."

I dialed the *Intelligencer*'s switchboard. It would be easier to be cross-examined by whoever was on the night desk.

I was relieved when Marty Maron picked up. He was easygoing most of the time, and he took my information calmly, saying, "Yeah, we heard some of this on the scanner. Thanks for the rest, Nora."

I hung up. Although I had a nagging feeling I had forgotten something, I decided I had done my duty. I gave Michael his phone back and picked up the glass of milk.

Michael watched me sip it, turning the duck over in one hand. For once he didn't make cracks about Gus. Instead, he said, "Maybe we ought to talk about your job."

"What about it?"

"You know. About after you have the baby and the other one gets here. Maybe you should take a break."

"I've got several weeks of maternity leave."

Choosing his words carefully, Michael said, "Nora, I don't like seeing you so upset like tonight. Maybe staying home for a while would be good for you. For everybody."

I swallowed the last of the milk and looked at him more carefully. He was making an effort to be steady, but his hands looked as if they were strangling the little duck's neck.

He said, "I'm just floating the idea out there."

"You want me to quit my job to stay home and raise our family?"

"It's not about what I want. But it's not a totally crazy suggestion, is it? I've got Gas N Grub up and running again. If we keep watching our expenses around here a little longer, we'll be okay with one income."

"So I should give up my career? Which I know isn't much of a career exactly, but it—well, it has become surprisingly important to me. I didn't expect that, but I—I feel good about what I'm doing. I can contribute to the city, in my own way."

"Which is great. I want you to be happy. But . . ."

I put my napkin back on the tray. "But?"

Michael lobbed the duck across the room and it landed accurately in the old armchair by the window. He avoided my gaze. It took him a long time to work up the right words, but finally he said, "I'm on a learning curve here. This is all new to me. Hell, I can break up a prison-yard brawl, if I have to, but living in a real home with you—with a washing machine and a refrigerator with actual food in it and flowers on the table—I'm trying to get my head around how to do it all right."

"You're the one who puts food in the fridge," I said.

"Thing is," he said just as carefully as before, "why are we having kids if we have to hire people to look after them? Is it supposed to be that way?"

There it was, out between us. His dream for a real family meant all the traditional things—including a stay-at-home wife. Maybe it was what I had imagined all along, too, after my upbringing in the rarified world of inherited money. But now . . . now my ideas were different. And not.

I set the tray on the nightstand. "We haven't talked about child care. Not really. We've joked around it a little. But nannies and babysitters and day care—if we don't go that route, one of us has to make some big sacrifices."

"I don't want you sacrificing anything," he said at once. "If one of us has to give up something, it should be me."

"Why?"

"Because," he said stubbornly.

My heart warmed again. He wanted to hang on to what we'd already created together, no matter what the cost. "If we're going to fight about this," I said, "you're going to need a better argument."

"I don't want to fight. But can you manage three kids on your own? I know you're good with Libby's kids, but . . . I don't think I can. Three little ones is a lot to handle."

"We won't have three children," I said gently. "Noah isn't ours, Michael. He's going back to his parents soon. And this time maybe he'll stay there."

Michael stretched out on his back on the bed. He put his hands behind his head and looked at the ceiling, saying nothing.

"We can't take Noah from Hart," I said with more emphasis.

He didn't respond.

I sighed and touched my forehead, wishing I could massage some easy solution into my brain. "I suppose I should quit my job. It would only be for a few years. After that, I can start over again. Maybe. If the newspaper still exists." I could hear the doubt in my own voice. Was I ready to make the sacrifice of my own budding career? Another issue was that I still had my parents' enormous tax debt to pay off. Could I let Michael shoulder that financial responsibility for me? Was it fair for my problem to become a burden for him, too?

"It could be a lot of years," Michael said before I could formulate that discussion. "I'm thinking we're going to have plenty more kids."

I smiled and laid my hand on his chest to feel his heartbeat. "Me, too. And we'll make it all work. Somehow."

He sent me a grin. "I'm not kidding. Four, six, eight. More? I'm thinking we could have a football team if we put our minds to it."

I figured I might as well say good-bye to my slim self forever, but I indulged him and asked, "What if they're all girls?"

"A softball team, then."

We smiled at each other, and then Michael rolled over and gathered me into his arms. One hand slid down to my belly, and he fondled Baby Girl. She was sleeping, though, and didn't kick. As for me, it felt good to be in his arms again.

His touch changed, and he tugged at the frilly hem of my borrowed nightie. In my ear, he said, "This thing is pretty sexy."

"I don't feel very sexy these days," I replied, snuggling back into the curve of his lean body. "Mostly, I feel like the winning pumpkin in one of those state fair competitions—you know, the big, lumpy gourd that can only be moved by a forklift. Emma called me Humpty Dumpty tonight. And it's been weeks since we . . . well."

"Emma has a lot of guts to make wisecracks. At the end, she was the size of a hippo, but she looked fine a couple of months later. You're not a pumpkin. And . . . I didn't think you were interested." He kissed my neck with slow attention. "I don't want to hurt you. Either one of you."

I smiled. "I don't think that's possible. Wait—what are you doing?"

With his other hand, he untied the ribbon at my shoulder, and

Libby's nightie began to fall apart around me like a magic trick. He murmured, "You're really not in the mood?"

I tried to catch the last remnants of frilly lace before I was completely exposed. "Your mother is right down the hall."

"We'll be quiet."

"Michael—"

"We haven't been communicating lately. You've been worrying about Lexie." He eased me over onto my back, his touch trailing appreciatively down to my breasts. "And I've been thinking too much about— Wow, these are different. I've been missing out."

When his warm mouth found my breast, I gave in and wound one arm around his shoulders. I slid my other hand to cup the back of his head. If he didn't mind my size, I didn't either anymore. We hadn't reached any conclusions about our coming family, but I didn't feel like hashing out the conundrum now. Sometimes it felt better to communicate without words. I closed my eyes and sighed.

An hour later when we were both dozing off, Michael's cell phone chirped on his side of the bed. He rolled over and grabbed it before the sound woke anyone else. He swung out of bed and took the phone into the bathroom. I heard him muttering to someone as he opened a bottle of Tums and shook out some tablets.

He came back to bed a minute later, shutting off the phone.

"Who was calling?" I asked. "The police?"

"No." He opened his palm and offered me an antacid as he slid back into bed. "Little Frankie."

"Your brother?" I couldn't keep the startled tone out of my voice and came fully awake. "That's all we need now."

"Go back to sleep." Michael tucked me against him again. "Maybe everything else is falling apart, but I've got Little Frankie under control."

I crunched the tablet and went back to sleep eventually, but I was aware that Michael lay awake for a long time. He was restless, and I knew he was thinking. About his bad brother? About our family? The crime wave in Bucks County?

Or about his mother?

CHAPTER FOURTEEN

Noah woke me in the morning with a boisterous yell. Michael was already doing his best Elvis impression in the shower, so I hurriedly slipped into my vintage Parisian bathrobe and went across the hall to attend to the baby. He was standing up in the crib, gripping the rail. When he saw me, his face split into a wide grin and he reached both hands for me.

I scooped him up and changed his sopping diaper while talking a lot of nonsense. He was happy to listen and kicked his chubby feet to make me laugh. I carried him downstairs and held him on my hip while warming a sippy cup of milk. When I put him in the borrowed high chair to drink it, I noticed a note had been slipped under the back door. It was written in Emma's scrawling hand.

"She must have come to feed her ponies before dawn," I said to Noah.

Spent half the night talking with the cops. None of them were cute. You okay? Call me.

I called Emma's cell phone while mixing Noah's cereal. I got her voice mail.

"I'm fine," I told her. "Thanks for looking after me last night. Next time you come over, you should stick around for breakfast."

When Michael came downstairs, dressed in his go-to-Mass shirt, he gave Baby Girl a good-morning caress, then pulled me into his arms, dipped me low and kissed me while I laughed. Noah watched us as if mesmerized.

"Any sign of my mother?" Michael asked, setting me on my feet.

"Would things be this quiet if she was awake?"

"Good point."

The three of us ate breakfast together in the cool kitchen. Then we took the baby outside to pick strawberries in the early-morning sunshine—me in my bathrobe, probably looking like a pregnant royal consort. From the crook of Michael's arm, Noah pointed out the rabbits that were busily decimating the sugar snap peas. I picked a bowl full of berries while the hem of my robe sucked up the dew from the grass.

Michael gave Noah a green pepper, and the baby threw it. Michael picked it up, and Noah threw it again.

"We've got a left-handed pitcher here," Michael called to me.

I watched them play their game. To my eye, Noah had a pretty good arm.

From his new enclosure on the other side of the peony border, Ralphie made longing noises. Our pet pig had grown to at least five hundred pounds, and he had broken out of every pen we'd built to keep him from rampaging all over the farm. His rooting had made a terrible mess of the lawn, so we had called a professional to build a sturdy corral out of steel and heavy-gauge wire mesh. We kept him penned up except when Michael took him for daily strolls in the pony pasture.

"I think this pen might hold him," Michael said, keeping an eye on Ralphie while the pig inquisitively nosed every bolt and bar for signs of weakness. He wanted his chance to chase the green pepper Noah was throwing.

"If it doesn't, we'll have to seriously consider sending him somewhere else."

Michael gave me a shocked stare. "Get rid of Ralphie?"

"He's not exactly a safe pet for children. And he's really starting to smell. Maybe he'd be happier at a zoo."

Michael frowned. "Maybe some barbecue restaurant needs a mascot. He'd make a good mascot, don't you think?"

Ralphie gave a long, loud pig snort as if to veto the idea. He was happy here with us.

I heard the phone ring inside the house and carried the bowl of strawberries into the kitchen to answer it. Out the window, I could see Michael and Noah throwing the green pepper over and over.

In my ear, Gus Hardwicke began to curse a blue streak.

I gathered he was furious that I hadn't phoned him personally with my information about discovering the nurse's body. In no mood to be verbally abused, I hung up. Upstairs, I heard the shower running. Bridget was awake.

Half a minute later, the phone rang again. But when I answered, it was not Gus, but Lexie's voice on the line.

"Sweetie," she said, sounding tense, "something's brewing at the Tuttle house. The police have been crawling all over the place like ants at a picnic! And there's yellow crime scene tape everywhere."

I told her about my misadventure with Emma and our discovery of Boom Boom's dead nurse.

"Dear, sweet heaven!" Lexie cried when I had described the events of my brief detecting excursion. "The nurse is dead? How did she die?"

"It looked like a heart attack," I said. "But of course the police think she was murdered."

Lexie gasped. "Do you think she suffered?"

"I'm pretty sure it was quick," I said.

At once, Lexie turned sympathetic. "What a shock for you. Sweetie, I'm so sorry you had to see that."

"To tell the truth, seeing the dead body wasn't the worst. You wouldn't believe the wall of pictures Jenny had put up in her music room." I told Lexie about the collage of defaced photographs of Boom Boom.

"What do you think it means?" Lexie asked.

"I think Boom Boom is lucky Jenny died first."

Shocked all over again, Lexie said, "You think Jenny wanted to kill her mother? Calling Dr. Freud!"

"It was very clear she hated Boom Boom."

"I've been known to make a wisecrack or two about my mother, but I never really— Oh Lord, there's someone ringing my doorbell. And yes, it's probably a police officer. I can see him through the window. No doubt he wants to know if I saw a villain fleeing across my lawn last night. I've got to go. Listen, have your groom call me later, will you, please? I need more information from him."

"Lexie, wait!" I had a sudden vision of Hostetler, Gus's snoopy reporter, finding his way to Lexie's front porch.

But she had hung up already. I redialed the number, but she didn't answer. While her phone rang, the bell on our security gate went off. I went to the window and peeked out. I didn't recognize the car idling at our gate, so I went to the console and pressed the intercom button. "Yes?"

"Miss Blackbird? It's me. Poppy."

Poppy Fontanna? Here?

When I didn't respond, she said, "Poppy Fontanna. From *Bluebird of Happiness*? Boom Boom sent me."

"Oh," I said. "Well, uh, come in."

I pushed the gate button, and it opened to allow a nondescript compact car to pass through. Behind it pulled a state police cruiser. The first car wavered to a stop on the lane, and a spritely figure popped out. She practically danced like a woodland nymph across the lawn to the front porch, swinging a tote bag as if it were a leprechaun's pot of gold. Warily, I opened the door to her. The police cruiser proceeded to the back of the house. I figured I'd let Michael cope with that problem.

Bouncing up the steps, Poppy smiled brightly and waved at me with all the enthusiasm of a newfound best friend.

"Nora! That's your name, right? I thought I'd stop by this morning and give you this banana bread! Fred baked it. He bakes all the time. It's a stress reliever. I got this one out of the freezer." She pushed past me into the house, handing over what felt like a brick wrapped in aluminum foil. "I heard you had a terrible shock last night while we were at rehearsal."

"Uh—"

"We wanted to make sure you're okay. You're okay, right? You look okay. Wow, what a lovely robe. You look like Christine in *Phantom*. That is, if she had a bun in the oven. Or a dozen buns. You're *really* pregnant, aren't you? Do I smell coffee?"

"Yes, but—"

"This is some house." She spun around, looking up. "It's like the set of *Jekyll and Hyde*. Very atmospheric. Unless that chandelier is going to fall down on us; then it's totally *Phantom*. Ha-ha! Kidding. How about some coffee? We could be just a couple of normal girlfriends having a chat."

Poppy seemed to have forgotten that the last time I'd seen her, she'd threatened to call the police to get rid of Lexie and me. This morning she was as cheery as . . . as an actress hoping to win some free publicity.

"Poppy, if you've come looking to score a mention in my newspaper column—"

"You have a column?" Her eyebrows disappeared up into her wig, and she popped her eyes wide enough to be seen from the cheap seats. "How fascinating! Oh, look, a piano! Do you play? I brought some music, if you'd like to hear me sing. I could use a good accompanist. Would you like to see me dance, too? I brought my shoes. I bet you could take some great pictures for your newspaper!"

The next thing I knew, I was pouring coffee and Poppy Fontanna was pulling on her tap shoes and thundering around my kitchen table like a madcap chorus girl. I peeked out the window in time to see Ricci climb out of his police cruiser and walk over to Michael in the garden, where Noah was still throwing things.

With a shine of perspiration starting on her face, Poppy stopped dancing long enough to open her large tote bag and pull out sheets of paper. "I can give you my whole résumé—here. See? All the Tuttle shows I've ever done, plus some regional theater and a couple of off-off-Broadway things, but you can skip those. They were stinkers. Not my fault, though. And here's my head shot. What do you think?"

"Very nice." I looked at her photo. She looked like a Muppet.

While she continued to sell herself to me, I opened Poppy's offering of banana bread and discovered a frozen lump that didn't look very appetizing. If Fred was baking to relieve tension, he was still very tense.

"I started out in a road show of *Annie*." Poppy continued reciting her accomplishments. "I played one of the orphan girls, and it was a magical beginning to my show-business career. Next I was in *Peter Pan* and then— Should you be taking notes?" she asked with a frown.

"How about I ask you about the new show?"

She perked up again. "Sure! What would you like to know?"

I pushed a cup of coffee into her hands. "Tell me about Boom Boom."

Her face fell. "Oh, she's had enough publicity to last a lifetime. Me, though—"

"First, tell me when she turned blue."

"You noticed that, huh?"

"It's hard to miss. What happened?"

"A while back, Jenny got excited about food supplements instead of eating actual, you know, food. She gave some to her mother."

"Why did Boom Boom turn blue, but Jenny didn't?"

"What do I look like? Dr. Oz?"

I assumed Jenny had deliberately used the supplements to sabotage her mother's career. "Tell me about Boom Boom's relationship with Jenny."

Suddenly cautious, Poppy sank into one of the kitchen chairs. She mustered an angelic smile. "They loved each other, of course."

I sat opposite her. "We both know that's not true. Jenny's gone, and there's a good chance Boom Boom won't ever set foot onstage again—making way for you to star in the next Toodles Tuttle musical. You have no reason to hold back information. So how about telling me the truth? What was really going on between those two?"

Poppy's smile broadened at my mention of her stepping into the lead role, but she tried to gain time to think by sipping coffee. I could see her debating a way to improvise the scene. At last, she gave up and said, "They hated each other. To the rest of us, it was pretty clear it was only a matter of time before one of them murdered the other."

"You think Boom Boom killed her daughter?"

Poppy shook her curls. "That's not what I mean. For years,

Jenny and Boom Boom argued about dieting. Boom Boom always yelled at Jenny for being fat. Started her on pills, sent her to the doctors who helped her get skinny. That's how Boom Boom stayed thin, too—pills. Plus they were both on heart and blood pressure medications—different prescriptions. And the supplements! The two of them popped pills like crazy. Sooner or later one of them was going to screw up and die." When she saw my puzzlement, she added, "That's why Higgie came to live at the house. After Boom Boom turned blue, it was obvious she needed help. Higgie's job was keeping all their pills straight."

"Boom Boom and Jenny got their pills mixed up?"

"Often," Poppy said.

"But the nurse ended up being the one who died."

"I know! Crazy, right?"

"Was Miss Higginbotham taking pills, too?"

"How should I know? Higgie needed to drop some weight. Maybe she figured she could help herself to Jenny's diet pills now that Jenny was gone. But she died instead."

"By accident?"

"Sure! Happens all the time. That's why I don't take any unnatural substances. My body is a temple." She regained her butter-won't-melt smile. "No sugar, no meat, no drugs. I do like a double martini once in a while, though. And if anybody tries to talk me out of it, I can show 'em a thing or two." She held up a fist.

I decided not to argue with her. "Okay, tell me about the boy in the photograph."

"The boy in the newspaper?" Her face closed like a trap door. "I'm not—I don't know anything about that."

"You've known Jenny for a long time, though, right? Your whole career? Did you know her when she was pregnant?"

"Pregnant? Jenny? Are you kidding me?" Poppy laughed unattractively. "That's not possible."

"Not possible?"

"Jenny never had a boyfriend. Not ever. With all the rest of us girls around, why would anybody look twice at her?" Unfazed by her own nastiness, Poppy added, "It's not like she was pretty or even very nice. She was a total grump most of the time—and completely obsessed with the shows. She worked, that's it. No boyfriends, no kids."

"I thought—well, it seemed to me that at least Fred was fond of Jenny."

Poppy's eyes turned to ice. "If he was, I'd have kicked his ass all the way to Chicago. Fred was *my* partner. He's still mine, and nobody else's. Maybe they were friends, just a tiny bit, but nothing else."

"Okay, my mistake," I said, backpedaling hastily. "But why do you think Jenny was carrying around a photograph of a little boy?"

"All I know is it wasn't her kid. We're a company, a theater company. Do you know how close a company works together? And we've been together for years. Oh, we had a revolving door of actors and musicians that rotated in and out, depending on the show, but the core group—that is, Fred and me and Boom Boom and Jenny and Toodles—we were really tight. There was this one time I went on the road to do the revival of *The Sound of Music*—believe it or not, I was a really good nun—but while I was gone, everybody else was working on a Toodles show, and they would have noticed something as obvious as Jenny being pregnant. Here, I've got pictures of me in my nun suit. Want to see?"

I thought of all the photographs of children in the desk in Jenny's private studio. "Poppy, are you absolutely sure Jenny never had a child? Or more?"

"Sure I'm sure. I mean, Toodles was an old hound dog, and Boom Boom wasn't an angel in her day, but Jenny? No fooling around for her. And look at you. It's really hard to hide being pregnant. Trust me, we would have known."

Poppy opened her portfolio and spread out a series of photo-graphs on the table. "Now, see? Here I am playing Miss Betty Brown in *The Flatfoot and the Floozy*. It got lousy reviews, but I think that's because Toodles wasn't nice to the press. See this one? I had to use a trapeze in that show."

I stared at the pictures without seeing anything. If Jenny wasn't David Kaminsky's mother, what was their relationship?

And who were all the other children in the photographs Jenny kept?

"Well?" Poppy finally asked. "How about it?"

I blinked. "How about what?"

"Featuring me in the newspaper, of course."

"That's not really up to me. My editor makes all the decisions."

Steamed, Poppy began stacking up her pictures again. "Well, you could have told me *that* ten minutes ago! It would have saved us both a lot of time!"

"Poppy—"

"And why all these questions? The police are bad enough, but why should I have to put up with you grilling me, too?"

"I wasn't—"

"What?" she demanded. "Do you think *I* killed Jenny? I'll have you know, when I was in *Little Shop of Horrors* in high school, the cast nominated me for Miss Congeniality! In a cast that small, that's a real accomplishment. Besides, none of this matters." She shoved the photos into her bag. "The cops told us there's a murderer living right next door."

"A—?"

"Yeah, in the house beside Boom Boom's. Some rich lady got out of prison, and she moved into the neighborhood. So of course she killed Jenny. It's going to be all over the front page tomorrow."

My heart gave a horrible thunk. I grabbed my cell phone. "Gus,"

I muttered as I savagely punched in Lexie's number, "you better not do what I think you're doing."

Poppy finished stuffing all of her items back into her bag. "This whole trip has clearly been a waste of my valuable time." She grabbed the slab of frozen banana bread off my counter and swept out of the kitchen. Over her shoulder, she said, "I can see I misjudged your reporting skills, Miss Blackbird. It's obvious you don't really want to write about good theater. If you change your mind, you know where to find me."

Poppy went out through the living room, and the front door banged shut so hard the chandelier over my head swayed.

Samir answered Lexie's phone.

"Samir," I said, almost hyperventilating. "Did Lexie let a man into the house? Is he a reporter? You have to stop her before she says anything."

"The police are here now," her houseman said, voice low. "A reporter came first, then the police."

"Samir, you have to find a way to get rid of the reporter—"

"They're questioning Miss Lexie about a murder," Samir interrupted. "I think I should call her lawyer."

"Yes, yes," I said, trying to keep my wits. "She shouldn't say anything without her lawyer. She had nothing to do with Jenny Tuttle's death, but they're going to make things awful for her." The police interview would be unpleasant, but the havoc Gus could wreak with headlines made me shudder.

"I've got to go," Samir said.

I dialed Gus next. "Don't you dare," I said while his phone rang in my ear. "Don't smear my friend, you bastard, or I'll strangle you with my bare hands."

"Tut-tut," said a voice behind me.

I spun around to see Bridget standing in my kitchen, dressed to kill and wearing enough makeup to audition for a drag revue. I hung up before my call to Gus went through. I could cope with only one egomaniac at a time. I said, "I'm not really in the mood, Bridget."

"Me neither," she said, dropping her handbag on my kitchen table. "Man, this place of yours is a dump. There's no air-conditioning! I once had a boyfriend who spent half his time in the sauna. A Swedish guy, used to own a big international furniture company. He'd be right at home, sweating here."

"A police officer is waiting outside," I said. "Probably looking for you."

"I saw him from upstairs." She stalked over to the window and peered out. "Where's my car?"

"Michael hid it in the barn."

"Smart guy, my boy, isn't he?"

"I'm not so sure aiding and abetting anyone is a good idea for him right now. He's still on probation, you know."

She laughed. "He's protecting his mommy. Can I get to the barn without being seen?"

"If you don't mind crawling through the pig pen. But even if you can reach your car, you can't drive out any other way except past the police."

"Then I have time for breakfast." She turned around and grinned at me. "I once had a boyfriend who was a famous French chef. The breakfasts he made could give a girl an orgasm."

Hardly in the mood to provide her with a food-induced sexual experience, I simply pointed at the coffee maker. She found a cup on the shelf and poured for herself. Sipping it, she went back to watching out the window. "What did the Poppet have to say?"

"You mean Poppy? We talked about Jenny Tuttle giving up a baby, as a matter of fact. But you'd know all about that, wouldn't you?"

"Judgmental, much?" she asked. "You sure have a lot of opinions for a girl with a leaky roof."

"I have a hard time imagining how you could have given up your son, that's all. Especially to the Abruzzo family."

"He turned out pretty good with them."

"You call nine years in prison 'pretty good,' but I call it a waste of his—"

"Oh, come off it. Maybe those nine years helped him calm down, grow up, figure out how to be a man."

"You couldn't have helped him do that?"

She laughed again, a harsh sound. Strolling around the kitchen, she made note of various items—the antique silver serving dish on display on a shelf, Michael's wine rack on the counter, the set of German kitchen knives that had come to me as a wedding present from a wealthy cousin. She picked up an etched glass jam jar with its matching delicate silver spoon inside, but set it down with a snort.

"Babycakes, maybe I didn't raise him, but you can thank me for teaching Mick a few things. Opening doors, *please* and *thank you*? I bet he still carries a clean handkerchief, right? I picked up stuff like that from my boyfriends and taught him all of it. I sent him books in jail, too. Lots of books. He finally had time to read, so I spent a fortune on books. So he's smart. And he knows how to treat a lady like a lady, am I right?"

"But—"

"Otherwise, Mick is the self-taught type. Most kids are. Your kids turn out to be who they are even if you're not a paragon of motherhood." Bridget's gaze had a cold glitter. "And you, a morally superior know-it-all girl with money and family and friends— you'd better walk a few miles in my Payless platforms before you shoot your mouth off."

"You could have kept him," I said quietly.

"You think he'd have turned out better if I raised him? Think again."

There was a bitter tone to her voice that surprised me. Until that moment, I had pegged her for a supremely confident woman who took no prisoners. Now, though, she suddenly looked her years. And as if she had a few regrets despite her tough talk.

I said, "He could use your help now. The police think you had something to do with Jenny Tuttle's death."

"I didn't," she snapped.

"I believe you," I replied just as curtly. "But the police are pressuring Michael."

"You want me to take the pressure off? By turning myself in?"

"By providing some information," I corrected. "Maybe you know something. Something that might implicate someone else."

"Someone like who?"

"Well . . . Ox Oxenfeld, for one."

She frowned. "What does he have to do with Jenny?"

"Maybe he didn't have anything to do with Jenny, but he certainly knows about financing the show. There's something strange going on with the money."

Half to herself, she said, "Big Frankie always said to follow the money."

"Yes, well, Boom Boom says she has a big investor—someone whose name she won't mention. Maybe you can find out from Ox who that person is."

"What would that accomplish?"

I held back an impatient sigh. "It would get the police thinking about someone other than you. They'd start widening their investigation."

She walked away from me. I held my tongue, letting her think. Back at the window, she said, "Cop's leaving." She turned around long enough to set down her coffee cup and grab her handbag. "I'm outta here. Thanks for the bed."

"Bridget—"

"No need to apologize for this dump," she cut me off. "I've stayed in worse places. I once had a boyfriend who lived in a tent on the beach. He was a great kisser. After a while, though, sand in your privates cancels out kissing. I'll let you know if I learn anything from Ox. It's time I checked back with him, anyway. He's probably ready to ditch your nutty sister for a real woman."

Libby and Bridget going head-to-head over a man was like the heavyweight championship fight. Somebody could sell tickets and make a fortune.

CHAPTER FIFTEEN

ran upstairs and pulled on my jeans—zipping them only as high as I could manage—and another of Libby's T-shirts, this one bright green with black polka dots. On the front it read I DELIVER. I caught a glimpse of myself in the mirror and moaned. I looked dangerously like a watermelon. While I struggled with my shoes, I tried calling Gus again. No answer.

I arrived downstairs just as Michael came in the back door with Noah, who had a big smooch of Bridget's red lipstick on his cheek. Michael was unable to stop himself from laughing at my shirt.

"It's awful," I agreed, taking the baby from his arms. "But tonight I'll wear Givenchy. Did Bridget get away without being arrested?"

"She waited until Ricci was out of sight; then she practically took the corner on two wheels." Michael poured himself another half cup of coffee. "I couldn't stop her."

"Me neither." I sat a squirming Noah down on the edge of the sink and clamped him tight while using a kitchen towel to swipe the lipstick from his cheek. "Did Ricci tell you about Lexie?"

"Yeah. She's being questioned, that's all." He tried to distract Noah from his impromptu bath by waggling his pink bunny in front of the squirming child. To me, Michael said, "Don't get worried about Lexie. She's got Cannoli on her side. And we both know she had nothing to do with the Tuttle murder. The cops will see that, too."

Noah gave a squawk, and I eased up on cleaning him. I slung him onto my hip. "What else did Ricci have to say?"

Michael gave Noah a big good-bye kiss on his forehead. "The tox screen came back on Jenny Tuttle. She died of an overdose of the drug her mother was taking to speed up her heart, combined with the energy drink and the diet pills. Today they're going to autopsy the Higginbotham lady to see if the same cocktail killed her, too. But here's the interesting part. They're going to test the cake that was on the floor. One of the scene investigators noticed bits of something colorful in the cake. Like, maybe the stuff capsules are made out of."

"Somebody mashed up pills and put them into the cake Higginbotham ate?"

"Something like that."

Fred, I thought. He was known to be a baker. Poppy had said he made the banana bread.

To Michael, I said, "Anything else?"

"Yeah." Michael gave me a good-bye kiss, too. "Ricci says the kid I socked last night is doing fine. Has a broken jaw and lost a couple of teeth, but he's sitting up and bitching about the liquid diet."

A broken jaw sounded horrible. And broken teeth? He had once been somebody's precious son, and now he had broken teeth?

Michael watched me absorb his news. He ruffled my hair. "Don't waste your feelings on a punk like that one. He'll serve some time on the weapons charge but be out sooner than anybody wants. Then I'll have to deal with him all over again." He reached for his keys.

"You missed Mass," I said, noting the time.

"Yeah. There's always tomorrow. Sorry, I have to run. A software guy's coming to show me some stuff for Gas N Grub. I'll be back midafternoon to take you downtown. You okay with the kid?"

"Of course."

He was in a rush, but he paused. "How about if you just relax with Noah? Not drive yourself nuts about all this murder stuff?"

"Sounds good to me."

He kissed me good-bye more thoroughly then. Afterward, Noah reached up to touch my mouth.

I said, "Do you think he's never seen his parents kiss?"

With a grunt of disgust for the Jones family dynamic, Michael withheld further comment and was gone.

Noah and I snuggled in the Adirondack chair, and both of us promptly fell asleep in the warm sun—me snoring while he dozed on my chest. I woke up when the phone rang again. I carried Noah inside to answer it and just missed the call. On the caller ID, I noted the number of the *Intelligencer*'s video manager, so I called him back.

Tremaine Jefferson and I brainstormed about what video to put into the paper's Sunday online edition. He thanked me for my input, and I asked if Gus was around. Tremaine didn't know, so we hung up. I typed up a quick social piece for Tremaine, then responded to some invitations. I was starting to get notices of events that would happen when I'd be on maternity leave, but I didn't feel I could decline some of them—especially the big gala fund-raiser for the children's hospital, which was not to be missed. I'd have to keep my hand in a little.

After a few more e-mails, I didn't need to check my watch to know it was long past lunchtime. Baby Girl was kicking me, famished.

I made a large sandwich for myself and a healthier lunch for Noah. We finished with strawberries, and Noah ended up with pink cheeks and chortling over his messy hands.

I puttered for a while, doing laundry and tidying up the kitchen. I tried calling Libby again, but she didn't pick up. Despite Michael's admonition to put murder out of my mind, I was soon thinking about Jenny Tuttle again. About who would have wanted her dead. The possibilities didn't make me happy.

Fred Fusby, the music director. He was the only person who seemed to prefer Jenny alive, but . . . I wondered if he had anything to do with the photos of children Jenny kept close by. But he was a baker and maybe he had something to do with Higgie's death.

Poppy Fontanna wanted to play the starring role, but Jenny had objected. Would hot-tempered Poppy have murdered Jenny to get a part?

Boom Boom Tuttle would have preferred the guaranteed success of a Toodles Tuttle show, not one created by a Broadway newcomer like Jenny. Might she have killed her own daughter to maintain the ruse that *Bluebird of Happiness* was her husband's final creative effort? Or maybe she was furious with Jenny for encouraging her to take whatever food supplements had turned her blue?

And what about Ox Oxenfeld? I wondered if he expected Boom Boom to die. The way he had rushed toward the bedroom when he heard the news that it was Jenny who had been found dead was suspicious to me. Had he killed her? To keep up the ruse that *Bluebird of Happiness* was another of Toodles Tuttle's musical masterpieces?

Actually, all of them wanted to pretend the new musical was composed by Toodles. Which one of them was crazy enough to kill Jenny to ensure the financial success of the show?

Then, of course, there was Bridget O'Halloran, who had sent threatening letters. Her heartless pursuit of a starring role in the face of a tragedy hinted at her lack of human kindness. Did she also have the capacity to kill for what she wanted? Did she have a violent tendency?

I tried to put my roiling mind to rest by cutting some hydrangeas and arranging them in a vase for the kitchen table. I wanted to make a gracious home for Michael, and I had also made an inner commitment to contemplating at least one beautiful thing every day. Fresh flowers fit the bill in both cases.

After that, I walked Noah down the lane and across the front pasture to the meadow. There, I had invited various neighbors to plant a community garden. In the evenings, I often saw the young couple from next door tending to their vegetable patch. Another gentleman from up the road had planted rows of sweet corn, and the tassels were already as tall as I. I hoped he might share a little of his harvest when the corn came in. Someone else was growing pumpkins. A zucchini crop was already out of control, too, with the vines curling up over the fence and escaping into the adjacent unmown field. All that growing food looked beautiful indeed.

Noah pointed out a groundhog, assuming, I'm sure, it was a bunny—his favorite animal. The groundhog raised his head, and I shouted to shoo him away from the garden. He scuttled into the bushes, triggering a weeping fit from Noah, so I carried the baby back to the house.

When we got home, I found a package left on the back porch by the postman. It turned out to be a box full of children's books sent to me by a Blackbird cousin whose children had outgrown them. Fourteen books with wonderful characters—Babar, Toad, Madeline, and more. I took them upstairs and read one to Noah when I put him down for his afternoon nap.

In my own bedroom, I picked up the phone and found a voice mail from Libby.

Her voice was cool. "I got your message, but I'm not ready to forgive you yet. I haven't learned anything else from Ox, by the way. He's a perfect lambkin, if you ask me. Hardly capable of murder. Do you have a copy of the recipe for that really good cheesecake Grandmama's last housekeeper used to make?"

Ox was capable of managing the cutthroat world of Broadway theater, so maybe he wasn't a perfect lambkin. I decided not to call Libby back yet. Instead, I crawled into my own bed to rest. I was sure I wouldn't fall asleep again, but I clonked off and woke up two hours later when Michael returned. He took care of the baby and ate a fast sandwich while I went into my closet.

Tonight I had hoped to wear a black vintage Givenchy slip dress that had belonged to a weight-battling movie star. It had been far too big for me a few months ago, but when I slipped it over my head and gave myself a critical stare, I was relieved to see it looked pretty darn good. The shoulders tied with lengths of black grosgrain ribbon, which I could adjust so that the empire-style waistline sat just above Baby Girl. The rest of the dress was a simple, loose-fitting sheath with a black lace overlay—a very Audrey Hepburn look, except for my baby bump. I was almost surprised to see how well it worked. But when does Givenchy not work?

I pulled my hair up to stay cool and kept Bridget in mind when I did my makeup a little more lavishly than usual. From the back of my closet, I dug out a pair of high Jimmy Choos.

Downstairs, Michael—an aficionado of black lace—came up behind me as I fixed my earrings in the hall mirror, and he brushed a kiss on the back my neck. "What's the occasion?"

"A very fashion-savvy crowd."

He met my gaze in the mirror and smiled. "You're gonna knock 'em dead."

Within the hour, I was on the train, headed for Philadelphia in plenty of time to reach my event of the evening. From the station, I walked across town—taking my time in my high heels. Even as dusk approached, the summer heat made the streets feel like a giant sweat lodge. All the tourist pedestrians around Franklin Square were dressed in shorts and T-shirts or light summer dresses, looking wilted. The music from the carousel blared, but when I got closer to the warehouse the Fashion Co-op had rented for the evening, I could hear thumping rock music two blocks away. The tourists thinned out, and I followed a steady stream of fashionistas heading toward the refurbished building.

Just as I reached the warehouse entrance, a clap of thunder rolled over the city, and a torrent of rain began to pound the sidewalk. The people around me groaned, but I was pleased to see the rain. The storm would cool things off. And I wouldn't have to water my garden with a hose. I ducked under the temporary party awning and slipped indoors.

One of the party cochairs was an old friend—Karen Shastri, five months pregnant with her first child. We compared bellies, and she gushed that she could hardly wait to quit her job and become a full-time mom.

"I just know it's going to be a wonderful experience!" She had a starry-eyed smile about motherhood. She introduced me to her husband, a well-known beer distributor in Philadelphia. He had provided all the beverages for the party—not just the beer, but fine wines and liquor, too: a sizable donation.

They were too busy to talk with me for long, so I roamed around until I found exactly whom I had hoped to see tonight—Delilah Fairweather, the best party planner in the city and my longtime good friend.

Delilah caught sight of me and squealed. She hung up on her cell phone caller without a good-bye and grabbed my belly between her long, elegant hands. She bent and gave Baby Girl big kisses, laughing, then kissed me, too. "Nora, you look fab! And what a great dress!"

"You look like a million," I told her. She had worn a very short cocktail dress in a dark African print that seemed to turn her skin to silk. "Delilah, I got my hair a little wet in the rain. Come with me somewhere to fix it?"

"My private lair," she said with a wink, sensing I wanted a private chat. "This way."

We skirted a runway that had been set up down the middle of the warehouse, with a long white carpet rolled out down the middle. From there, Delilah took me behind the scenes, where the tumult of backstage was in full swing. We dodged past the makeup tables, where models were having their faces painted on. Hairdressers plied blow-dryers, flatirons, brushes, spray and lots of gushing praise. We scurried through the dressing area, where one college-age designer after another was putting finishing touches on their designs while the models all jabbered to one another. Everyone seemed to shout at a fever pitch. If not for the ear-splitting party music, the guests would surely have heard the bedlam of last-minute preparations.

Delilah unlocked a door to a warehouse office where she had established a base of operations. We could hear the music vibrate through the walls.

"It's my biggest event of the summer," Delilah said while I fixed my hair in a cracked mirror hanging on one wall. She sat on a desk, crossed her legs and swung one elegant Louboutin. "You know most of the details—they're giving awards to up-and-coming fashion designers, but it's also a fund-raiser for that group that distributes first-day-of-school clothes to kids and job interview outfits to women who need them. Good stuff. It's a new group, and they wanted to partner with the Fashion Co-op to get more buzz going. Where's your phone? I'll give you all the important facts."

I pointed, and she grabbed my phone out of my bag. As she synced our phones, she said, "Good thing this new charity isn't on your hit list. They needed a great event to get started."

"Wait—my hit list?"

"A lot of people have been talking about that article you wrote. The ten best charities? Except it's the ten worst that should have been the headline." She shot me a sideways glance that I caught in the mirror. "Some people are pissed off, Nora."

"Because I told the truth?"

"You know as well as I do that this charitable stuff is big business."

"All the more reason donors should know when their money is going to a good cause—or is being diverted into other pockets."

"Yeah, I guess, but . . . hey, girl, don't cut into my business."

I turned away from the mirror. "I knew I wasn't going to make everybody happy with that article. But it's important information, Delilah. I felt I had to do it."

"I suppose so," my friend said without much enthusiasm. She went back to toying with our phones and changed the subject. "How are you feeling?"

"Great." I went back to fluffing my hair but made a mental note to bring up the subject again with Delilah when we'd have more time to explore the ramifications of my article on her business life. She worked with all charities—good and bad. Maybe I could help her choose wisely. Or maybe she had insider information that I needed to know, too. But she didn't want to talk seriously right now, so I said, "I slept through the first trimester, but now I'm going strong."

"Worried about delivery?"

"Not really. I've been taking yoga and getting some exercise. Most women seem to get through labor just fine. You did, right?"

"Keesa was no problem," Delilah said, "but I was a sweet young thing back then. You'll do great, though. And there's always the drugs. Trust me. Take whatever they offer, honey."

"It's what happens afterward that has me thinking."

Delilah looked up from our cell phones. "It's a little late to start wondering if you can handle being a mom."

I smiled ruefully. "After wanting a family for so long, I realize now I should have thought through the details more carefully."

She laughed with me. "Yeah, been there, done that! I couldn't wait to have Keesa, and then . . ."

"Then?"

"To be honest? I couldn't wait to get back to work. Don't get me wrong. I love being a mom. I love my daughter. But . . . for me, spending your whole day with a baby is just . . . boring. Don't quote me. I can hear the mommy screams now. I should spend every waking minute with my kid! But not everybody's the same. Spending months with a baby—that's the right choice for some, but it can drive other women bat-crap crazy. I'm just not the kind of mother who can stay home and make organic cheese sandwiches with cookie cutters and teach my kid to read and recycle. Screw that. I want to be out in the world! And knowing how to fill my needs makes me a better mother for Keesa."

"I'm not sure which kind of mother I am."

"You'll learn on the job, just like everyone else. I spend most of my time making parties for other people, and Keesa's a happy soul. And smart! Not to mention a lot more well adjusted than I ever was. Look at you and your sisters. Mama and Daddy Blackbird were never around much, but you're okay—better than most."

"Thanks," I said, knowing my parents were infamous in many circles. I feared they had stiffed Delilah for her fee on the last party they threw before skipping town.

"What about your Prince of Darkness? How's he doing with all this?"

"He's fine," I said with a smile. I got to the point of our private meeting. "In fact . . . we're getting married on Friday."

With a cry, Delilah jumped up and hugged me again. "Congrats, honey! I'm really happy for you. Your prince can scare the daylights out of people, but he was real nice to me at your birthday party. Can I throw you a reception?"

"Thank you, but no. We can't afford a party."

"There's a lot of that going around. With the Paine Investment Group problem, a lot of formerly loaded people are scrambling to pay the rent on their penthouses. But let me worry about what's affordable. I've got more than a few favors to collect in this town."

"Thank you, really, but no. Michael is still shy about my friends."

She snorted. "It's time he got over that. Nothing would make me happier than to throw you a party, Nora. Would I have all this work without you? All this glamour?" She spread her arms wide to indicate the cluttered warehouse office. "I owe all of my success to you!"

"You made your reputation all by yourself. Really, let's not have a party. We'd love to have you at the judge's chamber, though." I gave her the lowdown on the quiet wedding we had planned and added, "Just don't tell Libby, okay? Not until the last minute."

Delilah laughed. "You afraid your big sis is going to make everybody do the chicken dance?"

"I can handle the chicken dance. But she has more imagination than that—which scares me."

Delilah must have assumed I was kidding, because she laughed.

We went out to the party in time to see the parade of food that waiters brought out from the makeshift kitchen set up in a tent out back. The guests oohed and aahed as the flaming trays filled the room with light. Sparklers spouted bright cascades of color.

The live music began. The crowd shrieked with excitement and surged toward a stage that had been erected at the far end of the warehouse. Glaring lights came up. A once-very-famous rock band had been hired at substantial cost, I guessed. It took money to make money, I reminded myself—but this seemed over the top. I hoped someone on the committee had a relationship with the band and had scored a reduced price on the entertainment.

The live musicians revved up the crowd with their old hits. The balding lead singer strutted across the stage with his microphone, sending female guests of all ages into a frenzy of nostalgia. It was impossible not to dance along to the throbbing music. Baby Girl felt happy inside me.

Delilah had gone overboard with the sparkle. Strings of tiny lights dangled from the warehouse rafters. Huge ice sculptures glittered on tables covered with diaphanous fabrics. Guests carried glow sticks, and overhead a theatrical lighting system cast spinning disks of light across the crowd. A smoke machine billowed clouds of mist into the air. I counted up all the amenities and began to wonder how much money this new charity had spent to throw their party. And how much of what they hoped to raise actually went to buying winter coats and job interview clothes.

The crowd was mostly young, mostly very rich, with a sprinkling of fashion students in the mix. Their wild hair, lavish tattoos and unflattering clothes made them easily recognizable. I saw a lot of familiar faces among the nonstudents and chatted with many old friends. I wasn't the best-dressed person in attendance, but I was relieved to see I could still hold my own among the well-heeled.

After taking some pictures of the most au courant outfits, I went to the buffet table, where nobody was eating. Fashion people rarely did. But just in case, I was assured by a waiter, everything was gluten-free, organic, free-range, locally sourced, humanely slaughtered or grass fed. No peanuts, no soy and certainly no bacon. Amused, I nibbled a few carrots and accepted a glass of blended juices while talking with other guests.

My friend Chandler Ann appeared, dressed to the nines in a Tony Ward slip dress. She was with a couple of girlfriends in equally drop-dead party duds. Susan Shain wore a new Dior tank-top sundress, and Trish Connors was in an elaborately embellished Zac Posen frock. Shouting over the band, we exchanged compliments and harmless gossip about some of the clothes worn by other guests.

Chandler Ann took me aside when her friends went for more drinks. As soon as we were alone, she leaned close to make herself heard over the music. "Nora, I've been thinking a lot about Jenny Tuttle this week."

"Me, too," I confessed.

"Funny thing. I remembered something Jenny said just before she quit coming to my dad's clinic. Something about a woman who had threatened her. Do you think I should tell the police?"

"Yes, of course." Reluctantly, I reached for my cell phone. Even if my friend was about to implicate my future mother-in-law in a murder, it was the right thing to do. "I can give you the phone number of one of the state troopers on the case."

"Thanks. It may be nothing. But I remember Jenny coming for an appointment one day, and she was very upset. She said somebody she worked with was going to beat her up if she didn't give her a better role in a play."

"Who was it?" I asked before I could stop myself.

Chandler Ann frowned and said, "It was a funny name. Like a puppy or a flower. Daisy or Tulip or—"

"Poppy?"

"That's it! Anyway, Jenny seemed genuinely frightened. Like maybe this Poppy person could definitely do some harm. I don't want to be Chicken Little—claiming the sky is falling when it's really nothing—but—"

"It's something, not nothing. I think you should call the police." I quickly texted Ricci's phone number to Chandler Ann's phone. "It could be really important."

She continued to look doubtful. "I don't want to look foolish."

"You won't," I assured her.

Had I been alone with a murderer this morning? Had Poppy been the one to give Jenny too many medications? The music changed, and the band's lead singer shouted into his microphone that it was time for the fashion portion of the evening to begin. A few key people slipped backstage, and other guests began to find seats in the very limited number of chairs that were set up around the runway. Chandler Ann and I left the front-row seats for the guests, who fought their way into them; instead we snagged seats in the second row.

Next to me sat the middle-aged mother and sister of one of the young designers. Their excitement was contagious.

The lights flickered and dimmed. The tipsy committee chair came out into the spotlight to give a too-long introduction. She giggled and thanked her friends and giggled some more until finally the director of the new charity came to the microphone and lightly ended her ramble. He eased her off the runway to applause and whistles.

More recorded music blasted, and the show began. Skinny models sashayed along the runway, wearing one outlandish outfit after another. Heels were higher than it seemed humanly possible to walk on. I could see the bones of some great clothes—summer dresses, some fashion-forward separates, and a few really great gowns—but they were nearly obscured by the styling. Gigantic hats and chunky jewelry almost overshadowed the clothes. But that was the point of a fashion show—to entertain and show off. Later, the business of selling clothes that people might actually wear would take place in quiet offices around the city.

The crowd reacted to the spectacle with roars of cheering and rounds of applause. The family beside me jumped to their feet and clapped when their relative's designs went by. I cheered, too. They were all so happy.

But I found myself looking more carefully around at the people who had paid to come out for a good cause. I wondered if it had been altruism that brought them to the warehouse on a hot night. No, I was pretty sure they were here for the good times. And maybe to show off, to flaunt. Which was the way things worked in my world. Countless charities benefited from parties like this one. Some of them depended on a single big fund-raiser a year, so a good party meant the difference between continuing their good works or fading into the sunset.

This party felt . . . less about philanthropy, however, and more about excess. I had planned on featuring it prominently in my column because I knew the photos would be good. But now I had second thoughts about featuring an organization that was still so new. And one that had perhaps miscalculated in the balance between socializing and fund-raising. I couldn't help noticing that the managing director of the charity stood off to one side by himself, watching the show with a stiff smile on his face. I wondered if he knew he'd made a mistake and was already trying to figure out how to refocus his fun-loving board of directors and their tipsy chairperson.

Maybe parties that supported local food banks and regional cancer centers weren't as newspaper-friendly as fashion bashes, but at least donors could be sure their contributions went exactly where they intended their money to go. And maybe the ten best and ten worst charities list had made me a few enemies, but it was solid information worthy of newspaper inches. I just had to find a way to slip that information between the scandalous articles.

My phone vibrated, and I took a look at the screen.

Lexie.

I knew I wouldn't be able to hear her, so I let the call go to voice mail. But my concern for my friend soon got the best of me. When the lights signaled a break between designers, I said good-bye to

Chandler Ann and found Delilah for a good-night hug. She was too harried to talk, but she promised to see me on Friday.

"It's going to be a beautiful wedding," she shouted over the party noise. "I can feel it!"

On the way home on the train, I listened to Lexie's message.

"Sweetie," she said briskly, "I've been discovered. I have to pack my bags and go on the lam. Please don't be offended, but I'm going to keep my whereabouts a secret for a while. I'll call when I can."

I felt a stab of guilt. Had I somehow led Hostetler to Lexie's doorstep? It certainly sounded as if my best friend didn't trust me anymore.

CHAPTER SIXTEEN

took Sunday off from events, as usual, but wrote up pieces to go into the Monday and Tuesday print editions of the paper. After that, I exchanged e-mails with my online classmates to complete a journalism assignment. I felt good about my contribution. Maybe I wasn't a rookie anymore. I spent the rest of the day with Noah. Michael went to Mass and to tend to some business he clearly didn't want to talk about. I tried calling Libby but got no answer. Again.

I left another message. "Libby, I'm truly sorry about what I said about you and Ox Oxenfeld. You're right. I shouldn't judge. And I'm sorry that I don't have the housekeeper's cheesecake recipe, either. Try Pinterest."

She didn't call me back. Nor did Lexie. I tried not to worry.

Around noon, Emma called, sounding as if she were phoning from a wind tunnel, so I assumed she was outdoors somewhere. She said, "Did I leave my extra pair of boots at your place?"

"Give me a hint," I said. "Where should I look? In a closet? The basement? The attic?"

"If I'd left them in the attic, they'd be mouse food. Check the bedroom I usually use."

I had Noah on my hip as I carried the phone upstairs to look. "How's Cookie?"

"I jumped him this morning, and he's Superman. You should see him! If he doesn't pull my arms out of their sockets, he's the man of my dreams." Emma sounded very pleased.

I opened the bedroom door and discovered that Bridget had left the room a mess—the bed unmade and a half-empty wine bottle on the nightstand with a drinking glass. She had rooted through the closet and obviously had tried on Emma's riding boots. They were on the floor, askew.

"I found your boots," I said.

"You don't sound happy about it."

"Michael's mother spent a night here. This room looks like a tornado hit it."

"Tch-tch," Emma said. "I bet she didn't leave a hostess gift, either. Do you have your smelling salts?"

"She's not going to be your mother-in-law," I replied tartly.

"Surrender, Dorothy!" Emma sang a bar of the Wicked Witch of the West music and laughed. Then, "The cops called me to talk about what we saw at the Tuttle folly. They said they'd be in touch with you later."

"Are they any closer to discovering what happened?"

"I can't tell. They figured out what those bottles were, though. Not a collection of old glass, but containers of colloidal silver."

"I did some Googling, and colloidal silver sounded like the most likely possibility to turn Boom Boom blue. She must have taken it as a supplement."

"But Jenny obviously didn't," Emma said. "Yet the bottles were in Jenny's studio."

"Jenny was the one who encouraged her mother to take supplements."

"So she poisoned her mother? I mean, it has to take a lot of silver to turn somebody into a Sesame Street character. That must have put a damper on their relationship. Was turning blue enough to make Boom Boom want to kill her daughter?"

"Maybe so. What I don't understand is why the nurse was killed."

"Let the cops take care of it," Emma advised. "They seemed all excited about having a murder case to work on. It's more thrills than the usual teenager crap. I'll stop for my boots tomorrow, if I can."

We ended our call. Noah grabbed the phone from me, and I let him carry it back downstairs. To him, I said, "Your mother loves her new horse. I think that's a good sign."

I was relieved that the Sunday edition of the *Intelligencer* didn't have a front-page article about Lexie. When Monday's edition showed up without any mention of my friend, I started to think the long silence from Gus was suspicious. What was he working on? There were no penis stories, either, and even Jenny Tuttle's toxicology results didn't trigger more than a few inches of the front page.

On Monday afternoon while Noah napped, my friend Mary Jude telephoned from the office. "Nora, did I wake you?"

"No, of course not," I said, although I'd been considering taking a quick snooze before it was time to go to the preview of *Bluebird of Happiness*. "What's up, MJ?"

"I hate to ask," she said, "but I have to take Trevor to the emergency room. He needs a breathing treatment, and going to the hospital is the fastest way to get him some relief." She sounded unbelievably calm for a mother with a sick child. "But I'm supposed to be here two more hours to man the phones. We're still getting crazy calls about that photograph Mr. Hardwicke ran. Anyway, he says I can go home if I can find somebody to answer calls. I thought if you were coming in for an event tonight—"

"Sure. I can cover for you in an hour or so. Tell Gus I'll be there as soon as I can." Already, I was heading for my closet.

"Thanks, Nora. You're a lifesaver."

We hung up, and I took a superfast shower. I finished my hair and makeup just as Noah let out a preliminary squall. I stepped into the dress I planned to wear to tonight's preview. It was a short, strapless sheath of diaphanous blue chiffon, cut on the bias. From his resort-wear collection, it was Dior at the height of his genius. The décolletage would distract from the tight fit. Maybe it was a little overkill for a theater event, but two nights of lovemaking with Michael had made me think I should be making more of my bustline while I had it.

I went in to retrieve Noah from his crib. He was standing up and bawling full bore, but with one look at my flaunted bosom, his tears stopped rolling.

I said, "I know I look like Libby. Victoria's Secret will be calling me soon."

Noah put his hands on my breasts and gave a wavering sigh of appreciation.

"You're starting early," I said, removing his hands. I picked him up and changed his diaper.

I let Noah play with his pink bunny on the bed while I called Michael's cell phone. He said he was on his way.

In fifteen minutes, I stepped into my shoes and grabbed a light sweater for the office and a lime green embroidered silk pashmina that would work later for the theater preview. We went downstairs and were out the back door just as Michael pulled up in the bulletproof black Escalade. Our new car.

He came around the hood of the vehicle and stopped short at the sight of my low neckline. "What are you wearing?"

I stopped, too. "Is it too much?"

"It's a lot," he said on a laugh.

"Should I go change?"

"Nope." He came closer and dropped a smiling kiss on my mouth. "Noah seems to like it."

The baby was mashing his face into my bare cleavage and giggling. He left a puddle of drool behind. I handed him over for Michael to put in his car seat while I mopped myself up.

I convinced Michael to drop me at the train station again instead of driving me all the way into the city, so within the hour I was walking off the hot sidewalk and into the cool Pendergast Building.

On his phone, Skip Malone looked up from the Sports desk as I passed by. He nearly dropped his receiver. I waved.

Phones were ringing all over the newsroom, and the remaining reporters were busy taking calls. I set my bag down on Mary Jude's empty desk. She had left me an apple with a Post-it note stuck to it. Her hasty scrawl read *Thank you!*

The newsroom was chilly from the air-conditioning—a welcome relief after the humid walk from the station. I dug my sweater out of my bag and tugged it on. It didn't cover up my exposed cleavage, but it provided a little warmth. I took a bite of the apple and munched it.

A second later, Gus barged off the elevator. He strode straight across the room to the City desk, where he began to chew out one of the reporters there. When the reporter began a sniveling defense of himself, Gus looked up and met my gaze across the room. He did a double take and scowled.

Okay, so maybe I should have changed my outfit.

The phone on Mary Jude's desk rang, so I sat down, swallowed my mouthful of apple and picked up.

"*Philadelphia Intelligencer.* Nora Blackbird speaking."

"Uh, yeah," said a male voice. "Has anybody claimed the million dollars yet?"

"Million dollars? I don't know anything about that, sir."

"The morning dudes on the radio? They said you were giving away a million bucks to the kid in the picture."

"I think the radio dudes were misinformed, sir. The *Intelligencer* is not giving away money."

"Huh," he said. "I was just wondering, because that picture in the paper last week? It kinda looks like me when I was in school."

I sat up hastily. I remembered the group of similar photos I'd seen in Jenny Tuttle's desk. I grabbed a pencil and slipped open a notebook. "Can I have your name, sir?"

"I don't think so," he said with an edge of derision. "Not unless there's money involved."

"There's really not any— Look," I said, "I know this sounds weird, but could you just tell me one thing? Are you adopted?"

A long silence greeted that question. Finally, my caller said, "Yeah. So what?"

"We're putting together a story," I began, making it up as I went. "If you could answer a few—"

"I don't want to be in any story," he said and hung up.

I put my pencil down. Thinking, I took another bite of apple. What did all the photos of children mean? Ox and Poppy had declared that even one illegitimate baby was impossible, but I couldn't think of another possibility. Who were all the children in Jenny's desk drawer?

Tremaine Jefferson came up on the elevator and headed over to me. On Mary Jude's computer, he showed me the clips he had prepared from the group I'd sent him from the fashion party. We shared a laugh over some of the clothes and batted around some ideas for short videos that could be used later in the week. I made another suggestion—adding some still photos of well-dressed ladies from the Pelvic Health party, which he took in good humor.

When we finished, I said, "Tremaine, I've been invited to a preview of a new musical tonight. I was hoping you might come along and do some filming."

"You mean, it's a show? We can't film performances, Nora. Copyright issues."

"It's not a performance. At least, not yet. It's a work in progress. They want publicity to attract investors. It might be awful," I cautioned. "But we might get some fun footage. Think of it as a fishing trip. If it turns out badly, I'll buy you lunch someday soon."

He had come to trust me, so he agreed the excursion might be worth his time and promised to meet me downstairs in an hour. He went off to tweak his work.

Two minutes later, the phone rang again. Hoping it was another interesting call, I picked up right away. "*Philadelphia Intelligencer.* Nora Blackbird speaking."

"Hi," said a brisk female voice. "May I speak with Gus, please?"

I realized the hour had grown so late that Gus's assistant was no longer answering his phone. "Will you hold just a minute? He stepped away from his desk." I waved at Gus to get his attention. He pointedly ignored me.

The voice on the line sharpened. "Hang on. Did you say Nora Blackbird?"

"Yes, that's me."

"Well, hello!" Her tone turned friendly. "It's nice to know you actually exist. I'm Megan. Gus's sister."

It hit me that her accent, which I hadn't quite processed, was Australian. Her voice was low and throaty with a bubble of laughter in it.

She went on with enthusiasm. "Am I the first to welcome you into the fold?"

I almost choked on my apple. "Uh . . . ?"

She had a friendly chuckle. "Gus is a devilish good secret keeper. I was the one who wingled it out of him, did he say?"

"N-no," I said, still confused. "He didn't mention it."

"I don't have to tell you what a charmer he can be when he turns on the electricity, but what a bloody closemouthed bastard when he chooses. And a bludger in the romance department! So the news took us all by surprise. And then I saw your photograph! And you're expecting! Congratulations. I've been reading your column online. It's quite good, actually. I can see how he'd find you appealing. How did you reel him in?"

Something was very wrong, but all I could feel was my blood pressure spiking. "Well," I began.

"Dad was overjoyed, of course. Hearing about you put him over the moon. The rest of us were fair gob-smacked—seems we hardly know our Gus after all!" She barely drew a breath but kept on talking. "I'm sorry you couldn't make the trip with him to this outback, but in your condition, I understand completely. I don't suppose you might be a bit shy of us, too, maybe?"

"Not at all," I said. "But—"

"You'll be sure to come for Christmas. Dad does it up right—all the trimmings. His birthday is just a few days later, so he's always very festive."

She kept talking about Christmas, but I had stopped listening. I stood up from the desk and didn't care what anybody thought. I snapped my fingers at Gus. With annoyance, he looked up from his discussion—prepared to lambast me, I'm sure—but I sent him a poisonous glare that got his attention. I pointed at the phone as if to say *Important call*. He ambled in my direction.

I cut across Megan's rambling gush about lavish holiday meals and said into the phone, "Oh, here he is, Megan. Gus just got in. Hang on, will you?"

I hugged the receiver to my chest as Gus arrived in front of me. I snapped, "It's your sister. She seems to be under the impression that you and I are expected next Christmas. Is there something you haven't told me, Mr. Hardwicke?"

To my astonishment, Gus turned bright pink. And although he opened his mouth, no words came out.

I handed over the phone. He took it automatically, in a daze.

"Er, Meegs?" he said into the phone. "Let me call you back in five? No, five, I promise. I *promise*."

He put the phone down and said composedly to me, "In my office. Please."

It was the *please* that shook me. I followed him across the newsroom and into his sanctum.

He closed the door behind me, still very pink. "This is going to be difficult enough, but did you have to wear that particular dress to the office?"

"It's a Dior. Are you capable of finding something wrong with it?"

"Nothing's wrong with it. Except I can barely concentrate with all that—"

"Stop stalling. What in heaven's name was your sister talking about?"

Gus began to pace the floor. "This is very awkward."

"For which one of us?"

He put his hands into his trouser pockets and couldn't meet my glare. "Nora, I will preface the whole story by saying I never meant for things to get out of control the way they have, but my family is rather known for going big—"

"Gus! Is this the personal matter you've been trying not to tell me about? What in the world is going on?"

He gave up stonewalling. He stood still and said, "I told my family that you and I were seeing each other."

A Little Night Murder

If there had been so much as a stapler handy, I'd have thrown it at his head. Good for him that his office was empty of weapons. "Why?" I demanded.

Hastily, he lowered the blinds to prevent the entire newsroom from watching us. "It's not implausible. You're attractive," he said, perhaps deliberately misunderstanding my question. "As you know, I'm usually drawn to older women. They're easier to cope with, but you—"

"I'm going to be really hard to cope with in ten seconds. Why did you tell your family we were an item?"

"Because they wanted to hear it," he burst out, starting to lose control. "I needed an advantage to get assigned to this Philadelphia takeover, and you fit the bill. Megan was going to get the job if I didn't come up with an idea that made me the perfect choice to negotiate for my father. And they all thought adding you to the mix was a great strategy—an American with a pedigree those relics would appreciate. Besides, my father wants us all settled—that is, weighted down with ankle biters and generally stuck in the tar pit of life so we're prepared to take over his bloody empire if he drops dead tomorrow, but the main thing is this Philadelphia deal, which—"

"Stop!" I cried. "You want to buy a company, so you pretended to have a girlfriend?"

"It's not just a company. It's practically its own planet. I tried to explain to you last week when—well, other things popped up. By the way," he said, "you're not a girlfriend. As far as my family is concerned, you're my fiancée."

I let out a word that didn't usually cross my lips. "Gus! What were you thinking? They're going to find out you're not engaged to me."

"They're on the other side of the world! How can they find out?"

"She knew my name! She reads my column! She— Oh!" I was hit with an epiphany. "That's why you wanted the photo of me out of the online paper, isn't it? Because I was pregnant! You didn't want your family to think you had a baby on the way."

"My family is very old-fashioned about that sort of thing."

"What sort of thing? Children out of wedlock? Or bald-faced lies?"

"You're not going to have a stroke, are you? Because you're turning an alarming shade of— Look, if it's any consolation," he said, swiftly changing tactics, "they're delighted about you. Dad reckons you're a right sheila, and my brother Jack can hardly wait to meet you. Watch out for him, by the way. He'll poke anything in panties, but he's particularly wild about redheads."

"I'm not going to meet your brother! Or your father! Or anyone else! Ever! I'm staying right here in Philadelphia. And on Friday I'm marrying Michael."

"About that," Gus said.

I put up my hand to stop him. "No," I said. "You have no input on my wedding."

"Could I ask you to postpone it a few weeks? Or months?"

"You're joking, right?"

"Not really, no," he said grimly.

"Gus!" I pointed at the telephone. "You're going to phone your sister right now. And you're going to tell her the truth. I will have no part of your family politics. Tell them."

"I can't do that," he replied.

"I'm not giving you a choice!"

"It would kill my father," he said. "Do you want that on your conscience?"

"Don't try manipulating my feelings. That's not going to work."

"I'm being honest here. My father is not in the best of health.

The negotiations to buy that damn company have drained him. I know you're not the kind of woman who—"

"You're not going to worm your way out of this!"

"I need a week," he said. "To prepare them."

"Absolutely not."

"Four days."

"No."

"Okay, how about until Friday, then? Just— I need to do this carefully."

I let out a frustrated shriek and clapped both hands over my eyes to block out the whole stupid mess. When I had a grip on myself, I dropped my hands. "I'll give you until tomorrow."

"Thursday?" he bargained. "It's practically the middle of the night over there now. This will take time. It's a big family. And I need to rethink the negotiations."

I held my breath and wondered if I might explode. There was one person who was going to go ballistic over this situation, though, and I could already hear him shouting. And shouting wasn't going to be the worst part.

"Please breathe," Gus said.

At last, I said, "When Michael gets wind of this, don't take time to pack your bags. Get the first flight back to Australia. At the very least, he'll break your knees. At worst, you'll end up floating in the Atlantic in a variety of Tupperware containers."

"Understood," he said contritely. "Thank you for the warning. Meanwhile, I'd like to make it up to you."

I stepped back, afraid of what he thought "making it up to me" might include.

"Don't panic. This is good news. Stan Rosencrantz is retiring."

My temper flared again. "His name is Rosenstatz, not Rosencrantz. The least you could do is know the names of your employees."

"Whatever. He's retiring."

"How is Stan's retirement possibly good news? He loves the newspaper business!"

"He wants to leave while he still has what's left of his health. I want you to take his job—editing the Lifestyle section of the *Intelligencer*."

I stood very still and tried to make sense of what he'd just said. But I felt as if his words were suddenly swirling around in my head as if thrown by the centrifugal force of a roller coaster.

Finally, I said, "Can't you have one chair in this office?"

Gus opened the door and went out into the newsroom. He returned seconds later with the swivel chair from his assistant's desk. He took my elbow and guided me to sit down on it. I did so in the nick of time. A slosh of dark water had begun to surge around my feet. It rose up to my knees in a black flood that threatened to overwhelm me.

"Take a deep breath." Gus steadied me with both hands on my shoulders. His face swam before me, but his voice seemed very far away. "You're not going to faint, are you? You're white as foam."

I fought my way back to clarity. "Get your hands off me."

He let go of me and stepped back. He leaned against his desk and met my gaze, all trace of his embarrassment gone. "Well? Do you want the job or not?"

"I'm not qualified to assume Stan's job. He's a brilliant editor."

"He's a lame old coot with lousy digestion. It's long past time he went out to pasture. We need new ideas around here. You have proven yourself in the online edition. And you have your finger on the pulse of our readership. You're a born-and-bred Philadelphian, and I need that on the editorial side. We can work on your reticence when it comes to sensational ideas—"

"I loathe sensational ideas."

"You'll learn on the job. Bottom line? I'd like you to take on more responsibility."

Head clearing, I looked up at him through narrowed eyes. "You have another agenda, don't you?"

"Why would you say such a thing?" He endeavored to look innocent. "You're the girl for my money, Nora. And we work well together."

"We are not together in any sense of the word!"

"Right, right. Look, I'm not asking for an answer now. It means a raise, of course. And you won't start until fall, after your little Abruzzo is born. In fact, take a few extra weeks of maternity leave to energize yourself, and come back to a new career."

Gus had the audacity to smile down at me with the pleased look of a cat that had eaten a whole flock of canaries.

"There are days," I said, "when I think you are the devil."

"So you'll take the new job?"

"I'll have to talk it over with Michael and get back to you."

"Of course. I presume you'll refrain from telling him about my—our—that is, the relationship that you and I—"

"The ridiculous relationship that you made up? No, I'm not keeping that a secret from Michael." The idea of telling him, though, made my stomach plunge. Even though I was the innocent party, I dreaded having to explain the situation to him.

Gus went back out into the newsroom and returned with a paper cup of water. I sipped it without speaking. When he was satisfied that I wasn't going to sprawl out on the floor in a dead faint, he said, "Where are you going tonight?"

"The preview of the Tuttle musical."

"Where is it?"

I told him which theater and that I was going with Tremaine.

"Okay," he said. "I'll see you afterward, before you go home. I want to be sure you're all right. Can you walk?"

"Of course I can walk," I said, and tried to prove it. I went out of his office with a wobble, but when I realized everybody in the newsroom was watching with intense interest, I stiffened my spine, grabbed my bag and headed for the elevator.

I met Tremaine in the lobby of the building. He saw nothing amiss, so I congratulated myself on a quick recovery. More than anything, I wanted to bash Gus Hardwicke over the head with something lethal, and that wish strengthened my resolve. His preposterous engagement story enraged me. And the job offer? It was finally dawning on me that he'd probably used that to defuse my anger.

We reached Broad Street and the old rococo barn that was no longer one of the city's fine theatrical venues. It was still a beautiful place, though in need of a restoration. The marquee advertised a touring show that would come later in the month. For tonight, Ox Oxenfeld had rented the stage for the Tuttle preview.

Tremaine opened the door for me. Our route into the lobby was almost entirely blocked by a large easel bearing a handmade poster advertising *Bluebird of Happiness*. The poster depicted a much younger-looking non-blue Boom Boom Tuttle, her arms flung wide, her mouth gaping open as if she were hitting a glorious high note. The photo was surely decades old.

Edging around the poster, Tremaine said, "I'm not much of a theater person myself. You're going to have to tell me what to look for, Nora."

"Just take a few short videos of scenes from the show. Maybe we'll interview some of the cast later. I'll double-check with the producer, though, before we publish any photos or film."

The lobby was not thronged with an eager audience, all clutching tickets and pressing toward the open auditorium. Instead, a handful of men in suits brushed past me, talking with one another like bookies at a racetrack. And if the evening was supposed to be a memorial service as well as a theatrical performance, it looked as if mourners had been left off the guest list. Everyone seemed very businesslike.

Ox Oxenfeld came out of an open office door with a sheaf of papers in his hand. He caught sight of me and faltered.

"Hello, Ox," I said. "Is Boom Boom's big investor here tonight? I'd like to interview him."

"Uh, no," Ox said. "He isn't—that is, he couldn't make it. Excuse me, I have to—I must— Sorry. Later." He rushed over to the bookies. Hastily, he distributed the papers to them, and they all began to discuss financial matters.

"That's odd," I said, half to myself. "You'd think the primary investor would want to attend the first preview."

Tremaine and I headed across the faded carpet of the lobby. At the open double doors, a couple of long-legged showgirls in short, spangled costumes handed makeshift programs to me and Tremaine. The cast list had been printed on one side, a synopsis of the show on the other. No mention of Jenny.

Tremaine didn't bother glancing at his program. One look at the long legs of the dancers was all it took for him to hitch his camera out of its case. His smile turned enthusiastic. "Let's get started."

Inside the auditorium, the lights were on, and a small, restless audience talked noisily among themselves. I guessed they were potential investors, but also curious people from the theatrical community. I saw Nico Legarde standing by the front row of seats, speaking with a well-known local actor. I waved, and they waved back.

Tremaine and I found an open section of seats about halfway back on one side, and he set up his camera there. He pretended to do some test shots by filming the showgirls. They caught him in the act and strolled down the aisle to flirt with him.

I slid into a rump-sprung seat and looked at the stage. The curtains were open to reveal a half-constructed set. It was an interior of a house—a house of horrors, by the look of the crooked staircase and the fake cobwebs hanging from the chandelier. A large Palladian window at center stage had cracked panes and tattered draperies that swooped from a gilded pole. The room was decorated with whimsical props, though—an old butter churn wearing a top hat, a stuffed sailfish on the wall with a man's tie amusingly wrapped around its neck, a kite with a key dangling from its string.

A chubby man with a clipboard came along to call the showgirls backstage, so Tremaine squinted at the set with puzzlement. "What's this show about, Nora?"

"I don't know."

"Looks like Ben Franklin is going to drop in. Either him, or Dracula."

Fred Fusby came out from the wings and strode purposefully across the stage on his rubbery long legs. He headed for the lone piano. No orchestra had been engaged for the preview, I guessed. Fred spread his music on the stand and snapped on a light. He sat down at the bench and flexed his fingers. The audience understood his signal and quickly took their seats. Fred played a few bars of a pleasant melody. The auditorium lights dimmed, and a moment later the stage lighting came up. Spotlights pinpointed all the dilapidated details of the set, and I guessed the show had to be about a haunted house.

From the top of the crooked staircase, a wraithlike figure appeared. For a second, I assumed it was a ghost. But a light hit her, and I realized she was Boom Boom Tuttle in a flapper-style gown and a blond fright wig. Her face had been slathered with white makeup to diminish her blue coloring, but it hadn't quite worked. Her knees looked knobbier than ever, and her dancing shoes had heels too high for her to manage. Arching eyebrows had been painted on, and she wore false eyelashes along with rouge and matching lipstick. She swayed unsteadily, then clutched the banister to remain on her feet.

"Good evening," she said in a warbling voice that barely carried as far as the mezzanine. "Welcome to a newly discovered musical by the late, great Toodles Tuttle, my dear husband and the undisputed king of Broadway theater!"

A few murmurs around the auditorium hinted that the royal title she proposed might have been disputed just a little.

"I hope you brought your checkbooks," Boom Boom continued, "because we're still looking for a few smart investors. Tonight we're going to perform highlights from the show, just to give you a taste of what this production really could be. Sit back and enjoy!"

Fred Fusby cleared his throat meaningfully.

"Oh, yeah," Boom Boom added. "We're also remembering my daughter, Jenny. She was kinda helpful before she kicked the bucket. Now—on with the show!"

With that, Fred began banging on the piano and Boom Boom descended the rickety staircase. The audience held its breath as she teetered on her high heels. Two graceful male dancers leaped from the wings and rushed to assist her. By the time she had unsteadily reached the stage, more dancers came out and began to move around her. I settled back and tried to enjoy what I was watching. The choreography and music were lively and pleasant.

Then Boom Boom began to sing.

I couldn't understand a word.

But the action that played out on the stage began to make sense. Men in tuxedos danced or took turns passing trays of champagne glasses. Ladies in flapper dresses tap-danced and blew little plastic horns. It was supposed to be a New Year's Eve party, I realized. Boom Boom continued to sing inaudibly, and then two male dancers picked her up and spun her around. She did a hip wiggle and mimed embracing them. Her lascivious expression was ludicrous for a woman of her years.

Then Poppy Fontanna spun into view, grabbing a man in a white dinner jacket and pulling him away from his dance partner. The man was the recently hired choreographer, who had clearly been engaged at the last minute to perform in the preview. The rest of the cast faded back as the two of them tangoed, looking like a surefooted romantic couple. I had to admit, they were great. He dipped her. She kicked up one leg and pulled a funny face at the audience. Then Poppy danced offstage, and the man in the white dinner jacket came down to the front and sang. All he needed to make his life perfect was a new lady in his arms. His clear tenor was a welcome change from Boom Boom's shaky voice. He made a longing gesture in Poppy's direction before his previous partner came downstage to claim him.

Fending her off, he sang about his family history. How they had come on the *Mayflower* and how a young George Washington had left a foundling on their doorstep in a Paul Revere soup tureen. How Betsy Ross sewed their curtains. It didn't make a lot of sense, but I gathered he was proud of his family heritage.

From the front row, Nico Legarde glanced back at me. In the dark, I could not read his expression.

More great dancing. More upbeat music. Then Boom Boom took center stage and sang, but nobody could hear her. She was trying hard to be a sexy grande dame, I decided. A broad interpretation of a great lady gone to seed. Somebody gave her a champagne bottle, and she popped the cork, which soared across the stage and hit Fred Fusby squarely on the top of his bald head.

The audience laughed. Beside me, Tremaine snorted. The man in the white dinner jacket rushed onstage again, looking very handsome in the spotlight, and he valiantly tried to regain the audience's attention. He began to sing about love and bluebirds.

Suddenly it all made sense. The champagne cork, the man in the white dinner jacket, the tango, the magnificent house that had seen better days, the proud family heritage. I found myself boiling to my feet.

"Nora?" Tremaine asked. "You okay? What's wrong?"

"Bluebirds!" I pointed at the stage, not caring who heard me. "This show isn't about Bluebirds! It's about *Black*birds!"

"What?"

I could barely sputter out the words. "They're doing a show about my family!"

"Huh?"

I rarely lost my cool. I never made scenes. I couldn't stand melodrama. But suddenly I was a raving pregnant lunatic, shouting like a fishwife and shoving my way past Tremaine. "Stop filming! Turn off that camera!"

Tremaine stared at me as if I had grown an extra head. "Nora, have you gone crazy?"

"They're making fun of my parents! And Boom Boom is supposed to be—she's pretending to be Grandmama Blackbird—the loveliest, most kind, gracious lady who ever walked the earth, and *she's* making her out to be a horrible old— Let me go! I'm going to punch her in the nose!"

The whole audience turned around to watch me. The action onstage never stopped, but I couldn't hear anything except my own hysterical voice. The next thing I knew, Tremaine collared me as I tried to lunge past him, heading for the stage. He dragged me, kicking and shouting like a demented fury, up the aisle of the theater. I was vaguely aware of the audience watching my ranting exit. But I only wanted to run up onstage and knock Boom Boom down on her bony blue butt, once and for all.

Outside, Tremaine handed me off into a pair of strong arms, and in another minute, I was on the sidewalk, beating Gus Hardwicke on the chest.

He was laughing as he held me out of reach by my shoulders. "Keep this up, and somebody's going to call a cop."

"Do it!" I cried. "I want her arrested! I want all of them arrested! They can't do that to my family! To my grandmother! She was an elegant, lovely person who practiced *civility*, and they're pretending she was some kind of—some kind of *strumpet*!"

"A strumpet?" Gus burst into fresh laughter. "Who uses a word like *strumpet*?"

"And look what they're doing to my father! They're implying he was in love with someone other than my mother! See how he danced with the other woman? They're— It's obvious that Jenny Tuttle had a crush on him, and she—she made him into some kind of romantic hero. I won't let them do it, Gus! I swear I won't. Let go of me! I'm going back in there and—"

"You're not doing anything," he said reasonably as he restrained me, "except calm down. If you don't, you'll drop that baby right here on the street and Abruzzo really will have me executed. There you go. Breathe."

I sucked in a deep breath only because I had run out of air. When my head stopped spinning, I hauled off and clobbered Gus again just because he was within range.

He took the blow without wincing. "Feel better?"

I realized he still had a firm grip on my shoulders. I summoned my most commanding voice. "Turn me loose."

He eyed me sideways. "Are you going back inside to cause mayhem?"

"No," I said sulkily.

He set me back on my heels but positioned himself between me and the lobby doors in case I decided to make a break for it.

Tremaine came outside again, looking unnerved. He gave me my handbag. I accepted it with a very formal thank-you, and he returned to the theater with only one wary glance over his shoulder that said he feared I might turn into a screaming harpy all over again.

Gus said, "Better now?"

I tried to inhale another cleansing breath. "I'm still very angry."

"Let's get you out of here."

He hailed a taxi and settled me into the backseat. Gus stayed on his side of the seat, took out his phone and checked it. I looked at my phone, too, more to have a moment to regain my composure than to read messages. Sometime during the show, Michael had called, but I hadn't heard his ring. I read the text message.

Sorry—I hve thing 2 do. Take train home? 1 of my guys will pck u up @ station. Rwlns & grlfrnd here 2 bbysit. Roast chkn in oven.

Gus hadn't looked up from his phone. "Anything wrong?"

"Besides my family being subjected to libelous horror?"

Gus pocketed his phone. "Maybe because my family has been hit with more mud than Pompeii, it didn't seem that horrible to me. I came in late and certainly couldn't hear what that old lady was singing, but the show wasn't bad—as that kind of twaddle goes."

"Did you recognize Blackbird Farm?"

"The ruin of a house you live in? Not at first, but now that you mention it, I remember the place looking rather like the bulldozers should be called."

"That's my *home* you're talking about!" I put my face in my hands and moaned. "And my *grandmother*! Honestly, Gus, she was a refined lady. A cultured person who would rather be shot out of a cannon than be portrayed as some kind of crude, tasteless—"

"She sounds familiar," Gus said. "The refined lady part, that is." When I didn't respond, he added, "That's a compliment, you know. You're a throwback to a more gracious era."

I subsided into the seat. "For the first time in my life, I'm glad she's gone. I loved her, and I always wanted to be like her. She'd be appalled by this."

Gus reached over and took my hand. When I tried to pull away, he held on firmly. "Who's going to know the difference, Nora? I saw nothing that anyone would recognize as your family."

"We only saw the first fifteen minutes! Who knows what comes next?"

"Back up," he said, "What did you mean about Jenny Tuttle having a crush on your father?"

"Wasn't it obvious? He was the romantic lead! He left his wife to dance with Poppy!"

Light dawned on his face. "Crikey!"

"What?"

"Isn't it obvious? Your father was the father of Jenny Tuttle's child."

CHAPTER SEVENTEEN

f I were a trout, my mouth could not have fallen open so promptly. "He was not!"

"Are you sure?"

"Of course I'm sure!"

"Your father never had any affairs?"

I swallowed the answer to that question. Yes, my father had affairs, and yes, I knew he'd fathered at least one sibling who had not been raised with my sisters and me. My half-brother Tierney had showed up last summer. We weren't exactly close, but at least we acknowledged our bond. And our father's tendencies.

Firmly, I said, "David Kaminsky is not my brother. I'm absolutely certain he's not my father's son."

"Then whose son is he?"

"I don't know. Whatever Jenny felt about my father was purely wishful thinking on her part. And then she wrote about it!"

"You realize what you're saying, right?"

"What do you mean?"

"She wrote about it? Either you're not thinking straight," Gus chided, "or you're saying Jenny composed the show, not her father."

"That's exactly what I'm saying," I said. "There's no way Toodles could have written that story about my family. It's all from Jenny's point of view. Toodles never thought two moments about my father, but clearly Jenny was mad about him. And she disliked my mother—so she's making her out to be a fool in the show. And she must have truly hated my grandmother!"

"So why is the family pretending Toodles wrote the show?"

"Because with his name on it, the show would be a Broadway blockbuster no matter how good or bad it genuinely is. But if Jenny was the composer, there's no name recognition. It would be just another risky theatrical investment with lousy roles for the cast, who are all hoping for a vehicle to stardom." I said, "And it's all the motive for several people to kill Jenny."

"Are you serious?"

"Look, Jenny was preparing herself for the opening night. She relentlessly rehearsed the cast herself. She was losing weight, finding the right dress—which is the way any woman would want to present herself to the public, if she expected to be in the spotlight for the first time in her life. She was going to claim her work, and everybody in the cast knew she was going to do it. They had to stop her."

The cab pulled up to the Pendergast Building, and Gus helped me out of the backseat. He paid the driver while I stood unsteadily on the sidewalk. Suddenly, my anger was like sand that had drained out of an hourglass. When the last grain slipped out, I felt very weary. I desperately wanted to go home and eat roast chicken and then maybe a bowl of chocolate-chunk ice cream before burying my face in my pillow.

I sensed Gus watching me as he tucked his wallet back into his hip pocket. He said, "You look like a jumbuck just knocked you over."

"I am sure whatever a jumbuck is, it's no honor to be knocked over by one." I summoned my strength. "Did you call your sister back?"

"Her line was busy. Come on." He reached for my arm. "I'll take you home."

I avoided his touch. "There's no need for that. I'll take the train."

"I didn't mean your home. My apartment is only a couple of blocks from here."

"How convenient for you," I said. "But irrelevant to me."

He rearranged a lock of my hair. "We'll have a drink. Talk about the secret life of Jenny Tuttle. Not only did she have a love child with a player yet to be named, but she mooned over your papa and dared to outdo her famous father by writing a musical of her own. We'll bang out the story tonight, and it will be in print in the morning."

I shook my head firmly. "No, Gus."

"Which part don't you like? The love child? The musical? Or your papa?"

"The part about your apartment."

Lexie had said Gus was my work spouse—someone who could be my career partner, my supporter, one who kept me on the right track, encouraged me to be more than I thought I could. Just now, though, it felt a lot more dangerous than that. We faced each other with more truth in our faces than ever before.

"Nora," he said.

A horn tooted from the street, and we both looked around. Me with relief. Gus with annoyance.

A red pickup truck pulled to the curb, windows rolled down. My sister Emma called, "Hey, Sis! Are you hitchhiking again?

Haven't I warned you about the trouble you could get into with that?"

She burst out of the truck and came around the hood with her most confident, long-legged walk—a cigarette in one hand and her hair standing up in all directions. Evening had just fallen, and the headlights lit up her body like a searchlight. She was wearing boots and skintight riding breeches with a ragged T-shirt that looked as if she'd barely survived a zombie attack.

I thought I heard Gus make a noise in his throat.

"Well, well," she said to him, strolling closer. "You must be Crocodile Dundee. Where's your kangaroo?"

"Em," I said. "This is Gus Hardwicke. He's my boss, so behave yourself. Gus, this is my sister, Emma Blackbird."

I had dreaded the moment when these two met face-to-face. I couldn't keep them apart forever, but I'd held out hope for as long as possible. I fully expected thunder and lightning to come crashing out of the sky in some kind of cosmic sign of Shakespearean calamity, because my little sister was a force of nature where men were concerned. And Gus was almost her match.

Emma blew cigarette smoke and grinned with evil intent.

"Bugger me," Gus said, obviously impressed. "Hard to think you two swam out of the same gene pool."

Emma put her cigarette on her lip and shook his hand hard. "Nora's had more time to grow up and dry off. Me, I'm still in the primordial soup. How about you?"

"I'll take a plunge into just about anything."

She eyed his suit. "You look like you're selling fried chicken in that getup. No, I suppose with you it's shrimp on the barbie. You ever decide to see how the other half lives, Dundee, we'll do a little pub crawl, you and me."

I said, "If I get a vote, I think that's a very bad idea. Are you here to pick me up, Em?"

"Yeah," she said, still giving Gus a long study. "By now Mick's waiting at home after a long day of burying bodies in the Pine Barrens. Let's go."

I turned to Gus. "Thank you. For preventing me from making a bigger fool of myself tonight at the theater. I was ready to storm the stage."

"You're welcome," he said stiffly. "Storm avoided."

"Good night."

"It could have been better."

Emma blew another long, slow stream of blue smoke at Gus. "Don't kiss any koala bears."

He had no answer for that. He put his hands in his trouser pockets and watched in wonder as we climbed into my sister's truck.

Emma tooted her horn and roared away from the curb, heading for home. I collapsed into the seat and rested my head against the hard cushion. My heart was beating like a drum. "I can't remember ever being so happy to see you in my whole life. What brought you here at this precise moment, may I ask?"

"Mick called me, said you hadn't called him back, so he asked me to run down here to pick you up. I figured I'd check the Pendergast Building first." She threw her cigarette out the window. "I saw the way the Aussie was staring. He's got the hots for you!"

"He does not. Well, he does a little."

"You weren't exactly looking innocent either in that getup."

"This getup is a vintage Dior!"

"It makes you look like a pregnant pole dancer."

"Oh, for the love of—"

"It's not your usual style," she insisted. "And he noticed, too. What does Mick think of him? Have they met?"

"They hate each other."

Emma laughed delightedly. "I wouldn't want to be a guy on

Mick's bad side. Dundee could wake up some morning with his own severed dick in his hand."

"Don't be crude," I said.

She smothered her laughter into amused snorts. "You're such a goody-goody, Sis. You're always on your best behavior, and you always do the right thing. Except you have one major character flaw."

"Just one?"

"You like bad boys. You're in love with Mick, but you like Crocodile Dundee, too. Because he's a bad boy."

With a snap, I turned on the radio. The blaring music prevented further conversation until we were out of the city and headed into Bucks County. Emma sang along with the oldies, occasionally sending me amused glances. I thought about scoundrels adding piquancy and cursed to myself.

I didn't like bad boys. I loved Michael, yes, and perhaps his reputation wasn't as sterling as most men's. And Gus? Well, I . . . appreciated him. He could be pushy and annoying, but I enjoyed sparring with him. I felt nothing sexual for him, and I certainly didn't feel as if we shared values or life pursuits. I liked him and wanted to be his friend and certainly his coworker. But that was the sum total of so-called bad boys in my life.

Well, perhaps Todd had been no angel, either. And my college boyfriends were less Rhodes scholars and more the kind of men who broke into the field house late at night to liberate sporting equipment.

Oh, who was I kidding? I was drawn to the wrong men, and I couldn't explain it. I was a Blackbird female, and that's how we were. Nature worked in mysterious, infuriating ways, and my life was a testament to the perversity of the universe. I had made my choice, and to anyone keeping score, Michael was perhaps the baddest of the bad.

Finally I turned off the music. "You like bad boys, too."

She seemed delighted. "Guilty as charged."

"Are you going to tell me who it is? The man you're dating now?"

"I don't have to," she replied. "I'm going to pick him up in New Hope before I take you home. You're gonna meet him in person."

"Do I get a hint now?"

"Nope. What's going on with Libby? Is she making cheesecake for the old guy? What happened to the bug man? I thought he was getting rid of her termites and bringing her dinner. Playing with the kids. Making himself indispensable before making the final assault on Libby's virtue. Have you talked to him? Given him some pointers, maybe?"

"Why would I talk to Perry?"

"Because you're the only one sane enough to hold this family together. You should have a chat with the exterminator before Libby pushes Mr. AARP off into the sunset in his wheelchair."

"I have no intention of discussing anything personal with Perry Delbert. I barely know the man."

"Do you want Libby wasting the best years of her life with a coot who probably needs a penile implant?"

"Sex isn't everything in a relationship. And I thought you were on the other side of this argument! You said she should be thinking about her financial well-being."

"I was kidding. Libby needs a guy who'll light her fire, not just pay the electric bill, just like you and me. I asked around about Oxenfeld, by the way. He's rich and smart, but a social dud. She'd be bored with him in two weeks."

"What else did you learn about Ox?"

"What d'you mean?"

"I think he's mixed up in Jenny Tuttle's death."

Emma's foot faltered on the accelerator. "You mean, like maybe he killed her?"

"Maybe."

"Hey, I only heard that he was a smart producer. He doesn't lose his own money but makes a bundle using other people's cash to finance big shows. And he's never had a loser. That's a big accomplishment in show business. But are you thinking Libby might be in danger?"

"Em, I haven't heard from Libby since Saturday. Do you think she might—"

"Relax. I talked to her this afternoon. She's not being held hostage by a pudgy producer. She's just mad at you. And trying to score the world's best cheesecake recipe."

"Is she super mad at me?"

"Hey, if she's not talking to you, at least she's not planning your wedding, right? No, I think she's more annoyed that you're right about Oxenfeld not being her knight in shining armor. Just to spite you, she's still dating him. Which is loony tunes, but that's Libby for you. Talk to Perry, Sis."

When Emma chose to be insightful, she was often right on the money. I sank back down into the seat and groaned. "Why me?"

In New Hope, Emma took a dark side street and pulled up next to a fire hydrant on the corner by a disreputable tavern. She left the engine running and, whistling cheerfully, went inside to find her date. I waited in silence, mulling over murder and wondering what catastrophe was coming next.

It was a big one.

The door of the bar burst open, sending a shaft of toxic green light out into the street. And the man who came strolling out with Emma on his arm threw back his head and laughed with her. He was handsome, with dark, curly hair, broad shoulders and a wicked grin.

And he was none other than Little Frankie Abruzzo.

I barely held back a scream as Michael's brother opened the passenger door, leaned in and gave me a cocky hello.

A Little Night Murder

He said, "Last time I saw you, weren't you naked?"

If Emma had chosen an international terrorist to shack up with, I don't think she could have made a worse choice in boyfriends. Little Frankie climbed into the passenger seat, crowding me up against my sister and giving my knee a friendly fondle. He breathed beer in my face and leered down the front of my dress. "What's your name again?"

"She's Nora," Emma answered for me. "And she spooks easily, so take your hand off her leg, hotshot."

He laughed and threw his arm across the back of the seat behind me. With his finger, he toyed with my earlobe. I slapped his hand away, making him chortle.

We rode like that all the way to Blackbird Farm—the two of them laughing their heads off and me preventing Little Frankie's roving hands from undressing me. I desperately hoped Michael was already home and safely in bed, where he'd never need to know his brother was back in our lives.

CHAPTER EIGHTEEN

No such luck. Michael was pulling the Escalade through the security gate just as Emma drove into the lane at Blackbird Farm. She scooted her truck under the electronic arm before it came down, and we followed the Escalade around the house. If I wasn't mistaken, there was a new dent in the big SUV's rear bumper.

We all arrived at the back of the house and got out of our respective vehicles. Beside the barn sat the car Rawlins was driving these days. The only good news was that Bridget's convertible was nowhere to be seen. Clouds scudded across the half-moon overhead. There was just enough light for the brothers to recognize each other and take a long moment to plan their respective attacks.

"Oh, hell," Michael said to Little Frankie. "I thought you went back to Vegas."

"I misplaced my stake," his brother said with a grin.

"You mean, you lost it."

Frankie shrugged. "What does it matter? I need some cash, bro. You ready to pay me back?"

I could see Michael was in no mood for fun. He reached one hand into his pocket and came up with a quarter. He tossed it at Little Frankie, who caught it, turned over the coin and gave it a short inspection.

Michael was just barely holding on to his temper. Something had happened earlier, I could see. Now his brother had turned up unexpectedly. Michael was simmering hot.

Frankie missed all the signs and taunted him. "This must mean you're a little short, too, Mick. I guess it's time you found a place for me in the family hierarchy? I need a job—something cushy but lucrative."

Michael stood a couple of inches taller than his brother. I wasn't sure which one was older—Michael didn't like talking with me about his siblings, especially Little Frankie—but I guessed they were born only months apart. Growing up together, they had fought like wolverines. I didn't see any sign their relationship had improved. Michael's black eye seemed to give him an additional advantage in the threatening department.

He said, "Go home, Frank. Maybe Mom has some dishes you could wash."

The loose smile evaporated from Little Frankie's face. "I saved you when no bank would touch your sorry ass."

"And they say there's no more brotherly love."

"Now you're sitting pretty. You owe me."

"Your definition of pretty is faulty." Except he used a different word.

"Hey," Emma said.

"And you," Michael said to her, "should have better taste in men by now."

I said, "I'm hungry. Is anyone else hungry?"

They ignored me. Little Frankie had gone tense all over. Even his hands were balled into tight fists. He said to Michael, "Tell you what. I'll take a piece of Gas N Grub. Seems to me, I've got a right to a sizable chunk. Maybe the gasoline trade could use my particular brand of business acumen."

"Only you could screw up selling gas," Michael replied.

"Then set me up with a territory I can run the way I want to. My own section of the family store."

Michael pocketed his keys. "Run along, Frank."

"I'm not going anywhere. Either you cut me in, or I'm going to Pop."

"Visiting hours are on Saturdays." Michael touched my shoulder and turned me toward the house.

"This isn't over," Little Frankie said. "You hear me, Mick?"

Michael and I walked the length of the flagstones and went up the porch steps together. I heard Emma say, "Time to go, hotshot."

"I got rights," Little Frankie snapped at her. "He owes me, and he knows it."

I unlocked the back door, and Michael and I went into the kitchen. It smelled deliciously of roast chicken. But I wasn't hungry anymore. I heard doors slam, and Emma's truck revved up.

Michael and I faced each other beside the refrigerator. Neither one of us felt like smiling. I said, "He loaned you money to get us stable again. Can you pay him back?"

Michael shook his head. "Not even close. I just committed a quarter of a million dollars for new software."

"A quarter of a—! Michael, that's crazy."

He ran his hand around the back of his head and rubbed it. "Actually, Lexie convinced me it's a smarter way to go. In three months, the software will earn back what it cost and save me a bundle going forward."

"Three months is a long time to have your brother breathing down our necks."

He gathered me close. "My neck," he corrected.

A Little Night Murder

I laid my cheek against his shirt, glad to hold him, glad to feel his arms around me. "We're in this together, remember. For better or for worse."

"I'll figure out something."

"Tell me what happened to the Escalade."

He stiffened almost imperceptibly. "What?"

"I saw the bumper. There's a dent that wasn't there before. What happened?"

He loosened his hold on me. "Minor fender bender. Nothing to worry about."

We were interrupted by the arrival of Rawlins, who came through the butler's pantry talking to someone behind him. Michael and I parted in time to see Rawlins holding the hand of his ex-girlfriend Shawna.

I liked Shawna, and we chatted for a few minutes. If she saw something amiss, she didn't mention it. Instead, she told me she was excited about going back to Harvard in September. But it was clear she and Rawlins wanted to be alone, and maybe Michael and I were subconsciously communicating something was wrong. We thanked them for looking after Noah, and Michael slipped Rawlins some cash—more than a quarter. The teenagers were soon happily dashing down the back steps.

We could have finished our discussion then, but Michael headed for the oven, and I knew I needed time to calm myself, too. I went upstairs to change and check on the baby. Noah was sleeping soundly. I took off my dress and hung it in the closet.

By the time I went back downstairs in my bathrobe, Michael had pulled the chicken out of the oven and was sipping from a glass of wine while putting dinner together. He had fresh-picked green beans in a sauté pan and began slicing chicken off the bone. Over his shoulder, he asked, "Did you make it to that preview thing tonight? I don't suppose you saw Bridget there?"

"I didn't see her there, but maybe I missed her."

"She doesn't exactly blend into the scenery."

"True." I poured myself a glass of milk and sat down at the table. I told him all about *Bluebird of Happiness* and how it was a thinly disguised version of my family's story.

"Wow," he said, knife in one hand, dinner momentarily forgotten as I concluded my tale. "Can they legally do that?"

"Believe me, I'm going to consult a lawyer. As soon as I can afford one, that is."

Michael was already thinking ahead. "So this means the daughter wrote the musical, not her famous dad?"

"Right. But somebody killed her before she could launch her career." After a deep breath to gather my courage to reveal everything, I said, "There's more, Michael."

"More what?"

"Let's have dinner first, and then I'll tell you."

Maybe his temper wasn't yet under control after his brother's reappearance. His voice turned chilly. "Tell me now."

I got up from the table and pulled plates from the cupboard, silverware from the drawer. I helped myself to a slice of chicken and plucked a green bean from the hot pan with my fingers. To check if it was done, I bit into the bean and found it delicious, with a hint of butter and garlic.

Continuing to assemble my supper, I said, "Gus offered me a promotion today."

Michael's lazy eyes were narrow with suspicion. "If that was good news, you'd be happier about it. What kind of promotion?"

"It's a good one. Stan Rosenstatz has to retire. Gus wants me to take over as the editor of the Lifestyle section."

He leaned over and used the knife to spear another slice of chicken and add it to my plate. "What's the catch?"

"There's no catch. It's a good job—better than the one I have, with a raise and everything. For one, it will make things much easier around here when I go back to work after the babies are born. My hours would be more consistent. I wouldn't have to be out so late at night."

"You like going to parties," Michael observed.

I felt my smile waver. "Yes, it's a good excuse to drink champagne and talk to nice people."

"But it's time for a new challenge. Something that lights your fire. I get that."

"Gus has another agenda. And . . ." I hesitated but knew I had to keep going. "It came up today." I sat down at the table.

Michael stayed where he was and waited for the other shoe to drop.

I tried not to let his steady gaze unnerve me. I picked up my fork. "You know the Hardwickes are trying to buy more media assets in the U.S. They're trying to strike a deal with a Philadelphia conglomerate, except the conglomerate is run by a group of local characters who balk at selling to a foreign company."

"I read about it. Looks to me like old man Hardwicke just needs to offer another billion dollars to the pot."

Carefully, I said, "Money isn't the issue holding things up anymore. The sellers are patriotic. Very made-in-America, proud of their heritage. So the Hardwickes felt they needed an American connection to make themselves more appealing to the conglomerate."

"What kind of connection?"

"A family connection. A personal connection." Proceeding steadily, I said, "They thought it would be useful if one of the family had an ally in Philadelphia. Someone born here, the birthplace of freedom, that kind of thing."

"Wait a minute."

"It sounds completely stupid, the way I'm saying it. With the acquisition in mind, Gus told his father that he'd met someone. That he was engaged to someone who would make the Hardwicke empire more palatable to the seller. The whole family is very excited about this development. They think it's going to make the deal go through. They're hoping everyone can be one big happy—"

Darkly, Michael said, "Tell me this scheme has nothing to do with you."

"I knew nothing about it until today. Will you sit down, please?"

"It's really you?" His voice had an incredulous edge. "You and Hardwicke?"

"Obviously, it's *not* me, because I just learned about it. But—well, yes, Gus has led his family to believe he and I are—that we're together."

Michael exploded with a curse and began pacing. "That son of a bitch! He's been looking for a way to get into your pants ever since he first—"

"He's not getting into anything of mine," I said, "so let's not go there."

"He wants you to call off our wedding, doesn't he?"

"I told him that wasn't going to happen, but—"

"*But* . . . Are you serious?"

"Let me finish! I don't care what Gus or his family wants. I'm having nothing to do with their negotiations. I have insisted Gus tell his family the truth."

Michael laughed shortly and splashed more wine into his glass. "I'm sure he went straight to daddy and came clean."

"Not yet, but he will, I promise."

"And our wedding?"

I tried to swallow a bite of my dinner, but it got stuck in my throat. I sipped my milk, but it didn't help. My stomach felt as if it would reject anything I sent down there, anyway, so I sat up straight and said, "Tell me what happened to the Escalade."

The question brought him up short. "I already told you. I had a fender bender. Nothing serious."

"Where?"

"In New Hope."

"Who hit you?"

"Kid in an SUV."

"Was it one of the boys who attacked you at the ice cream shop?"

"No. I don't know. A kid—that's all I know. He came up behind me at a stoplight, rear-ended me and took off. I got his license number."

"Did you call the police?"

"Why am I getting the third degree? It was a minor traffic—"

"Were you hurt?"

"Nora—"

"Michael, this week you've been shot and punched in the eye and accosted by a boy with a gun, and now somebody has tried to mow you down with a truck—"

"I was winged, not shot. And it was my mother who hit me, nobody dangerous, and the truck thing was only—"

"Don't shout. Were you hurt?" I asked again.

He rubbed the back of his neck again and didn't answer.

I wished I could risk drinking a glass of wine. I looked up at the cobwebby chandelier above us. "Emma says I have a weakness for bad boys."

Low voiced, Michael said, "I've been good for you, Nora."

"What are you doing with Lexie?"

For another uncomfortable second, he didn't respond. Finally, he said, "I can't tell you."

I put my forehead down on the table. It was cool, and the kitchen was quiet. When I was pretty sure I could speak without shouting, I said, "I love you, Michael." I sat up again. "I want us to have our baby and a lot more after this one. I want you to make a wonderful success of Gas N Grub, and my job—well, whatever it is, I'll learn to love it." My voice began to rise again. "But I swear, if you get into trouble with this thing with Lexie, or you get yourself killed and leave me alone with children—"

"I don't believe this! You're really thinking of calling off the wedding."

"I don't want you hurt!"

"I'm not getting hurt!"

"You've done nothing *but* get hurt for a week! And now there's a gang of crazy teenagers trying to kill you!"

He drained his glass and set it on the counter. He said, "I'm going for a drive."

"Now?"

"Yes, now. If I don't, I'm going to say something neither one of us is going to like." He grabbed his keys.

I got up hastily from the table. "It's late. Your parole. You have to be home by midnight or—"

He shook his head. "I gotta get out of here."

"Michael, please. Don't go. I love you."

He stopped at the door and turned around. He came back to me, grabbed me around the waist and bent to kiss me on the mouth. It was a hard kiss, not gentle in the least. When he pulled back, his gaze was fiery blue. "I love you back."

He left.

I tried to eat a few bites of my healthy supper, but eventually I abandoned it on the table and instead dug a carton of ice cream out of the freezer. I used a spoon to eat right out of the carton. I thought about the phone call Michael had made to me just a few nights ago. He had been so happy to remind me that we'd be married on Friday. Now he was crushed, and it was all my fault.

To avoid bursting into tears, I cut the rest of the chicken off the bone and put the fragrant meat into the refrigerator. He'd come home soon, and we'd talk it through, I told myself. I washed the dishes while crunching a Tums. Any minute, he'd be back. He'd walk through the door with a wisecrack about Gus, and we'd make peace. I wiped the counters and poured detergent into the dishwasher. I pushed the "start" button and listened to the water slosh. Eventually, though, I turned off the kitchen lights and went upstairs. I checked on Noah and got ready for bed. I grabbed a book, plumped my pillow and climbed under the sheets to read.

I woke up when Baby Girl did a barrel roll. The book was still in my lap. I reached for Michael, but his side of the bed was cool.

With my heart in my throat, I pulled the clock off my night table. Nearly two in the morning—long past his midnight curfew. I hurried to the window and looked down. The Escalade wasn't in the backyard. Michael hadn't come home yet.

I called his cell phone. No answer.

An awful thought sent me plunking down on the bed. I didn't know why I hadn't thought of it before. Had Michael gone into the city? Had he gone looking for Gus?

CHAPTER NINETEEN

n the morning, Noah woke me with a happy yell, and I groggily pulled him out of his crib and changed him. He was delighted to see me but tugged at the bodice of my nightie to see more.

I said, "Are you turning into a bad boy, too?"

We went downstairs, and I sliced him a banana. I tried Michael's cell while our breakfast cooked. No answer. I wondered if I should call Gus, but I was afraid how that conversation might go.

When the house phone rang, I dashed across the kitchen to grab it.

But it was Libby's accusatory voice on the line. She said, "I haven't forgiven you yet."

"Libby! Are you—? I can't talk long."

"Forgive me for interrupting your life," she said frostily. "Call me back if you ever get a spare minute for your sister."

"No, wait! I'm sorry. I'm upset this morning. Michael. He— well—"

"Is something wrong?"

A Little Night Murder

I let out a quavering sigh. I knew it was wrong to trouble Libby with my problems, but I said, "We had an argument last night, and he left. He hasn't come home yet."

"What kind of argument? About your sex life? Because if that's the issue, I have a number of books and even a video that—"

"It wasn't about sex. It was about the curse. The Blackbird curse."

"What about it?"

I heard myself give a hiccough, and I realized I was fighting back tears again. I couldn't stop myself from blurting out, "Last week we got a marriage license. We have an appointment with a judge. We're getting married on Friday, and I even have a dress to wear and everything, but ever since we decided, he's been having one accident after another and I—I'm afraid something horrible has happened, Libby. He's badly hurt this time or—or—"

"He's not dead," she said with authority. "Calm down."

"I can't help it. I'm so worried—"

"I'm coming over right now. Hold on a little longer. I'll be there in a few minutes."

I should have been thrown into a panic. I had stupidly revealed my wedding plan to the one person who could hijack the whole thing and turn it into some kind of spectacle with sword-wielding gladiators and half-naked strippers and trained poodles, for all I knew. But this morning I was strangely comforted that my sister was on her way. Noah watched my face intently, trying to decipher how I was feeling. I didn't know myself.

The phone rang again, and I grabbed it.

In my ear, Michael said, "I'm allowed one phone call."

"You've been arrested?" I cried—relieved to hear his voice but panicked all over again. And a flicker of anger licked up from inside me, too. "What for?"

"Suspicion of DUI, whatever the hell that is." He sounded bad tempered. "Ricci stopped me about a mile from the farm. He didn't even give me a Breathalyzer. Just hauled me in here to cool down, he said." In a mutter, Michael added, "I had one glass of wine, that's it. Maybe one and a half. Anyway, I need you to call Cannoli and Sons."

Michael could have contacted them himself with his one phone call, but he'd chosen to call me instead. That thought gave me some reassurance. "Okay," I said. "I'll call them. Are you all right? Were you driving erratically?"

"Ricci seemed to think so." Michael was silent for a moment. Then he asked, "Has Bridget showed up there?"

"Bridget? No, should I be expecting her?"

"I don't know. They keep asking me about her. More than before."

"She's the reason you've been arrested?"

"I'm not arrested yet, just being held. Last night they asked me about Bridget and today the questions keep coming, which has me thinking this whole DUI thing is bogus. To get something out of me."

"You think they want Bridget?" I asked.

"Yeah, definitely. The cops still consider her the big suspect in your murder case." He blew a sigh and got quiet. The irritation dropped from his voice and Michael said with sincerity, "Sorry, Nora. For a lot of stuff."

"Me, too," I said, my heart filling up.

"Is the wedding back on?"

"Brace yourself. I accidentally spilled the beans to Libby."

"Uh-oh. Has she hired a brass band already?"

"Maybe. Sorry. How long are they going to keep you?"

"I dunno. Call Cannoli, please? We'll get started on the usual routine. I gotta go."

We hung up, and I sat down, trembling with relief. Michael hadn't gone roaring off to murder Gus. Nor had he driven himself into a telephone pole or been accosted by marauding teenage criminals. I was pretty sure Ricci had done me a favor by stopping Michael from whatever he'd stormed off to do last night.

With Noah on my hip, I looked through our collection of refrigerator magnets and found the business card with various numbers for Cannoli and Sons. Some people kept phone numbers for their plumbers or pizza delivery on the fridge, but we had lawyers and a bail bondsman.

To Noah, I said, "Trust me, this is not the kind of life I expected."

Left-handed, he threw a hunk of banana at the refrigerator.

I held Noah while I called the Cannoli offices. I spoke with Armand, Michael's good friend among all the Cannolis. He said he'd get right on the case. He sounded annoyingly delighted. He asked after the coming baby, and I told him we were right on schedule. He wished me well, and we hung up.

Libby's minivan pulled up behind the house. I wasn't sure whether to be sorry or relieved that I had given her the password to our new security gate.

She blew into the kitchen carrying her son Max. Libby put Max down and enveloped me in a warm hug. "Darling Nora, are you okay?"

"A little better. Michael just called." My throat contracted, making speech difficult. "He's been arrested."

"Arrested!" She held me by my shoulders and looked appalled.

"Not arrested," I corrected myself, dashing a tear from my cheek. "But he's with the police, being questioned."

"Well, that's a safe place to be, isn't it? Why, look, it's Noah!" She smiled brightly into the baby's face. "Hello, little sweet one.

Your cousin Max has come for a play date! And you have no idea how much he's looking forward to meeting someone in this family he can bully."

I snatched Noah closer. "Max isn't going to bully Noah."

"He's going to try," Libby predicted.

Max smiled up at me. He was eighteen months old and starting to look like a boy, not a baby anymore. He'd gotten a haircut recently, and it made him look like a tough guy. Except for his dimples. I tried to lean down to give him a kiss, but I couldn't get past my belly. I settled for ruffling his hair.

Libby watched me. "Are you really okay?"

"I'm getting there," I said, glad that my voice sounded stronger. "Thank you for coming, Libby. After the way I behaved toward you about Ox, I don't deserve it. I'm sorry for being such a jerk."

"Nonsense. We're all allowed a little slip of sanity now and then. A cutting remark one minute, and you're forgiven the next. That's what sisters do."

Libby was dressed in a tennis skirt and beaded sandals that made her legs look slim and tan and as smooth as if she'd endured a recent waxing as well as time in the tanning booth. Her hair had new highlights. Her bosom was barely contained by a stylish halter top printed with little alligators. A pair of gold bracelets I didn't recognize jingled on her arm, and a new gold necklace punctuated by tiny gold hearts decorated her neck. In other words, she looked like a Main Line housewife—or an aspiring one. I suppressed the urge to ask if she was already pricing mansions in upscale neighborhoods.

With a gleam in his eyes, Max toddled toward me, his predatory gaze fixed on Noah. Libby made no effort to discourage him.

I retreated around the table with Noah in my arms, but pretty soon Max was chasing us. "Just because Max's siblings pick on him doesn't mean we can't break the chain of behavior."

"That chain is too strong for me," Libby said. "I gave up refereeing my children years ago. Is there coffee?"

Over my shoulder, Noah threw a chunk of banana at Max, and it hit him square in the chest. Max wobbled to a halt, astonished.

I said, "You can make a fresh pot, if you like."

"Maybe I should make some muffins, too. We need to do some carbo loading if we're going to plan a wedding. That Man of Yours might be with the police, but he'll surely be out by Friday." Energized, Libby began bustling around my kitchen. "I presume the guest list is small, since the wedding is happening so soon. Have you booked a restaurant for dinner afterward? Or should we try to throw together something more daring? A champagne picnic would be perfect on a summer evening. Wait—could we commandeer one of those city tour buses? The double-decker kind! Do you think we could get someone to cater on a bus? Oh—and have you made arrangements for music? Because is there anything more romantic than a strolling violinist? I just heard the most wonderful young man playing the violin on the sidewalk out in front of the Ritz-Carlton the other night. We must brainstorm. No idea is too outré at this stage."

I held back a groan. Not only had the nutty wedding ideas started to fly, but she had been at the Ritz-Carlton at night. Probably with Ox.

Libby didn't notice my consternation and busied herself with the coffeemaker. "If you're having the wedding in a judge's chamber, we can't exactly go all out with decorations. But balloons make a big statement for not a lot of bother. Just pick a color and buy several dozen and—presto! Instant party! But I also love a pretty wedding—pink flowers, children in adorable clothes. Me in a flowing dress. What about a theme? How do you feel about a luau? Is that overdone—or on the cusp of wonderful? I would look great in a grass skirt!"

"Libby—"

"Right, right. First we should discuss the guest list. How many people are we talking? Two dozen or two hundred? I'm sure there are a few people who will be insulted if they're not invited. For instance, what about his mother?"

I groaned for real. "What about his mother?"

"Do you know she is sleeping in her convertible at the end of your driveway?"

I handed Noah to Libby and went hastily through the butler's pantry to the front door. I hauled it open and looked outside. Sure enough, the white convertible was parked beside my mailbox.

I went upstairs and pulled on a pair of yoga pants. I grabbed a T-shirt from the collection of Libby's hand-me-downs. I was getting to the bottom of the pile, so the more objectionable slogans were coming up. This one read MY OTHER KIDS HOPE THIS ONE'S A PONY. I didn't have time to be choosy and yanked it over my head.

I went down to the kitchen and said to my sister, "Can you look after Noah while I go get Bridget?"

Libby was already ensconced at my table with a cup of coffee and a stack of magazines she must have retrieved from my recycling bin. "Of course. Nora, dear, what would you think of a double wedding?"

I congratulated myself on not screaming. Instead, I put up one finger to delay what was coming next. "Hold that thought. I'll be right back."

I went out onto the back porch and was confronted by Libby's eight-year-old daughter, Lucy. She was barefoot and wearing a bathing suit and had an army surplus gas mask over her face. Nothing new, in other words. Her blond curls stuck out from under the straps of the mask. Her knees were covered with Band-Aids, and she held a sparkly magic wand in her hand, gripping it like a sword.

She pulled the gas mask up onto her head and said, "Aunt Nora, can I let Ralphie out to play?"

"When Michael gets back," I promised. I couldn't cope with both Lucy *and* a five-hundred-pound pig.

"I need a sworn enemy," she said very seriously. "Ralphie could be my sworn enemy, couldn't he?"

"Why do you need a sworn enemy, Luce?"

"I'm a pirate."

"I see."

"Is Uncle Mick a pirate? He looks like a pirate."

She was right. On the other hand, I sensed she was already on her way to developing an attraction to bad boys, too, so I said, "I'll be back in a minute, Lucy. We need to talk more about pirates."

"Okay." She sat down on the top step of the porch to wait.

I plodded my way down to the mailbox. I let myself out the security gate and approached the convertible cautiously. Peeking inside, I saw Bridget sprawled out in the driver's seat, which was fully reclined. An errant lock of her red hair was curled drunkenly around her nose. She had a snore like a buzz saw.

An empty beer can had been thrown onto the ground beside the car. A lone shoe lay beside the can. I picked up both items and leaned over her.

"Bridget?" I touched her shoulder gently. "Bridget?"

She gave a startled snort and flailed around for a second before grabbing the steering wheel and pulling herself to a sitting position. She wore a white off-the-shoulder sweater that had slipped far enough to show the straps of a lacy purple bra. Her matching purple skirt was hiked up high on her shapely thighs, and her other shoe was where it was supposed to be—on her foot. I noticed her toes were painted hot pink. Her fingernails were freshly done with a coordinating shade. Today she also wore a necklace that featured a very large diamond set inside two leaping dolphins that created the yin-yang symbol.

I handed her the other shoe and wondered if all her diamonds were gifts from the men with whom she had brief friendships. "Are you okay?" I asked.

She slipped her shoe back on. "Where's Harvey?"

"Who's Harvey?"

She yawned. Then, like a sleepy child, she rubbed both her eyes with her fists. When she stopped, she looked like a raccoon with a hangover.

She blinked as if the sunlight pained her. "I can't remember who Harvey was, but I think maybe I left him at the Best Western. Is there a Starbucks around here? Or is it just cows and pine trees, *Little House on the Prairie*?"

"Pretty much cows and trees," I agreed. "My sister is making coffee in the kitchen. Would you like to come inside?"

"The sister who's stealing Oxy away from me?"

"I'm not sure if she's actually—"

"It's okay." Bridget used a button to return her seat to the upright position. "Ox is kind of a snooze. Not my type, except for the audition potential. And he's the age when a guy starts looking for a nurse who'll change his diapers when the time comes. I've got too much living ahead of me to start down that road. She can have him. You got any Twizzlers?"

"Twizzlers? You mean, the candy?"

"Yeah, there's nothing like a Twizzler first thing in the morning. That, or a quickie. You have any? Twizzlers, I mean?"

"Sorry, no Twizzlers. But there's oatmeal. And Libby is threatening to make muffins."

Bridget rolled her eyes and adjusted the rearview mirror to get a look at her makeup. With a wince, she reached into another new handbag for her cosmetics. First she wiped away the previous day's layer of mascara by licking her thumb and smudging it off. Then she began repairing her face with a drugstore lipstick, more mascara and powder.

While she worked, I said, "Did you have any luck finding the mystery investor? The one who's financing *Bluebird of Happiness*?"

She gave me a measuring glance. "You've got your teeth into this Tuttle thing, haven't you? I kinda like that about you." She jerked her head in the direction of the passenger seat. "Hop in. Take a load off. I'll tell you the whole story. What I know so far, that is."

I went around the convertible and climbed in. She took the empty beer can from me and tossed it into the backseat.

"Here's the thing," she said, handing me the lipstick to hold while she applied mascara. "I paid calls on every single one of the potential investors that Oxy told me about—all the old-fart guys, plus one real stick-in-the-mud lady who threw in a few dollars to get the production started. And not one of them has met this mystery moneyman."

"So it's somebody only Boom Boom knows?"

Bridget raised a withering eyebrow. "She's the only one who claims to be communicating with him."

"Claims to—?"

For a moment, she eyed my shirt. "What does that mean, exactly? The kids are hoping for a pony?"

I looked down at my borrowed maternity shirt. "It's—well, it's a joke."

"Funny thing about humor. Not everybody likes the same joke. Me, I like a good dirty story. I once had a boyfriend who was a comedian—did late-night stand-up on cruise ships. Lemme tell you, he was the best in bed—always had me laughing. He loved aromatherapy, too, kinda wacky. But you probably get the vapors if somebody talks about sex around you."

"You've met my sister Libby, right? You need to get to know her better."

Bridget allowed a tiny smile. "I think maybe we should bust in on Boom Boom this morning and find out the truth about this secret investor. Big Frankie always said surprise is a good weapon. Wanna come?"

"Bridget, right now, the police are holding Michael—hoping he has information about your whereabouts."

"They're still looking for me? What for?"

"Because you're still a suspect in Jenny's death!"

"Why?" she demanded.

"Because you wrote letters to her. Letters that had a—well, an undercurrent of coercion."

"I had a boyfriend once who owned a TV network. He said honey was better than a stick, but in the bedroom he really preferred the stick—on his own backside, if you get my drift. Lots of coercion." She tucked her compact into her handbag and zipped it up. "Hell, you don't get ahead in show business unless you blow your own horn. Cops ought to know that."

"Maybe you should tell the police that yourself. If it's all a simple misunderstanding, it could be cleared up very easily. I wonder if you'd consider turning yourself in—that is, answering a few questions for the police—so Michael could be released."

She waved off that suggestion. "Every once in a while it does him good to get locked up—makes him think about what he has to do to stay out of jail, know what I mean?"

"But—"

"Buckle up, babycakes." Bridget grabbed her white-framed sunglasses off the rearview mirror where they'd been dangling and put them on her nose, then checked her reflection again and tousled her hair into a fluffy style. She started the convertible's engine. "I got a few things I want to straighten out with Boom Boom."

"I can't leave. Not right now. My sister is—"

"She won't miss you for a coupla minutes. Here. Put on some lipstick, will you?" She tossed her makeup bag at me. "And some mascara wouldn't hurt, either. You look a little pale this morning. Or maybe it's that shirt. Used to be, you could get real nice maternity clothes at Penney's. On the other hand, could be you just don't have good fashion sense. I could help you with that."

I buckled my seat belt, fearing the worst about Bridget's driving. I pegged her for a speed demon, but she drove the car quite sensibly. With the top down, the fresh air seemed to reinvigorate her, too.

I used the flip-down mirror to obey her makeup demands. Her shade of lipstick actually looked pretty great on me. We stopped at the Starbucks in New Hope to pick up a low-fat latte for Bridget.

"You sure you don't want a coffee?"

"Thank you, but no. I've given up caffeine until after the baby is born."

Bridget gave me a blank-faced look. "Well, while I was carrying Mickey, I gave up smoking pot, so that's something. Try some mascara."

A touch of mascara is always good for self-confidence. Emboldened, I said, "Do you mind telling me about Michael? When he was a baby?"

"Oh, I hardly saw him at all until he was five or six, when he could hold a conversation. Playgrounds—what a bore. Baseball games—even worse! But I liked taking him to restaurants. You can thank me for his good table manners. And how to decide on a wine? He could talk to a waiter about wine when he was twelve. He was a whosit—a prodigy."

"But when he was an infant. You didn't even . . . hold him?"

"Heck no, I had to get back to work right after he was born. In those days I had a boyfriend who ran a club in Atlantic City, sort of

305

a classy place, you know? He wanted me onstage when the fall season started, so I got back to fighting trim as soon as possible. Anyway, Mick was better off with Big Frankie. Frankie, he was a good father to his boys. They did all the sports and outdoor stuff—hunting and fishing. Mick got good at baseball. Or was it basketball? I forget which he told me about."

"But when Michael was a baby, did you ever—"

"What are you so worried about?" She finally tipped down her sunglasses to skewer me with a look. "Let me tell you, I read about this hormone—oxytocin. It's a whattayacallit—a female hormone that women get. It kicks in right after giving birth, and it makes us so we wake up when we hear a baby cry, and we go pick up the baby and take care of him. It's natural. So don't you worry. The hormones will take care of everything."

"But his mother. The woman who raised him, I mean, do you think she ever—"

"Big Frankie's wife? God, what a bitch. She was all about rules. Still is. Rules, rules, rules! So I figured my job was to give my boy some fun. Okay, my only rule was for myself—I wasn't going to use him to pick up guys. But for him—we did all kinds of goofy stuff together. Like go-karts. He loved go-karts. And the auto show—that was me who got him interested in cars, y'know. And I bought him Batman underpants every year for his birthday. What kid doesn't want to feel like Batman sometimes? I just did stuff that felt like fun. But you? The two of you'll do fine."

"I—I know we will."

Bridget glanced at me between sips of her latte. "Look, baby-cakes," she said, more kindly than before, "don't fret so much, okay? My Mickey, he's ten times the man his father is. And you? I can tell you're gonna be a great mom. You're the warm-and-fuzzy type. Except you're also the pit bull that doesn't give up. Which is a good combo. The two of you love each other like crazy, too. I can see that. Mick gets all mushy when he talks about you. Kids are going to make that kind of crazy love even better. It's a little late for second thoughts anyway. You can't stop what's coming, right?" She poked Baby Girl with one of her long fingernails and laughed.

"Right," I said, thinking her laugh sounded a lot like Michael's when he was really happy.

As we pulled up to the entrance to both driveways, I spotted several ominous vehicles parked in front of Lexie's house. Two large black SUVs and a plain blue sedan.

To Bridget, I said, "Pull up to Lexie's house, will you, please? Something's going on."

I heaved myself out of the low-slung car and went up the stone steps and between the tall columns to the front door. A moment after the bell chimed, Lexie's houseman appeared. He peeked through the glass panel on one side of the door before opening it. His face was not welcoming.

"Is Lexie okay?" I asked Samir.

He did not invite me in. Dressed in his crispest white shirt and dress slacks that he wore on formal occasions, he said, "Miss Lexie isn't here, Miss Blackbird."

But who was? And if Lexie was off the premises, where was she? I wanted to ask him questions, but cross-examining the help was not acceptable behavior, and we both knew it. I thanked him and returned unwillingly to the convertible.

Bridget was flicking through her cell phone for messages with one hand and sipping her latte with the other. When I opened the car door, she put her phone away. Pleased, she said, "I just remembered who Harvey is."

"Who is he?"

"Pack Man! He's the suitcase king—the guy who makes those

fancy rolling suitcases in those late-night TV commercials." Her face sparkled with delight. "You know—the suitcase that the big python squeezes? The python was rented, though, not his pet. I asked. If I'm going to get squeezed, I don't want it done by a snake. I met him at a sports bar last night. He was kinda cute. Now—what's up?"

I could hardly keep up with Bridget. "I'm not sure. My friend isn't home, but she has visitors."

"Federal visitors." Bridget pointed at the nearest SUV. "Those are government license plates."

They were. Not reporters, but federal employees. Which gave me another twist of anxiety.

"I didn't hook up with Big Frankie and not learn a few things," Bridget assured me. "Is your friend in some kind of trouble?"

"I thought she just got *out* of trouble. But now . . ."

Bridget patted my knee. "You shouldn't worry unless there's really something to worry about. There's a worry hormone, too, except I forget what it's called. But it's bad for your baby, so chill. Maybe your friend is just having a little party."

I doubted it. What concerned me even more than the possibility of Lexie being questioned by some kind of federal agency was that Michael might also be involved in whatever had brought the officers to her door.

Bridget spun her car around, and a moment later we were heading up the other driveway to the Tuttle house.

"Now, see here," Bridget said, shutting off the engine. "You better let me do the talking. I've got a way with show-business people. They don't always respond to please and thank-you and all that good-girl stuff."

"What are you planning to do?"

She gave me a wink and a grin. "We're gonna muscle these

people a little. You'll see. I learned a lot of things from Big Frankie. We'll get some answers."

Muscling sounded like a good idea to me. Foremost, I had a few things I wanted to make clear about using my family as a plot for a musical.

CHAPTER TWENTY

Bridget dropped her empty latte cup into the planter on the porch. We rang the bell three times before Fred Fusby finally opened the front door. He wore striped pajamas that showed several inches of bare, skinny ankle. Hastily, he had knotted an ascot around his neck. His hair stood up on end, and he could hardly open his eyes.

"Fred?" I said when Bridget failed to start her muscling. "Remember us?"

"Yeah," he said, scratching his head and squinting at my shirt to make sense of what it said. "Of course. What time is it? The preview ran long last night, and then we had notes."

"Notes?"

Bridget pushed past Fred and strode into the house. "Notes are when the director tells everybody what they did wrong." She spun on her heel and tilted up into Fred's sleepy face. "Isn't that right, handsome?"

He woke up fast. "Uh, right."

"How did everybody do? Boom Boom was a big blue bust, wasn't she?"

Uneasily, Fred said, "There's room for improvement. But that's what rehearsals are for."

"Hm." Bridget tapped her toe while giving Fred a long once-over. "You got any Twizzlers around the house, Fred?"

"Twizzlers? The candy? Uh, no."

"There's nothing like a Twizzler first thing in the morning. Except for one thing."

She grabbed Fred by the ascot and began pulling him in the direction of the cast's wing of the house. Obviously, Bridget knew her way around the Tuttle mansion. Fred followed her like a gangly wolfhound on a short leash.

I said to their disappearing backs, "Maybe I'll go look in on Boom Boom."

Bridget waved over her shoulder and kept going. I went up the staircase and found Boom Boom's room. I knocked, didn't hear a response, but decided to enter anyway.

The bedroom was empty. Boom Boom wasn't in the bathroom, either. I went to the window and peered down onto the terrace. There, on a lounge chair, Boom Boom lay sunning herself. At least, I assumed it was Boom Boom. I recognized her turban. She was completely wrapped in a bathrobe with a towel on her head, covering her face. A tall glass containing some amber-colored beverage stood on the table beside her. Boom Boom didn't move. She was probably exhausted after a night of ruining my grandmother's good name. I considered grabbing the nearest lamp and throwing it down at her.

But I refrained. Instead, I snooped through the collection of prescription bottles on her bedside table. There were so many—all with names of medications I didn't recognize—that surely anyone would have a hard time keeping them straight. I wondered how easily anyone living in the house could come into this room and steal a few pills without Boom Boom missing them.

Very easily.

I perched on the edge of the chair at the makeup mirror and pondered. Why had the nurse died? If someone laced her cake with a medication—who might have had a motive to do it? To shut her up, maybe? Or to punish her for killing Jenny? Had the nurse been part of a plan to kill Jenny? And had she died for it?

I heard raised voices from downstairs and went out onto the landing. I peered over the banister and saw Poppy Fontanna. She was wearing a set of striped pajamas that matched those Fred had had on. Poppy had tied a kerchief around her head, and it made her look like Rosie the Riveter in the old propaganda poster. She held a skillet in two hands like a tennis racquet.

"I step out of the bedroom to make him some pancakes, and this is what happens? You stay away from Fred, you crazy maniac!" she cried in her baby voice. "Get out and don't come back!"

In high heels, Bridget stood almost a foot taller than Poppy. "If you had what it takes to keep your man, he wouldn't come after me."

"He wasn't looking for you! He was minding his own business!" Poppy was panting with exertion. "Now, go away!"

"You're just scared I can beat you out of your role," Bridget taunted.

"I am not, you—you *amateur!*" Poppy lunged forward and managed to swat Bridget across her backside with the skillet. "I'm not letting anybody grab that role away from me—not you, not anybody! I'm done playing second banana!"

I headed downstairs to intervene. "Ladies, please!"

"You again," Poppy snapped at me. "Back to do more damage

with your poison pen? I read the review in this morning's paper. Thanks for nothing."

"I didn't write anything for this morning's paper."

"Oh, no? Then who butchered *Bluebird* before we even got the show on its feet? Wait till Boom Boom reads the review. She'll have you fired."

I pointed at the French doors. "She's out on the terrace. Let's go see what she has to say."

Everyone trooped out through the French doors. I followed as quickly as I could manage. By the time I got outside, Poppy had ripped the towel and the bathrobe off Boom Boom. Except Boom Boom wasn't there. What I had assumed was the old woman's sleeping body turned out to be a carefully constructed human form fashioned out of throw pillows.

"Where's Boom Boom?" Poppy shrieked with all the drama of a star in the spotlight.

"She's probably having breakfast," Fred said, putting his arm around Poppy to calm her.

"Or she's upstairs sleeping," Bridget supplied. "Jeez, calm down."

"Boom Boom's not upstairs," I reported. "But she can't have gone far. Not in the shape she's in. When was the last time anyone saw her?"

Fred said, "Last night, taking a curtain call. Except the audience had already left the theater. She's so blind she was bowing and throwing kisses to empty seats while the rest of us tried to figure out how to escape out the back without getting rotten fruit thrown at us."

Bridget grinned. "The show was a bomb, huh? I coulda told you that."

I said, "Did Boom Boom come home with the rest of you?"

"I wish she had," Poppy said bitterly. "We could have tossed the old blue broad over a bridge in the dark and been rid of her for good."

"So . . . where is she?" Bridget asked.

"I don't know, and I don't care," Poppy snapped, jutting her chin.

Bridget gave me a stink eye. "I have a bad feeling about this, babycakes."

I had a bad feeling, too. And not just because of Poppy's overheated acting.

We went out the front door just ahead of the cast-iron pan Poppy threw after us. It clanged on the sidewalk and bounced down the steps with a sound like church bells. Bridget jumped behind the wheel without opening the car door. I barely made it to the convertible by the time Bridget was revving the engine.

She floored the accelerator, and we shot down the driveway. I got my seat belt fastened just as we hit the road and took off like a bullet.

Bridget turned to me, blue gaze delighted. "How about that Fontanna girl? She's a piece of work, huh? I *like* her!"

"Eyes on the road, please!"

Bridget obeyed and slowed to the speed limit. "She's got a killer instinct, doesn't she? My money's on her for murdering Jenny. Who else could get mad enough to kill somebody?"

"She's certainly mad right now."

"Want to hear what I learned from Fred about the mystery investor? Yesterday Boom Boom announced that he *died*! She claimed he choked on a chicken bone and died."

"So Boom Boom really made him up. There is no mystery investor."

"Boom Boom had everybody snowed."

"She pretended to have a big investor so they could lure others into putting their money into the show. Question is, was it just

Boom Boom's plan? Or were they all in on the fraud? And," I said, "maybe they were all in on the murders, too."

"Jeez," said Bridget, delighted. "You've got quite a criminal mind, haven't you?"

On the way home, Bridget sang show tunes at the top of her lungs.

CHAPTER TWENTY-ONE

She dropped me at Blackbird Farm and resisted all my efforts to get her to stay for breakfast. Or to call the police and turn herself in. She seemed completely unaffected by the idea of Michael languishing in jail while she avoided an interrogation.

"Why won't she answer a few simple questions?" Libby demanded. "In my experience, talking to the police can sometimes be very pleasant."

I couldn't contain my exasperation. "I can only guess she must have something to hide."

I noticed Libby was packing a selection of my magazines into her handbag while Max whimpered from the safety of the high chair. Noah was on the floor, trying his darnedest to pull himself to an upright position and climb up to Max to torment him. He had a raptorlike gleam in his eyes.

To Libby, I said, "Can't you stay for lunch?"

Libby shook her head. "I think Max has had enough tension for one day. I'm taking him home before Noah gives him some kind of inferiority complex. You should try some socialization techniques with that boy, Nora. Before he needs a serious psychological intervention for his aggression."

I thought Noah looked quite happy. He gave me a big grin while making a grab for Max's dangling foot. Max shrieked with panic.

"Besides," Libby said, "I need time to process a few wedding ideas. You know, to formulate a creative plan. You want your wedding to be memorable, right? Well, I'm the girl for that job!"

"Libby, we're hoping for a quiet wedding, just family and—"

"Nonsense! You'll regret a quiet wedding—take it from me. My second wedding was a complete disappointment. I have always been sorry I decided against the jugglers."

I needed time to formulate a better argument if I was going to win this battle. Or I could count on Libby getting distracted by something else. She had the attention span of a hummingbird. There was no telling where she might decide to devote her considerable energies. I plucked up Noah, and we walked outside, where Lucy had occupied herself by climbing a tree to keep a lookout for pirates. Libby coaxed her down and herded both children to her minivan. I waved good-bye.

I bent down and picked up a green pepper from the garden. Noah threw it after Max.

Noah and I had lunch, and I put him down for a nap. While he crooned to himself in the crib, I took a phone call from Armand Cannoli.

"Sorry, Nora," he said. "The police are keeping Mick a little longer. I'm working on his release, but they can hold him for twenty-four hours without charges."

"That means he won't be released until tonight?" I checked my watch and tried not to panic. I needed to get to work in a few hours.

"Looks that way," Cannoli said. "Unless you know the whereabouts of his mother?"

"She was just here. But she took off. I don't know where she was headed."

"Next time you see her, call 911, okay?"

We signed off, and I sat for a moment, trying to stay calm and to think of whom I could ask to babysit Noah while I went to work.

I got on the phone and quickly understood why so many of my women friends went into hysterical rants when talking about the difficulties of finding child care. I scrolled through my address book and made call after call. Libby was busy. Rawlins had taken his girlfriend on a picnic and could not be raised. Assorted neighborhood friends either didn't answer or had good excuses. As the clock ticked, I found myself feeling more and more desperate. With Michael in jail, I was in big trouble. I realized we were definitely going to need in-house help when the babies arrived.

As a last resort, I called Emma and caught her eating lunch after a long morning of working with Cookie.

She crunched salad in my ear. "In jail, huh?"

"Michael has not been arrested. He's just being held for questioning."

"Either way, that's what he gets for being mean to his brother."

"Neither one of them was exactly big on brotherly kindness."

"Whatever. I'm not babysitting."

"Emma, I'm desperate."

"I'll pick you up and take you to work, but that's all I'm doing."

"What do I do with Noah?"

"Take him with you. Or call in sick. Lots of people do when their sitters cancel."

"Not anybody who works for Gus Hardwicke."

She arrived early at Blackbird Farm, and she checked on her ponies while I struggled to put Noah's car seat into her pickup truck. A hand-me-down stroller went into the back of the truck, and I stowed a diaper bag loaded down with all the things I hoped would help me survive any child-related catastrophe. I had thrown on a stretchy maternity dress and ballet flats—purely functional clothes. I added a large garden-party hat—complete with ribbons and a big poof of feathers on one side. Noah was fascinated by the hat.

On the drive into Philadelphia, Emma and I soon reached the conclusion that we could not discuss the Abruzzo brothers without fighting. Noah played with his toes and sang to himself.

"He's a cute kid," Emma said. "But I'm not going to take care of him."

"You looked after Libby's twins when they were his age."

"And look how that turned out. Do you know they're working on a cadaver this summer? They've even given it a name—Kanye. They have a cadaver for a friend!"

"Someday, think how good that's going to look on a medical school application."

"Or a court order." Emma shook her head firmly. "I don't have a good influence on kids."

"You underestimate yourself."

"I'll wait until he can walk and talk. And order from the kids' menu."

"That's almost exactly what Bridget O'Halloran said."

Emma asked me to describe Michael's mother, and I told her what I had observed about her—including her penchant for leopard print, her mercurial temper and her habit of pushing people's buttons just to watch their reaction. But also her sense of humor and her tenacity.

"She's a handful," I said when I had listed all her good and bad points.

"Is she a hooker?" Emma asked, as blunt as ever. "Frank says she's a call girl. At her age, that's pretty impressive."

It took me a while to decide how to answer the question. "She sees a lot of men. And she has expensive taste in cars and clothes and jewelry that somebody indulges. But that doesn't mean she's a call girl. Does it?"

My little sister shrugged. "How come you didn't ask her to babysit?"

"Because I'm not crazy," I said at once. "There's no way she's going to ever look after our children. You should have seen the way she punched Michael the other day."

"I hear he's pretty good with a punch when it's called for, too. That doesn't make him a bad dad."

"She's not babysitter material. Trust me on that."

Emma pulled up in front of the Fu Manchu restaurant, and I climbed out of the truck. My abandonment sent Noah into a weeping fit. With his cries ringing in my ears, I left my hat on the passenger seat and trundled up the narrow stairs to Krissie Wong's apartment. She had my dresses ready, and I paid her quickly.

I said, "Would you like me to take Jenny Tuttle's dresses, too?"

"Oh, I should have told you," Krissie replied. "I ended up sending them with the *Bluebird of Happiness* costumes. That little lady took them—Poppy was her name. She was much nicer this time. She even brought me a loaf of banana bread. She said she baked it herself."

"She did?" Last I'd heard, Poppy was saying Fred was the baker. Now she was baking for Krissie? Which was the truth? Thinking the cake might be laced with diet pills, I said, "Just to be on the safe side, maybe you shouldn't eat that bread."

"You think I'm crazy?" Krissie asked with a grin. "I never eat anything clients bring to me. I live over a restaurant, remember? I'm real fussy when it comes to sanitation."

I returned to the truck and gave Noah his binky to calm him down. At the Pendergast Building, Emma helped me get the stroller out and opened up. Noah seemed mildly interested in her, but he was happy to be in my arms as we waved good-bye and headed inside. He wanted nothing to do with the stroller, so I held him. With a struggle, I dragged the stroller and my dresses and the baby through the security checkpoints. Both guards made a fuss over Noah. He was a big hit with the other passengers in the elevator, too.

When we arrived in the newsroom, Gus looked up from the desk where he was conferring with one of the crime reporters.

"No," he said as soon as his stormy gaze fell on Noah. "No kids, not ever. This isn't a nursery school, it's a place of business."

Left-handed, Noah pulled out his binky and threw it at Gus. It hit Gus's tie and left a splotch of drool on the silk.

"This wouldn't happen," I said while Gus glared at his tie, "if we had an on-site day-care center." I hung up my dresses on the edge of the partition between the City desk and the Lifestyle cubicles.

"We have no money for a day-care center. Now, get that troll out of here."

Mary Jude hotfooted it over to us from her desk. "Ooh, a baby! Nora, he's beautiful! Can I hold him?"

"Give it to her," Gus said. "And meet me in my office." He turned on his heel and walked away.

Noah's face puckered when I handed him over to Mary Jude, but she was ready with an apple slice. He grabbed it, intrigued. "I was just having my snack," she said to me. "We'll share. What's his name? Whose baby is he?"

I took off my hat and left it on my desk. "His name is Noah. And—well, he's the baby my sister gave up last winter."

"So why is he with you?"

"Good question," I said.

Gus barked my name from his office door, so I left Noah in Mary Jude's arms and obeyed his summons.

He closed the door, still holding out his tie and glowering at the spot on it. "Have you considered the job offer I extended to you?"

"I'm still considering it."

"You discussed it with your thug?"

"Michael and I talked, yes. He thinks you have another motive besides my career advancement."

Gus dropped his tie back into place and smoothed it. "I hear he's in jail."

I should have known Gus would have his ear to the ground where Michael was concerned. He had staffers who listened to police scanners all the time. Half the *Intelligencer*'s crime stories came directly from the radio.

"Michael has not been arrested," I said primly. "He's answering questions to help the police with an investigation."

"And his mother's on the lam. There are BOLOs out in three states. Have you seen her?"

My turn to glare. "Are you asking me in a professional capacity? Or personal? Because I have a few personal questions to ask you, Gus. For one, have you cleared the air with your family yet? Confessed your sins? Told them you fabricated a fiancée?"

He managed a superior expression. "My sister Megan is coming to Philadelphia. She'll be here Saturday. I'd like you to meet her. She's a great wit. The two of you will get along fine."

"Gus! I have not forgiven you for dragging me into your family problem. I want out—completely and cleanly. Why is she coming?"

"She's the lead dog on my father's legal team. Negotiations are heating up with the shilly-shallying Americans. She'll give that mob a gobful." He smirked at the idea of his assertive sister strong-arming the competition. "While she's here, though, she'd like to meet you. What about dinner?"

I wanted to shriek. "Didn't you hear me? I want no part of your family. I will not be used as a pawn in your business deal. And I'm busy on Saturday."

"Ah. Honeymooning?"

If he tied me down to pound bamboo slivers under my fingernails, I was not going to tell Gus anything else. I could imagine him bursting in on our wedding with guns blazing—or whatever Aboriginal weapon Australians preferred. So I diverted him. "Wouldn't you rather hear what I've learned about the Tuttle murder?"

"Murders, plural." Gus folded his arms over his chest and prepared to be unimpressed. "Okay, shoot."

After deciding that I owed no favors to anyone who was part of a show that embarrassed my family, I intended to share with him everything I had learned. I outlined what I had sussed out since I'd last seen him: how any number of the cast might have wanted Jenny Tuttle dead. How the police were investigating cake laced with drugs. How the mystery investor in Ox Oxenfeld's production was very likely imaginary—dreamed up to defraud other investors. And the collection of photos I had found in Jenny Tuttle's desk.

"Photos?" he demanded.

"Lots of them. Lots of kids. I didn't count."

"Where are these photos?"

"In the desk where I found them. I'm not stealing evidence out from under the police, Gus. Question is, who are all those children?"

"I'll be stuffed!" He was delighted. "We have a sex scandal after all! When I came to this city, I was prepared to be bored out of my skull with how provincial it is. But now and then it's an interesting place, after all."

I leaned against the door. "The penis stories are beneath you."

He grinned at me, good humor restored. "By God, Nora, I'll

make a reporter of you yet. How will we find out about all the children in the photos you found?"

"First someone needs to review the calls that came in to the *Intelligencer* when you ran the original photo of David Kaminsky. The staff assumed they were all crank callers, but some of them might have been on the up-and-up. I talked to one caller myself—he said he was adopted, but we didn't get any further than that before he hung up. The children in the photos—they're not Jenny's children, that's for sure. I don't think she could have concealed one pregnancy, let alone a lot."

"So why was she keeping their pictures around?"

I took a deep breath and said, "I wonder if they aren't her siblings."

"Siblings? You mean—Boom Boom's offspring?"

"No, I think Toodles is their father. He had a notorious access to chorus girls."

"Toodles? Are you out of your mind? He wrote ooey-gooey musicals that would make Captain von Trapp want to brush his teeth! He can't have a boatload of illegitimate kids in his closet."

"Kids weren't the only surprises in his closet," I said, thinking of Nico's story that Toodles had been the life of many parties. "Toodles is the only option that makes sense. But one step at a time. We need to confirm some facts. Have you heard from David Kaminsky?"

"Only from his lawyers, unfortunately." Gus was pacing with excitement over the developing story. "They're playing it cool, probably organizing an assault on the Tuttle bank accounts."

"They're going to be disappointed if the Tuttle fortune has to be split a dozen different ways."

"A dozen! By God, the Music Man got around, didn't he?" Cackling with glee, he grabbed his phone. "I'm putting a couple of the City desk guys on this now. They can make the phone calls for the investor story, do the follow-up. And I'll find a team to start reviewing all the calls that came in about the Kaminsky photo. We'll have some paragraphs put together by the time you finish your events tonight."

"I only have one. Art in the Garden. It's outdoors at the garden of a friend of my grandmother's. She opens it every year for a local artists' cooperative to display their work. The party is a hot ticket."

"It sounds like a crashing bore to me, but get going." He shooed me away with one hand and finished dialing with the other.

"Gus," I said in the doorway, "I'm serious about being no part of your family's business situation. I am out. You have to talk to them."

"Sure, sure." He had the receiver to his ear. "Toddle along. Work to do."

Noah was happily gnawing on one of Mary Jude's apple slices, and he lifted it high in his chubby fist to show it to me. I gave him a kiss and pretended to take a bite of his apple, and he giggled.

Mary Jude said, "This is one happy little boy."

My cell phone rang in my bag. Hoping it was Michael calling to say he was out of police custody, I grabbed it, my heart lifting.

I was surprised to hear Hart Jones on the other end of the line.

My hopeful heart sank like a stone when he asked me if I had time to meet him for a drink. I had been enjoying a few minutes of triumph about the Tuttle story, but Hart's voice sobered me instantly. I checked my watch and agreed.

Dismayed, I grabbed my hat, tucked Noah into his stroller and thanked Mary Jude for her help. I rolled Noah onto the elevator.

I stopped first at a trendy children's clothing shop just two blocks from the Pendergast Building. Since Michael and I had picked up Noah at the Jones house under such hasty circumstances, we didn't have many clothes for the baby at the farm. I'd been laundering the few items we did have to keep him decently dressed. Now it seemed like a good idea to find him something nice to wear home with his father. His T-shirt and shorts looked spattered with drool and bits of apple skin—as if we'd been neglectful of him.

In the shop, I slipped through the sale rack and struck gold when I pulled out an adorable set of blue shorts with a matching sailor shirt. While I changed Noah's diaper and dressed him in his new finery, the shopkeeper found a matching pair of navy blue sneakers and little sailor hat that gave Noah a jaunty look. He wasn't a pirate—not yet, anyway—but he was a very cute midshipman.

I tried to be enthusiastic, but my heart ached as I finished dressing him. Noah snatched off the hat and threw it at the shopkeeper, but after a few more tries, he agreed to wear it.

Twenty minutes later when I wheeled him into the bar at the Four Seasons, he was sound asleep.

I looked around the room crowded with bankers enjoying a drink at the end of the day. I spotted Hart Jones sitting nervously alone at a table by the window. I saw right away that he was twisting his wedding ring. He stood up when Noah and I reached the table. Hart wore an expensive charcoal suit with a crisp shirt and an Hermès tie. He seemed unnerved when he realized I had the baby with me.

"Thanks for meeting me, Nora." Hart brushed a quick kiss on my cheek. He leaned over the stroller and saw that his son was asleep. Hart reached to touch him but thought better of waking the baby and pulled his hand back.

The waiter brought Hart a beer, and I asked for an orange juice and some peanuts.

Hart and I sat down. I took off my hat and perched it on the stroller handle.

Uncomfortable, Hart said again, "Thanks for meeting me."

"Of course. I'd have brought all of Noah's things if I thought we were going to—"

"No," he said. "That's not why I called."

He surprised me. I asked, "How's Penny?"

Hart toyed with a cocktail napkin. "I took her to the facility on Sunday. She agreed to stay in rehab. She hates it, but she knows she needs to be there."

"That's good, right?"

"Right." Again, he glanced down at Noah in the stroller as if to reassure himself the baby was still sleeping. Without meeting my eye, he asked, "How's Emma? Have you seen her lately?"

The question surprised me all over again. Not that Hart was curious about the mother of his child, but that he asked about her in the same second he spoke about his wife.

"She's okay," I said warily.

"Is she drinking?"

"Maybe a little." There was no point in lying to him.

He grinned with admiration. "She's a party girl."

"She has a problem," I said, refusing to acknowledge that my sister's drinking might be a commendable thing. "But I think she's on a good path right now."

"I hear she's riding again."

"Yes. And it's going well. She's getting into top condition and working very hard. Paddy Horgan has assigned her a new horse. They could go far. As long as she doesn't get sidetracked."

Hart didn't respond, but he had the grace to look chagrined. He took a nervous slug of his beer.

The waiter reappeared in record time with my orange juice and a plate with assorted nuts, crackers and three kinds of sliced cheese. I popped a piece of cheddar and a few almonds.

Crunching the nuts, I decided I didn't want to make anything easy for Hart. The best strategy seemed to be waiting for him to decide he was brave enough to discuss what he'd brought me here to talk about.

His shoulders lost some of their courage. Finally, he said, "I've been working on a big deal at the firm."

Not news. I sipped orange juice and waited for more.

"It's complicated—the kind of deal I wish I could ask Lexie Paine about. She'd know how to handle the details."

"She's not working these days."

"Oh, I know that," he said hurriedly. "I didn't mean—that is, I was just saying it's complicated."

I leaned forward. "Hart, it's just me. I can be your friend, if you like. But you have to be honest with me. Are we here to talk about everything else? Or about your son?"

He sighed, and his shoulders slumped further. He toyed unhappily with his beer glass but didn't drink. "How's Noah doing?"

"He's sleeping well, eating his head off. He's . . . happy."

Hart wagged his head. "I know. That's great. You've been great for Noah. Even your—even Abruzzo—you've both been great. Don't think we don't appreciate what the two of you have done for us. But it's—it all makes this even harder for me to— Look, I know being with Penny and me isn't always good for Noah. Not when she's out of control. And I—maybe I'm not much of a parent, either."

"Noah is a wonderful little boy," I said gently. "If you had time to just be with him—"

"That's just it. I don't have time."

"He's your son, Hart." Maybe my tone was too harsh, but I couldn't take it back.

Hart didn't hear the reproof in my voice. He took a deep breath and then spoke in a rush. "I've been offered—that is, part of this deal I'm working on is a project with almost unlimited potential for me. I could have my own division in a couple of years. It involves politics and banking and all the things I'm good at. I can sink my teeth into this, make it my own. I really think I can make an impact."

"What does all this mean?"

He gave up explaining and said flatly, "The job is in Brussels."

I couldn't speak, couldn't react. My brain was suddenly clanging like an emergency alarm. *Brussels!*

Hart continued to babble about his huge opportunity. A shot at something very big. A job he couldn't pass up. The chance of a lifetime. A career maker.

My throat closed up tight. I tried to take a sip of orange juice, but my hand was shaking so hard I couldn't manage the glass. I set it down on the table and nearly spilled it. Hart caught the glass—his quick reaction saving both of us from getting soaked. *No, no, please, no.* I couldn't say the words. But the idea of Noah going halfway around the world from us—it was too hard to bear. I thought of Michael and what he'd say in this moment. His response wouldn't be civil. He'd be furious. He'd take action—maybe the legally wrong action, but right for us. Right for Noah. I felt as if I was betraying him by letting Noah go with Hart now—maybe forever—without Michael being able to say good-bye.

I felt tears welling up in my eyes.

Hart stopped talking, shocked at my reaction.

I reached for a cocktail napkin and tried to stop the tears from ruining my makeup—a foolish reaction, perhaps, but easier to stand than the idea of losing Noah.

I said, "Sorry. I—we're very fond of Noah. I know I should be congratulating you on the job—it sounds like something you really want. But—I'll be honest. It gets harder and harder to give him back to you after he stays with us. We love him. We really do. Not just me, but Michael, too."

Quietly, Hart murmured, "I know."

"I've been afraid, actually, that someday we wouldn't be able to hand him over to you. He's almost ours, but not quite. It's—it's very hard. We want him at our house. We do love him."

Hart hunched forward and grasped my hand. "That makes this easier."

I dabbed my eyes. "What?"

"Nora, if Penny and I are going to make our marriage work, I think we need to be together. Just the two of us. Without Noah. Having him with us doesn't help Penny with her addiction. In fact, I think he makes things worse for her. So we're thinking we should go to Brussels. The two of us. To start over."

"The two of you?" I couldn't understand what he was saying.

"I don't have any right to ask you this. But you have a way with him. You and Abruzzo both. If you could keep him for a year—maybe two years, if that's how long the job lasts—Penny and I could get our marriage under control." Hart kept talking, unaware that I stared at him with my mouth open. "We never really had a honeymoon. We took Noah the same week as the wedding. It was too soon. Too much to handle. And Penny's problem wasn't under control. But if she and I had a chance to—"

"You want us to take care of Noah while you go to Brussels?"

"A year. Maybe two. He'll never remember, will he? He's less than a year old. Kids are resilient."

"Resilient?" I repeated, barely hanging on to my good manners. "Hart, he's a baby, not a dog you can give back if you can't house-break him."

Hart sat back, his mouth snapping shut.

I said, "You're asking us to take Noah but give him back when you return?"

"Well, yes." As if his words were perfectly logical, Hart said, "You can't keep him, Nora. He's my son."

"Nobody recognizes that fact more than I do. But you're asking us to be . . ."

To be as hard-hearted as he and Penny were.

Noah stirred in the stroller, and we both turned to look down at him. He didn't wake, but his sailor hat tipped drunkenly over one eye. I reached down and slipped off the hat. Underneath it, his hair was wet and curled into sweaty whorls. If I woke him now and gave him the hat, I knew Noah's first reaction would be to throw the damn thing straight at his father.

I couldn't hold back a shaky smile.

I knew what Michael's vote would be.

I said, "We'll take him, Hart. We'll keep him for as long as you want us to."

And maybe longer, I thought. Michael just needed to think of a strategy. He'd have a year—maybe two—to come up with a way to . . . coerce Hart and Penny into letting us have Noah forever. And when that time came, I'd be standing right beside him with Noah locked in my arms.

I don't remember saying good-bye to Hart, or how we parted. My head buzzed with anger and outrage and adrenaline. On the way out of the bar, pushing Noah in the stroller and feeling my blood hot in my veins, I felt more determined than I ever had in my whole life. No way was I ever giving up Noah. Not in a year or two years, not ever.

At the revolving door I bumped into Jamie Scaithe, a former associate of my late husband's from the cocaine days. I'd had a couple of unpleasant dates with him after Todd died. Jamie had a fancy new haircut designed to disguise his receding hairline, and he was dressed on trend in a tight-fitting suit and expensive shoes. His wristwatch flashed in the sunlight.

He didn't recognize me until my hat tilted and he saw my face. Then Jamie reeled back from me as if shocked, but laughing. "God, Nora, look how fat you are!"

I was going to push past him without speaking, but he blocked my way. I'd always suspected Jamie wasn't just a consumer of cocaine, but a dealer, too. He came from a rich Philadelphia family, but he hadn't inherited much of their money—his parents had good instincts, I thought. He had a lavish lifestyle, though. The kind that I had come to decide was distasteful in its excess.

His face was smug as he looked down at me. "I guess I dodged a bullet when you refused my dinner invitations. You'd probably have eaten me broke. How many kids do you have now?" He made it sound as if I were running a pig farm.

"Will you let me pass, please? I'm late for an engagement."

He continued to laugh. "I've never seen a girl so fat before. Let me feel that bowling ball."

He reached and almost put his hand on Baby Girl. Maybe I had endured one too many touches by strangers, but this was the last straw. I slapped his hand hard.

He pulled back as if bitten, face shocked.

If I had worried about how I might settle into motherhood, those doubts evaporated in a heartbeat. I wasn't afraid anymore. I had my priorities straight. I said, "Keep your dirty hands off my family."

CHAPTER TWENTY-TWO

took Noah to the garden party at the house of my grandmother's friend, who greeted me fondly and gushed over the baby in his sailor suit. We chatted for only a minute before she had to move on to other guests, leaving me to wander in the garden. Although compact, her urban oasis was a masterpiece of topiaries and statuary and stone containers that gleamed with the patina of old age and long, loving use. Tiers of immaculately mulched flowers had been expertly chosen in subtle waves of color to please the most discerning of eyes. The intoxicating scent of all those wonderful flowers filled the air, which seemed full of swooping birds, too. The art hanging from overhead wires strung between the shady trees was vibrant and playful, and the strolling guests clutched price lists while they admired everything. If ever I had an opportunity to contemplate beauty, this was it. I found one perfect Peace rose and showed it to Noah, who put his pudgy fingers to the soft petals. After that, I took photos for the newspaper and talked briefly to a few friends.

I soon bumped into Michael and Gail Rosen, a couple who could always be relied upon to support the local children's hospital. Michael, a CPA wearing a snappy summer suit, and Gail, a retired teacher in a crisp dress with her triple strands of pearls, were sipping cool drinks and admiring a splashy canvas of bicycles finger-painted in primary colors.

He turned away from the painting with a shake of his head. "Not that one, Gail. We'll find another way to donate. Nora!" He gave me a kiss on the cheek and said with concern, "Should you be out in this heat?"

Gail hugged me. "We're trying not to melt."

"Why aren't you two out on the golf course on such a beautiful day?" I asked, teasing.

"Oh, we wouldn't miss this party for anything. Honey," she said to her husband, "why don't you find something cold for Nora to drink?"

"I'm fine, really—"

"I'll be back in a minute," he promised. "I think my wife is hinting she needs some girl time."

When he went off into the crowd, Gail said, "This gives me a minute to ask you about Lexie. Is she all right? I assume you're in touch with her?"

Since her husband worked in the financial world, which was still in an uproar about the fall of Lexie's firm, I said cautiously, "She's okay."

"I don't approve of what she did," Gail said. "Nobody could. It was awful that her partner stole from clients, but that doesn't excuse pushing him off a ledge. She's going to make restitution to the investors, isn't she?"

"I can't really say, Gail."

"No, of course not. You're being discreet. One of my daughters went to school with her, you may remember, so I think I know

Lexie well enough to guess she's going to do the right thing. I hope you'll tell her that although many clients are furious about what happened—justifiably so—there are also some of us who still respect her. Her charity work was especially admirable. And you know I'm a big advocate of women in business. I hate seeing a good one go down. So we're rooting for her to get back on her feet."

"Thank you, Gail."

"I hope she comes back better than ever."

I hoped so, too. I didn't say I was worried that my friend was dabbling in the dark arts.

Gail deftly changed the subject to Noah. She crouched down to talk directly to him in the stroller, and he responded with a grin. She was telling me about her granddaughters when her husband returned with a frosty glass of iced tea for me, and while I gratefully sipped it, we chatted pleasantly about the pictures hanging around us. The Rosens were very nice people, the backbone of charitable giving. I left them discussing the attributes of various paintings.

I wheeled Noah around to look at some of the sculptures and listen to the music of a youth string trio, but my heart wasn't in it. I was too rocked by Hart's proposal that Michael and I take Noah. Long before the party got fully under way, and without even bothering to find anyone to say thank you or good-bye to, Noah and I headed home.

Usually, I used the travel time to write my newspaper pieces, but Noah was too much of a distraction today. He demanded my attention. Juggling him, I finally checked my phone and discovered a text message from Michael.

Ill pick u up at train station.

I showed the phone's screen to Noah. "See? He'll be home with us tonight."

Noah grabbed the phone and sucked on it.

By the time the train reached Doylestown, Noah was asleep in my arms, and it was a struggle to get the stroller and everything else off the train and into the station. My feet were swollen. Baby Girl was doing a tap dance on my bladder. But I looked around for Michael with happy anticipation.

Instead, it was Armand Cannoli, Michael's lawyer, who came striding up from the dark parking lot.

I must have looked terribly disappointed, because he said, "I'm so sorry. I used Mick's phone to text you."

"Where is he? In jail still?"

"Not exactly. Here, I brought my car. I have my son's car seat, too. It might be the wrong size, but— No, don't lift that yourself. Let me help."

When we were finally settled in Cannoli's big Mercedes and he was driving me home, he explained.

"The original charges were all bogus," he said. "Mick wasn't driving under the influence, of course. The cops just wanted some leverage to find out about his mother. When that didn't work, I thought they were going to turn him loose this afternoon, but that's when the feds showed up."

"The feds? You mean the FBI?" My voice rose as dread surged up from inside me. "What for? What do they want with him?"

"I don't know, and Mick wasn't talking. They took him away, and now—"

"The FBI took him away where? Why? He hasn't done anything wrong." Federal charges were much more serious than the rest. My head was suddenly full of horrible thoughts of penitentiaries and grimly long sentences that might doom our future, and I felt sick.

Cannoli tried to soothe me. "I'm working on finding out everything. What's his relationship with Lexie Paine? He mentioned her name to me, then decided to clam up. I can't help him if he won't let me."

I felt a pit start to open in my stomach. My worst fears were coming true. Michael and Lexie had concocted something illegal together, and now it was coming apart. "I don't know what they're doing. They wouldn't tell me." Probably to keep me out of their conspiracy.

Gently, Armand asked, "Do you know if it's legal?"

I had asked Michael the same question. What had his answer been? *Legal in some countries.* Had he been joking?

If Michael had chosen to keep secrets from his lawyer, I had to trust there were good reasons for me to do the same. So I didn't answer.

Instead, I asked, "Where are they keeping him?"

"I won't know until morning."

"A jail somewhere? Locked up?'

"Probably."

If my whole chest were being squeezed in a vise, I couldn't have felt more panicked. "Will they let him go before Friday?"

"Friday? I don't know, Nora."

"Armand, we have an appointment to get married that evening."

"How delightful," Cannoli said warmly. "No wonder he's pacing like a caged lion. Congratulations. Nora, I'll move mountains to get him to the church on time, I promise. I'll pull in favors— whatever it takes. He'll be waiting at the altar. Don't worry."

I was only somewhat comforted. "I met an FBI agent last year. Do you think it would do any good for me to call him and—"

"Let us handle it." Cannoli's voice was gentle. "We've never failed Mick before. We'll save his bacon again."

On Wednesday morning, I put on another of Libby's awful maternity T-shirts. This one read ALL I WANTED WAS A BACK RUB.

I figured nobody would see me, so I was safe. I read the *Intelligencer* while feeding Noah his breakfast. There was no story about Michael, thank heaven.

The story about the Tuttles was splashed above the fold, with pictures of Jenny and David Kaminsky arranged side by side so readers could make their own decisions about family resemblance. A sidebar story outlined the possibility that Boom Boom Tuttle had invented her mystery moneyman to drain as much working capital as possible from other investors. Did I care anymore? Not really. If all the Tuttles ended up in a soup kitchen, that was all right with me. I hated the idea of any of them cashing in on the Blackbird family.

I flipped the newspaper over, and there was a grainy photo of Lexie, probably taken from a helicopter. She was stretched out in a lounge chair in her bathing suit, sunning herself by the luxurious pool. The headline: LIVING THE GOOD LIFE.

For the first time in my pregnancy, I felt my belly twinge. I put my hand on Baby Girl and silently cursed Gus. The story would sell a lot of papers that day. And raise the ire of people who had lost their life's savings to the Paine Investment Group. It made Lexie look like an uncaring criminal who had stolen from her clients to feather her own considerable nest.

Rubbing the tight muscle in my belly, I phoned the newspaper when I was pretty sure Gus would be in. His assistant transferred me, and Gus picked up on the fourth ring, as if he was deliberately keeping me in suspense.

Instead of hello, he asked, "Did you get home safely last night?"

His concern surprised me. "Of course. Why wouldn't I?"

"You left here with enough infant paraphernalia to cripple a pack mule."

"I managed just fine."

In a different tone, he said, "I heard about Abruzzo."

I didn't answer. I had a hard time believing Gus could have

heard about Michael's trouble with federal investigators from a police scanner. He must have informants in higher places.

Gus said, "Are you okay?"

"No, of course I'm not okay. I saw your photo of Lexie. I can't bear to read what you've written about her."

"Everywhere I go, people badger me about when we're going to do a full-blown exposé on your friend. I had to toss a little chum into the water to—"

"Gus," I said, "I'm going to take a few days off. I have several photos and extra stories we can use until I get back to work. Tremaine and I can make arrangements by phone for the online edition. But I'm not coming in. I can't handle this anymore."

"Handle what?"

"The way you treat people. The way you conduct business."

"Let me come out there to your outpost in the country." Gus tried hard to sound kind. "We'll discuss your promotion. Or—"

"No, Gus."

"I'm coming to see you," he said. "I can be there in an hour."

"I'll call the police if you do."

"You left a garment bag here. It's got a couple of dresses in it, Mary Jude says. I'll bring it."

"I'll pick it up myself sometime. You're not welcome here."

"I'm trying to help!"

"Keep working on the Tuttle story. There's one more angle I should have mentioned. I think it's possible Boom Boom is missing. Either missing or she's in danger."

His voice changed. "What kind of danger?"

"She wasn't at the Tuttle house yesterday, so somebody needs to start looking. Hostetler's probably the man for the job," I said bitterly. "And he's finished with his other assignment, right?" Before Gus could ask more questions, I disconnected and sat for a moment, angry and frightened.

Noah threw his banana at me and smiled brightly.

I did my best to wipe the worry from my face. If I felt as if my life was falling apart, I owed it to Noah to pretend otherwise. Surely the primary principle of good parenting was making a child feel protected and loved at all times.

For the next couple of days, though, I looked after Noah never far from a telephone. I stopped reading the newspapers. I phoned Lexie, but she didn't answer. I talked to the Cannolis on a regular basis, and they assured me that Michael planned on showing up for our wedding. But they couldn't tell me exactly how that miracle might happen.

If not for my sisters, I think I'd have gone crazy. But Libby came every morning and brought Max, who grew more and more intimidated by Noah. Emma arrived at the end of her workday, bringing take-out food. Talking a lot about her progress with Cookie, she helped me in the garden. My sisters did their level best to keep me on an even keel.

On Friday morning, Libby insisted on taking me out for a bridal breakfast. "It will get your mind off everything."

"I'd rather just stay here by the phone, Libby—"

"I have something to discuss. Something delicate," she said, "and I'd like to do it in public, if you don't mind."

"Why? I'm warning you, Libby—in my current state of mind, I'm willing to make a scene just about anywhere."

She smiled. "A quick breakfast. Who doesn't need waffles once in a while?"

We took Noah and Max along in the hope of negotiating a peace treaty between them. The line was too long at the pancake house, so we ended up at the Rusty Sabre. When we were settled at our usual table in the back room by the window overlooking the canal, Libby took a deep breath.

"I know you're going to be disappointed," she said, "but I've decided a double wedding is a mistake. For both of us."

I tried to rearrange my relieved face and took a moment to compose the best response. Carefully, I said, "Are you sure?"

She took my hand in both of hers and clasped it on the tablecloth. "Dear Nora. I know you want to share your happiness with me, but I think it's best if we each have our own day in the sun. What bride doesn't want to be the star of the show?"

"Let me guess," I said. "Ox has decided he doesn't want to be married."

She released my hand. "Well, of course he wants to marry me! He just hasn't asked yet, that's all. So no double wedding. Are you very disappointed?"

With complete honesty, I said, "I'll only be disappointed if Michael is still in custody at six this evening."

"Darling, the FBI will release That Man of Yours today," Libby assured me. "Don't give it a moment's worry."

I sighed, feeling very low. Allowing myself a moment to wallow in self-pity, I said, "I haven't heard from him in days. And the Cannolis have stopped calling me. Which probably means bad news. When we get home, I think I should phone the judge's office to cancel."

"Oh, dear! I've already put a down payment on the mime! And the musicians I found—maybe I'd better check on their cancellation policy. Do you mind if I step outside?" Agitated, she already had her cell phone in hand and was getting up from the table.

When she left, I said to Max and Noah, "When it comes time for you two to get married, be sure to check the bride's family for mental health issues."

I had made the mistake of grabbing a newspaper off the hostess's desk. I gave the boys each a handful of Cheerios to keep them occupied, and I opened the paper—not the *Intelligencer*, but the city's respected news source. On page three, I found the piece that flatly described the FBI's interest in Michael, "a known criminal with extensive ties to organized crime and a probable connection to the tarnished Paine Investment Group."

I suddenly felt as if my brain were on fire.

"That's it!" I threw down the paper and leaped to my feet, practically colliding with my sister as she returned to the table. "Libby, I'm going into the city. I'm going this minute. There's an FBI agent I met last year. I'm going to talk to him and get some answers."

"Nora, your hormones have rendered you incapable of rational thought. Sit down and—"

"I can't stand it! I can't wait around any longer! This is supposed to be my wedding day!" I cried, "I'm going straight to the FBI myself!"

Libby tried to talk me out of going. But in the end she drove me to the station, and she promised to look after Noah until I got back.

I took the train into Philadelphia.

It was only when I climbed the steps out of the station that I realized I was wearing one of Libby's shirts. This one read CAN YOU TELL ME IF MY SHOES MATCH? I groaned. In sneakers and my yoga capri pants, I wouldn't have caused a moment's surprise at the pancake house, but I hardly made the picture of an upstanding citizen the FBI should pay attention to. I almost slapped my forehead. My hormones were definitely on a rampage.

There was no time to go back home to change. So I figured I'd have to stop to buy something suitable to wear. Through light morning pedestrian traffic, I waddled toward the federal building with the plan of ducking into a department store along the way. My credit card could withstand the hit if there was a maternity section in the store. If there wasn't—so many retailers had relegated the extraordinary sizes to their online catalogs—I'd have to improvise to avoid appearing to be a crazy woman.

I crossed the street and headed for the store but found myself passing alongside the theater where I had gone to see the preview of *Bluebird of Happiness.*

I paused to catch my breath and glanced down the alley behind the theater.

I could have sworn I saw the tall, distinctive figure of Fred Fusby unlocking a side door. He slipped inside before I could be sure.

Fred? Going back to the theater, the scene of the crime against the arts?

I headed down the alley, passing litter and two parked taxicabs. The drivers were leaning against the trunk of the first car and eyed my shirt with amusement. They watched me go to the steel door marked STAGE DOOR. I tried the handle and found it hanging on the latch. Perhaps foolishly, I let myself into the old theater.

A small backstage lobby lay just inside the door, illuminated by the exit sign and a single bare lightbulb swinging from the cracked ceiling. I breathed the musty scent of a large space left empty for long periods of time. A desk sat to the left of the door—the spot where the stage-door guard normally kept watch. Today, the chair was empty, the walkie-talkie abandoned. Beside the desk, a wide staircase ran up. Opposite the desk, a narrower staircase led down into darkness. Straight ahead was a velvet curtain. I peeked through it and saw the darkened auditorium of the theater. Only the light of the exit signs cast a dim glow across the rows of seats. The hushed silence of the big open space was eerie. Overhead, I saw the shadows of the private boxes and the looming curve of the upper balcony. There was no movement, however, and no sound. Not even the distant noise of the city penetrated the theater's thick walls.

I tugged the velvet curtain closed. Where had Fred gone? I had no intention of blundering around all by myself. But I steadied my breath and took a few tentative steps up the wide staircase to get the lay of the land. On a wide landing, I found myself standing just a few yards from the empty stage, where the remnants of the *Bluebird of Happiness* set were cast in dim light. I could see no human being on the stage.

But if I looked up the rest of the flight of stairs, I could plainly see a hallway lined with a dozen open doors. Dressing rooms? A lone light was shining in the last room at the end of the corridor. I could hear Fred speaking to someone there. Quietly, I edged up the stairs toward his familiar voice. My sneakers made no noise on the smooth linoleum floor as I eased down the narrow hallway toward the light.

When I reached the halfway point, I heard Boom Boom's voice. She sounded even more warbly than before. And frightened.

"Look, I brought food," Fred was saying. He sounded weepy and apologetic. "It should make you feel better."

I fumbled my cell phone out of my bag, prepared to call 911. But a noise in the dark dressing room next to me nearly stopped my heart in my chest.

A human voice. Strained. Muffled. Scared.

Instinct told me someone needed help. With my pulse pounding, I leaned into the small room. On the floor, I could make out the shape of a chair knocked on its side. Tied to the chair was a person. Lying on her side on the floor, she strained to turn her head toward me.

Bridget O'Halloran. Her mouth taped shut, her wrists and ankles bound with electrical cord. Her eyes were wide but flashing with fury.

"Bridget!" I whispered, dropping to my knees and reaching to free her.

She grunted and wriggled, jerking her head in the direction of the door. I got the message and quietly closed the door behind myself. In the dark, I scrabbled for the cell phone on the floor and turned it on. By the faint blue light of the screen, I could see well enough to try loosening the electrical cords wrapped around Bridget's ankles. She wiggled angrily, and I realized she wanted the tape off her mouth.

"I don't want to hurt you," I whispered.

From down the hall, I heard Fred say, "Did you hear something?"

I froze. Bridget's glare intensified, though, so I gingerly picked the edge of the tape from her cheek. When I got it loosened, I carefully tried to peel the tape back, but she gave an impatient jerk of her head that tore the tape from her mouth.

She gasped, teeth clenched, then snapped as quietly as she could manage, "It took you long enough! Where have you been?"

"Shh! I just—"

"Never mind that now! Get me loose."

Again, we heard Fred speak. Then he walked out into the hallway. Both of us held as still as rabbits for an agonizing minute. We heard Fred return to Boom Boom's dressing room and resume their conversation.

"Damn," Bridget whispered. "I gotta pee something awful! No, no, untie my wrists first."

I broke a nail, then another, as I pried the tight cords apart to free her hands. When I ripped the last loop away, she flexed her fingers and shook both hands to get the circulation going again. Then she contorted her body to help me untie her feet.

"What happened?" I demanded as softly as I could while we worked together. "Why are you here? What's going on? I hear Boom Boom and Fred—"

"What time is it?"

"Almost noon."

"What day is this?"

"Friday. How long have you—"

"I got here Thursday afternoon," Bridget reported. "I followed

Poppy, that little stinker. I knew she was some kind of rat, and sure enough, she had Boom Boom here—"

"Wait. Boom Boom is a prisoner?"

"Yes. Poppy's in cahoots with Fred to keep her here. I tried to get away, but most of the doors are locked around this joint. And then somebody hit me over the head in the dark, dammit. I almost conked out, it hurt so bad." She used one hand to carefully touch her scalp, and she winced. "These people mean business, lemme tell you. They must have grabbed me while I was still confused. When I figured out what was going on, they had me tied to this chair. I knocked it over trying to get loose, and then—oh, man! Where's the nearest bathroom in this hellhole? Do you know?"

"We'll find one. How badly are you hurt? Can you stand up?"

"I'm fine. These people really piss me off!" Bridget was already clambering to her feet. She had lost her shoes. She reached down and hauled me to an upright position. "We gotta get out of here. If these maniacs get ahold of you, babycakes, Mick will be really mad at me."

"Fred's here now," I whispered. "He's talking to Boom Boom."

"Gotcha." Bridget eased open the door and peeked out. "Stay here. I'm going to find a john, and then we'll blow this joint!"

"I'm coming with you," I said firmly. "While you're in the bathroom, I'll call 911."

We scampered silently back down the hall. Well, Bridget scampered. I lumbered. We went down the steps, and she darted through the velvet curtain into the empty theater. With my phone in one hand, I went after her. But I heard a thunk and assumed she'd fallen in the gloom, so I blundered through the curtain to rescue her, only to have my phone knocked from my hand.

Then Poppy Fontana swung a long aluminum pole like a baseball bat, aiming for my head. I ducked back through the curtain and instinctively used the fabric to entangle the pole.

Bridget cursed, and then Poppy cried out as if injured.

Bridget burst back through the curtain and grabbed my hand. "Let's go!"

Bridget dragged me up the three wide steps and out onto the shadowy stage. I staggered clumsily in her wake until we reached the back of the stage, where a series of ropes ran upward into the gloom over our heads. Each rope was tied with nautical precision around what looked like an upside-down bowling pin. Bridget grabbed one of the ropes.

"Here," she said, thrusting my arm through a strap attached to the rope. "Hold on and don't let go. This will all be over in a second."

"What will be over?" I cried. Because I could see Poppy dashing out onto the stage in pursuit of us, the lethal pole in her hands.

Bridget grabbed the other strap with one hand and used her other arm to get a solid grip around me—holding me firmly by my armpit. I felt the bottom fall out of my stomach as she kicked the bowling pin with one foot, knocking the lever sideways.

Instantly, we were off our feet and propelled upward into the darkness, ropes hissing around us as we took off as if on a rocket. My feet sailed sideways in midair. I screamed.

"Take it easy! It's the old fly loft," Bridget said breathlessly as we zoomed smoothly up. "Just hang on."

I had no intention of letting go. I saw the stage grow smaller and we jetted upward, then jerked to a stop with our heads just a few feet from a grimy steel beam. We dangled there for a heartbeat, high above the stage.

"Hope you're not afraid of heights." Bridget angled herself sideways and found a ledge with her bare foot. "There's a place to stand here. Feel it?"

"I won't fit!" I cried, unable to suck in a breath of air. "I'm too big!"

"You're not going to fall," Bridget said sternly. "I won't let you. Keep your head, babycakes. Put your feet over here. No, here, feel it?"

I found the ledge with both sneakers, but I was afraid to let go of the strap around my wrist. I panted. "We're going to be trapped up here."

"We're not trapped. I know my way around a theater. C'mon, I thought you had more nerve than this."

Her words stiffened my spine. I had a lot of nerve. But I was afraid for Baby Girl. The stage was at least thirty feel below us— maybe more. If I fell, both Baby Girl and I would be seriously hurt. I edged onto the ledge, which turned out to be a metal catwalk high above the stage. Finally, I let go of the strap and clamped both hands around the catwalk's thin metal railing. "Now what?"

"This way." She jerked her head to the right. "I think."

"You *think*?"

"There's always a way out to the roof from a catwalk."

"The *roof*!"

From far below, Poppy Fontanna shouted, "You might as well come down here, you two. I know you're up there. All I have to do is cut this rope, and you'll be flatter than Boom Boom's singing!"

Out of the side of her mouth, Bridget said to me, "Who's calling who flat?"

"Wait." I caught Bridget's arm.

From our vantage point, we could hear more voices, and soon Boom Boom came lurching into view. On her skinny blue legs and wearing fuzzy slippers, she could hardly keep her balance. She looked weaker than ever. She still wore elaborate stage makeup, but it had melted down her face, making her look like an old, sad blue clown.

Beside her, Poppy steamed with fury. She had lost her wig, but her anger was enough to send her pacing around the stage. Then the performance lights blazed on, and Fred hurried into view, wiping tears with his handkerchief. He looked decades older than when I'd last seen him. All three of them put their hands to their foreheads to peer through the bright lights to where we had disappeared.

Perched on the catwalk beside me, Bridget whispered, "They can't see us up here in the dark."

"I told them to come down," Poppy said to her cohorts, her voice carrying easily up to us. "I don't know what they think they're going to do up there. Take a nap or something?"

Fred gave a sob. "Everything's come unraveled. We should get our passports and go to Cuba."

"What good will that do?" Boom Boom quavered. "Nobody's ever heard of Toodles there. We'll never get this show off the ground if there's no audience."

"You old fool," Poppy snapped. "This show closed before it opened! If you hadn't killed Jenny, we'd be halfway to Broadway by now. But you ran scared."

"She was going to tell!" Boom Boom whined. "She was going to ruin everything for us. Who'd want to see a show written by a nobody? Besides, she tried to kill me first! She almost poisoned me to death! How am I going to make my comeback if I'm blue?"

"Comeback," Poppy spat. "The only place you'll ever see your stupid name in lights is in a courtroom."

"Take it easy on her, Poppy." Fred's voice broke. "You're only making things worse."

"And you!" Poppy swung on him wrathfully. "You had to go bake a poison cake and bump off poor old Higgie! What a dumb plan! Who made things worse?"

"She knew everything," Fred moaned. "She was going to tell the police what Boom Boom did. She was going to end the show for sure."

"Shut up," Poppy said. She looked up into the darkness again, her face hard. "This show isn't over yet. It's still my best chance to get back on Broadway. We need to get those two snoops down here and shut them up. Anybody got a gun?"

Bridget whispered, "That's an exit cue if I ever heard one. Let's go."

Poppy said, "Fred, there's got to be a gun in the stage-door desk. Go get it."

I said, "I—I'm not sure I can move my hands."

"Sure you can." Bridget pried my fingers loose.

She pulled me along the catwalk. Below us on the stage, the three conspirators went on trying to decide how to lure us down. Fred disappeared, but I was too concerned about keeping my feet on solid metal to worry about him.

When we reached the end of the catwalk, Bridget cursed. "No exit here," she said.

Her voice sounded different. I whispered, "Are you okay?"

"I gotta pee something fierce. But we have to go back the other way. And I can't get past you, so you'll have to lead."

I edged along the catwalk, my hand clamped to Bridget's. Once I thought I felt her lose her balance.

"Keep going," she urged when I faltered. "Here," she said at last. "See it?"

I looked up and spotted what looked like a hatch in a submarine—a small, square door in the grimy ceiling with a red lever attached. The lever was secured by a padlock.

Bridget groaned. "It can't be locked!"

But it was.

"Wait a minute," I said. I felt around the edges of the hatch with my fingers. The narrow rim was filthy, but I kept blindly reaching until my hand struck a small hook. I could feel a key hanging from it. "The door must be locked from the inside so nobody can break in from the roof. Here."

A Little Night Murder

I lifted the key off the hook. But at that moment, Bridget lost her balance. She made a funny sound in her throat. I gasped and turned to her. Her face looked slack and sweaty. I tried to steady her, but her knees buckled. In the dark, she suddenly sank down on the catwalk.

"I'm okay," she insisted. "Just a little light-headed."

"Bridget, you're hurt!"

"I'll be okay," she insisted, but gingerly felt her scalp. "My head hurts like hell. Just—hurry up and get us out of here, will you?"

I reached up and inserted the key into the padlock. It sprang open. I dropped the padlock over the catwalk and heard it hit the stage a moment later. I pulled on the door's red lever, but it was stuck fast. I had to swing on it, using my weight to break the lever free. Finally, it popped with a clang.

From the stage, Poppy shouted up at us, "Come down out of there!" Then, "Hurry up and load that thing, Fred."

Bridget pulled herself upright. "As soon as you open the door, the sunlight will come in. They'll be able to see us. So make it quick."

I gulped down my fear and shoved up on the hatch with all my strength. It flew open and crashed onto the roof. Sunlight blazed down on us, and I was sure we were sitting ducks. That knowledge should have instantly sent me scrambling up the narrow ladder and through the small door, but I couldn't maneuver my bulky body. The ladder was too narrow. The hatch looked too small. I tried to get my feet onto the steps, but I slipped and fell back. If not for Bridget, I might have gone careening over the metal handrail and plunged to my death.

I said, "I can't make it. You go first."

"I'll pull you up," she promised.

I grabbed her foot just as I often did when I boosted Emma into a saddle. I realized Bridget wasn't as nimble as she'd been a few minutes ago. She was weaker, too. But she gamely grabbed the ladder and heaved herself up through the open hatch.

We heard shouts from below. I wasn't sure if it was Poppy ordering Fred to use the gun or what, but I knew my life was in danger—and Baby Girl's, too. When Bridget put her hand down to me, I seized it. I swung wide, gasping, but with her help, I managed to struggle up the ladder. It was a tight squeeze through the hatch. Suddenly I was out in the sunshine, sprawled on my hands and knees in some gritty black mess, gasping fresh air, dizzy from the bright light.

Beside me, Bridget collapsed. She fell to her knees first, then toppled down like a sack of potatoes, out cold.

"Bridget? Bridget!"

I staggered up and slammed the hatch closed again. If Poppy and Fred were armed, I didn't want them climbing out of there to shoot at us on the roof.

"Bridget? Bridget? Wake up!" I tapped her cheek, but her eyes rolled up, and her head lolled. She was flat on her back, arms and legs askew, her body inert. Her hair was a tangled mess, and I could see the gloss of dark blood on her scalp.

And it was hot on the flat roof. Very hot. The summer sun beat down on the gelatinous goo that made up the roof's waterproof material, which radiated a wet heat so intense that I could hardly draw a breath.

I looked around. Other buildings surrounded the theater—but the closest ones were smaller. Nobody could see us. The taller buildings were too far away to hail. I forced myself to cross the roof to the edge—sneakers sticking to the tarlike roof—and I looked down at the street below. My head spun as I gripped the top of the stone railing and peered over the edge of the theater. Bizarrely, I felt as if I might get sucked over the side of the building. But I had no choice. I had to shout for help. It was up to me to call for assistance.

I yelled and waved my arms. Pedestrians kept passing by. Vehicles moved up and down Broad Street without stopping. I shouted. I shouted some more. Finally, someone looked up. Someone else used a cell phone. At last, a police car pulled to the curb. A knot of people gathered below me. Eventually, a fire truck arrived, lights spinning, siren screaming. Only then did I stop shouting.

I rushed back to Bridget and tried to revive her. Kneeling in the grit beside her, I shielded her from the sunlight and spoke a lot of nonsense. "We're going to be okay," I said over and over. "C'mon, Bridget. You can't give up now."

At last she blinked at me. "Boy," she said, voice weak, "I really have to pee."

"Hang on," I commanded. "The fire department is coming. They're going to rescue us. And take you to the hospital."

"You go, too," she said, trying to smile. "We have to make sure my grandbaby is okay."

I put my other hand on Baby Girl and smiled down at Michael's mother. "She's strong. I have a feeling she's going to take after you."

CHAPTER TWENTY-THREE

he fire rescue and the hospital were a blur. But I knew I was okay and Baby Girl was the picture of health, and I told the ER staff that I wasn't the one who needed their first attention. They looked doubtfully at my belly and reluctantly attended to Bridget, who finally got her bathroom break and then began flirting with the neurologist who came to examine her.

I let the doctors check me out, and they reassured me Baby Girl was fine. I talked to the police, too, trying to make myself sound sane. I had the brainstorm of asking them to call Ricci, who was able to convey the pertinent facts about Jenny Tuttle's death and the necessity of arresting Boom Boom and Fred and Poppy.

At last, I noticed the time. After five o'clock.

Bridget saw my expression and grinned. "Better run, babycakes. Give your groom a kiss from me."

"We'll come to see you afterward," I promised.

"The hell you will," she said. "Not on your wedding night.

Besides, I don't want you cramping my style around here. I might pick myself up a nice young doctor."

I gave her a hug and rushed out of the hospital and down the street as fast as I could manage. I had lost my handbag and my cell phone, but not my determination. No way was I going to miss my wedding. By the time I reached the city building where Judge Scotto maintained her chambers, I had to hang on to the door handle to catch my breath.

"Nora!"

I turned, and there was my worst nightmare—Gus.

He rushed to my side. "My God, should I call an ambulance? That's blood!"

"It's not mine. I'm fine," I panted. "I can't be late."

He had one hand under my elbow. "You're going to faint."

"No, I'm not. I'm going to get married."

"What the hell are you wearing?"

I looked down at myself. I was still in Libby's shirt. The one that read CAN YOU TELL ME IF MY SHOES MATCH?

"Oh, heavens," I said. "I've worn some of the most beautiful dresses in the world, and I'm going to get married in *this*?"

"Let's get you out of the heat." Gus opened the door and helped me into the blissfully cool lobby. Marble floors, marble walls, marble staircase. High above, light shone through skylights down into the lobby, which was big enough to fly a kite in. In front of the security desk milled a noisy mob of people who sorted themselves out to be my dearest friends.

Mary Jude Yashurik ran up to me. "Oh, Nora, we've been calling you for hours. We thought—I'm so glad to see you! Here, I brought your dress."

I nearly burst into tears of gratitude at the sight of my lovely dress still safely encased in its plastic bag. I wasn't going to have to recite my vows wearing Libby's ridiculous T-shirt, after all. "Thank you, thank you! Have you seen Michael? Did he make it?"

My sister Emma skidded up to us next. "He's not here yet. You okay? Where the hell have you been?"

"It's— We— I'm fine. But Michael—"

"Don't worry," Emma said. "He'll be here. He wouldn't miss it. You know that."

"Nora!" Libby's wail echoed in the cavernous lobby. "Oh, thank heaven you're okay."

She crushed me against her bosom and wept. "We thought the most awful things. Maybe the FBI arrested you or—"

I barely managed to get my head out of her cleavage before she smothered me. Behind her surged all of her children—the twins looking furtive, Lucy wearing a filthy tutu. Rawlins held Noah in his arms. Shawna balanced Max against her shoulder, keeping him a safe distance from Noah. All of them were smiling. Standing off to one side was Ox Oxenfeld, seeming nervous in a suit with a rose in his lapel, and Delilah, grinning broadly. All of them were ready for a wedding.

My wedding. My heart began to flutter. It might actually happen, after all! If only Michael could get here in time.

"C'mon," Emma snapped, elbowing everyone out of her way so she could grab me. "Let's get you cleaned up and into your dress. I'll help."

"We'll all help!" Libby cried.

I felt grubby but full of hope. "How much time do we have?"

"Ten minutes," Emma reported.

"Michael—"

"He's coming," Libby said with certainty. "Let's move!"

We all looked at the long flight of marble stairs that led up to the mezzanine floor, and we instantly knew there was no way I could climb all those stairs.

The security guard waved us to the elevator. "This way, ladies. You must be the bride," he said kindly to me. "Better hurry. We lock up in ten minutes." His gaze fell to my belly, and his eyes popped wide. "Wow, you better step on it!"

My friends bundled me into the elevator, and as the doors closed I caught a glimpse of Gus and Ox dubiously eyeing each other while the children milled around them.

On the mezzanine floor, we all tumbled into a ladies' room, and everyone pitched in to transform me from a bedraggled wretch into a glowing bride. Emma stripped me down to my granny panties and helped me scrub off the roof grime. Libby carefully pulled my dress from its garment bag. Delilah brushed out my hair and got to work on it with a rat-tailed comb and a can of hairspray conjured from her enormous bag. Mary Jude had her makeup brushes out, and she daubed my face with color.

Everybody spoke at once.

"We were terrified when we didn't hear from you—"

"Libby called your phone over and over and finally Poppy Fontanna answered—"

"She was so rude and hung up—"

"Then a police officer answered, and he said you'd been taken to a hospital!"

As I popped my head out of the dress, I asked, "Has anybody heard from Lexie?"

"Not yet," Emma reported.

"But Michael," I said. "He's on his way, right?"

"Nothing's going to stop him," Emma insisted. "Stop worrying."

My sisters exchanged a glance. I knew they were concerned. The clock was ticking as they helped fasten my dress.

"It's almost time!" Libby trilled when all the buttons were done up. "Ready, everyone?"

I hoped the dress was every inch what I'd intended it to be—ladylike, with a hint of sex appeal in the back. There was no hiding how low my center of gravity had become, but surely the dress was pretty and feminine.

"Wait!" Delilah shouted. "Do you have everything? Something borrowed?"

"No—I don't."

"Here." She yanked off her wristwatch. "Put this on. Something old?"

"Take my diamond earrings," Libby said, immediately unscrewing them from her lobes. "I inherited them from Grandmama."

"Something new?"

Emma said, "I've got a stick of gum in my pocket." She handed it over to much laughter, and I tucked it into my cleavage.

"Something blue?" Delilah asked.

I held up my right hand, where I always wore Grandmama Blackbird's sapphire ring. The blue stone flashed in the bathroom light. The sight of the ring made me choke up suddenly. I had loved her dearly, and she was here with me at my wedding.

They all stood back and looked at me for a long moment. I held my breath.

Then, "Well?"

Libby gave a sniffle and groped in her handbag for a tissue. "You look lovely, Nora!"

I tried to get a glimpse of myself in the tiny mirror over the sink, but it was no use. My face glowed, and that was enough.

A moment later, they hustled me out of the ladies' room. A crowd had gathered on the mezzanine. Everyone milled around in confusion until Gus stepped forward.

"Nora," he said, "we've got to talk."

Emma gave him a stiff-armed block. "Not now, Crocodile Dundee."

"But—"

"Where is the judge's chamber?" Libby asked.

"Down there." I pointed. Tall oak doors with transoms lined the imposing marble corridor. "Second door on the right. But where's Michael?" I felt close to tears and fought them down. "They're going to close the building soon. If he's not here—"

We heard a commotion in the lobby below, and everyone leaned over the balustrade to see what was happening. A mob of police officers, federal agents and at least one canine unit burst into the building—the dog barking his head off. In their midst was Michael. Behind him charged his parole officer, state trooper Ricci and all the Cannolis.

I felt my trembling knees give way, but Emma was there to hold me up. "See? No worries," she said to me. Then she shouted, "Hey, Mick! Up here!"

He looked up, and the storm blew off his face. The security team held him long enough to check his pockets, but half a dozen police officers stepped forward to speak for him. He broke loose and headed for the long staircase. Taking the stairs two at a time, he came leaping up to me.

In another instant, I was in his arms, holding back tears of relief.

"You okay?" He touched my face. "Baby Girl, too? God, you look beautiful."

"We're fine. Don't worry. Oh, Michael, are you—? In custody? Arrested?"

He laughed. "No, I'm great. Lexie and I— Well, it's over now. I'll tell you later. Let's do this."

He had found time to climb into his best go-to-court dark suit, and for a second Noah didn't recognize him. But then the baby began to howl. He flung his arms out to Michael, and Rawlins could barely hold him. Michael scooped up Noah and held him in one arm, me in the other.

I felt as though we were pushed along by a wave of joyous friends and family—everybody talking and laughing as we dashed into the judge's chamber. She was there, tall and stately in her solemn robe, with her smiling clerk standing by. The room was lined with bookshelves and had a high ceiling with white trim.

It was almost too small for everyone, but one last person squeezed her way through the door and ducked under Michael's elbow to come up at my side.

"Lexie!"

"Sweetie," she said, "you need a bouquet!"

My dearest friend had brought me a lovely nosegay of all my favorites—peonies and tulips and calla lilies—all pink and white—with baby's breath and hosta leaves, tied up with a creamy satin ribbon. Teary eyed, she gave me a kiss on the cheek, and I let go of Michael long enough to hug my longtime trusted friend. I had been afraid I'd lost her again, but here she was.

"Thank you, Lex." The words caught in my throat. "Thank you for being here."

"I wouldn't miss it for anything."

The judge clapped her hands lightly. "Are we ready to proceed?"

Michael managed to pass Noah off to Rawlins, who handed the baby a stuffed bunny to keep him entertained. Then Michael took my hand and looked down at me, a happy gleam in his gaze. His eye might still be black and blue, but it didn't mean a thing. To me, he was every inch my Prince Charming.

At long last, we were together. I smiled up at him, trembling a little, but so sure and ready to be his wife, his partner, his soul mate forever, that I thought my heart would burst. In the company of all our dearest friends, I felt buoyant, blissful, bewitched by joy. Baby Girl gave me a nudge to say she was ready, too. In minutes, we were going to be a family. For better or for worse. Forever.

"Now, then," said the judge with grave authority. The buzz in the room subsided at her command. She glanced around the room at the gathered throng, and finally she smiled. Everyone fell silent, as if holding one big breath.

When she had everyone's attention, she said, "Before we proceed, I need to ask the traditional question. Is there any person present who has reason to believe these two should not be joined in matrimony?"

She asked it lightly, in jest, and a politely amused silence passed.

"Uh . . ." At the back of the room, Gus Hardwicke cleared his throat. "That person would be me."

Everyone turned to him, and I felt Michael go tense. I squeezed him into stillness.

Gus edged his way through the crowd while drawing a long envelope from his pocket. "Your Honor, I apologize for waiting until this unfortunately melodramatic moment, but—"

"Hardwicke," Michael said with more good humor than I thought possible, "take a hike."

"Gus, please," I said.

Gus extended the envelope to the judge. "Nora cannot go through with this."

"But—"

"Because she's already married," he said. "To me."

The room spun, and every voice rose in protest. It was impossible. Ridiculous. Untrue.

While the hubbub grew, the judge opened the envelope and extracted an official document on vellum. I caught a glimpse of florid signatures and a blue ribbon affixed to a gold seal.

"It's unorthodox," Gus continued, "but completely legal. It's a marriage by proxy from Paraguay. I was there earlier this summer, you see. It's one of the few non-Muslim countries that allows such marriages, and I thought while I was there, why not—"

Michael moved like a tiger, and I was certain Gus was going to die horribly right there in the judge's chamber. Instantly, Gus was down on the desk on his back, gasping for air. I flung myself between them. So did Emma, and soon the Cannolis were throwing elbows, too. Ricci waded in and took a punch on the chin.

The melee sorted itself out as the judge shouted for order. I clutched Michael and pulled him off Gus.

The judge continued to frown over the document. "I've never actually seen one of these," she murmured. "I've heard of them, of course, but . . ."

"I assure you, it's legal." Gus stood up and straightened his tie again. "Nora is my wife. If she marries this thug, she'll be committing bigamy. I'm sorry, Nora. I tried to tell you."

I found my voice. "I never agreed to any such thing. I can't be married—not without my own consent."

The judge hummed, shaking her head. "Actually, Miss Blackbird, Paraguay does have a lock on the market for this kind of thing, and I fear—"

"No," Michael said. "Hardwicke—!"

Another fistfight. Louder, more violent. Some of the women screamed and ducked out of the room. Michael sent Gus hurtling against a bookcase, and a shower of books and knickknacks hit him across the shoulders. Libby pulled me back against the window, shielding me with Lucy and Max. The judge shouted. Her assistant grabbed a phone and called for security.

Ricci pulled his sidearm and his handcuffs.

Emma jammed herself in front of Michael and with all her strength forced him to back away from Gus.

"I'm sorry," the judge said with obvious regret. "I can't perform this ceremony today. We'll need time to consider this matter."

I felt my whole being deflate. The Cannolis descended upon the judge, interrupting each other with a dozen legal arguments, but she shook her head decisively. "No," she said. "We'll do this an-other day."

I don't remember leaving the room. Maybe I blacked out and someone helped me into the hallway. I remember Michael scooping up my bouquet and pressing it into my hands. His touch was warm on my bare shoulders, but I knew he was angry. Furious. Around us, our friends all spoke at once, expressing shock and regret and trying to reassure us.

"Another day—"

"It's a little setback—"

"Nothing to worry about—"

But I felt dreadful.

And all I could see was Gus's smug grin as he tucked the enve-lope back into his pocket and headed down the corridor with a jaunty stroll. Michael started after him, but I held him back.

At the top of the long staircase, Rawlins stood holding Noah. My nephew must have wisely taken Noah out of the room when the first fight broke out. Rawlins stood quietly, Noah in his arms, both of them watching Gus head down the corridor toward them.

I saw an especially intent look on Noah's face. The baby watched Gus approach, eyes fixed and suspicious. All his Blackbird genes were there in his expression. At just the right moment, Noah threw his pink bunny at Gus.

He missed.

Gus turned back and blew a kiss to me.

And tangled up his feet in the bunny. In the next second, he tripped. He lost his balance. Teetered on the top step.

It was the curse. The Blackbird curse. I knew it as surely as any-thing I had ever known.

Gus might have fallen on one knee if he hadn't been standing on the top step of the long, long staircase. He threw his arms wide, but—as if in slow motion—he went airborne. And fell. Down, down, down he went—striking one marble step after another, rolling, tumbling, cracking bones, breaking his nose, falling, falling, falling all the way to the very bottom, where his limp body came to rest at the foot of the security desk.

People cried out and rushed to help. The crowd from the mezzanine hurried down in a wave, and the security team from the lobby ran to the rescue.

Only Michael and I remained at the top of the stairs, holding each other tight, holding our breath, holding our worst fears barely at bay.

"Holy shit." Michael sounded dazed. "That's some curse you've got, Nora Blackbird."

CHAPTER TWENTY-FOUR

"He's alive," Lexie said the following afternoon at her mother's pool, where friends and family had gathered in the sunshine to celebrate our non-marriage. She set her cell phone down on the glass-topped table. "I just spoke with his nurse. Thank heaven he didn't die. That would have been too horrible."

Champagne had been poured. Hamburgers were ready to be grilled for lunch. Everyone had brought dishes to share. It was a modest non-wedding reception, but it was festive and lively. The children played in the pool while the adults sat at the umbrella table and shook their heads. We had been waiting for news of Gus's condition and, after hearing he wasn't going to die, we all shared sighs of relief.

"He's young," Emma said, helping herself to a pickle. "I've seen worse accidents with guys who fall off horses and get trampled. Betcha he makes a full recovery."

"It's going to take months," I said. "Two compound fractures! A concussion. For heaven's sake, he lost three teeth!"

"Who cares about a few broken bones?" Michael asked, back from lighting the gas grill. For the last eighteen hours, he hadn't let me out of his sight. He had his arm around me again. "Hardwicke coulda been dead."

Lexie tilted her hat back to study Michael with amusement. "Do you believe in the curse now, sweetie?"

"It's kinda hard not to," Michael said. "All along, I figured the curse was some kind of big, karmic coincidence—you know, nothing but bad timing. But he was publicly married to Nora for less than a minute before he took a header down those stairs."

"So what are you going to do?" Lexie asked. "Live in sin forever?"

Michael shook his head. "We're gonna get married, one way or another. I'm not going to be a low-rent baby daddy. We've got six weeks before the baby is born to figure something out." He reached for my hand and kissed it. His eyes were bluer than the summer sky, filled with love but also determination. "Can we find an exorcist? Or maybe a voodoo warlock? Hell, I'll go looking for Dumbledore, if that's what it takes."

I rested my head on his shoulder. "Maybe Libby will have some ideas. Where is she?"

"Late," Emma reported. "But she's coming. She's bringing the ice cream."

"And Nora," Lexie said, "what happened with Boom Boom and Fred?"

After yesterday's adventure, I felt revived following a good night's sleep and a morning of doing nothing more than talking on the telephone. "I spoke with the police. After Bridget and I escaped from the theater, all three of them tried to make a run for the airport. But Boom Boom fell asleep in the cab, and the driver thought she had died, so he called the police, who came right away. Fred and Poppy were caught at the airport. As far as I know, they're in custody until the police sort out everything."

"Boom Boom really killed her own daughter?"

"I think she sees it differently. Jenny tried to poison her first, and Boom Boom felt she was acting in self-defense by substituting the wrong pills and causing Jenny's heart attack. Then Fred killed the nurse to keep her quiet about Jenny's death so the show could go on. But Poppy was the one who set the whole thing in motion when she discovered Jenny was going to contact all of Toodles's children."

"The children Toodles fathered with all those chorus girls?" Emma said. "They were adopted out?"

"Yes. Toodles wanted his children to go to families who were interested in music or theater, so he made sure they were all well placed. Jenny knew about them all—she may have helped get them into the kind of homes Toodles wanted for them. She was going to gather them all together for the opening of *Bluebird of Happiness* as a kind of publicity stunt. When Poppy told Boom Boom about the plan, Boom Boom decided to kill Jenny."

Lexie said, "She probably guessed all those children would sue for a financial settlement of some kind—another reason for stopping Jenny from contacting all her half siblings."

I said, "It will take a long time to make sense of it all."

"What I want to know, Mick," Emma said, "is where the hell you and Lexie have been these last several days."

Lexie sighed. "I'm afraid it was all my fault. Sweetie," she said to me, "I sincerely wish I could have told you everything. But the vow of secrecy was part of my release agreement. I promised to help gather evidence against some Wall Streeters who have been very naughty. Your groom provided a lot of the details we needed."

I eyed Michael. "Details? What kind of details?"

When he shrugged modestly, Lexie said, "I had the financial expertise to know what kind of financial information the investigators wanted, but I didn't have the . . . the right insight into the criminal mind to know where to look. So we put our heads together and got the job done."

Michael said, "We were going to tell you all about it, but things fell into place faster than we thought they would. The cops wanted Lexie and me off the street while they did the takedown, which is why I almost missed the wedding. If everything fell apart, Lexie was going back in jail. For her sake, we wanted to be sure it all went according to the plan."

"So you're out for good?" I asked my friend. "You're safe?"

"I may be asked to help in the future," she admitted. "I intend to assist my former clients to regain as much of their losses as possible, but that will take time. And I might not be successful. But this—helping to bring down the criminals who cheat clients on a much broader scale—I can contribute there."

"And you?" I asked Michael. "Are your duties finished?"

Lexie spoke when he hesitated. "He has a delightfully devious mind." She patted his arm with affection. "I couldn't have done it without you. I'm just dreadfully sorry it meant they had to drag you into custody this week. I did everything but dance on the table to get you released in time for your wedding." To me, she said, "It was your state trooper friend who managed your groom's timely release."

Michael said, "I hate owing favors to the cops."

To Michael, I said, "I thought you were money laundering. Or offshore gambling."

He sipped champagne. "There are some intriguing ideas I'm still thinking about."

"Legal?"

He winked at me. "In some countries."

"I could tell your mother on you," I said. "She might make you go straight."

"Nah. She likes a bad boy as much as you do."

Last night, after checking with the hospital to make sure Bridget would recover fully and was going home to bed with one of her boyfriends, I had asked Michael about his Batman underpants. He had laughed and said he thought we'd better start looking for superhero underwear for Noah.

Lexie asked, "And what happened with the local troublemakers you were helping the police with?"

Michael shrugged. "I don't think they're going to be much of a problem anymore."

"The kids went to jail?"

"One will, but sometimes it's easier to fight crime with . . . bigger crime."

I guessed, "The Abruzzo family is back in business."

"Not the whole family. I gave permission for some of the old rackets to start up again. My cousins will chase the kids back to playing hopscotch."

"By intimidating them," I said.

Michael flipped one hand back and forth, but finally said, "Yeah."

Emma said, "And let me guess. Little Frankie is running the show."

"A greatly reduced show," Michael said. "He'd screw up something big, but he might make this work. I'll give him time. Maybe he'll go to jail or end up wandering around in a bathrobe pretending he's crazy, but—well, we'll see what he can do without getting a bunch of cousins arrested."

Emma slugged beer and didn't say anything. I wondered if she had real feelings for Little Frankie. I feared she hoped he was Michael—a man she could trust if she overlooked a few liabilities. Or would

Little Frankie become one of the men she discarded when she got bored?

"Speaking of legal," Lexie said while Emma digested the idea of a new branch of the Abruzzo crime family, "Nora, what are you going to do about your marriage to Gus?"

"Cannoli is looking into what it will take to get a Paraguayan proxy annulled," I said. "Gus wanted to help his family with their negotiations to buy a media company. If marrying me could help his father win over the other owners, Gus was willing to do it—for a short time. I'm sure he considered the marriage a joke, really."

Emma and Michael exchanged skeptical glances.

"Who's going to run the *Intelligencer* while he's recuperating?" Lexie asked.

"They're bringing back the previous editor from retirement—just for a few weeks."

"And what about your promotion to the Lifestyle section?"

With Michael quietly watching, I said, "If I can do something worthwhile with it, I'd like to try. I don't want the job if it's going to be a constant fight against printing salacious things that hurt people or promoting hateful ideas. But I think I can make good things happen. Whether Gus comes back to work at the *Intelligencer* or not—that's part of my decision, too. I don't think I can work for him anymore."

Lexie swooped down and gave me a kiss. "Sweetie, it's all wonderful. If I can help you with your career plan, I'm happy to do it."

"I want a job flexible enough that I can enjoy my family." I gave Baby Girl a rub.

In a few short weeks, she'd be here. Baby Girl and her sister, too, along with Noah. Michael and I were going to have our hands full. Happily full. I looked forward to a couple of months of enjoying our new family before going back to work. It felt as if paradise was on our horizon at last.

A Little Night Murder

If I'd been having misgivings about bringing new life into the world, I was feeling better about it now. Maybe I wasn't going to be the perfect mother, but who could claim that distinction? Motherhood took all configurations now, and I would fit somewhere on the spectrum. I was newly committed to raising children who would be happy and kind. Who might contribute something good to the world. Who could contemplate beauty. Who would know the meaning of love.

Michael leaned over and gave me a warm kiss.

From the pool, Noah let out a squawk. Rawlins carried him to the edge of the pool, and the baby flung himself onto the terrace stones. Leaving a wet trail behind, he crawled across the terrace and grabbed Michael's leg. He hauled himself upright to the delighted laughter of the rest of us, then held his arms up to be lifted. Michael obediently pulled the baby up onto his lap, dribbling pool water on both of us. Noah puckered up and insistently leaned toward me for a kiss. I gave him one back, and then he kissed Michael, too. He laughed in delight at his new trick.

I took Michael's hand, and he squeezed mine in return. We had time to find a way to make Noah ours forever.

"Whoo-hoo!" Libby's voice carried through the house. A moment later she burst through the French doors and came out onto the pool terrace, dragging Ox Oxenfeld behind her. She wore a pink wedding gown and carried a nosegay of matching flowers. The gown was all swoops of pink tulle and a neckline that plunged almost as low as the skirt was slit high. She was radiant.

"Libby, what have you done?" I cried.

She glowed with pleasure and curled her arm around Ox's. "We're married! Oxy proposed, and we decided not to wait. Isn't it romantic?"

Emma and Lexie jumped up to congratulate the happy couple, but I remained seated at the table with Michael and Noah.

"Heaven help him," Michael said, watching Ox. "That guy's not going to survive the weekend."

"But we're going to find a way for you to survive for a long time," I said.

"Right," Michael replied. "Foiling the Blackbird curse—that's my top priority. We're going to have a long and happy life together, Nora Blackbird."